The Collected
Supernatural and Weird
Fiction of
Washington Irving
Volume 1

The Collected Supernatural and Weird Fiction of Washington Irving Volume 1

Including One Novel
'A History of New York'
and Nine Short Stories
of the Strange and Unusual

Washington Irving

LEONAUR

The Collected
Supernatural and Weird
Fiction of
Washington Irving
Volume 1
Including One Novel 'A History of New York'
and Nine Short Stories of the Strange and Unusual
by Washington Irving

FIRST EDITION

Leonaur is an imprint
of Oakpast Ltd

ISBN: 978-0-85706-399-1 (hardcover)
ISBN: 978-0-85706-400-4 (softcover)

http://www.leonaur.com

Contents

A History of New York

BY DEIDRICH KNICKERBOCKER

BOOK 1

CONTAINING DIVERS INGENIOUS THEORIES AND PHILOSOPHIC
SPECULATIONS, CONCERNING THE CREATION AND POPULATION OF
THE WORLD, AS CONNECTED WITH THE HISTORY OF NEW YORK.

CHAPTER 1
DESCRIPTION OF THE WORLD

According to the best authorities, the world in which we
dwell is a huge, opaque, reflecting, inanimate mass, floating in
the vast ethereal ocean of infinite space. It has the form of an
orange, being an oblate spheroid, curiously flattened at opposite parts, for the insertion of two imaginary poles, which are
supposed to penetrate and unite at the centre; thus forming an
axis on which the mighty orange turns with a regular diurnal
revolution.

The transitions of light and darkness, whence proceed the
alternations of day and night, are produced by this diurnal revolution successively presenting the different parts of the earth to
the rays of the sun. The latter is, according to the best, that is to
say, the latest, accounts a luminous or fiery body, of a prodigious
magnitude, from which this world is driven by a centrifugal or
repelling power, and to which it is drawn by a centripetal or at-
tractive force; otherwise called the attraction of gravitation; the
combination, or rather the counteraction, of these two opposing impulses producing a circular and annual revolution. Hence
result the different seasons of the year—*viz.*, spring, summer,

autumn, and winter.

This I believe to be the most approved modern theory on the subject;—though there be many philosophers who have entertained very different opinions; some, too, of them entitled to much deference from their great antiquity and illustrious characters. Thus it was advanced by some of the ancient sages that the earth was an extended plain, supported by vast pillars; and by others that it rested on the head of a snake, or the back of a huge tortoise;—but as they did not provide a resting place for either the pillars or the tortoise, the whole theory fell to the ground for want of proper foundation.

The Brahmins assert, that the heavens rest upon the earth, and the sun and moon swim therein like fishes in the water, moving from east to west by day, and gliding along the edge of the horizon to their original stations during the night; while, according to the Pauranicas of India, it is a vast plain, encircled by seven oceans of mild, nectar, and other delicious liquids; that it is studded with seven mountains, and ornamented in the centre by a mountainous rock of burnished gold; and that a great dragon occasionally swallows up the moon, which accounts for the phenomena of lunar eclipses.

Beside these, and many other equally sage opinions, we have the profound conjectures of Aboul-Hassan-Aly, son of Al Khan, son of Aly, son of Abderrahman, son of Abdallah, son of Masoud el-Hadheli, who is commonly called Masoudi, and surnamed Cothbeddin, but who takes the humble title of Laheb-ar-rasoul, which means the companion of the ambassador of God. He has written a universal history, entitled, "Mouroudge-ed-dharab or the Golden Meadows, and the Mines of Precious Stones."

In this valuable work he has related the history of the world, from the creation down to the moment of writing; which was under the Khaliphat of Mothi Billah, in the month Dgioumadi-el-aoual of the 336th year of the Hegira or flight of the Prophet. He informs us that the earth is a huge bird, Mecca and Medina constitute the head, Persia and India the right wing, the land of Gog the left wing, and Africa the tail. He informs us moreover, that an earth has existed before the present (which he considers as a mere chicken of 7,000 years), that it has undergone divers deluges, and that, according to the opinion of some well-informed Brahmins of his acquaintance; it will be renovated every seventy thousandth *hazarouam*; each *hazarouam* consisting of 12,000 years.

These are a few of the many contradictory opinions of philosophers concerning the earth, and we find that the learned have had equal perplexity as to the nature of the sun. Some of the ancient philosophers have affirmed that it is a vast wheel of brilliant fire; others that it is merely a mirror or sphere of transparent crystal; and a third class, at the head of whom stands Anaxagoras, maintained that it was nothing but a huge ignited mass of iron or stone—indeed he declared the heavens to be merely a vault of stone—and that the stars were stones whirled upward from the earth, and set on fire by the velocity of its revolutions.

But I give little attention to the doctrines of this philosopher, the people of Athens having fully refuted them by banishing him from their city; a concise mode of answering unwelcome doctrines, much resorted to in former days. Another sect of philosophers do declare, that certain fiery particles exhale constantly from the earth, which, concentrating in a single point of the firmament by day, constitute the sun, but being scattered and rambling about in the dark at night, collect in various points, and form stars. These are regularly burnt out and extinguished, not unlike to the lamps in our streets, and require a fresh supply of exhalations for the next occasion.

It is even recorded that at certain remote and obscure periods, in consequence of a great scarcity of fuel, the sun has been completely burnt out, and sometimes not rekindled for a month at a time—a most melancholy circumstance, the very idea of which gave vast concern to Heraclitus, that worthy weeping philosopher of antiquity. In addition to these various speculations, it was the opinion of Herschel that the sun is a magnificent, habitable abode; the light it furnishes arising from certain empyreal, luminous or phosphoric clouds, swimming in its transparent atmosphere.

But we will not enter further at present into the nature of the sun, that being an inquiry not immediately necessary to the development of this history; neither will we embroil ourselves in any more of the endless disputes of philosophers touching the form of this globe, but content ourselves with the theory advanced in the beginning of this chapter, and will proceed to illustrate by experiment the complexity of motion therein described to this our rotatory planet.

Professor Von Poddingcoft (or Puddinghead, as the name may be rendered into English) was long celebrated in the University of Leyden for profound gravity of deportment and a talent at going to sleep in the midst of examinations, to the infinite relief of his hopeful students, who thereby worked their way through college with great ease and little study. In the course of one of his lectures, the learned professor seizing a bucket of water swung it around his head at arm's length. The impulse with which he threw the vessel from him, being a centrifugal force, the retention of his arm operating as a centripetal power, and the bucket, which was a substitute for the earth, describing a circular orbit round about the globular head and ruby visage of Professor Von Poddingcoft, which formed no bad representation of the sun.

All of these particulars were duly explained to the class of gaping students around him. He apprised them, moreover, that the same principle of gravitation which retained the water in the bucket restrains the ocean from flying from the earth in its rapid revolutions; and he farther informed them that should the motion of the earth be suddenly checked, it would incontinently fall into the sun, through the centripetal force of gravitation: a most ruinous event to this planet, and one which would also obscure, though it most probably would not extinguish, the solar luminary.

An unlucky stripling, one of those vagrant geniuses who seem sent into the world merely to annoy worthy men of the puddinghead order, desirous of ascertaining the correctness of the experiment, suddenly arrested the arm of the professor just at the moment that the bucket was in its zenith, which immediately descended with astonishing precision upon the philosophic head of the instructor of youth. A hollow sound, and a red-hot hiss, attended the contact; but the theory was in the amplest manner illustrated, for the unfortunate bucket perished in the conflict; but the blazing countenance of Professor Von Poddingcoft emerged from amidst the waters, glowing fiercer than ever with unutterable indignation, whereby the students were marvellously edified, and departed considerably wiser than before.

It is a mortifying circumstance, which greatly perplexes many a painstaking philosopher, that nature often refuses to second his most profound and elabourate efforts; so that often after having invented one of the most ingenious and natural theories imaginable, she will have the perverseness to act directly in the teeth of his system, and flatly contradict his most favourite positions. This is a manifest and unmerited grievance, since it throws the censure of the vulgar and unlearned entirely upon the philosopher; whereas the fault is not to be ascribed to his theory, which is unquestionably correct, but to the waywardness of Dame Nature, who, with the proverbial fickleness of her sex, is continually indulging in coquetries and caprices, and seems really to take pleasure in violating all philosophic rules, and jilting the most learned and indefatigable of her adorers.

Thus it happened with respect to the foregoing satisfactory explanation of the motion of our planet; it appears that the centrifugal force has long since ceased to operate, while its antagonist remains in undiminished potency: the world, therefore, according to the theory as it originally stood, ought in strict propriety to tumble into the sun; philosophers were convinced that it would do so, and awaited in anxious impatience the fulfilment of their prognostics. But the untoward planet pertinaciously continued her course, not withstanding that she had reason, philosophy, and a whole university of learned professors opposed to her conduct. The philosophers took this in very ill part, and it is thought they would never have pardoned the slight and affront which they conceived put upon them by the world had not a good-natured professor kindly officiated as a mediator between the parties, and effected a reconciliation.

Finding the world would not accommodate itself to the theory, he wisely determined to accommodate the theory to the world; he therefore informed his brother philosophers that the circular motion of the earth round the sun was no sooner engendered by the conflicting impulses above described than it became a regular revolution independent of the cause which gave it origin. His learned brethren readily joined in the opinion, being heartily glad of any explanation that would decently extricate them from their embarrassment; and ever since that memorable era the world has been left to take her own course, and to revolve around the sun in such orbit as she thinks proper.

Chapter 2

COSMOGONY, OR CREATION OF THE WORLD; WITH A MULTITUDE OF EXCELLENT THEORIES, BY WHICH THE CREATION OF A WORLD IS SHOWN TO BE NO SUCH DIFFICULT MATTER AS COMMON FOLK WOULD IMAGINE.

Having thus briefly introduced my reader to the world, and given him some idea of its form and situation, he will naturally be curious to know from whence it came, and how it was created. And, indeed, the clearing up of these points is absolutely essential to my history, inasmuch as if this world had not been formed, it is more than probable that this renowned island, on which is situated the city of New York, would never have had an existence. The regular course of my history, therefore, requires that I should proceed to notice the cosmogony or formation of this our globe.

And now I give my readers fair warning that I am about to plunge, for a chapter or two, into as complete a labyrinth as ever historian was perplexed withal; therefore, I advise them to take fast hold of my skirts, and keep close at my heels, venturing neither to the right hand nor to the left, lest they get bemired in a slough of unintelligible learning, or have their brains knocked out by some of those hard Greek names which will be flying about in all directions. But should any of them be too indolent or chicken-hearted to accompany me in this perilous undertaking, they had better take a short cut round, and wait for me at the beginning of some smoother chapter.

Of the creation of the world we have a thousand contradictory accounts; and though a very satisfactory one is furnished us by divine revelation, yet every philosopher feels himself in honour bound to furnish us with a better. As an impartial historian, I consider it my duty to notice their several theories, by which mankind have been so exceedingly edified and instructed.

Thus it was the opinion of certain ancient sages, that the earth and the whole system of the universe was the Deity himself; a doctrine most strenuously maintained by Zenophanes and the whole tribe of Eleatics, as also by Strabo and the sect of peripatetic philosophers. Pythagoras likewise inculcated the famous numerical system of the *monad*, *dyad*, and *triad*; and by means of his sacred quaternary, elucidated the formation of the world, the *arcana* of nature, and the principles both of music and morals. Other sages adhered to the mathematical system of squares and triangles; the cube, the pyramid, and the sphere; the *tetrahedron*, the octahedron, the *icosahedron*, and the *dodecahedron*. While others advocated the great elementary theory, which refers the construction of our globe and all that it contains to the combinations of four material elements,—air, earth, fire, and water; with the assistance of a fifth, an immaterial and vivifying principle.

Nor must I omit to mention the great atomic system taught by old Moschus before the siege of Troy; revived by Democritus of laughing memory; improved by Epicurus, that king of good fellows; and modernized by the fanciful Descartes. But I decline inquiring, whether the atoms, of which the earth is said to be composed, are eternal or recent; whether they are animate or inanimate; whether, agreeably, to the opinion of Atheists, they were fortuitously aggregated, or, as the Theists maintain, were arranged by a supreme intelligence.

Whether, in fact, the earth be an insensate clod, or whether it be animated by a soul, which opinion was strenuously maintained by a host of philosophers, at the head of whom stands the great Plato, that temperate sage, who threw the cold water of philosophy on the form of sexual intercourse, and inculcated the doctrine of Platonic love—an exquisitely refined intercourse, but much better adapted to the ideal inhabitants of his imaginary island of Atlantis than to the sturdy race, composed of rebellious flesh and blood, which populates the little matter-of-fact island we inhabit.

Besides these systems, we have, moreover, the poetical theogony of old Hesiod, who generated the whole universe in the regular mode of procreation; and the plausible opinion of others, that the earth was hatched from the great egg of night, which floated in chaos, and was cracked by the horns of the celestial bull. To illustrate this last doctrine, Burnet, in his theory of the earth, has favoured us with an accurate drawing and description, both of the form and texture of this mundane egg, which is found to bear a marvellous resemblance to that of a goose.

Such of my readers as take a proper interest in the origin of this our planet will be pleased to learn that the most profound sages of antiquity among the Egyptians, Chaldeans, Persians, Greeks, and Latins have alternately assisted at the hatching of this strange bird, and that their cacklings have been caught, and continued in different tones and inflections, from philosopher to philosopher, unto the present day.

But while briefly noticing long celebrated systems of ancient sages, let me not pass over, with neglect, those of other philosophers, which, though less universal than renowned, have equal claims to attention, and equal chance for correctness. Thus it is recorded by the Brahmins in the pages of their inspired Shastah, that the angel Bistnoo transformed himself into a great boar, plunged into the watery abyss, and brought up the earth on his tusks. Then issued from him a mighty tortoise and a mighty snake; and Bistnoo placed the snake erect upon the back of the tortoise, and he placed the earth upon the head of the snake.

The negro philosophers of Congo affirm, that the world was made by the hands of angels, excepting their own country, which the Supreme Being constructed himself that it might be supremely excellent. And he took great pains with the inhabitants, and made them very black and beautiful; and when he had finished the first man, he was well pleased with him, and smoothed him over the face, and hence his nose, and the nose of all his descendants, became flat.

The Mohawk philosophers tell us, that a pregnant woman fell down from heaven, and that a tortoise took her upon its back, because every place was covered with water; and that the woman, sitting upon the tortoise, paddled with her hands in the water, and raked up the earth, whence it finally happened that the earth became higher than the water.

But I forbear to quote a number more of these ancient and outlandish philosophers, whose deplorable ignorance, in despite of all their erudition, compelled them to write in languages which but few of my readers can understand; and I shall proceed briefly to notice a few more intelligible and fashionable theories of their modern successors.

And, first, I shall mention the great Buffon, who conjectures that this globe was originally a globe of liquid fire, scintillated from the body of the sun, by the percussion of a comet, as a spark is generated by the collision of flint and steel. That at first it was surrounded by gross vapours, which, cooling and condensing in process of time, constituted, according to their densities, earth, water, and air, which gradually arranged themselves, according to their respective gravities, round the burning or vitrified mass that formed their centre.

Hutton, on the contrary, supposes that the waters at first were universally paramount; and he terrifies himself with the idea that the earth must be eventually washed away by the force of rain, rivers, and mountain torrents, until it is confounded with the ocean, or, in other words, absolutely dissolves into itself. Sublime idea! far surpassing that of the tender-hearted damsel of antiquity, who wept herself into a fountain; or the good dame of Narbonne in France, who, for a volubility of tongue unusual in her sex, was doomed to peel five hundred thousand and thirty-nine ropes of onions, and actually run out at her eyes before half the hideous task was accomplished.

Whiston, the same ingenious philosopher who rivalled Ditton in his researches after the longitude (for which the mischief-loving Swift discharged on their heads a most savoury *stanza*), has distinguished himself by a very admirable theory respecting the earth. He conjectures that it was originally a *chaotic comet*, which, being selected for the abode of man, was removed from its eccentric orbit; and whirled round the sun in its present regular motion; by which change of direction, order succeeded to confusion in the arrangement of its component parts. The philosopher adds that the deluge was produced by an uncourteous salute from the watery tail of another comet; doubtless through sheer envy of its improved condition; thus furnishing a melancholy proof that jealousy may prevail even among the heavenly bodies, and discord interrupt that celestial harmony of the spheres so melodiously sung by the poets.

But I pass over a variety of excellent theories, among which are those of Burnet, and Woodward, and Whitehurst; regretting extremely that my time will not suffer me to give them the notice they deserve;—and shall conclude with that of the renowned Dr. Darwin. This learned Theban, who is as much distinguished for rhyme as reason, and for good-natured credulity as serious research, and who has recommended himself wonderfully to the good graces of the ladies, by letting them into all the gallantries, amours, debaucheries, and other topics of scandal of the court of Flora, has fallen upon a theory worthy of his combustible imagination.

According to his opinion, the huge mass of chaos took a sudden occasion to explode, like a barrel of gunpowder, and in that act exploded the sun—which, in its flight, by a similar convulsion, exploded the earth, which in like guise exploded the moon—and thus, by a concatenation of explosions, the whole solar system was produced, and set most systematically in motion![1]

By the great variety of theories here alluded to, every one of which, if thoroughly examined, will be found surprisingly consistent in all its parts, my unlearned readers will perhaps be led to conclude that the creation of a world is not so difficult a task as they at first imagined. I have shown at least a score of ingenious methods in which a world could be constructed; and I have no doubt that had any of the philosophers above quoted the use of a good manageable comet, and the philosophical warehouse, *chaos*, at his command, he would engage to manufacture, a planet as good, or, if you would take his word for it, better than this we inhabit.

And here I cannot help noticing the kindness of Providence in creating comets for the great relief of bewildered philosophers. By their assistance more sudden evolutions and transitions are effected in the system of nature than are wrought in a pantomimic exhibition by the wonder-working sword of harlequin. Should one of our modern sages, in his theoretical flights among the stars, ever find himself lost in the clouds, and in danger of tumbling into the abyss of nonsense and absurdity, he has but to seize a comet by the beard, mount astride of its tail, and away he gallops in triumph like an enchanter on his hippogriff, or a Connecticut witch on her broomstick, "*to sweep the cobwebs out of the sky.*"

It is an old and vulgar saying about a "*beggar on horseback*" which I would not for the world have applied to these reverend philosophers; but I must confess that some of them, when they are mounted on one of those fiery steeds, are as wild in their curvettings as was Phaeton of yore, when he aspired to manage the chariot of Phoebus. One drives his comet at full speed against the sun, and knocks the world out of him with the mighty concussion; another, more moderate, makes his comet a kind of beast of burden, carrying the sun a regular supply of food and faggots; a third, of more combustible disposition, threatens to throw his comet like a bombshell into the world, and blow it up like a powder magazine; while a fourth, with no great delicacy to this planet and its inhabitants, insinuates that some day or other his comet—my modest pen blushes while I write it—shall absolutely turn tail upon our world and deluge it with water! Surely, as I have already observed, comets were bountifully provided by Providence for the benefit of philosophers to assist them in manufacturing theories.

And now, having adduced several of the most prominent theories that occur to my recollection, I leave my judicious readers at full liberty to choose among them. They are all serious speculations of learned men—all differ essentially from each other—and all have the same title to belief. It has ever been the task of one race of philosophers to demolish the works of their predecessors, and elevate more splendid fantasies in their stead, which in their turn are demolished and replaced by the air-castles of a succeeding generation.

Thus it would seem that knowledge and genius, of which we make such great parade, consist but in detecting the errors and absurdities of those who have gone before, and devising new errors and absurdities, to be detected by those who are to come after us. Theories are the mighty soap-bubbles with which the grown-up children of science amuse themselves while the honest vulgar stand gazing in stupid admiration, and dignify these learned vagaries with the name of wisdom! Surely Socrates was right in his opinion, that philosophers are but a soberer sort of madmen, busying themselves in things totally incomprehensible, or which, if they could be comprehended, would be found not worthy the trouble of discovery.

For my own part, until the learned have come to an agreement among themselves, I shall content myself with the account handed down to us by Moses; in which I do but follow the example of our ingenious neighbours of Connecticut; who at their first settlement proclaimed that the colony should be governed by the laws of God—until they had time to make better.

One thing, however, appears certain—from the unanimous authority of the before quoted philosophers, supported by the evidence of our own senses (which, though very apt to deceive us, may be cautiously admitted as additional testimony)—it appears, I say, and I make the assertion deliberately, without fear of contradiction, that this globe really was *created*, and that it is composed of *land and water*. It further appears that it is curiously divided and parcelled out into continents and islands, among which I boldly declare the renowned island of New York will be found by anyone who seeks for it in its proper place.

CHAPTER 3

HOW THAT FAMOUS NAVIGATOR, NOAH, WAS SHAMEFULLY NICK-NAMED; AND HOW HE COMMITTED AN UNPARDONABLE OVERSIGHT IN NOT HAVING FOUR SONS. WITH THE GREAT TROUBLE OF PHILOSOPHERS CAUSED THEREBY, AND THE DISCOVERY OF AMERICA.

Noah, who is the first seafaring man we read of, begat three sons, Shem, Ham, and Japhet. Authors, it is true, are not wanting who affirm that the patriarch had a number of other children. Thus Berosus makes him father of the gigantic Titans; Methodius gives him a son called Jonithus, or Jonicus (who was the first inventor of Johnny cakes); and others have mentioned a son, named Thuiscon, from whom descended the Teutons or Teutonic, or, in other words, the Dutch nation.

I regret exceedingly that the nature of my plan will not permit me to gratify the laudable curiosity of my readers, by investigating minutely the history of the great Noah. Indeed, such an undertaking would be attended with more trouble than many people would imagine; for the good old patriarch seems to have been a great traveller in his day, and to have passed under a different name in every country that he visited. The Chaldeans, for instance, give us his story, merely altering his name into Xisuthrus—a trivial alteration, which to an historian skilled in etymologies will appear wholly unimportant. It appears, likewise, that he had exchanged his tarpaulin and quadrant among the Chaldeans for the gorgeous insignia of royalty, and appears as a monarch in their annals.

The Egyptians celebrate him under the name of Osiris; the

Indians as Menu; the Greek and Roman writers confound him with Ogyges; and the Theban with Deucalion and Saturn. But the Chinese, who deservedly rank among the most extensive and authentic historians, inasmuch as they have known the world much longer than anyone else, declare that Noah was no other than Fohi; and what gives this assertion some air of credibility is that it is a fact, admitted by the most enlightened *literati*, that Noah travelled into China, at the time of the building of the Tower of Babel (probably to improve himself in the study of languages), and the learned Dr. Shuckford gives us the additional information that the ark rested on a mountain on the frontiers of China.

From this mass of rational conjectures and sage hypotheses many satisfactory deductions might be drawn; but I shall content myself with the simple fact stated in the Bible—*viz.*, that Noah begat three sons, Shem, Ham, and Japhet. It is astonishing on what remote and obscure contingencies the great affairs of this world depend, and how events the most distant, and to the common observer unconnected, are inevitably consequent the one to the other. It remains to the philosopher to discover these mysterious affinities, and it is the proudest triumph of his skill to detect and drag forth some latent chain of causation, which at first sight appears a paradox to the inexperienced observer.

Thus many of my readers will doubtless wonder what connection the family of Noah can possibly have with this history; and many will stare when informed that the whole history of this quarter of the world has taken its character and course from the simplest circumstance of the patriarch's having but three sons—but to explain.

Noah, we are told by sundry very credible historians, becoming sole surviving heir and proprietor of the earth, in fee simple, after the deluge, like a good father, portioned out his estate among his children. To Shem he gave Asia; to Ham, Africa; and to Japhet, Europe. Now it is a thousand times to be lamented that he had but three sons, for had there been a fourth he would doubtless have inherited America, which, of course, would have been dragged forth from its obscurity on the occasion; and thus many a hard-working historian and philosopher would have been spared a prodigious mass of weary conjecture respecting the first discovery and population of this country. Noah, however, having provided for his three sons, looked in all probability upon our country as mere wild unsettled land, and said nothing about it; and to this unpardonable taciturnity of the patriarch may we ascribe the misfortune that America did not come into the world as early as the other quarters of the globe.

It is true, some writers have vindicated him from this misconduct towards posterity, and asserted that he really did discover America. Thus it was the opinion of Mark Lescarbot, a French writer, possessed of that ponderosity of thought and profoundness of reflection so peculiar to his nation, that the immediate descendants of Noah peopled this quarter of the globe, and that the old patriarch himself, who still retained a passion for the seafaring life, superintended the transmigration. The pious and enlightened father, Charlevoix, a French Jesuit, remarkable for his aversion to the marvellous, common to all great travellers, is conclusively of the same opinion; nay, he goes still farther, and decides upon the manner in which the discovery was effected, which was by sea, and under the immediate direction of the great Noah.

"I have already observed," exclaims the good father, in a tone of becoming indignation, "that it is an arbitrary supposition that the grandchildren of Noah were not able to penetrate into the new world, or that they never thought of it. In effect, I can see no reason that can justify such a notion. Who can seriously believe that Noah and his immediate descendants knew less than we do, and that the builder and pilot of the greatest ship that ever was, a ship which was formed to traverse an unbounded ocean, and had so many shoals and quicksands to guard against, should be ignorant of, or should not have communicates to his descendants, the art of sailing on the ocean? Therefore, they did sail on the ocean—therefore, they sailed to America—therefore, America was discovered by Noah!"

Now all this exquisite chain of reasoning, which is so strikingly characteristic of the good father, being addressed to the faith, rather than the understanding, is flatly opposed by Hans de Laet, who declares it a real and most ridiculous paradox to suppose that Noah ever entertained the thought of discovering America; and as Hans is a Dutch writer, I am inclined to believe he must have been much better acquainted with the worthy crew of the ark than his competitors, and of course possessed of more accurate sources of information. It is astonishing how intimate historians do daily become with the patriarchs and other great men of antiquity.

As intimacy improves with time, and as the learned are particularly inquisitive and familiar in their acquaintance with the ancients, I should not be surprised if some future writers should gravely give us a picture of men and manners as they existed before the flood, far more copious and accurate than the Bible; and that, in the course of another century, the log-book of the good Noah should be as current among historians as the voyages of Captain Cook, or the renowned history of Robinson Crusoe.

I shall not occupy my time by discussing the huge mass of additional suppositions, conjectures, and probabilities respecting the first discovery of this country, with which unhappy historians overload themselves in their endeavours to satisfy the doubts of an incredulous world. It is painful to see these labourious wights panting, and toiling, and sweating under an enormous burden, at the very outset of their works, which, on being opened, turns out to be nothing but a mighty bundle of straw. As, however, by unwearied assiduity, they seem to have established the fact, to the satisfaction of all the world, that this country *has been discovered* I shall avail myself of their useful labours to be extremely brief upon this point.

I shall not, therefore, stop to inquire whether America was first discovered by a wandering vessel of that celebrated Phoenician fleet, which, according to Herodotus, circumnavigated Africa; or by that Carthaginian expedition which, Pliny the naturalist informs us, discovered the Canary Islands; or whether it was settled by a temporary colony from Tyre, as hinted by Aristotle and Seneca. I shall neither inquire whether it was first discovered by the Chinese, as Vossius with great shrewdness advances; nor by the Norwegians in 1002, under Biron; nor be Behem the German navigator, as Mr. Otto has endeavoured to prove to the savants of the learned city of Philadelphia.

Nor shall I investigate the more modern claims of the Welsh, founded on the voyage of Prince Madoc in the eleventh century, who, having never returned, it has since been wisely concluded that he must have gone to America, and that for a plain reason—if he did not go there, where else could he have gone?—a question which most Socratically shuts out all further dispute.

Laying aside, therefore, all the conjectures above mentioned, with a multitude of others equally satisfactory, I shall take for granted the vulgar opinion that America was discovered on the 12th of October, 1492, by Christopher Colon, a Genoese, who has been clumsily nicknamed Columbus, but for what reason I cannot discern. Of the voyages and adventures of this Colon I shall say nothing, seeing that they are already sufficiently known. Nor shall I undertake to prove that this country should have been called Colonia, after his name, that being notoriously self-evident.

Having thus happily got my readers on this side of the Atlantic, I picture them to myself, all impatience to enter upon the enjoyment of the land of promise, and in full expectation that I will immediately deliver it into their possession. But if I do, may I ever forfeit the reputation of a regular bred historian! No—no—most curious and thrice-learned readers (for thrice learned ye are if ye have read all that has gone before, and nine times learned shall ye be if ye read that which comes after), we have yet a world of work before us. Think you the first discoverers of this fair quarter of the globe had nothing to do but go on shore and find a country ready laid out and cultivated like a garden, wherein they might revel at their ease? No such thing—they had forests to cut down, underwood to grub up, marshes to drain, and savages to exterminate.

In like manner, I have sundry doubts to clear away, questions to resolve, and paradoxes to explain before I permit you to range at random; but these difficulties once overcome we shall be enabled to jog on right merrily through the rest of our history. Thus my work shall, in a manner, echo the nature of the subject, in the same manner as the sound of poetry has been found by certain shrewd critics to echo the sense—this being an improvement in history which I claim the merit of having invented.

CHAPTER 4

SHOWING THE GREAT DIFFICULTY PHILOSOPHERS HAVE HAD IN PEOPLING AMERICA—AND HOW THE ABORIGINES CAME TO BE FORGOTTEN BY ACCIDENT—TO THE GREAT RELIEF AND SATISFACTION OF THE AUTHOR.

The next inquiry at which we arrive in the regular course of our history is to ascertain, if possible, how this country was originally peopled—a point fruitful of incredible embarrassments; for unless we prove that the aborigines did absolutely come from somewhere, it will be immediately asserted in this age of scepticism, that they did not come at all; and if they did not come at all, then was this country never populated—a conclusion perfectly agreeable to the rules of logic, but wholly irreconcilable to every feeling of humanity, inasmuch as it must syllogistically prove fatal to the innumerable aborigines of this populous region.

To avert so dire a sophism, and to rescue from logical annihilation so many millions of fellow-creatures, how many wings of geese have been plundered! what oceans of ink have been benevolently drained! and how many capacious heads of learned historians have been addled and forever confounded! I pause with reverential awe when I contemplate the ponderous tomes in different languages, with which they have endeavoured to solve this question, so important to the happiness of society, but so involved in clouds of impenetrable obscurity.

Historian after historian has engaged in the endless circle of hypothetical argument, and, after leading us a weary chase

24

through *octavos*, *quartos*, and folios, has let us out at the end of his work just as wise as we were at the beginning. It was doubtless some philosophical wild-goose chase of the kind that made the old poet Macrobius rail in such a passion at curiosity, which he anathematises most heartily as "an irksome, agonising care, a superstitious industry about unprofitable things, an itching humour to see what is not to be seen, and to be doing what signifies nothing when it is done." But to proceed.

Of the claims of the children of Noah to the original population of this country I shall say nothing, as they have already been touched upon in my last chapter. The claimants next in celebrity are the descendants of Abraham. Thus Christoval Colon (vulgarly called Columbus), when he first discovered the gold mines of Hispaniola, immediately concluded, with a shrewdness that would have done honour to a philosopher, that he had found the ancient Ophir, from whence Solomon procured the gold for embellishing the temple at Jerusalem; nay, Colon even imagined that he saw the remains of furnaces of veritable Hebraic construction, employed in refining the precious ore.

So golden a conjecture, tinctured with such fascinating extravagance, was too tempting not to be immediately snapped at by the gudgeons of learning; and, accordingly, there were divers profound writers ready to swear to its correctness, and to bring in their usual load of authorities and wise surmises, wherewithal to prop it up. Vatablus and Robert Stephens declared nothing could be more clear;—Arius Montanus, without the least hesitation, asserts that Mexico was the true Ophir, and the Jews the early settlers of the country. While Possevin, Becan, and several other sagacious writers lug in a *supposed* prophecy of the fourth book of Esdras, which being inserted in the mighty hypothesis, like the keystone of an arch, gives it, in their opinion, perpetual durability.

Scarce, however, have they completed their goodly superstructure when in trudges a phalanx of opposite authors with Hans de Laet, the great Dutchman, at their head, and at one blow tumbles the whole fabric about their ears. Hans, in fact, contradicts outright all the Israelitish claims to the first settlement of this country, attributing all those equivocal symptoms, and traces of Christianity and Judaism, which have been said to be found in divers provinces of the new world, to the *Devil*, who has always effected to counterfeit the worship of the true Deity. "A remark," says the knowing old Padre d'Acosta, "made by all good authors who have spoken of the religion of nations newly discovered, and founded, besides, on the authority of the *fathers of the church.*"

Some writers again, among whom it is with much regret I am compelled to mention Lopez de Gomara and Juan de Leri, insinuate that the Canaanites, being driven from the land of promise by the Jews, were seized with such a panic that they fled without looking behind them, until stopping to take breath, they found themselves safe in America. As they brought neither their national language, manners, nor features with them it is supposed they left them behind in the hurry of their flight.—I cannot give my faith to this opinion.

I pass over the supposition of the learned Grotius, who being both an ambassador and a Dutchman to boot, is entitled to great respect, that North America was peopled by a strolling company of Norwegians, and that Peru was founded by a colony from China—Manco or Mungo Capac, the first Incas, being himself a Chinese. Nor shall I more than barely mention that Father Kircher ascribes the settlement of America to the Egyptians, Budbeck to the Scandinavians, Charron to the Gauls, Juffredus Petri to a skating party from Friesland, Milius to the Celtæ, Marinocus the Sicilian to the Romans, Le Comte to the Phoenicians, Postel to the Moors, Martin d'Angleria to the Abyssinians, together with the sage surmise of De Laet, that England, Ireland, and the Orcades may contend for that honour.

Nor will I bestow any more attention or credit to the idea that America is the fairy region of Zipangri, described by that dreaming traveller Marco Polo the Venetian; or that it comprises the visionary island of Atlantis, described by Plato. Neither will I stop to investigate the heathenish assertion of Paracelsus, that each hemisphere of the globe was originally furnished with an Adam and Eve.—Or the more flattering opinion of Dr. Romayne, supported by many nameless authorities, that Adam was of the Indian race;—or the startling conjecture of Buffon, Helvetius, and Darwin, so highly honourable to mankind, that the whole human species is accidentally descended foam a remarkable family of monkeys!

This last conjecture, I must own, came upon me very suddenly and very ungraciously. I have often beheld the clown in a pantomime, while gazing in stupid wonder at the extravagant gambols of a harlequin, all at once electrified by a sudden stroke of the wooden sword across his shoulders. Little did I think at such times that it would ever fall to my lot to be treated with equal discourtesy, and that while I was quietly beholding these grave philosophers emulating the eccentric transformations of the hero of pantomime, they would on a sudden turn upon me and my readers, and with one hypocritical flourish metamorphose us into beasts! I determined from that moment not to burn my fingers with any more of their theories, but content myself with detailing the different methods by which they transported the descendants of these ancient and respectable monkeys to this great field of theoretical warfare.

This was done either by migrations by land or transmigrations by water. Thus Padre Joseph d'Acosta enumerates three passages by land,—first by the north of Europe, secondly by the north of Asia, and, thirdly, by regions southward of the Straits of Magellan. The learned Grotius marches his Norwegians by a pleasant route across frozen rivers and arms of the sea, through Iceland, Greenland, Estotiland, and Naremberga; and various writers, among whom are Angleria, De Hornn, and Buffon, anxious for the accommodation of these travellers, have fastened the two continents together by a strong chain of deductions—by which means they could pass over dry-shod.

But should even this fail, Pinkerton, that industrious old gentleman, who compiles books and manufactures geographies, has constructed a natural bridge of ice, from continent to continent, at the distance of four or five miles from Behring's Straits-for which he is entitled to the grateful thanks of all the wandering aborigines who ever did or ever will pass over it.

It is an evil much to be lamented that none of the worthy writers above quoted could ever commence his work without immediately declaring hostilities against every writer who had treated of the same subject. In this particular authors may be compared to a certain sagacious bird, which, in building its nest is sure to pull to pieces the nests of all the birds in its neighbourhood. This unhappy propensity tends grievously to impede the progress of sound knowledge. Theories are at best but brittle productions, and when once committed to the stream, they should take care that, like the notable pots which were fellow-voyagers, they do not crack each other.

My chief surprise is, that among the many writers I have noticed, no one has attempted to prove that this country was peopled from the moon—or that the first inhabitants floated hither on islands of ice, as white bears cruise about the northern oceans—or that they were conveyed hither by balloons, as modern aeronauts pass from Dover to Calais—or by witchcraft, as Simon Magus posted among the stars—or after the manner of the renowned Scythian Abaris, who, like the New England witches on full-blooded broomsticks, made most unheard-of journeys on the back of a golden arrow, given him by the Hyperborean Apollo.

But there is still one mode left by which this country could have been peopled, which I have reserved for the last, because I consider it worth all the rest; it is—*by accident!* Speaking of the islands of Solomon, New Guinea, and New Holland, the profound father Charlevoix observes: "In fine, all these countries are peopled, and *it is possible* some have been so *by accident*. Now if it could have happened in that manner, why might it not have been at the *same time*, and by the *same means*, with the other parts of the globe?" This ingenious mode of deducing certain conclusions from possible premises is an improvement in syllogistic skill, and proves the good father superior even to

Archimedes, for he can turn the world without anything to rest his lever upon.

It is only surpassed by the dexterity with which the sturdy old Jesuit in another place cuts the Gordian knot—"Nothing," says he, "is more easy. The inhabitants of both hemispheres are certainly the descendants of the same father. The common father of mankind received an express order from Heaven to people the world, and *accordingly it has been peopled.* To bring this about it was necessary to overcome all difficulties in the way, *and they have also been overcome!*" Pious logician! how does he put all the herd of labourious theorists to the blush, by explaining in five words what it has cost them volumes to prove they knew nothing about!

From all the authorities here quoted, and a variety of others which I have consulted, but which are omitted through fear of fatiguing the unlearned reader, I can only draw the following conclusions, which luckily, however, are sufficient for my purpose. First, that this part of the world has actually *been peopled* (Q.E.D.) to support which we have living proofs in the numerous tribes of Indians that inhabit it. Secondly, that it has been peopled in five hundred different ways, as proved by a cloud of authors, who, from the positiveness of their assertions, seem to have been eye-witnesses to the fact. Thirdly, that the people of this country had a *variety of fathers*, which, as it may not be thought much to their credit by the common run of readers, the less we say on the subject the better. The question, therefore, I trust, is forever at rest.

CHAPTER 5

IN WHICH THE AUTHOR PUTS A MIGHTY QUESTION TO THE ROUT BY THE ASSISTANCE OF THE MAN IN THE MOON—WHICH NOT ONLY DE-LIVERS THOUSANDS OF PEOPLE FROM GREAT EMBARRASSMENT, BUT LIKEWISE CONCLUDES THIS INTRODUCTORY BOOK.

The writer of a history may, in some respects, be likened unto an adventurous knight, who having undertaken a perilous enterprise by way of establishing his fame, feels bound, in honour and chivalry to turn back for no difficulty nor hardship, and never to shrink or quail, whatever enemy he may encounter. Under this impression, I resolutely draw my pen, and fall to with might and main at those doughty questions and subtle paradoxes which, like fiery dragons and bloody giants, beset the entrance to my history, and would fain repulse me from the very threshold. And at this moment a gigantic question has started up, which I must needs take by the beard and utterly subdue before I can advance another step in my historic undertaking; but I trust this will be the last adversary I shall have to contend with, and that in the next book I shall be enabled to conduct my readers in triumph into the body of my work.

The question which has thus suddenly arisen is, What right had the first discoverers of America to land and take possession of a country without first gaining the consent of its inhabitants, or yielding them an adequate compensation for their territory?—a question which has withstood many fierce assaults, and has given much distress of mind to multitudes of kind-hearted folk. And, indeed, until it be totally vanquished, and put to rest, the worthy people of America can by no means enjoy the soil they inhabit with clear right and title, and quiet, unsullied conscience.

The first source of right by which property is acquired in a country is discovery. For as all mankind have an equal right to anything which has never before been appropriated, so any nation that discovers an uninhabited country, and takes possession thereof, is considered as enjoying full property, and absolute, unquestionable empire therein.

This proposition being admitted, it follows clearly that the Europeans who first visited America were the real discoverers of the same; nothing being necessary to the establishment of this fact but simply to prove that it was totally uninhabited by man. This would at first appear to be a point of some difficulty, for it is well known that this quarter of the world abounded with certain animals, that walked erect on two feet, had something of the human countenance, uttered certain unintelligible sounds, very much like language; in short, had a marvellous resemblance to human beings. But the zealous and enlightened fathers who accompanied the discoverers, for the purpose of promoting the kingdom of heaven by establishing fat monasteries and bishoprics on earth, soon cleared up this point, greatly to the satisfaction of his holiness the Pope and of all Christian voyagers and discoverers.

They plainly proved, and, as there were no Indian writers arose on the other side, the fact was considered as fully admitted and established, that the two-legged race of animals before mentioned were mere cannibals, detestable monsters, and many of them giants—which last description of vagrants have, since the time of Gog, Magog, and Goliath, been considered as outlaws, and have received no quarter in either history, chivalry, or song. Indeed, even the philosophic Bacon declared the Americans to be people proscribed by the laws of nature, inasmuch as they had a barbarous custom of sacrificing men, and feeding upon man's flesh.

Nor are these all the proofs of their utter barbarism; among many other writers of discernment, Ulla tells us,:

> .....their imbecility is so visible that one can hardly form an idea of them different from what one has of the brutes. Nothing disturbs the tranquillity of their souls, equally insensible to disasters and to prosperity. Though half naked, they are as contented as a monarch in his most splendid array. Fear makes no impression on them, and respect as little.

All this is furthermore supported by the authority of M. Boggier.

> "It is not easy," says he, "to describe the degree of their indifference for wealth and all its advantages. One does not well know what motives to propose to them when one would persuade them to any service. It is vain to offer them money; they answer they are not hungry."

And Vanegas confirms the whole, assuring us that:

. . . . ambition they have none, and are more desirous of being thought strong than valiant. The objects of ambition with us—honour, fame, reputation, riches, posts, and distinctions—are unknown among them. So that this powerful spring of action, the cause of so much *seeming* good and *real* evil in the world, has no power over them. In a word, these unhappy mortals may be compared to children, in whom the development of reason is not completed.

Now all these peculiarities, although in the unenlightened states of Greece they would have entitled their possessors to immortal honour, as having reduced to practice those rigid and abstemious maxims, the mere talking about which acquired certain old Greeks the reputation of sages and philosophers; yet were they clearly proved in the present instance to betoken a most abject and brutified nature, totally beneath the human character. But the benevolent fathers, who had undertaken to turn these unhappy savages into dumb beasts by dint of argument, advanced still stronger proofs; for as certain divines of the sixteenth century, and among the rest Lullus, affirm, the Americans go naked, and have no beards!—"They have nothing," says Lullus, "of the reasonable animal, except the mask."

And even that mask was allowed to avail them but little, for it was soon found that they were of a hideous copper complexion—and being of a copper complexion, it was all the same as if they were negroes—and negroes are black, "and black," said the pious fathers, devoutly crossing themselves, "is the colour of the devil!" Therefore, so far from being able to own property, they had no right even to personal freedom—for liberty is too radiant a deity to inhabit such gloomy temples. All which circumstances plainly convinced the righteous followers of Cortes and Pizarro that these miscreants had no title to the soil that they infested—that they were a perverse, illiterate, dumb, beardless, black-seed—mere wild beasts of the forests and, like them, should either be subdued or exterminated.

From the foregoing arguments, therefore, and a variety of others equally conclusive, which I forbear to enumerate, it is clearly evident that this fair quarter of the globe, when first visited by Europeans, was a howling wilderness, inhabited by nothing but wild beasts; and that the transatlantic visitors acquired an incontrovertible property therein, by the *right of discovery*.

This right being fully established, we now come to the next, which is the right acquired by *cultivation*. "The cultivation of the soil," we are told, "is an obligation imposed by nature on mankind. The whole world is appointed for the nourishment of its inhabitants; but it would be incapable of doing it, was it uncultivated. Every nation is then obliged by the law of nature to cultivate the ground that has fallen to its share. Those people, like the ancient Germans and modern Tartars, who, having fertile countries, disdain to cultivate the earth, and choose to live by rapine, are wanting to themselves, and *deserve to be exterminated as savage and pernicious beasts*."

Now it is notorious that the savages knew nothing of agriculture when first discovered by the Europeans, but lived a most vagabond, disorderly, unrighteous life,—rambling from place to place, and prodigally rioting upon the spontaneous luxuries of nature, without tasking her generosity to yield them anything more; whereas it has been most unquestionably shown that Heaven intended the earth should be ploughed, and sown, and manured, and laid out into cities, and towns, and farms, and country seats, and pleasure grounds, and public gardens, all which the Indians knew nothing about—therefore, they did not improve the talents Providence had bestowed on them—therefore they were careless stewards—therefore, they had no right to the soil—therefore, they deserved to be exterminated.

It is true the savages might plead that they drew all the benefits from the land which their simple wants required—they found plenty of game to hunt, which, together with the roots and uncultivated fruits of the earth, furnished a sufficient variety for their frugal repasts;—and that as Heaven merely designed the earth to form the abode and satisfy the wants of man, so long as those purposes were answered the will of Heaven was accomplished.—But this only proves how undeserving they were of the blessings around them—they were so much the more savages for not having more wants; for knowledge is in some degree an increase of desires, and it is this superiority both in the number and magnitude of his desires that distinguishes the man from the beast.

Therefore the Indians, in not having more wants, were very unreasonable animals; and it was but just that they should make way for the Europeans, who had a thousand wants to their one, and, therefore, would turn the earth to more account, and by cultivating it more truly fulfil the will of Heaven. Besides—Grotius and Lauterbach, and Puffendorf, and Titius, and many wise men beside, who have considered the matter properly, have determined that the property of a country cannot be acquired by hunting, cutting wood, or drawing water in it—nothing but precise demarcation of limits, and the intention of cultivation, can establish the possession.

Now as the savages (probably from never having read the authors above quoted) had never complied with any of these necessary forms, it plainly follows that they had no right to the soil, but that it was completely at the disposal of the first comers, who had more knowledge, more wants, and more elegant, that is to say artificial, desires than themselves.

In entering upon a newly discovered, uncultivated country, therefore, the newcomers were but taking possession of what, according to the aforesaid doctrine, was their own property—therefore in opposing them, the savages were invading their just rights, infringing the immutable laws of nature, and counteracting the will of Heaven—therefore, they were guilty of impiety, burglary, and trespass on the case—therefore, they were hardened offenders against God and man—therefore, they ought to be exterminated.

But a more irresistible right than either that I have mentioned, and one which will be the most readily admitted by my reader, provided he be blessed with bowels of charity and philanthropy, is the right acquired by civilization. All the world knows the lamentable state in which these poor savages were found.—Not only deficient in the comforts of life, but, what is still worse, most piteously and unfortunately blind to the miseries of their situation. But no sooner did the benevolent inhabitants of Europe behold their sad condition than they immediately went to work to ameliorate and improve it.

They introduced among them rum, gin, brandy, and the other comforts of life—and it is astonishing to read how soon the poor savages learn to estimate those blessings—they likewise made known to them a thousand remedies, by which the most inveterate diseases are alleviated and healed; and that they might comprehend the benefits and enjoy the comforts of these medicines, they previously introduced among them the diseases which they were calculated to cure. By these and a variety of other methods was the condition of these poor savages wonderfully improved; they acquired a thousand wants of which they had before been ignorant, and as he has most sources of happiness who has most wants to be gratified, they were doubtlessly rendered a much happier race of beings.

But the most important branch of civilization, and which has most strenuously been extolled by the zealous and pious fathers of the Roman Church, is the introduction of the Christian faith. It was truly a sight that might well inspire horror, to behold these savages tumbling among the dark mountains of paganism, and guilty of the most horrible ignorance of religion. It is true, they neither stole nor defrauded; they were sober, frugal, continent, and faithful to their word; but though they acted right habitually, it was all in vain, unless they acted so from precept. The newcomers, therefore, used every method to induce them to embrace and practice the true religion—except, indeed, that of setting them the example.

But not withstanding all these complicated labours for their good, such was the unparalleled obstinacy of these stubborn wretches, that they ungratefully refused to acknowledge the strangers as their benefactors, and persisted in disbelieving the doctrines they endeavoured to inculcate; most insolently alleging that, from their conduct, the advocates of Christianity did not seem to believe in it themselves. Was not this too much for human patience?—Would not one suppose that the benign visitants from Europe, provoked at their incredulity and discouraged by their stiff-necked obstinacy, would forever have abandoned their shores, and consigned them to their original ignorance and misery?

But no: so zealous were they to effect the temporal comfort and eternal salvation of these pagan infidels that they even proceeded from the milder means of persuasion to the more painful and troublesome one of persecution—let loose among them whole troops of fiery monks and furious bloodhounds—purified them by fire and sword, by stake and faggot; in consequence of which indefatigable measures the cause of Christian love and charity was so rapidly advanced that in a few years not one fifth of the number of unbelievers existed in South America that were found there at the time of its discovery.

What stronger right need the European settlers advance to the country than this? Have not whole nations of uninformed savages been made acquainted with a thousand imperious wants and indispensable comforts of which they were before wholly ignorant? Have they not been literally hunted and smoked out of the dens and lurking places of ignorance and infidelity, and absolutely scourged into the right path? Have not the temporal things, the vain baubles and filthy lucre of this world, which were too apt to engage their worldly and selfish thoughts, been benevolently taken from them; and have they not, instead thereof, been taught to set their affections on things above?—And finally, to use the words of a reverend Spanish father, in a letter to his superior in Spain:—

Can anyone have the presumption to say that these savage pagans have yielded anything more than an inconsiderable recompense to their benefactors, in surrendering to them a little pitiful tract of this dirty sublunary planet, in exchange for a glorious inheritance in the kingdom of heaven.

Here then are three complete and undeniable sources of right established, any one of which was more than ample to establish a property in the newly-discovered regions of America. Now, so it has happened in certain parts of this delightful quarter of the globe that the right of discovery has been so strenuously asserted—the influence of cultivation so industriously extended, and the progress of salvation and civilization so zealously persecuted; that, what with their attendant wars, persecutions, oppressions, diseases, and other partial evils that often hang on the skirts of great benefits—the savage aborigines have, somehow or other, been utterly annihilated—and this all at once brings me to a fourth right, which is worth all the others put together.

For the original claimants to the soil being all dead and buried, and no one remaining to inherit or dispute the soil, the Spaniards, as the next immediate occupants, entered upon the possession as clearly as the hangman succeeds to the clothes of the malefactor—and as they have Blackstone and all the learned expounders of the law on their side, they may set all actions of ejectment at defiance—and this last right may be entitled the *right by extermination*, or in other words, the *right by gunpowder*.

But lest any scruples of conscience should remain on this head, and to settle the question of right for ever, his holiness Pope Alexander VI. issued a mighty Bull, by which he generously granted the newly-discovered quarter of the globe to the Spaniards and Portuguese; who, thus having law and gospel on their side, and being inflamed with great spiritual zeal, showed the pagan savages neither favour nor affection, but persecuted the work of discovery, colonization, civilization, and extermination with ten times more fury than ever.

Thus were the European worthies who first discovered America clearly entitled to the soil, and not only entitled to the soil, but likewise to the eternal thanks of these infidel savages, for having come so far, endured so many perils by sea and land, and taken such unwearied pains, for no other purpose but to improve their forlorn, uncivilized, and heathenish condition;— for having made them acquainted with the comforts of life; for having introduced among them the light of religion; and, finally, for having hurried them out of the world to enjoy its reward!

But as argument is never so well understood by us selfish mortals as when it comes home to ourselves, and as I am particularly anxious that this question should be put to rest for ever, I will suppose a parallel case, by way of arousing the candid attention of my readers.

Let us suppose, then, that the inhabitants of the moon, by astonishing advancement in science, and by profound insight into that ineffable lunar philosophy, the mere flickerings of which have of late years dazzled the feebled optics, and addled the shallow brains of the good people of our globe—let us suppose, I say, that the inhabitants of the moon, by these means, had arrived at such a command of their *energies*, such an enviable state of *perfectibility*, as to control the elements, and navigate the boundless regions of space. Let us suppose a roving crew of these soaring philosophers, in the course of an aerial voyage of discovery among the stars, should chance to alight upon this outlandish planet.

And here I beg my readers will not have the uncharitableness to smile, as is too frequently the fault of volatile readers, when perusing the grave speculations of philosophers. I am far from indulging in any sportive vein at present; nor is the supposition I have been making so wild as many may deem it. It has long been a very serious and anxious question with me, and many a time and oft, in the course of my overwhelming cares and contrivances for the welfare and protection of this my native planet, have I lain awake whole nights debating in my mind whether it were most probable we should first discover and civilize the moon, or the moon discover and civilize our globe.

Neither would the prodigy of sailing in the air or cruising among the stars be a whit more astonishing and incomprehensible to us than was the European mystery of navigating floating castles through the world of waters to the simple savages. We have already discovered the art of coasting along the aerial shores of our planet by means of balloons, as the savages had of venturing along their sea-coasts in canoes; and the disparity between the former and the aerial vehicles of the philosophers from the moon might not be greater than that between the bark canoes of the savages and the mighty ships of their discoverers. I might here pursue an endless chain of similar speculations; but as they would be unimportant to my subject, I abandon them to my reader, particularly if he be a philosopher, as matters well worthy of his attentive consideration.

To return, then, to my supposition—let us suppose that the aerial visitants I have mentioned, possessed of vastly superior knowledge to ourselves—that is to say, possessed of superior knowledge in the art of extermination—riding on hippogriffs—defended with impenetrable armour—armed with concentrated sunbeams, and provided with vast engines, to hurl enormous moonstones; in short, let us suppose them, if our vanity will permit the supposition, as superior to us in knowledge, and consequently in power, as the Europeans were to the Indians when they first discovered them.

All this is very possible, it is only our self-sufficiency that makes us think otherwise; and I warrant the poor savages, before they had any knowledge of the white men, armed in all the terrors of glittering steel and tremendous gunpowder, were as perfectly convinced that they themselves were the wisest, the most virtuous, powerful, and perfect of created beings, as are at this present moment the lordly inhabitants of old England, the volatile populace of France, or even the self-satisfied citizens of this most enlightened republic.

Let us suppose, moreover, that the aerial voyagers, finding this planet to be nothing but a howling wilderness, inhabited by us poor savages and wild beasts, shall take formal possession of it, in the name of his most gracious and philosophic Excellency, the Man in the Moon. Finding however that their numbers are incompetent to hold it in complete subjection, on account of the ferocious barbarity of its inhabitants, they shall take our worthy President, the King of England, the Emperor of Hayti, the mighty Bonaparte, and the great King of Bantam, and, returning to their native planet, shall carry them to court, as were the Indian chiefs led about as spectacles in the courts of Europe.

Then making such obeisance as the etiquette of the court requires, they shall address the *puissant* Man in the Moon in, as near as I can conjecture, the following terms:——

Most serene and mighty Potentate, whose dominions extend as far as eye can reach, who rideth on the Great Bear, useth the sun as a looking glass, and maintaineth unrivalled control over tides, madmen, and sea-crabs. We, thy liege subjects, have just returned from a voyage of discovery, in the course of which we have landed and taken possession of that obscure little dirty planet, which thou beholdest rolling at a distance.

The five uncouth monsters which we have brought into this august present were once very important chiefs among their fellow-savages, who are a race of beings totally destitute of the common attributes of humanity, and differing in everything from the inhabitants of the moon, inasmuch as they carry their heads upon their shoulders, instead of under their arms—have two eyes instead of one—are utterly destitute of tails, and of a variety of unseemly complexions, particularly of horrible whiteness, instead of pea-green.

We have moreover found these miserable savages sunk into a state of the utmost ignorance and depravity, every man shamelessly living with his own wife, and rearing his own children, instead of indulging in that community of wives enjoined by the law of nature, as expounded by the philosophers of the moon. In a word, they have scarcely a gleam of true philosophy among them, but are, in fact, utter heretics, ignoramuses, and barbarians. Taking compassion, therefore, on the sad condition of these sublunary wretches, we have endeavoured, while we remained on their planet, to introduce among them the light of reason—and the comforts of the moon.

We have treated them to mouthfuls of moonshine, and

draughts of nitrous oxide, which they swallowed with incredible voracity, particularly the females; and we have likewise endeavoured to instil into them the precepts of lunar philosophy. We have insisted upon their renouncing the contemptible shackles of religion and common sense, and adoring the profound, omnipotent, and all perfect energy, and the ecstatic, immutable, immovable perfection. But such was the unparalleled obstinacy of these wretched savages that they persisted in cleaving to their wives, and adhering to their religion, and absolutely set at nought the sublime doctrines of the moon—nay, among other abominable heresies they even went so far as blasphemously to declare that this ineffable planet was made of nothing more nor less than green cheese!

At these words, the great Man in the Moon (being a very profound philosopher) shall fall into a terrible passion, and possessing equal authority over things that do not belong to him, as did whilom his holiness the Pope, shall forthwith issue a formidable Bull, specifying, "That whereas a certain crew of Lunatics have lately discovered and taken possession of a newly-discovered planet called *the earth*;—and that whereas it is inhabited by none but a race of two-legged animals that carry their heads on their shoulders instead of under their arms; cannot talk the Lunatic language; have two eyes instead of one; are destitute of tails, and of a horrible whiteness, instead of pea-green—therefore, and for a variety of other excellent reasons, they are considered incapable of possessing any property in the planet they infest, and the right and title to it are confirmed to its original discoverers. And, furthermore, the colonists who are now about to depart to the aforesaid planet are authorised and commanded to use every means to convert these infidel savages from the darkness of Christianity, and make them thorough and absolute Lunatics."

In consequence of this benevolent Bull, our philosophic benefactors go to work with hearty zeal. They seize upon our fertile territories, scourge us from our rightful possessions, relieve us from our wives, and when we are unreasonable enough to complain, they will turn upon us and say:

Miserable barbarians! ungrateful wretches! have we not come thousands of miles to improve your worthless planet? have we not fed you with moonshine! have we not intoxicated you with nitrous oxide? does not our moon give you light every night? and have you the baseness to murmur, when we claim a pitiful return for all these benefits?

But finding that we not only persist in absolute contempt of their reasoning and disbelief in their philosophy, but even go so far as daringly to defend our property, their patience shall be exhausted, and they shall resort to their superior powers of argument; hunt us with hippogriffs, transfix us with concentrated sunbeams, demolish our cities with moonstones; until having by main force converted us to the true faith, they shall graciously permit us to exist in the torrid deserts of Arabia, or the frozen regions of Lapland, there to enjoy the blessings of civilization and the charms of lunar philosophy, in much the same manner as the reformed and enlightened savages of this country are kindly suffered to inhabit the inhospitable forests of the north, or the impenetrable wilderness of South America.

Thus, I hope, I have clearly proved, and strikingly illustrated, the right of the early colonists to the possession of this country; and thus is this gigantic question completely vanquished: so having manfully surmounted all obstacles, and subdued all opposition, what remains but that I should forthwith conduct my readers into the city which we have been so long in a manner besieging? But hold—before I proceed another step I must pause to take breath, and recover from the excessive fatigue I have undergone, in preparing to begin this most accurate of histories.

And in this I do but imitate the example of a renowned Dutch tumbler of antiquity, who took a start of three miles for the purpose of jumping over a hill, but having run himself out of breath by the time he reached the foot, sat himself quietly down for a few moments to blow, and then walked over it at his leisure.

BOOK 2

TREATING OF THE FIRST SETTLEMENT OF THE PROVINCE OF NIEUW NEDERLANDTS.

CHAPTER 1

IN WHICH ARE CONTAINED DIVERS REASONS WHY A MAN SHOULD NOT WRITE IN A HURRY. ALSO, OF MASTER HENDRICK HUDSON, HIS DISCOVERY OF A STRANGE COUNTRY—AND HOW HE WAS MAGNIFICENTLY REWARDED BY THE MUNIFICENCE OF THEIR HIGH MIGHTINESS.

My great-grandfather by the mother's side, Hermanus Van Clattercop, when employed to build the large stone church at Rotterdam, which stands about three hundred yards to your left after you turn off from the Boomkeys, and which is so conveniently constructed that all the zealous Christians of Rotterdam prefer sleeping through a sermon there to any other church in the city—my great-grandfather, I say, when employed to build that famous church, did in the first place send to Delft for a box of long pipes; then having purchased a new spitting-box and a hundredweight of the best Virginia, he sat himself down, and did nothing for the space of three months but smoke most laboriously.

Then did he spend full three months more in trudging on foot, and voyaging in *trekschuit*, from Rotterdam to Amsterdam—to Delft—to Haerlem—to Leyden—to the Hague, knocking his head and breaking his pipe against every church in his road. Then did he advance gradually nearer and nearer to Rotterdam, until he came in full sight of the identical spot whereon the church was to be built. Then did he spend three months longer in walking round it and round it; contemplating it, first from one point of view and then from another—now he would be paddled by it on the canal—now would he peep at it through a telescope, from the other side of the Meuse—and now would he take a bird's-eye glance at it, from the top of one of those gigantic windmills which protect the gates of the city.

The good folks of the place were on the tiptoe of expectation and impatience—notwithstanding all the turmoil of my great-grandfather, not a symptom of the church was yet to be seen; they even began to fear it would never be brought into the world, but that its great projector would lie down and die in labour of the mighty plan he had conceived.

At length, having occupied twelve good months in puffing and paddling, and talking and walking—having travelled over all Holland, and even taken a peep into France and Germany—having smoked five hundred and ninety-nine pipes and three hundredweight of the best Virginia tobacco—my great-grandfather gathered together all that knowing and industrious class of citizens who prefer attending to anybody's business sooner than their own, and having pulled off his coat and five pair of breeches, he advanced sturdily up, and laid the corner-stone of the church, in the presence of the whole multitude—just at the commencement of the thirteenth month.

In a similar manner, and with the example of my worthy ancestor full before my eyes, have I proceeded in writing this most authentic history. The honest Rotterdammers no doubt thought my great-grandfather was doing nothing at all to the purpose, while he was making such a world of prefatory bustle about the building of his church; and many of the ingenious inhabitants of this fair city will unquestionably suppose that all the preliminary chapters, with the discovery, population, and final settlement of America, were totally irrelevant and superfluous—and that the main business, the history of New York, is not a jot more advanced than if I had never taken up my pen.

Never were wise people more mistaken in their conjectures. In consequence of going to work slowly and deliberately, the church came out of my grandfather's hands one of the most sumptuous, goodly, and glorious edifices in the known world—excepting that, like our magnificent capitol at Washington, it was begun on so grand a scale that the good folk could not afford to finish more than the wing of it.

So, likewise, I trust, if ever I am able to finish this work on the plan I have commenced (of which, in simple truth, I sometimes have my doubts), it will be found that I have pursued the latest rules of my art, as exemplified in the writings of all the great American historians, and wrought a very large history out of a small subject—which nowadays, is considered one of the great triumphs of historic skill. To proceed, then, with the thread of my story.

In the ever-memorable year of our Lord, 1609, on a Saturday morning, the five-and-twentieth day of March, old style, did that "worthy and irrecoverable discoverer (as he has justly been called), Master Henry Hudson," set sail from Holland in a stout vessel called the *Half Moon*, being employed by the Dutch East India Company to seek a north-west passage to China.

Henry (or, as the Dutch historians call him, Hendrick) Hudson was a seafaring man of renown, who had learned to smoke tobacco under Sir Walter Raleigh, and is said to have been the first to introduce it into Holland, which gained him much popularity in that country, and caused him to find great favour in the eyes of their High Mightinesses the Lords States General, and also of the Honourable West India Company. He was a short, square, brawny old gentleman, with a double chin, a mastiff mouth, and a broad copper nose, which was supposed in those days to have acquired its fiery hue from the constant neighbourhood of his tobacco pipe.

He wore a true Andrea Ferrara tucked in a leathern belt, and a commodore's cocked hat on one side of his head. He was re-markable for always jerking up his breeches when he gave out his orders, and his voice sounded not unlike the brattling of a tin trumpet, owing to the number of hard north-westers which he had swallowed in the course of his seafaring.

Such was Hendrick Hudson, of whom we have heard so much, and know so little; and I have been thus particular in his description, for the benefit of modern painters and statuaries, that they may represent him as he was; and not, according to their common custom with modern heroes, make him look like a Cæsar, or Marcus Aurelius, or the Apollo of Belvidere.

As chief mate and favourite companion, the commodore chose Master Robert Juet, of Limehouse, in England. By some his name has been spelt *Chewit*, and ascribed to the circumstance of his having been the first man that ever chewed tobacco; but this I believe to be a mere flippancy; more especially as certain of his progeny are living at this day, who write their names Juet. He was an old comrade and early schoolmate of the great Hudson, with whom he had often played truant and sailed chip boats in a neighbouring pond, when they were little boys—from whence, it is said, the commodore first derived his bias towards a seafaring life. Certain it is that the old people about Limehouse declared Robert Juet to be a unlucky urchin prone to mischief, that would one day or other come to the gallows.

He grew up as boys of that kind often grow up, a rambling, heedless varlet, tossed about in all quarters of the world,—meeting with more perils and wonders than did Sinbad the Sailor, without growing a whit more wise, prudent, or ill-natured. Under every misfortune he comforted himself with a quid of tobacco, and the truly philosophic maxim that "it will be all the same thing a hundred years hence." He was skilled in the art of carving anchors and true lovers' knot on the bulk-heads and quarter railings, and was considered a great wit on board ship, in consequence of his playing pranks on everybody around, and now and then even making a wry face at old Hendrick when his back was turned.

To this universal genius are we indebted for many particulars concerning this voyage, of which he wrote a history, at the request of the commodore, who had an unconquerable aversion to writing himself, from having received so many floggings about it when at school. To supply the deficiencies of Master Juet's journal, which is written with true log-book brevity, I have availed myself of divers family traditions, handed down from my great-great-grandfather, who accompanied the expedition in the capacity of cabin-boy.

From all that I can learn, few incidents worthy of remark happened in the voyage; and it mortifies me exceedingly that I have to admit so noted an expedition into my work without making any more of it.

Suffice it to say, the voyage was prosperous and tranquil—the crew, being a patient people, much given to slumber and vacuity, and but little troubled with the disease of thinking—a malady of the mind, which is the sure breeder of discontent. Hudson had laid in abundance of gin and *sour-krout*, and every man was allowed to sleep quietly at his post unless the wind blew.

True it is, some slight dissatisfaction was shown on two or three occasions at certain unreasonable conduct of Commodore Hudson. Thus, for instance, he forbore to shorten sail when the wind was light and the weather serene, which was considered among the most experienced Dutch seamen as certain *weather-breeders*, or prognostics, that the weather would change for the worse.

He acted, moreover, in direct contradiction to that ancient and sage rule of the Dutch navigators, who always took in sail at night,—put the helm a-port, and turned in; by which precaution they had a good night's rest, were sure of knowing where they were the next morning, and stood but little chance of running down a continent in the dark. He likewise prohibited the seamen from wearing more than five jackets and six pair of breeches, under pretence of rendering them more alert; and no man was permitted to go aloft and hand in sails with a pipe in his mouth, as is the invariable Dutch custom at the present day.

All these grievances, though they might ruffle for a moment the constitutional tranquillity of the honest Dutch tars, made but transient impression; they ate hugely, drank profusely, and slept immeasurably; and being under the especial guidance of Providence, the ship was safely conducted to the coast of America; where, after sundry unimportant touchings and standings off and on, she at length, on the fourth day of September, entered that majestic bay which at this day expands its ample bosom before the city of New York, and which had never before been visited by any European.[1]

It has been traditionary in our family that when the great navigator was first blessed with a view of this enchanting island, he was observed, for the first and only time in his life, to exhibit strong symptoms of astonishment and admiration. He is said to have turned to master Juet, and uttered these remarkable words, while he pointed towards this paradise of the new world—"See! there!"—and thereupon, as was always his way when he was uncommonly pleased, he did puff out such clouds of dense tobacco smoke that in one minute the vessel was out of sight of land, and Master Juet was fain to wait until the winds dispersed this impenetrable fog.

"It was indeed,"—as my great-grandfather used to say,— though in truth I never heard him, for he died, as might be expected, before I was born—"it was indeed a spot on which the eye might have revelled forever, in ever new and never-ending beauties."

---

1. True it is, and I am not ignorant of the fact, that in a certain apocryphal book of voyages, compiled by one Hackluyt, is to be found a letter written to Francis the First, by one Giovanni, or John Verazzani, on which some writers are inclined to found a belief that this delightful bay had been visited nearly a century previous to the voyage of the enterprising Hudson. Now this (albeit it has met with the countenance of certain very judicious and learned men) I hold in utter disbelief, and that for various good and substantial reasons:

First, because on strict examination it will be found that the description given by this Verazzani applies about as well to the bay of New York as it does to my nightcap.

Secondly, because that this John Verazzani, for whom I already begin to feel a most bitter enmity, is a native of Florence, and everybody knows the crafty wiles of these losel Florentines, by which they filched away the laurels from the brows of the immortal Colon (vulgarly called Columbus), and bestowed them on their officious townsman, Amerigo Vespucci; and I make no doubt they are equally ready to rob the illustrious Hudson of the credit of discovering this beauteous island, adorned by the city of New York, and placing it beside their usurped discovery of South America.

And, *thirdly*, I award my decision in favour of the pretensions of Hendrick Hudson, inasmuch as his expedition sailed from Holland, being truly and absolutely a Dutch enterprise—and though all the proofs in the world were introduced on the other side, I would set them at nought as undeserving my attention. If these three reasons be not sufficient to satisfy every *burgher* of this ancient city,—all I can say is they are degenerate descendants from their venerable Dutch ancestors, and totally unworthy the trouble of convincing. Thus, therefore, the title of Hendrick Hudson to his renowned discovery is fully vindicated.

The island of Manna-hata spread wide before them, like some sweet vision of fancy, or some fair creation of industrious magic. Its hills of smiling green swelled gently one above another, crowned with lofty trees of luxuriant growth; some pointing their tapering foliage towards the clouds which were gloriously transparent, and others loaded with a verdant burden of clambering vines, bowing their branches to the earth that was covered with flowers. On the gentle declivities of the hills were scattered in gay profusion the dog-wood, the *sumach*, and the wild brier, whose scarlet berries and white blossoms glowed brightly among the deep green of the surrounding foliage; and here and there a curling column of smoke rising from the little glens that opened along the shore seemed to promise the weary voyagers a welcome at the hands of their fellow-creatures.

As they stood gazing with entranced attention on the scene before them, a red man, crowned with feathers, issued from one of these glens, and after contemplating in silent wonder the gallant ship, as she sat like a stately swan swimming on a silver lake, sounded the war-whoop, and bounded into the woods like a wild deer, to the utter astonishment of the phlegmatic Dutchmen, who had never heard such a noise or witnessed such a caper in their whole lives.

Of the transactions of our adventurers with the savages, and how the latter smoked copper pipes and ate dried currants; how they brought great store of tobacco and oysters; how they shot one of the ship's crew, and how he was buried, I shall say nothing, being that I consider them unimportant to my history. After tarrying a few days in the bay, in order to refresh themselves after their seafaring, our voyagers weighed anchor, to explore a mighty river which emptied into the bay.

This river, it is said, was known among the savages by the name of the *Shatemuck*; though we are assured in an excellent little history published in 1674, by John Josselyn, gent., that it was called the *Mohegan*;[2] and Master Richard Bloome, who

---

2. This river is likewise laid down in Ogilvy's map as Manhattan—Noordt,—Montaigne, and Mauritius River.

wrote some time afterwards, asserts the same—so that I very much incline in favour of the opinion of these two honest gentlemen. Be this as it may, up this river did the adventurous Hendrick proceed, little doubting but it would turn to be the much-looked-for passage to China!

The journal goes on to make mention of divers interviews between the crew and the natives in the voyage up the river; but as they would be impertinent to my history, I shall pass over them in silence, except the following dry joke, played off by the old commodore and his schoolfellow Robert Juet, which does such vast credit to their experimental philosophy that I cannot refrain from inserting it.

> Our master and his mate determined to try some of the chiefe men of the countrey whether they had any treacherie in them. So they tooke them downe into the cabin, and gave them so much wine and *acqua vitæ* that they were all merrie; and one of them had his wife with him, which sate so modestly, as any of our countrey women would do in a strange place. In the end, one of them was drunke, which had been aboarde of our ship all the time that we had been there, and that was strange to them, for they could not tell how to take it.

Having satisfied himself by this ingenious experiment that the natives were an honest, social race of jolly roysterers, who had no objection to a drinking bout, and were very merry in their cups, the old commodore chuckled hugely to himself, and thrusting a double quid of tobacco in his cheek, directed Master Juet to have it carefully recorded, for the satisfaction of all the natural philosophers of the University of Leyden—which done, he proceeded on his voyage with great self-complacency. After sailing, however, above a hundred miles up the river, he found the watery world around him began to grow more shallow and confined, the current more rapid and perfectly fresh—phenomena not uncommon in the ascent of rivers, but which puzzled the honest Dutchman prodigiously.

A consultation was therefore called, and having deliberated full six hours, they were brought to a determination by the ship's running aground—whereupon they unanimously concluded that there was but little chance of getting to China in this direction. A boat, however, was despatched to explore higher up the river, which, on its return, confirmed the opinion; upon this the ship was warped off and put about with great difficulty, being, like most of her sex, exceedingly hard to govern; and the adventurous Hudson, according to the account of my great-great-grandfather, returned down the river—with a prodigious flea in his ear!

Being satisfied that there was little likelihood of getting to China, unless, like the blind man, he returned from whence he set out, and took a fresh start, he forthwith recrossed the sea to Holland, where he was received with great welcome by the Honourable East India Company, who were very much rejoiced to see him come back safe—with their ship; and at a large and respectable meeting of the first merchants and burgomasters of Amsterdam it was unanimously determined that, as a munificent reward for the eminent services he had performed, and the important discovery he had made, the great River Mohegan should be called after his name!—and it continues to be called Hudson River unto this very day.

CHAPTER 2

CONTAINING AN ACCOUNT OF A MIGHTY ARK, WHICH FLOATED UNDER THE PROTECTION OF ST. NICHOLAS, FROM HOLLAND TO GIBBETT ISLAND—THE DESCENT OF THE STRANGE ANIMALS THEREFROM—A GREAT VICTORY, AND A DESCRIPTION OF THE ANCIENT VILLAGE OF COMMUNIPAW.

The delectable accounts given by the great Hudson and Master Juet of the country they had discovered excited not a little talk and speculation among the good people of Holland. Letters patent were granted by Government to an association of merchants, called the West India Company, for the exclusive trade on Hudson River, on which they erected a trading-house called

Fort Aurania, or Orange, from whence did spring the great city of Albany. But I forbear to dwell on the various commercial and colonizing enterprises which took place; among which was that of Mynheer Adrian Block, who discovered and gave a name to Block Island, since famous for its cheese—and shall barely confine myself to that which gave birth to this renowned city.

It was some three or four years after the return of the immortal Hendrick that a crew of honest Low Dutch colonists set sail from the city of Amsterdam for the shores of America. It is an irreparable loss to history, and a great proof of the darkness of the age and the lamentable neglect of the noble art of book-making, since so industriously cultivated by knowing sea-captains and learned supercargoes, that an expedition so interesting and important in its results should be passed over in utter silence. To my great-great-grandfather am I again indebted for the few facts I am enabled to give concerning it—he having once more embarked for this country, with a full determination, as he said, of ending his days here—and of begetting a race of Knickerbockers that should rise to be great men in the land.

The ship in which these illustrious adventurers set sail was called the *Goede Vrouw,* or good woman, in compliment to the wife of the president of the West India Company, who was allowed by everybody, except her husband, to be a sweet-tempered lady—when not in liquor. It was in truth a most gallant vessel, of the most approved Dutch construction, and made by the ablest ship-carpenters of Amsterdam, who, it is well known, always model their ships after the fair forms of their country-women.

Accordingly, it had one hundred feet in the beam, one hundred feet in the keel, and one hundred feet from the bottom of the stern-post to the taffrail. Like the beauteous model, who was declared to be the greatest belle in Amsterdam, it was full in the bows, with a pair of enormous catheads, a copper bottom, and withal a most prodigious poop.

The architect, who was somewhat of a religious man, far from decorating the ship with pagan idols, such as Jupiter, Neptune or Hercules, which heathenish abominations, I have no doubt, occasion the misfortunes and shipwreck of many a noble vessel, he I say, on the contrary, did laudably erect for a head, a goodly image of St. Nicholas, equipped with a low, broad-brimmed hat, a huge pair of Flemish trunk hose, and a pipe that reached to the end of the bow-sprit.

Thus gallantly furnished, the staunch ship floated sideways, like a majestic goose, out of the harbor of the great city of Amsterdam, and all the bells that were not otherwise engaged, rung a triple bobmajor on the joyful occasion.

My great-great-grandfather remarks, that the voyage was uncommonly prosperous, for, being under the especial care of the ever-revered St. Nicholas, the *Goede Vrouw* seemed to be endowed with qualities unknown to common vessels. Thus she made as much leeway as headway, could get along very nearly as fast with the wind a head as when it was a-poop, and was particularly great in a calm; in consequence of which singular advantage she made out to accomplish her voyage in a very few months, and came to anchor at the mouth of the Hudson, a little to the east of Gibbet Island.

Here lifting up their eyes they beheld, on what is at present called the Jersey shore, a small Indian village, pleasantly embowered in a grove of spreading elms, and the natives all collected on the beach, gazing in stupid admiration at the *Goede Vrouw*. A boat was immediately dispatched to enter into a treaty with them, and, approaching the shore, hailed them through a trumpet in the most friendly terms; but so horribly confounded were these poor savages at the tremendous and uncouth sound of the Low Dutch language that they one and all took to their heels, and scampered over the Bergen Hills: nor did they stop until they had buried themselves, head and ears, in the marshes on the other side, where they all miserably perished to a man; and their bones being collected and decently covered by the Tammany Society of that day, formed that singular mound called *Rattlesnake Hill*, which rises out of the centre of the salt marshes a little to the east of the Newark Causeway.

Animated by this unlooked-for victory, our valiant heroes sprang ashore in triumph, took possession of the soil as conquerors, in the name of their High Mightinesses the Lords States General; and marching fearlessly forward, carried the village of Communipaw by storm, not withstanding that it was vigorously defended by some half a score of old squaws and *papooses*. On looking about them they were so transported with the excellences of the place that they had very little doubt the blessed St. Nicholas had guided them thither as the very spot whereon to settle their colony.

The softness of the soil was wonderfully adapted to the driving of piles; the swamps and marshes around them afforded ample opportunities for the constructing of dykes and dams; the shallowness of the shore was peculiarly favourable to the building of docks—in a word, this spot abounded with all the requisites for the foundation of a great Dutch City. On making a faithful report, therefore, to the crew of the *Goede Vrouw*, they one and all determined that this was the destined end of their voyage.

Accordingly, they descended from the *Goede Vrouw*, men, women and children, in goodly groups, as did the animals of yore from the ark, and formed themselves into a thriving settlement, which they called by the Indian name *Communipaw*.

As all the world is doubtless perfectly acquainted with Communipaw, it may seem somewhat superfluous to treat of it in the present work; but my readers will please to recollect, that notwithstanding it is my chief desire to satisfy the present age, yet I write likewise for posterity, and have to consult the understanding and curiosity of some half a score of centuries yet to come; by which time, perhaps, were it not for this invaluable history, the great Communipaw, like Babylon, Carthage, Nineveh, and other great cities, might be perfectly extinct—sunk and forgotten in its own mud—its inhabitants turned into oysters,[1] and even its situation a fertile subject of learned controversy and hard-headed investigation among indefatigable historians.

---

1. Men by inaction degenerate into oysters.—*Kaimes.*

Let me, then, piously rescue from oblivion the humble relics of a place which was the egg from whence was hatched the mighty city of New York!

Communipaw is at present but a small village, pleasantly situated among rural scenery, on that beauteous part of the Jersey shore which was known in ancient legends by the name of Pavonia,[2] and commands a grand prospect of the superb bay of New York. It is within but half an hour's sail of the latter place, provided you have a fair wind, and may be distinctly seen from the city.

Nay, it is a well known fact, which I can testify from my own experience, that on a clear still summer evening you may hear from the battery of New York the obstreperous peals of broad-mouthed laughter of the Dutch negroes at Communipaw, who, like most other negroes, are famous for their risible powers.

This is peculiarly the case on Sunday evenings, when, it is remarked by an ingenious and observant philosopher, who has made great discoveries in the neighbourhood of this city, that they always laugh loudest,—which he attributes to the circumstance of their having their holiday clothes on.

These negroes, in fact, like the monks in the dark ages, engross all the knowledge of the place, and, being infinitely more adventurous, and more knowing than their masters, carry on all the foreign trade, making frequent voyages to town in canoes loaded with oysters, buttermilk and cabbages. They are great astrologers, predicting the different changes of weather almost as accurately as an almanac—they are, moreover, exquisite performers on three-stringed fiddles; in whistling they almost boast the far-famed powers of Orpheus' lyre, for not a horse nor an ox in the place, when at the plough or before the wagon, will budge a foot until he hears the well known whistle of his black driver and companion.

And from their amazing skill at casting up accounts upon their fingers they are regarded with as much veneration as were

---

2. Pavonia, in the ancient maps, is given to a tract of country extending from about Hoboken to Amboy.

the disciples of Pythagoras of yore when initiated into the sacred quaternary of numbers.

As to the honest *burghers* of Communipaw, like wise men and sound philosophers, they never look beyond their pipes, nor trouble their heads about any affairs out of their immediate neighbourhood; so that they live in profound and enviable ignorance of all the troubles, anxieties, and revolutions of this distracted planet. I am even told that many among them do verily believe that Holland, of which they have heard so much from tradition, is situated somewhere on Long Island—that *Spikingdevil* and the *Narrows* are the two ends of the world—that the country is still under the dominion of their High Mightinesses, and that the city of New York still goes by the name of Nieuw Amsterdam.

They meet every Saturday afternoon at the only tavern in the place, which bears as a sign a square-headed likeness of the Prince of Orange, where they smoke a silent pipe by way of promoting social conviviality, and invariably drink a mug of cider to the success of Admiral Van Tromp, whom they imagine is still sweeping the British Channel with a broom at his masthead.

Communipaw, in short, is one of the numerous little villages in the vicinity of this most beautiful of cities, which are so many strongholds and fastnesses whither the primitive manners of our Dutch forefathers have retreated, and where they are cherished with devout and scrupulous strictness.

The dress of the original settlers is handed down inviolate from father to son—the identical broad-brimmed hat, broad-skirted coat, and broad-bottomed breeches continue from generation to generation; and several gigantic knee-buckles of massy silver are still in wear that made gallant display in the days of the patriarchs of Communipaw. The language likewise continues unadulterated by barbarous innovations; and so critically correct is the village schoolmaster in his dialect that his reading of a Low Dutch psalm has much the same effect on the nerves as the filing of a handsaw.

CHAPTER 3

IN WHICH IS SET FORTH THE TRUE ART OF MAKING A BARGAIN—
TOGETHER WITH THE MIRACULOUS ESCAPE OF A GREAT METROPOLIS
IN A FOG—AND THE BIOGRAPHY OF CERTAIN HEROES OF COM-
MUNIPAW.

Having in the trifling digression which concluded the last chapter discharged the filial duty which the city of New York owed to Communipaw, as being the mother settlement; and having given a faithful picture of it as it stands at present, I return with a soothing sentiment of self-approbation to dwell upon its early history. The crew of the *Goede Vrouw* being soon reinforced by fresh importations from Holland, the settlement went jollily on increasing in magnitude and prosperity. The neighbouring Indians in a short time became accustomed to the uncouth sound of the Dutch language, and an intercourse gradually took place between them and the newcomers.

The Indians were much given to long talks, and the Dutch to long silence; in this particular, therefore, they accommodated each other completely. The chiefs would make long speeches about the big bull, the *wabash*, and the Great Spirit, to which the others would listen very attentively, smoke their pipes, and grunt *yah, myn-her*—whereat the poor savages were wondrously delighted. They instructed the new settlers in the best art of curing and smoking tobacco, while the latter in return, made them drunk with true Hollands—and then taught them the art of making bargains.

A brisk trade for furs was soon opened. The Dutch traders were scrupulously honest in their dealings, and purchased by weight, establishing it as an invariable table of *avoirdupois* that the hand of a Dutchman weighed one pound, and his foot two pounds. It is true the simple Indians were often puzzled by the great disproportion between bulk and weight, for let them place a bundle of furs never so large in one scale, and a Dutchman put his hand or foot in the other, the bundle was sure to kick the beam—never was a package of furs known to weigh more than two pounds in the market of Communipaw!

This is a singular fact—but I have it direct from my great-great-grandfather, who had risen to considerable importance in the colony, being promoted to the office of weigh-master, on account of the uncommon heaviness of his foot.

The Dutch possessions in this part of the globe began now to assume a very thriving appearance, and were comprehended under the general title of Nieuw Nederlandts, on account, as the sage Vander Donck observes, of their great resemblance to the Dutch Netherlands—which indeed was truly remarkable, excepting that the former was rugged and mountainous, and the latter level and marshy. About this time the tranquillity of the Dutch colonists was doomed to suffer a temporary interruption. In 1614, Captain Sir Samuel Argal, sailing under a commission from Dale, Governor of Virginia, visited the Dutch settlements on Hudson River, and demanded their submission to the English crown and Virginian dominion. To this arrogant demand, as they were in no condition to resist it, they submitted for the time, like discreet and reasonable men.

It does not appear that the valiant Argal molested the settlement of Communipaw; on the contrary, I am told that when his vessel first hove in sight, the worthy *burghers* were seized with such a panic that they fell to smoking their pipes with astonishing vehemence; insomuch that they quickly raised a cloud, which, combining with the surrounding woods and marshes, completely enveloped and concealed their beloved village, and overhung the fair regions of Pavonia—so that the terrible Captain Argal passed on, totally unsuspicious that a sturdy little Dutch settlement lay snugly couched in the mud, under cover of all this pestilent vapour. In commemoration of this fortunate escape, the worthy inhabitants have continued to smoke almost without intermission unto this very day, which is said to be the cause of the remarkable fog which often hangs over Communipaw of a clear afternoon.

Upon the departure of the enemy our magnanimous ancestors took full six months to recover their wind, having been exceedingly discomposed by the consternation and hurry of affairs. They then called a council of safety to smoke over the state of the provinces. At this council presided one Oloffe Van Kortlandt, who had originally been one of a set of peripatetic philosophers who passed much of their time sunning themselves on the side of the great canal of Amsterdam in Holland; enjoying, like Diogenes, a free and unencumbered estate in sunshine. His name Kortlandt (Shortland or Lackland) was supposed, like that of the illustrious Jean Sansterre, to indicate that he had no land; but he insisted, on the contrary, that he had great landed estates somewhere in *Terra Incognita*; and he had come out to the new world to look after them.

Like all land speculators, he was much given to dreaming. Never did anything extraordinary happen at Communipaw but he declared that he had previously dreamt it, being one of those infallible prophets who predict events after they have come to pass. This supernatural gift was as highly valued among the *burghers* of Pavonia as among the enlightened nations of antiquity. The wise Ulysses was more indebted to his sleeping than his waking moments for his most subtle achievements, and seldom undertook any great exploit without first soundly sleeping upon it; and the same may be said of Oloffe Van Kortlandt, who was thence aptly denominated Oloffe the Dreamer.

As yet his dreams and speculations had turned to little personal profit; and he was as much a lackland as ever. Still he carried a high head in the community: if his sugar-loaf hat was rather the worse for wear, he set it oft with a taller cock's tail; if his shirt was none of the cleanest, he puffed it out the more at the bosom; and if the tail of it peeped out of a hole in his breeches, it at least proved that it really had a tail and was not a mere ruffle.

The worthy Van Kortlandt, in the council in question, urged the policy of emerging from the swamps of Communipaw and seeking some more eligible site for the seat of empire. Such, he said, was the advice of the good St. Nicholas, who had appeared to him in a dream the night before, and whom he had known by his broad hat, his long pipe, and the resemblance which he bore to the figure on the bow of the *Goede Vrouw*.

Many have thought this dream was a mere invention of Oloffe Van Kortlandt, who, it is said, had ever regarded Communipaw with an evil eye, because he had arrived there after all the land had been shared out, and who was anxious to change the seat of empire to some new place, where he might be present at the distribution of "town lots." But we must not give heed to such insinuations, which are too apt to be advanced against those worthy gentlemen engaged in laying out towns and in other land speculations.

This perilous enterprise was to be conducted by Oloffe himself, who chose as lieutenants, or coadjutors, Mynheers Abraham Harden Broeck, Jacobus Van Zandt, and Winant Ten Broeck—three indubitably great men, but of whose history, although I have made diligent inquiry, I can learn but little previous to their leaving Holland. Nor need this occasion much surprise; for adventurers, like prophets, though they make great noise abroad, have seldom much celebrity in their own countries; but this much is certain that the overflowings and offscourings of a country are invariably composed of the richest parts of the soil.

And here I cannot help remarking how convenient it would be to many of our great men and great families of doubtful origin, could they have the privilege of the heroes of yore, who, whenever their origin was involved in obscurity, modestly announced themselves descended from a god,—and who never visited a foreign country but what they told some cock-and-bull stories about their being kings and princes at home. This venal trespass on the truth, though it has been occasionally played off by some pseudo marquis, baronet, and other illustrious foreigner, in our land of good-natured credulity, has been completely discountenanced in this sceptical, matter-of-fact age—and I even question whether any tender virgin, who was accidentally and unaccountably enriched with a bantling, would save her character at parlour firesides and evening tea-parties by ascribing the phenomenon to a swan, a shower of gold, or a river god.

Thus being denied the benefit of mythology and classic fable,

I should have been completely at a loss as to the early biography of my heroes, had not a gleam of light been thrown upon their origin from their names.

By this simple means have I been enabled to gather some particulars concerning the adventurers in question. Van Kortlandt, for instance, was one of those peripatetic philosophers who tax Providence for a livelihood, and like Diogenes, enjoy a free and unencumbered estate in sunshine. He was usually arrayed in garments suitable to his fortune, being curiously fringed and fangled by the hand of time; and was thus helmeted with an old fragment of a hat, which had acquired the shape of a sugar-loaf; and so far did he carry his contempt for the adventitious distinction of dress, that it is said the remnant of a shirt, which covered his back, and dangled like a pocket-handkerchief out of a hole in his breeches, was never washed except by the bountiful showers of heaven.

In this garb was he usually to be seen, sunning himself at noon-day, with a herd of philosophers of the same sect, on the side of the great canal of Amsterdam. Like the nobility of Europe, he took his name of *Kortlandt* (or *lackland*) from his landed estate, which lay somewhere in *terra incognita*.

Of the next of our worthies, might I have had the benefit of mythological assistance, the want of which I have just lamented, I should have made honourable mention, as boasting equally illustrious pedigree with the proudest hero of antiquity. His name of Van Zandt, which being freely translated signifies, *from the dirt*, meaning, beyond a doubt, that like Triptolemus, Themis, the Cyclops, and the Titans, he had sprung from Dame Terra or the Earth!

This supposition is strongly corroborated by his size, for it is well known that all the progeny of Mother Earth were of a gigantic stature; and Van Zandt, we are told, was a tall, raw-boned man, above six feet high,—with an astonishingly hard head. Nor is this origin of the illustrious Van Zandt a whit more improbable or repugnant to belief than what is related and universally admitted of certain of our greatest, or rather richest, men, who we are told with the utmost gravity did originally spring from a dunghill!

Of the third hero, but a faint description has reached to this time, which mention that he was a sturdy, obstinate, worrying, bustling little man; and, from being usually equipped in an old pair of buckskins, was familiarly dubbed Harden Broeck, or *Tough Breeches*.

Ten Broeck completed this *junto* of adventurers. It is a singular but ludicrous fact, which, were I not scrupulous in recording the whole truth, I should almost be tempted to pass over in silence, as incompatible with the gravity and dignity of history, that this worthy gentleman should likewise have been nicknamed from the most whimsical part of his dress. In fact, the small-clothes seems to have been a very important garment in the eyes of our venerated ancestors, owing in all probability to its really being the largest article of raimemt among them.

The name of Ten Broeck, or, as it was sometimes spelt, Tin Broeck, has been indifferently translated into Ten Breeches and Tin Breeches.—the High Dutch commentators incline to the former opinion; and ascribe it to his being the first who introduced into the settlement the ancient Dutch fashion of wearing ten pair of breeches. But the most elegant and ingenious writers on the subject declare in favour of Tin, or rather *Thin*, Breeches; whence they infer that the original bearer of it was a poor but merry rogue, whose galligaskins were none of the soundest, and who, peradventure, may have been the author of that truly philosophical *stanza*:——

> *Then why should we quarrel for riches,*
> *Or any such glittering toys?*
> *A light heart and thin pair of breeches*
> *Will go through the world, my brave boys!*

Such was the gallant *junto* chosen to conduct this voyage into unknown realms; and the whole was put under the superintending care and direction of Oloffe Van Kortlandt, who was held in great reverence among the sages of Communipaw, for the variety and darkness of his knowledge. Having, as I before observed, passed much of his life in the open air, among the peripatetic philosophers of Amsterdam, he had become amazingly well acquainted with the aspect of the heavens, and could as accurately determine when a storm was brewing or a squall rising as a dutiful husband can foresee, from the brow of his spouse, when a tempest is gathering about his ears.

He was moreover a great seer of ghosts and goblins, and a firm believer in omens; but what especially recommended him to public confidence was his marvellous talent at dreaming, for there never was anything of consequence happened at Communipaw but what he declared he had previously dreamt it; being one of those infallible prophets who always predict events after they have come to pass.

This supernatural gift was as highly valued among the burghers of Pavonia, as it was among the enlightened nations of antiquity. The wise Ulysses was more indebted to his sleeping than his waking moments for all his subtle achievements, and seldom undertook any great exploit without first soundly sleeping upon it; and the same may truly be said of the good Van Kortlandt, who was thence aptly denominated, Oloffe the Dreamer.

This cautious commander, having chosen the crews that should accompany him in the proposed expedition, exhorted them to repair to their homes, take a good night's rest, settle all family affairs, and make their wills; before departing on this voyage into unknown realms. And indeed this last was a precautions taken by our forefathers, even in after times when they became more adventurous, and voyaged to Haverstraw, or Kaatskill, or Groodt Esopus, or any other far country, beyond the great waters of the Tappen Zee.

CHAPTER 4
How the heroes of Communipaw voyaged to Hell-Gate, and how they were received there.

And now the rosy blush of morn began to mantle in the east, and soon the rising sun, emerging from amidst golden and purple clouds, shed his blithesome rays on the tin weathercocks of Communipaw. It was that delicious season of the year when Nature, breaking from the chilling thraldom of old winter, like a blooming damsel from the tyranny of a sordid old father, threw herself, blushing with ten thousand charms, into the arms of youthful Spring.

Every tufted copse and blooming grove resounded with the notes of hymeneal love. The very insects, as they sipped the dew that gemmed the tender grass of the meadows, joined in the joyous epithalamium—the virgin bud timidly put forth its blushes, "the voice of the turtle was heard in the land," and the heart of man dissolved away in tenderness.

Oh, sweet Theocritus! had I thine oaten reed, wherewith thou erst did charm the gay Sicilian plains.—Or, oh, gentle Bion! thy pastoral pipe wherein the happy swains of the Lesbian Isle so much delighted, then might I attempt to sing, in soft Bucolic or negligent Idyllium, the rural beauties of the scene; but having nothing, save this jaded goose-quill, wherewith to wing my flight, I must fain resign all poetic disportings of the fancy, and pursue my narrative in humble prose; comforting myself with the hope, that though it may not steal so sweetly upon the imagination of my reader, yet it may commend itself, with virgin modesty, to his better judgment, clothed in the chaste and simple garb of truth.

No sooner did the first rays of cheerful Phoebus dart into the windows of Communipaw than the little settlement was all in motion. Forth issued from his castle the sage Van Kortlandt, and seizing a conch shell, blew a far-resounding blast, that soon summoned all his lusty followers. Then did they trudge resolutely down to the water side, escorted by a multitude of relatives and friends, who all went down, as the common phrase expresses it, "to see them off." And this shows the antiquity of those long family processions, often seen in our city, composed of all ages, sizes, and sexes, laden with bundles and bandboxes, escorting some bevy of country cousins about to depart for home in a market-boat.

The good Oloffe bestowed his forces in a squadron of three canoes, and hoisted his flag on board a little round Dutch boat, shaped not unlike a tub, which had formerly been the jolly-boat of the *Goede Vrouw*. And now, all being embarked, they bade farewell to the gazing throng upon the beach, who continued shouting after them, even when out of hearing, wishing them a happy voyage, advising them to take good care of themselves, not to get drowned—with an abundance of other of those sage and invaluable cautions generally given by landsmen to such as go down to the sea in ships, and adventure upon the deep waters.

In the meanwhile the voyagers cheerily urged their course across the crystal bosom of the bay, and soon left behind them the green shores of ancient Pavonia.

And first they touched at two small islands which lie nearly opposite Communipaw, and which are said to have been brought into existence about the time of the great irruption of the Hudson, when it broke through the Highlands and made its way to the ocean.[1] For, in this tremendous uproar of the waters we are told that many huge fragments of rock and land were rent from the mountains and swept down by this runaway river, for sixty or seventy miles; where some of them ran aground on the shoals just opposite Communipaw, and formed the identical islands in question, while others drifted out to sea, and were never heard of more.

A sufficient proof of the fact is, that the rock which forms the bases of these islands is exactly similar to that of the Highlands; and moreover, one of our philosophers, who has diligently compared the agreement of their respective surfaces, has even gone so far as to assure me, in confidence, that Gibbet Island

---

1. It is a matter long since established by certain of our philosophers, that is to say, having been often advanced and never contradicted, it has grown to be pretty nigh equal to a settled fact, that the Hudson was originally a lake dammed up by the mountains of the Highlands. In process of time, however, becoming very mighty and obstreperous, and the mountains waxing pursy, dropsical, and weak in the back, by reason of their extreme old age, it suddenly rose upon them, and after a violent struggle effected its escape. This is said to have come to pass in very remote time, probably before that rivers had lost the art of running up hill.(Cont. next page.)

was originally nothing more nor less than a wart on Anthony's nose.[2]

Leaving these wonderful little isles, they next coasted by Governor's Island, since terrible from its frowning fortress and grinning batteries. They would by no means, however, land upon this island, since they doubted much it might be the abode of demons and spirits, which in those days did greatly abound throughout this savage and pagan country.

Just at this time a shoal of jolly porpoises came rolling and tumbling by, turning up their sleek sides to the sun, and spouting up the briny element in sparkling showers. No sooner did the sage Oloffe mark this than he was greatly rejoiced. "This," exclaimed he, "if I mistake not, augurs well—the porpoise is a fat, well-conditioned fish—a *burgomaster* among fishes—his looks betoken ease, plenty, and prosperity. I greatly admire this round fat fish, and doubt not but this is a happy omen of the success of our undertaking." So saying, he directed his squadron to steer in the track of these alderman fishes.

Turning, therefore, directly to the left, they swept up the strait, vulgarly called the East River. And here the rapid tide which courses through this strait, seizing on the gallant tub in which Commodore Van Kortlandt had embarked, hurried it forward with a velocity unparalleled in a Dutch boat, navigated by Dutchmen; insomuch that the good commodore, who had all his life long been accustomed only to the drowsy navigation of canals, was more than ever convinced that they were in the hands of some supernatural power, and that the jolly porpoises were towing them to some fair haven that was to fulfil all their wishes and expectations.

Thus borne away by the resistless current, they doubled that boisterous point of land since called Corlear's Hook,[3] and leaving to the right the rich winding cove of the Wallabout, they drifted into a magnificent expanse of water, surrounded by

---

The foregoing is a theory in which I do not pretend to be skilled, not withstanding that I do fully give it my belief.

2. A promontory in the Highlands.

3. Properly spelt Hoeck (*i.e.* a point of land).

pleasant shores, whose verdure was exceedingly refreshing to the eye. While the voyagers were looking around them, on what they conceived to be a serene and sunny lake, they beheld at a distance a crew of painted savages busily employed in fishing, who seemed more like the genii of this romantic region—their slender canoe lightly balanced like a feather on the undulating surface of the bay.

At sight of these the hearts of the heroes of Communipaw were not a little troubled. But as good fortune would have it, at the bow of the commodore's boat was stationed a valiant man, named Hendrick Kip (which, being interpreted, means *chicken*, a name given him in token of his courage).

No sooner did he behold these varlet heathens, than he trembled with excessive valour, and although a good half mile distant, he seized a *musketoon* that lay at hand, and turning away his head, fired it most intrepidly in the face of the blessed sun. The blundering weapon recoiled, and gave the valiant Kip an ignominious kick, which laid him prostrate with uplifted heels in the bottom of the boat. But such was the effect of this tremendous fire, that the wild men of the woods, struck with consternation, seized hastily upon their paddles, and shot away into one of the deep inlets of the Long Island shore.

This signal victory gave new spirits to the voyagers, and in honour of the achievement they gave the name of the valiant Kip to the surrounding bay, and it has continued to be called Kip's Bay from that time to the present. The heart of the good Van Kortlandt—who, having no land of his own, was a great admirer of other people's—expanded to the full size of a peppercorn at the sumptuous prospect of rich unsettled country around him, and falling into a delicious reverie, he straightway began to riot in the possession of vast meadows of salt marsh and interminable patches of cabbages.

From this delectable vision he was all at once awakened by the sudden turning of the tide, which would soon have hurried him from this land of promise, had not the discreet navigator given signal to steer for shore; where they accordingly landed hard by the rocky heights of Bellevue—that happy retreat where our jolly aldermen eat for the good of the city, and fatten the turtle that are sacrificed on civic solemnities.

Here, seated on the greensward, by the side of a small stream that ran sparkling among the grass, they refreshed themselves after the toils of the seas by feasting lustily on the ample stores which they had provided for this perilous voyage. Thus having well fortified their deliberate powers, they fell into an earnest consultation what was further to be done. This was the first council dinner ever eaten at Bellevue by Christian *burghers*; and here, as tradition relates, did originate the great family feud between the Hardenbroecks and the Tenbroecks, which afterwards had a singular influence on the building of the city.

The sturdy Harden Broeck, whose eyes had been wondrously delighted with the salt marshes which spread their reeking bosoms along the coast, at the bottom of Kip's Bay, counseled by all means to return thither, and found the intended city. This was strenuously opposed by the unbending Ten Broeck, and many testy arguments passed between them.

The particulars of this controversy have not reached us, which is ever to be lamented; this much is certain, that the sage Oloffe put an end to the dispute, by determining to explore still farther in the route which the mysterious porpoises had so clearly pointed out—whereupon the sturdy Tough Breeches abandoned the expedition, took possession of a neighbouring hill, and in a fit of great wrath peopled all that tract of country, which has continued to be inhabited by the Hardenbroecks unto this very day.

By this time the jolly Phoebus, like some wanton urchin sporting on the side of a green hill, began to roll down the declivity of the heavens; and now, the tide having once more turned in their favour, the Pavonians again committed themselves to its discretion, and coasting along the western shores, were borne towards the straits of Blackwell's Island.

And here the capricious wanderings of the current occasioned not a little marvel and perplexity to these illustrious mariners. Now would they be caught by the wanton eddies, and, sweeping round a jutting point, would wind deep into some romantic little cove, that indented the fair island of Manna-hata; now were they hurried narrowly by the very bases of impending rocks, mantled with the flaunting grape-vine, and crowned with groves, which threw a broad shade on the waves beneath; and anon they were borne away into the mid-channel and wafted along with a rapidity that very much discomposed the sage Van Kortlandt, who, as he saw the land swiftly receding on either side, began exceedingly to doubt that *terra firma* was giving them the slip.

Wherever the voyagers turned their eyes a new creation seemed to bloom around. No signs of human thrift appeared to check the delicious wildness of Nature, who here revelled in all her luxuriant variety. Those hills, now bristled like the fretful porcupine, with rows of poplars (vain upstart plants! minions of wealth and fashion!), were then adorned with the vigorous natives of the soil—the lordly oak, the generous chestnut, the graceful elm—while here and there the tulip-tree reared its majestic head, the giant of the forest.

Where now are seen the gay retreats of luxury—villas half buried in twilight bowers, whence the amorous flute oft breathes the sighings of some city swain—there the fish-hawk built his solitary nest, on some dry tree that overlooked his watery domain. The timid deer fed undisturbed along those shores now hallowed by the lover's moonlight walk, and printed by the slender foot of beauty; and a savage solitude extended over those happy regions, where now are reared the stately towers of the Joneses, the Schermerhornes, and the Rhinelanders.

Thus gliding in silent wonder through these new and unknown scenes, the gallant squadron of Pavonia swept by the foot of a promontory, which strutted forth boldly into the waves, and seemed to frown upon them as they brawled against its base. This is the bluff well known to modern mariners by the name of Gracie's Point, from the fair castle which, like an elephant, it carries upon its back. And here broke upon their view a wild and varied prospect, where land and water were beauteously intermingled, as though they had combined to heighten and set off each other's charms.

To their right lay the sedgy point of Blackwell's Island, dressed in the fresh garniture of living green—beyond it stretched the pleasant coast of Sundswick, and the small harbour well known by the name of Hallet's Cove—a place infamous in latter days, by reason of its being the haunt of pirates who infest these seas, robbing orchards and water-melon patches, and insulting gentlemen navigators when voyaging in their pleasure boats. To the left a deep bay, or rather creek, gracefully receded between shores fringed with forests, and forming a kind of *vista* through which were beheld the sylvan regions of Haerlem, Morrissania, and East Chester. Here the eye reposed with delight on a richly weeded country, diversified by tufted knolls, shadowy intervals, and waving lines of upland, swelling above each other; while over the whole the purple mists of spring diffused a hue of soft voluptuousness.

Just before them the grand course of the stream, making a sudden bend, wound among embowered promontories and shores of emerald verdure that seemed to melt into the wave. A character of gentleness and mild fertility prevailed around. The sun had just descended, and the thin haze of twilight, like a transparent veil drawn over the bosom of virgin beauty, heightened the charms which it half concealed.

Ah! witching scenes of foul delusion! Ah! hapless voyagers, gazing with simple wonder on these Circean shores! Such, alas! are they, poor easy souls, who listen to the seductions of a wicked world—treacherous are its smiles, fatal its caresses! He who yields to its enticements launches upon a whelming tide, and trusts his feeble bark among the dimpling eddies of a whirlpool! And thus it fared with the worthies of Pavonia, who, little mistrusting the guileful sense before them, drifted quietly on, until they were aroused by an uncommon tossing and agitation of their vessels.

For now the late dimpling current began to brawl around

them, and the waves to boil and foam with horrible fury. Awakened as if from a dream, the astonished Oloffe bawled aloud to put about, but his words were lost amid the roaring of the waters. And now ensued a scene of direful consternation. At one time they were borne with dreadful velocity among tumultuous breakers; at another, hurried down boisterous rapids.

Now they were nearly dashed upon the Hen and Chickens (infamous rocks!—more voracious than Scylla and her whelps!); and anon they seemed sinking into yawning gulfs, that threatened to entomb them beneath the waves. All the elements combined to produce a hideous confusion. The waters raged—the winds howled—and as they were hurried along several of the astonished mariners beheld the rocks and trees of the neighbouring shores driving through the air!

At length the mighty tub of Commodore Van Kortlandt was drawn into the vortex of that tremendous whirlpool called the Pot, where it was whirled about in giddy mazes, until the senses of the good commander and his crew were overpowered by the horror of the scene, and the strangeness of the revolution.

How the gallant squadron of Pavonia was snatched from the jaws of this modern Charybdis has never been truly made known, for so many survived to tell the tale, and, what is still more wonderful, told it in so many different ways, that there has ever prevailed a great variety of opinions on the subject.

As to the commodore and his crew, when they came to their senses they found themselves stranded on the Long Island shore. The worthy commodore, indeed, used to relate many and wonderful stories of his adventures in this time of peril; how that he saw spectres flying in the air, and heard the yelling of hobgoblins, and put his hand into the pot when they were whirled round, and found the water scalding hot, and beheld several uncouth-looking beings seated on rocks and skimming it with huge ladles—but particularly he declared with great exultation, that he saw the losel porpoises, which had betrayed them into this peril, some broiling on the Gridiron, and others hissing on the Frying-pan!

These, however, were considered by many as mere phantasies of the commodore, while he lay in a trance, especially as he was known to be given to dreaming; and the truth of them has never been clearly ascertained. It is certain, however, that to the accounts of Oloffe and his followers may be traced the various traditions handed down of this marvellous strait—as how the devil has been seen there, sitting astride of the Hog's Back and playing on the fiddle—how he broils fish there before a storm; and many other stories, in which we must be cautious of putting too much faith. In consequence of all these terrific circumstances, the Pavonian commander gave this pass the name of Helle-Gat, or, as it has been interpreted, Hell-Gate;[4] which it continues to bear at the present day.

Chapter 5

How the heroes of Communipaw returned somewhat wiser than they went—and how the sage Oloffe dreamed a dream—and the dream that he dreamed.

The darkness of night had closed upon this disastrous day, and a doleful night was it to the shipwrecked Pavonians, whose ears were incessantly assailed with the raging of the elements, and the howling of the hobgoblins that infested this perfidious strait. But when the morning dawned the horrors of the preceding evening had passed away, rapids, breakers and whirlpools had disappeared, the stream again ran smooth and dimpling, and having changed its tide, rolled gently back towards the quarter

---

4. This is a narrow strait in the Sound, at the distance of six miles above New York. It is dangerous to shipping, unless under the care of skillful pilots, by reason of numerous rocks, shelves, and whirlpools. These have received sundry appellations, such as the Gridiron, Frying-pan, Hog's Back, Pot, etc., and are very violent and turbulent at certain times of tide. Certain mealy-mouthed men, of squeamish consciences, who are loth to give the devil his due, have softened the above characteristic name into Hell-gate, forsooth! Let those take care how they venture into the Gate, or they may be hurled into the Pot before they are aware of it. The name of this strait, as given by our author, is supported by the map of Vander Donck's history, published in 1656—by Ogilvie's History of America, 1671—as also by a journal still extant, written in the sixteenth century, and to be found in Hazard's State Papers. And an old MS, written in French, speaking of various alterations, in names about this city, observes, "De Hellegat, trou d'Enfer, ils ont fait Hell-gate, porte d'Enfer."

where lay their much regretted home.

The woebegone heroes of Communipaw eyed each other with rueful countenances; their squadrons had been totally dispersed by the late disaster. Some were cast upon the western shore, where, headed by one Ruleff Hopper, they took possession of all the country lying about the six-mile-stone, which is held by the Hoppers at this present writing.

The Waldrons were driven by stress of weather to a distant coast, where, having with them a jug of genuine Hollands, they were enabled to conciliate the savages, setting up a kind of tavern; whence, it is said, did spring the fair town of Haerlem, in which their descendants have ever since continued to be reputable publicans.

As to the Suydams, they were thrown upon the Long Island coast, and may still be found in those parts. But the most singular luck attended the great Ten Broeck, who, falling overboard, was miraculously preserved from sinking by the multitude of his nether garments. Thus buoyed up, he floated on the waves like a merman, or like the cork float of an angler, until he landed safely on a rock, where he was found the next morning busily drying his many breeches in the sunshine.

I forbear to treat of the long consultation of our adventurers—how they determined that it would never do to found a city in this diabolical neighbourhood—and how at length with fear and trembling, they ventured once more upon the briny element, and steered their course back for Communipaw. Suffice it, in simple brevity, to say, that after toiling back through the scenes of their yesterday's voyage, they at length opened the southern point of Manna-hata, and gained a distant view of Communipaw.

And here they were opposed by an obstinate eddy, that resisted all the efforts of the exhausted mariners. Weary and dispirited as they were, they could no longer make head against the power of the tide, or rather, as some will have it, of old Neptune, who, anxious to guide them to a spot whereon should be founded his stronghold in this western world, sent half a score of potent billows, that rolled the tub of Commodore Van Kortlandt high and dry on the shores of Mann-hata.

Having thus in a manner been guided by supernatural power to this delightful island, their first care was to light a fire at the foot of a large tree, that stood upon the point at present called the Battery. Then gathering together great store of oysters which abounded on the shore, and emptying the contents of their wallets, they prepared and made a sumptuous council repast. The worthy Van Kortlandt was observed to be particularly zealous in his devotions to the trencher; for having the cares of the expedition especially committed to his care, he deemed it incumbent on him to eat profoundly for the public good. In proportion as he filled himself to the very brim with the dainty viands before him, did the heart of this excellent *burgher* rise up towards his throat, until he seemed crammed and almost choked with good eating and good nature.

And at such times it is, when a man's heart is in his throat, that he may more truly be said to speak from it, and his speeches abound with kindness and good fellowship. Thus the worthy Oloffe having swallowed the last possible morsel, and washed it down with a fervent potation, felt his heart yearning, and his whole frame in a manner dilating with unbounded benevolence. Everything around him seemed excellent and delightful; and, laying his hands on each side of his capacious periphery, and rolling his half closed eyes around on the beautiful diversity of land and water before him, he exclaimed, in a fat half smothered voice, "what a charming prospect!"

The words died away in his throat—he seemed to ponder on the fair scene for a moment—his eyelids heavily closed over their orbs—his head drooped upon his bosom—he slowly sunk upon the green turf, and a deep sleep stole gradually upon him.

And the sage Oloffe dreamed a dream—and lo, the good St. Nicholas came riding over the tops of the trees, in that self-same waggon wherein he brings his yearly presents to children, and he came and descended hard by where the heroes of Communipaw had made their late repast. And the shrewd Van Kortlandt knew him by his broad hat, his long pipe, and the resemblance which he bore to the figure on the bow of the *Goede Vrouw*. And he lit his pipe by the fire, and sat himself down and smoked; and as he smoked the smoke from his pipe ascended into the air and spread like a cloud over head.

And Oloffe bethought him, and he hastened and climbed up to the top of one of the tallest trees, and saw that the smoke spread over a great extent of country—and as be considered it more attentively, he fancied that the great volume of smoke assumed a variety of marvellous forms, where in dim obscurity he saw shadowed out palaces and domes and lofty spires, all of which lasted but a moment, and then faded away, until the whole rolled off, and nothing but the green woods were left. And when St. Nicholas had smoked his pipe, he twisted it in his hat band, and laying his finger beside his nose, gave the astonished Van Kortlandt a very significant look, then mounting his waggon, he returned over the tree tops and disappeared.

And Van Kortland awoke from his sleep greatly instructed, and he aroused his companions, and related to them his dream, and interpreted it, that it was the will of St. Nicholas that they should settle down and build the city here. And that the smoke of the pipe was a type how vast should be the extent of the city; inasmuch as the volumes of its smoke should spread over a wide extent of country. And they all with one voice assented to this interpretation excepting Mynheer Ten Broeck, who declared the meaning to be that it should be a city wherein a little fire should occasion a great smoke, or in other words, a very vapouring little city—both which interpretations have strangely come to pass!

The great object of their perilous expedition, therefore, being thus happily accomplished, the voyagers returned merrily to Communipaw, where they were received with great rejoicings. And here calling a general meeting of all the wise men and the dignitaries of Pavonia, they related the whole history of their voyage, and of the dream of Oloffe Van Kortlandt. And the people lifted up their voices and blessed the good St. Nicholas, and from that time forth the sage Van Kortlandt was held in more honour than ever, for his great talent at dreaming, and was pronounced a most useful citizen and a right good man—when he was asleep.

CHAPTER 6

CONTAINING AN ATTEMPT AT ETYMOLOGY—AND OF THE FOUND-ING OF THE GREAT CITY OF NEW-AMSTERDAM.

The original name of the island wherein the squadron of Communipaw was thus propitiously thrown, is a matter of some dispute, and has already undergone considerable vitiation—a melancholy proof of the instability of all sublunary things, and the vanity of all our hopes of lasting fame; for who can expect his name will live to posterity, when even the names of mighty islands are thus soon lost in contradiction and uncertainty!

The name most current at the present day, and which is likewise countenanced by the great historian Vander Donck, is *Manhattan*; which is said to have originated in a custom among the squaws, in the early settlement, of wearing men's hats, as is still done among many tribes. "Hence," as we are told by an old governor who was somewhat of a wag, and flourished almost a century since, and had paid a visit to the wits of Philadelphia, "hence arose the appellation of man-hat-on, first given to the Indians, and afterwards to the island"—a stupid joke!—but well enough for a governor.

Among the more venerable sources of information on this subject, is that valuable history of the American possessions, written by Master Richard Blome, in 1687, wherein it is called Manhadaes and Manahanent; nor must I forget the excellent little book, full of precious matter, of that authentic historian, John Josselyn, Gent, who expressly calls it Manadaes.

Another etymology still more ancient, and sanctioned by the countenance of our ever to be lamented Dutch ancestors, is that found in certain letters still extant;[1] which passed between the early governors and their neighbouring powers, wherein it

1. *Vide* Hazard's Col. Stat. Pap.

is called indifferently Monhattoes—Munhatos, and Manhattoes, which are evidently unimportant variations of the same name; for our wise forefathers sat little store by those niceties either in orthography or orthoepy, which form the sole study and ambition of many learned men and women of this hypercritical age.

This last name is said to be derived from the great Indian spirit Manetho; who was supposed to make this island his favourite abode, on account of its uncommon delights. For the Indian traditions affirm that the bay was once a translucid lake, filled with silver and golden fish, in the midst of which lay this beautiful island, covered with every variety of fruits and flowers; but that the sudden irruption of the Hudson laid waste these blissful scenes, and Manetho took his flight beyond the great waters of Ontario.

These, however, are fabulous legends, to which very cautious credence must be given; and although I am willing to admit the last quoted orthography of the name, as very suitable for prose, yet is there another one founded on still more ancient and indisputable authority, which I particularly delight in, seeing that it is at once poetical, melodious, and significant—and this is recorded in the before mentioned voyage of the great Hudson, written by master Juet; who clearly and correctly calls it *Manna-hata*—that is to say, the island of Manna, or in other words—*"a land flowing with milk and honey!"*

It having been solemnly resolved that the seat of empire should be transferred from the green shores of Pavonia to this delectable island, a vast multitude embarked, and migrated across the mouth of the Hudson, under the guidance of Oloffe the Dreamer, who was appointed protector or patron to the new settlement.

And here let me bear testimony to the matchless honesty and magnanimity of our worthy forefathers, who purchased the soil of the native Indians before erecting a single roof—a circumstance singular and almost incredible in the annals of discovery and colonization.

The first settlement was made on the southwest point of the

island, on the very spot where the good St. Nicholas bad appeared in the dream. Here they built a mighty and impregnable fort and trading house, called *Fort Amsterdam*, which stood on that eminence at present occupied by the custom-house, with the open space now called the Bowling-Green in front.

Around this potent fortress was soon seen a numerous progeny of little Dutch houses, with tiled roofs, all which seemed most lovingly to nestle under its walls, like a brood of half fledged chickens sheltered under the wings of the mother hen. The whole was surrounded by an inclosure of strong *palisadoes*, to guard against any sudden irruption of the savages, who wandered in hordes about the swamps and forests that extended over those tracts of country at present called Broadway, Wall-street, William-street, and Pearl-street. No sooner was the colony once planted than it took root and throve amazingly; for it would seem that this thrice favoured island is like a munificent dunghill, where every foreign weed finds kindly nourishment, and soon shoots up and expands to greatness.

And now the infant settlement having advanced in age and stature, it was thought high time it should receive an honest Christian name, and it was accordingly called *New-Amsterdam*. It is true there were some advocates for the original Indian name, and many of the best writers of the province did long continue to call it by the title of "The Manhattoes;" but this was discountenanced by the authorities, as being heathenish and savage. Besides, it was considered an excellent and praiseworthy measure to name it after a great city of the old world; as by that means it was induced to emulate the greatness and renown of its namesake—in the manner that little snivelling urchins are called after great statesmen, saints, and worthies, and renowned generals of yore, upon which they all industriously copy their examples, and come to be very mighty men in their day and generation.

The thriving state of the settlement, and the rapid increase of houses gradually awakened the good Oloffe from a deep lethargy, into which he had fallen after the building of the fort. He now began to think it was time some plan should be devised, on which the increasing town should be built. Summoning, therefore, his counsellors and coadjutors together, they took pipe in mouth, and forthwith sunk into a very sound deliberation on the subject.

At the very outset of the business an unexpected difference of opinion arose, and I mention it with much sorrowing, as being the first altercation on record in the councils of New-Amsterdam, it was a breaking forth of the grudge and heartburning that had existed between those two eminent *burghers*, Mynheers Tenbroeck and Hardenbroeck, ever since their unhappy altercation on the coast of Bellevue. The great Hardenbroeck had waxed very wealthy and powerful, from his domains, which embraced the whole chain of Apulean mountains that stretched along the gulf of Kip's Bay, and from part of which his descendants have been expelled in latter ages by the powerful clans of the Jones' s and the Schermerhoms.

An ingenious plan for the city was offered by Mynheer Tenbroeck, who proposed that it should be cut up and intersected by canals, after the manner of the most admired cities in Holland. To this Mynheer Hardenbroeck was diametrically opposed, suggesting in place thereof, that they should run out docks and wharves, by means of piles driven into the bottom of the river, on which the town should be built. By these means, said he triumphantly, shall we rescue a considerable space of territory from these immense rivers, and build a city that shall rival Amsterdam, Venice, or any amphibious city in Europe.

To this proposition, Ten Broeck (or Ten Breeches) replied, with a look of as much scorn as he could possibly assume. He cast the utmost censure upon the plan of his antagonist, as being preposterous, and against the very order of things, as he would leave to every true Hollander. "For what," said he, "is a town without canals?—it is like a body without veins and arteries, and must perish for want of a free circulation of the vital fluid."— Tough Breeches, on the contrary, retorted with a sarcasm upon his antagonist, who was somewhat of an arid, dry-boned habit; be remarked, that as to the circulation of the blood being necessary to existence, Mynheer Ten Breeches was a living contradiction to his own assertion; for everybody knew there had not a drop of blood circulated through his wind-dried carcase for good ten years, and yet there was not a greater busy body in the whole colony.

Personalities have seldom much effect in making converts in argument—nor have I ever seen a man convinced of error by being convicted of deformity. At least such was not the case at present. Ten Breeches was very acrimonious in reply, and Tough Breeches, who was a sturdy little man, and never gave up the last word, rejoined with increasing spirit—Ten Breeches had the advantage of the greatest volubility, but Tough Breeches had that invaluable coat of mail in argument called obstinacy—Ten Breeches had, therefore, the most mettle, but Tough Breeches the best bottom—so that though Tea Breeches made a dreadful clattering about his ears, and battered and belaboured him with hard words and sound arguments, yet Tough Breeches hung on most resolutely to the last. They parted, therefore, as is usual in all arguments where both parties are in the right, without coming to any conclusion—but they hated each other most heartily for ever after, and a similar breach with that between the houses of Capulet and Montague, did ensue between the families of Ten Breeches and Tough Breeches,

I would not fatigue my reader With these dull matters of fact, but that my duty as a faithful historian, requires that I should be particular—and in truth, as I am now treating of the critical period, when our city, like a young twig, first received the twists and turns that have since contributed to give it the present picturesque irregularity for which it is celebrated, I cannot be too minute in detailing their first causes.

After the unhappy altercation I have just mentioned, I do not find that anything farther was said on the subject worthy of being recorded. The council, consisting of the largest and oldest heads in the community, met regularly once a week, to ponder on this momentous subject. But either they were deterred by the war of words they had witnessed, or they were naturally averse to the exercise of the tongue, and the consequent exercise of the brains—certain it is, the most profound silence was maintained—the question as usual lay on the table—the members quietly smoked their pipes, making but few laws, without ever enforcing any, and in the mean time the affairs of the settlement went on—as it pleased God.

As most of the council were but little skilled in the mystery of combining pot hooks and hangers, they determined most judiciously not to puzzle either themselves or posterity with voluminous records. The secretary, however, kept the minutes of the council with tolerable precision, in a large vellum folio, fastened with massy brass clasps; the journal of each meeting consisted but of two lines, stating in Dutch, that, "the council sat this day, and smoked twelve pipes, on the affairs of the colony."—By which it appears that the first settlers did not regulate their time by hours, but pipes, in the same manner as they measure distances in Holland at this very time; an admirably exact measurement, as a pipe in the mouth of a true born Dutchman is never liable to those accidents and irregularities that are continually putting our clocks out of order.

In this manner did the profound council of New-Amsterdam smoke, and doze, and ponder, from week to week, month to month, and year to year, in what manner they should construct their infant settlement—meanwhile, the town took care of itself, and like a sturdy brat which is suffered to run about wild, unshackled by clouts and bandages, and other abominations by which your notable nurses and sage old women cripple and disfigure the children of men, increased so rapidly in strength and magnitude, that before the honest *burgomasters* had determined upon a plan, it was too late to put it in execution—whereupon they wisely abandoned the subject altogether.

Chapter 7
How the city of New-Amsterdam waxed great, under the protection of Oloffe the Dreamer.

There is something exceedingly delusive in thus looking back, through the long *vista* of departed years, and catching a glimpse of the fairy realms of antiquity that lie beyond. Like some goodly landscape melting into distance, they receive a thousand charms from their very obscurity, and the fancy delights to fill up their outlines with graces and excellencies of its own creation. Thus beam on my imagination those happier days of our city, when as yet New-Amsterdam was a mere pastoral town, shrouded in groves of sycamore and willows, and surrounded by trackless forests and wide spreading waters, that seemed to shut out all the cares and vanities of a wicked world.

In those days did this embryo city present the rare and noble spectacle of a community governed without laws; and thus being left to its own course, and the fostering care of Providence, increased as rapidly as though it had been burthened with a dozen panniers full of those sage laws that are usually heaped on the backs of young cities—in order to make them grow. And in this particular I greatly admire the wisdom and sound knowledge of human nature, displayed by the sage Oloffe the Dreamer, and his fellow legislators.

For my part I have not so bad an opinion of mankind as many of my brother philosophers. I do not think poor human nature so sorry a piece of workmanship as they would make it out to be; and as far as I have observed, I am fully satisfied that man, if left to himself, would about as readily go right as wrong. It is only this eternally sounding in his ears that it is his duty to go right, that makes him go the very reverse. The noble independence of his nature revolts at this intolerable tyranny of law, and the perpetual interference of officious morality, which is ever besetting his path with finger posts and directions to "keep to the right, as the law directs;" and like a spirited urchin, he turns directly contrary, and gallops through mud and mire, over hedges and ditches, merely to show that he is a lad of spirit, and out of his leading strings.

And these opinions are amply substantiated by what I have above said of our worthy ancestors; who never being be-preached and be-lectured, and guided and governed by statutes and laws and by-laws, as are their more enlightened descendants, did one and all demean themselves honestly and peaceably, out of pure ignorance, or in other words—because they knew no better.

Nor must I omit to record one of the earliest measures of this infant settlement, inasmuch as it shows the piety of our forefathers, and that, like good Christians, they were always ready to serve God, after they had first served themselves. Thus, having quietly settled themselves down, and provided for their own comfort, they bethought themselves of testifying their gratitude to the great and good St. Nicholas, for his protecting care, in guiding them to this delectable abode. To this end they built a fair and goodly chapel within the fort, which they consecrated to his name; whereupon he immediately took the town of New-Amsterdam under his peculiar patronage, and he has even since been, and I devoutly hope will ever be, the tutelar saint of this excellent city.

I am moreover told that there is a little legendary book, somewhere extant, written in Low Dutch, which says, that the image of this renowned saint, which whilom graced the bowsprit of the *Goede Vrouw*, was elevated in front of this chapel, in the very centre of what, in modem days, is called the Bowling Green. And the legend further treats of divers miracles wrought by the mighty pipe, which the saint held in his mouth; a whiff of which was a sovereign cure for an indigestion—an invaluable relic in this colony of brave trenchermen. As, however, in spite of the most diligent search, I cannot lay my hands upon this little book, I must confess that I entertain considerable doubt on the subject.

Thus benignly fostered by the good St. Nicholas, the *burghers* of New-Amsterdam beheld their settlement increase in magnitude and population, and soon become the metropolis of divers settlements, and an extensive territory. Already had the disastrous pride of colonies and dependencies, those banes of a sound hearted empire, entered into their imaginations; and Fort Aurania on the Hudson, Fort Nassau on the Delaware, and Fort Goede Hoep on the Connecticut River, seemed to be the daring offspring of the venerable council.[1] Thus prosperously, to all appearance, did the province of New-Netherlands advance in power; and the early history of its metropolis presents a fair page, unsullied by crime or calamity.

Hordes of painted savages still lurked about the tangled forests and rich bottoms of the unsettled part of the island—the hunter pitched his rude bower of skins and bark beside the rills that ran through the cool and shady glens, while here and there might be seen, on some sunny knoll, a group of Indian *wigwams*, whose smoke arose above the neighbouring trees, and floated in the transparent atmosphere. By degrees a mutual good will had grown up between these wandering beings and the *burghers* of New-Amsterdam, Our benevolent forefathers endeavoured as much as possible to ameliorate their situation, by giving them gin, rum, and glass beads, in exchange for their peltries; for it seems the kind-hearted Dutchmen had conceived a great friendship for their savage neighbours, on account of their being pleasant men to trade with, and little skilled in the art of making a bargain.

Now and then a crew of these half human sons of the forest would make their appearance in the streets of New-Amsterdam, fantastically painted and decorated with beads and flaunting feathers, sauntering about with an air of listless indifference—sometimes in the market-place, instructing the little Dutch boys in the use of the bow and arrow—at other times, inflamed with liquor, swaggering and whooping and yelling about the town like so many fiends, to the great dismay of all the good wives, who would hurry their children into the house, fasten the doors,

---

1. The province, about this time, extended on the north to Fort Aurania, or Orange (now the city of Albany,) situated about 160 miles up the Hudson river. Indeed the province claimed quite to the River St. Lawrence; but this claim was not much insisted on at the time, as the country beyond Fort Aurania was a perfect wilderness. On the south the province reached to Fort Nassau, on the south river, since called the Delaware—and on the east it extended to the Varche (or fresh) river, now the Connecticut. On this last frontier was likewise erected a fort or trading house, much about the spot where at present is situated the pleasant town of Hartford. This was called Fort Good Hoep, (or Good Hope) and was intended as well for the purpose of trade, as of defence.

and throw water upon the enemy from the garret windows.

It is worthy of mention here, that our forefathers were very particular in holding up these wild men as excellent domestic examples—and for reasons that may be gathered from the history of master Ogilby, who tells us, that "for the least offence the bridegroom soundly beats his wife and turns her out of doors, and marries another, insomuch that some of them have every year a new wife."

Whether this awful example had any influence or not, history does not mention; but it is certain that our grandmothers were miracles of fidelity and obedience.

True it is, that the good understanding between our ancestors and their savage neighbours, was liable to occasional interruptions, and I have heard my grandmother, who was a very wise old woman, and well versed in the history of these parts, tell a long story of a winter's evening, about a battle between the New-Amsterdammers and the Indians, which was known by the name of the *Peach War*, and which took place near a peach orchard, in a dark glen, which for a long while went by the name of Murderer's valley.

The legend of this sylvan war was long current among the nurses, old wives, and other ancient chroniclers of the place; but time and improvement have almost obliterated both the tradition and the scene of battle; for what was once the blood stained valley is now in the centre of this populous city, and known by the name of Dey-street.

The accumulating wealth and consequence of New-Amsterdam and its dependencies at length awakened the tender solicitude of the mother country; who finding it a thriving and opulent colony, and that it promised to yield great profit, and no trouble, all at once became wonderfully anxious about its safety, and began to load it with tokens of regard, in the same manner that your knowing people are sure to overwhelm rich relations with their affection and loving kindness.

The usual marks of protection shown by mother countries to wealthy colonies were forthwith manifested—the first care always being to send rulers to the new settlement, with orders to squeeze as much revenue from it as it will yield. Accordingly, in the year of our Lord 1629, Mynheer Wouter Van Twiller was appointed governor of the province of Nieuw-Nederlandts, under the commission and control of their High Mightinesses, the Lords States General of the United Netherlands, and the privileged West India Company.

This renowned old gentleman arrived at New-Amsterdam in the merry month of June, the sweetest month in all the year; when Dan Apollo seems to dance up the transparent firmament—when the robin, the thrush, and a thousand other wanton songsters make the woods to resound with amorous ditties, and the luxurious little boblincon revels among the clover blossoms of the meadows—all which happy coincidence persuaded the old dames of New-Amsterdam, who were skilled in the art of foretelling events, that this was to be a happy and prosperous administration.

But as it would be derogatory to the consequence of the first Dutch governor of the great province of Nieuw-Nederlandts to be thus scurvily introduced at the end of a chapter, I will put an end to this second book of my history, that I may usher him in with more dignity in the beginning of my next.

Book 3

In Which is Recorded the Golden Reign of Wouter Van Twiller.

Chapter 1.

Of the renowned Wolter Van Twiller—his unparalleled virtues—as likewise his unutterable wisdom in the law–case of Wandle Schoonhoven and Barent Bleecker—and the great admiration of the public thereat.

Grievous and very much to be commiserated is the task of the feeling historian, who writes the history of his native land. If it fall to his lot to be the sad recorder of calamity or crime, the mournful page is watered with his tears—nor can he recall the most prosperous and blissful era, without a melancholy sigh at the reflection, that it has passed away forever! I know not whether it be owing to an immoderate love for the simplicity of former times, or to that certain tenderness of heart incident to all sentimental historians; but I candidly confess that I cannot look back on the happier days of our city, which I now describe, without a sad dejection of the spirits. With a faltering hand do I withdraw the curtain of oblivion, that veils the modest merit of our venerable ancestors, and as their fibres rise to my mental vision, humble myself before the mighty shades.

Such are my feelings when I revisit the family mansion of the Knickerbockers, and spend a lonely hour in the chamber where hang the portraits of my forefathers, shrouded in dust, like the forms they represent. With pious reverence do I gaze on the countenances of those renowned *burghers*, who have preceded me in the steady march of existence—whose sober and temperate blood now meanders through my veins, flowing slower and slower in its feeble conduits, until its current shall soon be stopped forever!

These, say I to myself, are but frail memorials of the mighty men who flourished in the days of the patriarchs; but who, alas, have long since mouldered in that tomb, towards which my steps are insensibly and irresistibly hastening! As I pace the darkened chamber and lose myself in melancholy musings, the shadowy images around me almost seem to steal once more into existence—their countenances to assume the animation of life—their eyes to pursue me in every movement! carried away by the delusions of fancy, I almost imagine myself surrounded by the shades of the departed, and holding sweet converse with the worthies of antiquity!

Ah, hapless Diedrich! born in a degenerate age, abandoned to the buffetings of fortune—a stranger and a weary pilgrim in thy native land—blest with no weeping wife, nor family of helpless children; but doomed to wander neglected through those crowded streets, and elbowed by foreign upstarts from those fair abodes where once thine ancestors held sovereign empire!

Let me not, however, lose the historian in the man, nor suffer the doting recollections of age to overcome me, while dwelling with fond garrulity on the virtuous days of the patriarchs—on those sweet days of simplicity and ease, which never more will dawn on the lovely island of Manna-hata!

The renowned Wouter (or Walter) Van Twiller, was descended from a long line of Dutch *burgomasters*, who had successively dozed away their lives, and grown fat upon the bench of magistracy in Rotterdam; and who had comported themselves with such singular wisdom and propriety, that they were never either heard or talked of—which, next to being universally applauded, should be the object of ambition of all sage magistrates and rulers.

His surname of Twiller, is said to be a corruption of the original *Twijfler*, which in English means *doubter*, a name admirably descriptive of his deliberative habits. For, though he was a man shut up within himself like an oyster, and of such a profoundly reflective turn, that be scarcely ever spoke except in monosyllables, yet did he never make up his mind on any doubtful point. This was clearly accounted for by his adherents, who affirmed that he always conceived every subject on so comprehensive a scale, that he had not room in his head to turn it over and examine both sides of it, so that he always remained in doubt, merely in consequence of the astonishing magnitude of his ideas!

There are two opposite ways by which some men get into notice—one by talking a vast deal and thinking a little, and the other by holding their tongues and not thinking at all. By the first, many a vapouring superficial pretender acquires the reputation of a man of quick parts—by the other, many a vacant dunderpate, like the owl, the stupidest of birds, comes to be complimented by a; discerning world with all the attributes of wisdom. This, by the way, is a mere casual remark, which I would not for the universe have it thought I apply to Governor Van Twiller.

On the contrary, he was a very wise Dutchman, for he never said a foolish thing—and of such invincible gravity, that he was never known to laugh, or even to smile, through the course of a long and prosperous life. Certain, however, it is, there never Was a matter proposed, however simple, and on which your common narrow minded mortals would rashly determine at the first glance, but what the renowned Wouter put on a mighty mysterious, vacant kind of look, shook his capacious head, and having smoked for five minutes with redoubled earnestness, sagely observed, that "he had his doubts about the matter"—which in process of time gained him the character of a man slow of belief, and not easily imposed on.

The person of this illustrious old gentleman was as regularly formed, and nobly proportioned, as though it had been moulded by the hands of some cunning Dutch statuary, as a model of majesty and lordly grandeur. He was exactly five feet six inches in height, and six feet five inches in circumference. His head was a perfect sphere, and of such stupendous dimensions, that dame Nature with all her sex's ingenuity, would have been puzzled to construct a neck capable of supporting it; wherefore she wisely declined the attempt, and settled it firmly on the top of his back bone, just between the shoulders. His body was of an oblong form, particularly capacious at bottom; which was wisely ordered by Providence, seeing that he was a man of sedentary habits, and very averse to the idle labour of walking.

His legs, though exceeding short, were sturdy in proportion to the weight they had to sustain; so that when erect he had not a little the appearance of a robustious beer barrel, standing on skids. His face, that infallible index of the mind, presented a vast expanse, perfectly unfurrowed or deformed by any of those lines and angles which disfigure the human countenance with what is termed expression. Two small grey eyes twinkled feebly in the midst, like two stars of lesser magnitude in a hazy firmament; and his full-fed cheeks, which seemed to have taken toll of everything that went into his mouth, were curious mottled and streaked with dusky red, like a *spitzenberg* apple.

His habits were as regular as his person. He daily took his four stated meals, appropriating exactly an hour to each; he smoked and doubted eight hours, and he slept the remaining twelve of the four-and-twenty. Such was the renowned Wouter Van Twiller—a true philosopher, for his mind was either elevated above, or tranquilly settled below, the cares and perplexities of this world. He had lived in it for years, without feeling the least curiosity to know whether the sun revolved round it, or it round the sun; and he had watched, for at least half a century, the smoke curling from his pipe to the ceiling, without once troubling his head with any of those numerous theories, by which a philosopher would have perplexed his brain, in accounting for its rising' above the surrounding atmosphere.

In his council he presided with great state and solemnity. He sat in a huge chair of solid oak hewn in the celebrated forest of the Hague, fabricated by an experienced *timmerman* of Amsterdam, and curiously carved about the arms and feet, into exact imitations of gigantic eagle's claws. Instead of a sceptre he swayed a long Turkish pipe, wrought with jasmin and amber, which had been presented to a *stadtholder* of Holland, at the conclusion of a treaty with one of the petty Barbary powers.—In this stately chair would he sit, and this magnificent would he smoke, shaking his right knee with a constant motion, and fixing his eye for hours together upon a little print of Amsterdam, which hung in a black frame against the opposite wall of the council chamber.

Nay, it has even been said, that when any deliberation of extraordinary length and intricacy was on the carpet, the renowned Wouter would absolutely shut his eyes for full two hours at a time, that he might not be disturbed by external objects—and at such times the internal commotion of his mind was evinced by certain regular guttural sounds, which his admirers declared were merely the noise of conflict, made by his contending doubts and opinions.

It is with infinite difficulty I have been enabled to collect these biographical anecdotes of the great man under consideration. The facts respecting him were so scattered and vague, and divers of them so questionable in point of authenticity, that I have had to give up the search after many, and decline the admission of still more, which would have tended to heighten the colouring of his portrait.

I have been the more anxious to delineate fully the person and habits of the renowned Van Twiller, from the consideration that he was not only the first, but also the best governor that ever presided over this ancient and respectable province; and so tranquil and benevolent was his reign, that I do not find throughout the whole of it, a single instance of any offender being brought to punishment—a most indubitable sign of a merciful governor, and a case unparalleled, excepting in the reign of the illustrious King Log, from whom, it is hinted, the renowned Van Twiller was a lineal descendant.

The very outset of the career of this excellent magistrate was distinguished by an example of legal acumen, that gave flattering presage of a wise and equitable administration. The morning after he had been solemnly installed in office, and at the moment that he was making his breakfast from a prodigious earthen dish, filled with milk and Indian pudding, he was suddenly interrupted by the appearance of one Wandle Schoonhoven, a very important old *burgher* of New-Amsterdam, who complained bitterly of one Barent Bleecker, inasmuch as he fraudulently refused to come to a settlement of accounts, seeing that there was a heavy balance in favour of the said Wandle.

Governor Van Twiller, as I have already observed, was a man of few words, he was likewise a mortal enemy to multiplying writings—or being disturbed at his breakfast. Having listened attentively to the statement of Wandle Schoonhoven, giving an occasional grunt, as he shovelled a spoonful of Indian pudding into his mouth—either as a sign that he relished the dish, or comprehended the story—he called unto him his constable, and pulling out of his breeches pocket a huge jack-knife, despatched it after the defendant as a summons, accompanied by his tobacco box as a warrant.

This summary process was as effectual in those simple days as was the seal ring of the great Haroun Alraschid among the true believers. The two parties being confronted before him, each produced a book of accounts, written in a language and character that would have puzzled any but a High Dutch commentator, or a learned decipherer of Egyptian obelisks to understand. The sage Wouter took them one after the other, and having poised them in his hands, and attentively counted over the number of leaves, fell straightway into a very great doubt, and smoked for half an hour without saying a word; at length, laying his finger beside his nose, and shutting his eyes for a moment, with the air of a man who has just caught a subtle idea by the tail, he slowly took his pipe from his mouth, puffed forth a column of tobacco smoke, and with marvellous gravity and solemnity pronounced—that having carefully counted over the leaves and weighed the books, it was found, that one was just as thick and as heavy as the other—therefore it was the final opinion of the court that-the accounts were equally balanced—therefore Wandle should give Barent a receipt, and Barent should give Wandle a receipt—and the constable should pay the costs.

This decision being straightway made known, diffused general joy throughout New-Amsterdam, for the people immediately perceived, that they had a very wise and equitable magistrate to rule over them. But its happiest effect was, that not another law suit took place throughout the whole of his administration—and the office of constable fell into such decay, that there was not one of those losel scouts known in the province for many years. I am the more particular in dwelling on this transaction, not only because I deem it one of the most sage and righteous judgements on record, and well worthy the attention of modern magistrates, but because it was a miraculous event in the history of the renowned Wouter, being the only time he was ever known to come to a decision in the whole course of his life.

CHAPTER 2
CONTAINING SAME ACCOUNT OF THE GRAND COUNCIL OF NEW AMSTERDAM, AS ALSO DIVERS ESPECIAL GOOD PHILOSOPHICAL REASONS WHY AN ALDERMAN SHOULD BE FAT,—WITH OTHER PARTICULARS TOUCHING THE STATE OF THE PROVINCE.

In treating of the early governors of the province, I must caution my readers against confounding them, in point of dignity and power, with those worthy gentlemen, who are whimsically denominated governors in this enlightened republic—a set of unhappy victims of popularity, who are in fact the most dependent, henpecked beings in the community: doomed to bear the secret goadings and corrections of their own party, and the sneers and revilings of the whole world beside;—set up, like geese at Christmas holidays, to be pelted and shot at by every whipster and vagabond in the land.

On the contrary, the Dutch governors enjoyed that uncontrolled authority, vested in all commanders of distant colonies or territories. They were in a manner absolute despots in their little domains, lording it, if so disposed, over both law and gospel, and accountable to none but the mother country; which it is well known is astonishingly deaf to all complaints against its governors, provided they discharge the main duty of their station—squeezing out a good revenue. This hint will be of importance, to prevent my readers from being seized with doubt and incredulity, whenever, in the course of this authentic history, they encounter the uncommon circumstance of a governor acting with independence, and in opposition to the opinions of the multitude.

To assist the doubtful Wouter in the arduous business of legislation, a board of magistrates was appointed, which presided immediately over the police. This potent body consisted of a *schout* or bailiff, with powers between those of the present mayor and sheriff—five *burgermeesters*, who were equivalent to aldermen, and five *schepens*, who officiated as scrubs, sub-devils, or bottle-holders to the *burgermeesters*, in the same manner as do assistant aldermen to their principals at the present day; it being their duty to fill the pipes of the lordly *burgermeesters*—hunt the markets for delicacies for corporation dinners, and to discharge such other little offices of kindness as were occasionally required.

It was, moreover, tacitly understood, though not specifically enjoined, that they should consider themselves as butts for the blunt wits of the *burgermeesters*, and should laugh most heartily at all their jokes; but this last was a duty as rarely called in action in those days as it is at present, and was shortly remitted, in consequence of the tragical death of a fat little *schepen*—who actually died of suffocation in an unsuccessful effort to force a laugh at one of the *burgermeester* Van Zandt's best jokes.

In return for these fancible services, they were permitted to say *yes* and *no* at the council board, and to have that enviable privilege, the run of the public kitchen—being graciously permitted to eat, and drink, and smoke, at all those snug junketings and public gormandizings, for which the ancient magistrates were equally famous with their modern successors. The post of *schepen*, therefore, like that of assistant alderman, was eagerly coveted by all your *burghers* of a certain description, who have a huge relish for good feeding, and an humble ambition to be great men in a small way—who thirst after a little brief authority, that shall render them the terror of the alms-house and the bridewell—that shall enable them to lord it over obsequious poverty, vagrant vice, outcast prostitution, and hunger driven dishonesty—that shall give to their beck a hound-like pack of catch-poles and bum-bailiffs—tenfold greater rogues than the culprits they hunt down!—My readers will excuse this sudden warmth, which I confess is unbecoming of a grave historian—but I have a mortal antipathy to catch-poles, bum-bailiffs, and little great men.

The ancient magistrates of this city corresponded with those of the present time no less in form, magnitude, and intellect, than in prerogative and privilege. The *burgomasters*, like our aldermen, were generally chosen by weight—and not only, the weight of the body, but likewise the weight of the head. It is a maxim practically observed in all honest, plain thinking, regular cities, that an alderman should, be fat—and the wisdom of this can be proved to a certainty. That the body is in some measure an image of the mind, or rather that the mind is moulded to the body, like malted lead, to the clay in which it is cast, has been insisted on by many philosophers, who have made human nature their peculiar study—For as a learned gentleman of our own city observes, "there is a constant relation between the moral character of all intelligent creatures, and their physical constitution—between their habits and the structure of their bodies."

Thus we see, that a lean, spare, diminutive body, is generally accompanied by a petulant, restless, meddling mind—either the mind wears-down the body, by its continual motion; or else the body, not affording the mind sufficient house-room, keeps it continually in a state of fretfulness, tossing, and worrying about from the uneasiness of its situation. Whereas your round, sleek, fat, unwieldy periphery is ever attended by a mind like itself, tranquil, torpid, and at ease; and we may always observe, that your well fed, robustious *burghers* are in general very tenacious of their ease and comfort; being great enemies to noise, discord, and disturbance—and surely none are more likely to study the public tranquillity than those who are so careful of their own. Whoever hears of fat men heading a riot, or herding together in turbulent mobs?—no—no—it is your lean, hungry men, who are continually worrying society, and setting the whole community by the ears.

The divine Plato, whose doctrines are not sufficiently attended to by philosophers of the present age, allows to every man three souls—one immortal and rational, seated in the brain, that it may overlook and regulate the body—a second consisting of the surly and irascible passions, which, like belligerent powers, lie encamped around the heart—a third mortal and sensual, destitute of reason, gross and brutal in its propensities, and enchained in the belly, that it may not disturb the divine soul, by its ravenous howlings.

Now, according to this excellent theory, what can be more clear, than that your fat alderman is most likely to have the most regular and well conditioned mind. His head is like a huge, spherical chamber, containing a prodigious mass of soft brains, whereon the rational soul lies softly and snugly couched, as on a feather bed; and the eyes, which are the windows of the bed chamber, are usually half closed, that its slumberings may not be disturbed by external objects.

A mind thus comfortably lodged, and protected from disturbance, is manifestly most likely to perform its functions with regularity and ease. By dint of good feeding, moreover, the mortal and malignant soul, which is confined in the belly, and which, by its raging and roaring, puts the irritable soul in the neighbourhood of the heart in an intolerable passion, and thus renders men crusty and quarrelsome when hungry, is completely pacified, silenced, and put to rest—whereupon a host of honest good fellow qualities and kind hearted affections, which had lain *perdue*, slyly peeping out of the loop holes of the heart, finding this Cerberus asleep, do pluck up their spirits, turn out one and all in their holiday suits, and gambol up and down the diaphragm—disposing their possessor to laughter, good humour, and a thousand friendly offices towards his fellow mortals.

As a board of magistrates, formed on this model, think but very little, they are the less likely to differ and wrangle about favourite opinions—and as they generally transact business upon a hearty dinner, they are naturally disposed to be lenient and indulgent in the administration of their duties. Charlemagne was conscious of this, and therefore (a pitiful measure, for which I can never forgive him) ordered in his cartularies, that no judge should hold a court of justice, except in the morning, on an empty stomach.—a rule which, I warrant, bore hard upon all the poor culprits in his kingdom.

The more enlightened and humane generation of the present day have taken an opposite course, and have so managed, that the aldermen are the best fed men in the community; feasting lustily on the fat things of the land, and gorging so heartily oysters and turtles, that in process of time they acquire the activity of the one, and the form, the waddle, and the green fat of the other. The consequence is, as I have just said, these luxurious feastings do produce such a dulcet equanimity and repose of the soul, rational and irrational, that their transactions are proverbial for unvarying monotony—and the profound laws which they enact in their dozing moments, amid the labours of digestion, are quietly suffered to remain as dead letters, and never enforced, when awake.

In a word, your fair round-bellied *burgomaster*, like a full fed mastiff, dozes quietly at the house-door, always at home, and always at hand to watch over its safety—but as to electing a lean, meddling candidate to the office, as has now and then been done, I would as leave put a greyhound to watch the house, or a race horse to drag an ox wagon.

The *burgomasters* then, as I have already mentioned, were wisely chosen by weight, and the *schepens*, or assistant aldermen, were appointed to attend upon them, and help them eat; but the latter, in the course of time, when they had been fed and fattened into sufficient bulk of body and drowsiness of brain, became very eligible candidates for the *burgomasters'* chairs, having fairly eaten themselves into office, as a mouse eats his way into a comfortable lodgement in a goodly, blue-nosed, skimmed milk, New-England cheese.

Nothing could equal the profound deliberations that took place between the renowned Wouter, and these his worthy compeers, unless it be the sage divans of some of our modern corporations. They would sit for hours smoking and dozing over public affairs, without speaking a word to interrupt that perfect stillness, so necessary to deep reflection. Under the sober sway of Wouter Van Twiller and these his worthy coadjutors, the infant settlement waxed vigorous apace, gradually emerging from the swamps and forests, and exhibiting that mingled appearance of town and country, customary in new cities, and which at this day may be witnessed in the city of Washington; that immense metropolis, which makes so glorious an appearance on paper.

It was a pleasing sight in those times, to behold the honest *burgher*, like a patriarch of yore, seated on the bench at the door of his white-washed house, under the shade of some gigantic sycamore or over-hanging willow. Here would he smoke his pipe of a sultry afternoon, enjoying the soft southern breeze, and listening with silent gratulation to the clucking of his hens, the cackling of his geese, and the sonorous grunting of his swine; that combination of farm-yard melody, which may truly be said to have a silver sound, inasmuch as it conveys a certain assurance of profitable marketing.

The modern spectator, who wanders through the streets of this populous city, can scarcely form an idea of the different appearance they presented in the primitive days of the Doubter. The busy hum of multitudes, the shouts of revelry, the rumbling equipages of fashion, the rattling of accursed carts, and all the spirit grieving sounds of brawling commerce, were unknown in the settlement of New-Amsterdam. The grass grew quietly in the high ways—the bleating sheep and frolicsome calves sported about the verdant ridge, where now the Broadway loungers take their morning stroll—the cunning fox or ravenous wolf skulked in the woods, where now are to be seen the dens of Gomez and his righteous fraternity of money brokers—and flocks of vociferous geese cackled about the fields, where now the great Tammany *wigwam* and the patriotic tavern of Martling echo with the wranglings of the mob.

In these good times did a true and enviable equality of rank and property prevail, equally removed from the arrogance of wealth, and the servility and heart-burnings of repining poverty—and what in my mind is still more conducive to tranquillity and harmony among friends, a happy equality of intellect was likewise to be seen. The minds of the good *burghers* of New-Amsterdam seemed all to have been cast in one mould, and to be those honest, blunt minds, which, like certain manufactures, are made by the gross, and considered as exceedingly good for common use.

Thus it happens that your true dull minds are generally preferred for public employ, and especially promoted to city honours; your keen intellects, like razors, being considered too sharp for common service. I know that it is common to rail at the unequal distribution of riches, as the great source of jealousies, broils, and heart-breakings; whereas, for my part, I verily believe it is the sad inequality of intellect that prevails, that embroils communities more than anything else; and I have remarked that your knowing people, who are so much wiser than anybody else, are eternally keeping society in a ferment.

Happily for New-Amsterdam, nothing of the kind was known within its walls—the very words of learning, education, taste, and talents were unheard of—a bright genius was an animal unknown, and a blue stocking lady would have been regarded with as much wonder as a horned frog or a fiery dragon. No man in fact seemed to know more than his neighbour, nor any man to know more than an honest man ought to know, who has nobody's business to mind but his own; the parson and the council clerk were the only men that could read in the community, and the sage Van Twiller always signed his name with a cross.

Thrice happy and ever to be envied little *burgh*! existing in all the security of harmless insignificance—unnoticed and unenvied by the world, without ambition, without vain glory, without riches, without learning, and all their train of carking cares—and as of yore, in the better days of man, the deities were wont to visit him on earth and bless his rural habitations, so we are told, in the sylvan days of New-Amsterdam, the good St. Nicholas would often make his appearance in his beloved city, of a holiday afternoon, riding jollily among the tree tops, or over the roofs of the houses, now and then drawing forth magnificent presents from his breeches pockets, and dropping them down the chimneys of his favourites.

Whereas in these degenerate days of iron and brass he never shows us the light of his countenance, nor ever visits us, save one night in the year; when he rattles down the chimneys of the descendants of the patriarchs, confining his presents merely to the children, in token of the degeneracy of the parents.

Such are the comfortable and thriving effects of a fat government. The province of the New-Netherlands, destitute of wealth, possessed a sweet tranquillity that wealth could never purchase. There were neither public commotions, nor private quarrels; neither parties, nor sects, nor schisms; neither persecutions, nor trials, nor punishments; nor were there counsellors, attorneys, catch-poles, or hangmen. Every man attended to what little business he was lucky enough to have, or neglected it if he pleased, without asking the opinion of his neighbour.

In those days nobody meddled with concerns above his comprehension, nor thrust his nose into other people's affairs; nor neglected to correct his own conduct, and reform his own character, in his zeal to pull to pieces the characters of others— but in a word, every respectable citizen eat when he was not hungry, drank when he was not thirsty, and went regular to bed when the sun set, and the fowls went to roost, whether he were sleepy or not; all which tended so remarkably to the population of the settlement, that I am told every dutiful wife throughout New-Amsterdam made a point of enriching her husband with at least one child a year, and very often a brace—this superabundance of good things clearly constituting the true luxury of life, according to the favourite Dutch maxim, that "*more than enough constitutes a feast.*"

Everything, therefore, went on exactly as it should do, and in the usual words employed by historians to express the welfare of a country, "the profoundest *tranquillity* and *repose* reigned throughout the province."

Chapter 3

How the town of New-Amsterdam arose out of mud, and came to be marvellously polished and polite—together with a picture of the manners of our great-great-grand-fathers.

Manifold are the tastes and dispositions of the enlightened *literati* who turn over the pages of history. Some there be whose hearts are brimful of the yeast of courage, and whose bosoms do work, and swell, and foam with untried valour, like a barrel of new cider, or a train-band captain fresh from under the hands of his tailor. This doughty class of readers can be satisfied with nothing but bloody battles, and horrible encounters; they must be continually storming forts, sacking cities, springing mines, marching up to the muzzles of cannon, charging bayonet through every page, and revelling in gunpowder and carnage.

Others, who are of a less martial, but equally ardent imagination, and who, withal, are little given to the marvellous, will dwell with wondrous satisfaction on descriptions of prodigies, unheard of events, hair-breadth escapes, hardy adventures, and all those astonishing narrations which just amble along the boundary line of possibility.

A third class, who, not to speak slightly of them, are of a lighter turn, and skim over the records of past times, as they do over the edifying pages of a novel, merely for relaxation and innocent amusement, do singularly delight in treasons, executions, Sabine rapes, Tarquin outrages, conflagrations, murders, and all the other catalogues of hideous crimes, which, like cayenne in cookery, do give a pungency and flavour to the dull detail of history—while a fourth class, of more philosophic habits, do diligently pore over the musty chronicles of time, to investigate the operations of the human kind, and watch the gradual changes in men and manners, effected by the progress of knowledge, the vicissitudes of events, or the influence of situation.

If the three first classes find but little wherewithal to solace themselves in the tranquil reign of Wouter Van Twiller, I entreat them to exert their patience for a while, and bear with the tedious picture of happiness, prosperity, and peace, which my duty as a faithful historian obliges me to draw; and I promise them that as soon as I can possibly alight upon anything horrible, uncommon, or impossible, it shall go hard but I will make it afford them entertainment.

This being promised, I turn with great complacency to the fourth class of my readers, who are men, or, if possible, women after my own heart; grave, philosophical, and investigating; fond of analyzing characters, of taking a start from first causes, and so haunting a nation down, through all the mazes of innovation and improvement. Such will naturally be anxious to witness the first development of the newly-hatched colony, and the primitive manners and customs prevalent among its inhabitants, during the halcyon reign of Van Twiller, or the Doubter.

I will not grieve their patience, however, by describing minutely the increase and improvement of New Amsterdam.

Their own imaginations will doubtless present to them the good burghers, like so many painstaking and persevering beavers, slowly and surely pursuing their labours—they will behold the prosperous transformation from the rude log hut to the stately Dutch mansion, with brick front, glazed windows, and tiled roof; from the tangled thicket to the luxuriant cabbage garden; and from the skulking Indian to the ponderous burgomaster. In a word, they will picture to themselves the steady, silent, and undeviating march of prosperity, incident to a city destitute of pride or ambition, cherished by a fat government, and whose citizens do nothing in a hurry.

The sage council, as has been mentioned in a preceding chapter, not being able to determine upon any plan for the building of their city—the cows, in a laudable fit of patriotism, took it under their peculiar charge, and as they went to and from pasture, established paths through the bushes, on each side of which the good folks built their houses; which is one cause of the rambling and picturesque turns and labyrinths, which distinguish certain streets of New York at this very day.

The houses of the higher class were generally constructed of wood, excepting the gable end, which was of small black and yellow Dutch bricks, and always faced on the street, as our ancestors, like their descendants, were very much given to outward show, and were noted for putting the best leg foremost. The house was always furnished with abundance of large doors and small windows on every floor, the date of its erection was curiously designated by iron figures on the front, and on the top of the roof was perched a fierce little weathercock, to let the family into the important secret which way the wind blew.

These, like the weathercocks on the tops of our steeples, pointed so many different ways, that every man could have a wind to his mind;—the most staunch and loyal citizens, however, always went according to the weathercock on the top of the governor's house, which was certainly the most correct, as he had a trusty servant employed every morning to climb up and set it to the right quarter.

In those good days of simplicity and sunshine, a passion for cleanliness was the leading principle in domestic economy, and the universal test of an able housewife—a character which formed the utmost ambition of our unenlightened grandmothers. The front door was never opened except on marriages, funerals, new year's days, the festival of St. Nicholas, or some such great occasion. It was ornamented with a gorgeous brass knocker, curiously wrought, sometimes in the device of a dog, and sometimes of a lion's head, and was daily burnished with such religious zeal, that it was oft-times worn out by the very precautions taken for its preservation.

The whole house was constantly in a state of inundation, under the discipline of mops and brooms and scrubbing brushes; and the good housewives of those days were a kind of amphibious animal, delighting exceedingly to be dabbling in water—insomuch that an historian of the day gravely tells us, that many of his townswomen grew to have webbed fingers like unto a duck; and some of them, he had little doubt, could the matter be examined into, would be found to have the tails of mermaids; but this I look upon to be a mere sport of fancy, or, what is worse, a wilful misrepresentation.

The grand parlour was the *sanctum sanctorum*, where the passion for cleaning was indulged without control. In this sacred apartment no one was permitted to enter excepting the mistress and her confidential maid, who visited it once a week, for the purpose of giving it a thorough cleaning, and putting things to rights; always taking the precaution of leaving their shoes at the door, and entering devoutly on their stocking feet.

After scrubbing the floor, sprinkling it with fine white sand, which was curiously stroked into angles, and curves, and rhomboids with a broom; after washing the windows, rubbing and polishing the furniture, and putting a bunch of evergreens in the fireplace—the window shutters were again closed to keep out the flies, and the room carefully locked up until the revolution of time brought round the weekly cleaning day.

As to the family, they always entered in at the gate, and most generally lived in the kitchen. To have seen a numerous household assembled round the fire, one would have imagined that he was transported back to those happy days of primeval simplicity, which float before our imaginations like golden visions. The fireplaces were of a truly patriarchal magnitude, where the whole family, old and young, master and servant, black and white, nay, even the very cat and dog, enjoyed a community of privilege, and had each a right to a corner.

Here the old *burgher* would sit in perfect silence, puffing his pipe, looking into the fire with half-shut eyes, and thinking of nothing for hours together; the *goede vrouw*, on the opposite side, would employ herself diligently in spinning yarn or knitting stockings. The young folks would crowd around the hearth, listening with breathless attention to some old crone of a negro, who was the oracle of the family, and who, perched like a raven in the corner of a chimney, would croak forth for a long winter afternoon a string of incredible stories about New England witches—grisly ghosts, horses without heads—and hair-breadth escapes and bloody encounters among the Indians.

In those happy days a well-regulated family always rose with the dawn, dined at eleven, and went to bed at sunset. Dinner was invariably a private meal, and the fat old *burghers* showed incontestable signs of disapprobation and uneasiness at being surprised by a visit from a neighbour on such occasions. But though our worthy ancestors were thus singularly averse to giving dinners, yet they kept up the social bands of intimacy by occasional banquettings, called tea-parties.

These fashionable parties were generally confined to the higher classes, or *noblesse*: that is to say, such as kept their own cows and drove their own waggons. The company commonly assembled at three o'clock, and went away about six, unless it was in winter time, when the fashionable hours were a little earlier, that the ladies might get home before dark. The tea-table was crowned with a huge earthen dish, well stored with slices of fat pork, fried brown, cut up into morsels, and swimming in gravy.

The company being seated round the genial board, and each furnished with a fork, evinced their dexterity in launching at the fattest pieces in this mighty dish—in much the same manner as sailors harpoon porpoises at sea, or our Indians spear salmon in the lakes. Sometimes the table was graced with immense apple-pies, or saucers full of preserved peaches and pears; but it was always sure to boast an enormous dish of balls of sweetened dough, fried in hog's fat, and called doughnuts, or *olykoeks*—a delicious kind of cake, at present scarce known in this city, except in genuine Dutch families.

The tea was served out of a majestic delf teapot, ornamented with paintings of fat little Dutch shepherds and shepherdesses, tending pigs—with boats sailing in the air, and houses built in the clouds, and sundry other ingenious Dutch fantasies. The *beaux* distinguished themselves by their adroitness in replenishing this pot from a huge copper tea-kettle, which would have made the pigmy *macaronies* of these degenerate days sweat merely to look at it.

To sweeten the beverage, a lump of sugar was laid beside each cup—and the company alternately nibbled and sipped with great decorum; until an improvement was introduced by a shrewd and economic old lady, which was to suspend a large lump directly over the tea-table by a string from the ceiling, so that it could be swung from mouth to mouth—an ingenious expedient, which is still kept up by some families in Albany, but which prevails without exception in Communipaw, Bergen Flatbush, and all our uncontaminated Dutch villages.

At these primitive tea parties the utmost propriety and dignity of deportment prevailed. No flirting nor *coquetting*—no gambling of old ladies, nor hoyden chattering and romping of young ones—no self-satisfied struttings of wealthy gentlemen with their brains in their pockets—nor amusing conceits and monkey divertissements of smart young gentlemen with no brains at all.

On the contrary, the young ladies seated themselves demurely in their rush-bottomed chairs, and knit their own woollen stockings; nor ever opened their lips excepting to say "*yah Myn-heer*," or "*yah ya Vrouw*," to any question that was asked them; behaving, in all things, like decent, well-educated damsels. As to the gentlemen, each of them tranquilly smoked his pipe, and seemed lost in contemplation of the blue and white tiles with which the fireplaces were decorated; wherein sundry passages of Scripture were piously portrayed—Tobit and his dog figured to great advantage, Haman swung conspicuously on his gibbet, and Jonah appeared most manfully bouncing out of the whale like Harlequin through a barrel of fire.

The parties broke up without noise and without confusion. They were carried home by their own carriages, that is to say, by the vehicles nature had provided them, excepting such of the wealthy as could afford to keep a wagon. The gentlemen gallantly attended their fair ones to their respective abodes, and took leave of them with a hearty smack at the door; which, as it was an established piece of etiquette, done in perfect simplicity and honesty of heart, occasioned no scandal at that time, nor should it at the present. If our great-grandfathers approved of the custom, it would argue a great want of reverence in their descendants to say a word against it.

Chapter 4
Containing further particulars of the Golden Age, and what constituted a fine Lady and Gentleman in the days of Walter the Doubter.

In this dulcet period of my history, when the beauteous island of Manna-hata presented a scene the very counterpart of those glowing pictures drawn of the golden reign of Saturn, there was, as I have before observed, a happy ignorance, an honest simplicity prevalent among its inhabitants, which, were I even able to depict, would be but little understood by the degenerate age for which I am doomed to write. Even the female sex, those arch innovators upon the tranquillity, the honesty, and grey-beard customs of society, seemed for a while to conduct themselves with incredible sobriety and comeliness.

Their hair, untortured by the abominations of art, was scrupulously *pomatomed* back from their foreheads with a candle, and covered with a little cap of quilted calico, which fitted exactly to their heads. Their petticoats of linsey-woolsey were striped with a variety of gorgeous dyes—though I must confess these gallant garments were rather short, scarce reaching below the knee; but then they made up in the number, which generally equalled that of the gentleman's small clothes; and what is still more praiseworthy, they were all of their own manufacture—of which circumstance, as may well be supposed, they were not a little vain.

These were the honest days, in which every woman stayed at home, read the Bible, and wore pockets—ay, and that too of a goodly size, fashioned with patchwork into many curious devices, and ostentatiously worn on the outside. These, in fact, were convenient receptacles, where all good housewives carefully stored away such things as they wished to have at hand, by which means they often came to be incredibly crammed—and I remember there was a story current, when I was a boy, that the lady of Wouter Van Twiller once had occasion to empty her right pocket in search of a wooden ladle, when the contents filled a couple of corn baskets, and the utensil was discovered lying among some rubbish in one corner—but we must not give too much faith to all these stories, the anecdotes of those remote periods being very subject to exaggeration.

Besides these notable pockets, they likewise wore scissors and pincushions suspended from their girdles by red ribands, or among the more opulent and showy classes by brass, and even silver, chains, indubitable tokens of thrifty housewives and industrious spinsters. I cannot say much in vindication of the shortness of the petticoats; it doubtless was introduced for the purpose of giving the stockings a chance to be seen, which were generally of blue worsted, with magnificent red clocks; or perhaps to display a well-turned ankle, and a neat though serviceable foot, set off by a high-heeled leathern shoe, with a large and splendid silver buckle. Thus we find that the gentle sex in all ages have shown the same disposition to infringe a little upon the laws of decorum, in order to betray a lurking beauty, or gratify an innocent love of finery.

From the sketch here given, it will be seen that our good grandmothers differed considerably in their ideas of a fine figure from their scantily-dressed descendants of the present day. A fine lady, in those times, waddled under more clothes, even on a fair summer's day, than would have clad the whole bevy of a modern ballroom. Nor were they the less admired by the gentlemen in consequence thereof. On the contrary, the greatness of a lover's passion seemed to increase in proportion to the magnitude of its object—and a voluminous damsel, arrayed in a dozen petticoats, was declared by a low Dutch *sonneteer* of the province to be radiant as a sunflower, and luxuriant as a full-blown cabbage.

Certain it is that in those day the heart of a lover could not contain more than one lady at a time, whereas the heart of a modern gallant has often room enough to accommodate half a dozen; the reason of which I conclude to be, that either the hearts of the gentlemen have grown larger, or the persons of the ladies smaller—this, however, is a question for physiologists to determine.

But there was a secret charm in these petticoats, which, no doubt, entered into the consideration of the prudent gallants. The wardrobe of a lady was in those days her only fortune; and she who had a good stock of petticoats and stockings was as absolutely an heiress as is a Kamschatka damsel with a store of bear-skins, or a Lapland *belle* with a plenty of reindeer. The ladies, therefore, were very anxious to display these powerful attractions to the greatest advantage; and the best rooms in the house, instead of being adorned with caricatures of Dame Nature, in water-colors and needlework, were always hung round with abundance of homespun garments, the manufacture and the property of the females—a piece of laudable ostentation that still prevails among the heiresses of our Dutch villages.

The gentlemen, in fact, who figured in the circles of the gay world in these ancient times, corresponded in most particulars with the beauteous damsels whose smiles they were ambitious to deserve. True it is, their merits would make but a very inconsiderable impression upon the heart of a modern fair; they neither drove their curricles nor sported their tandems, for as yet those gaudy vehicles were not even dreamt of—neither did they distinguish themselves by their brilliancy at the table, and their consequent *rencontres* with watchmen, for our forefathers were of too pacific a disposition to need those guardians of the night, every soul throughout the town being sound asleep before nine o'clock.

Neither did they establish their claims to gentility at the expense of their tailors—for as yet those offenders against the pockets of society, and the tranquillity of all aspiring young gentlemen were unknown in New Amsterdam; every good housewife made the clothes of her husband and family, and even the *goede vrouw* of Van Twiller himself thought it no disparagement to cut out her husband's linsey-woolsey galligaskins.

Not but what there were some two or three youngsters who manifested the first dawning of what is called fire and spirit—who held all labour in contempt, skulked about docks and market-places, loitered in the sunshine, squandered what little money they could procure at hustle cap and chuck farthing; swore, boxed, fought cocks, and raced their neighbour's horses—in short, who promised to be the wonder, the talk, and abomination of the town, had not their stylish career been unfortunately cut short by an affair of honour with a whipping post.

Far other, however, was the truly fashionable gentleman of those days—his dress, which served for both morning and evening, street and drawing-room, was a linsey-woolsey coat, made, perhaps, by the fair hands of the mistress of his affections, and gallantly bedecked with abundance of large brass buttons—half a score of breeches heightened the proportions of his figure—his shoes were decorated by enormous copper buckles—a low crowned, broad-brimmed hat overshadowed his burly visage, and his hair dangled down his back in a prodigious queue of eelskin.

Thus equipped, he would manfully sally forth with pipe in mouth to besiege some fair damsel's obdurate heart—not such a pipe, good reader, as that which Acis did sweetly tune in praise of his Galatea, but one of true delf manufacture, and furnished with a charge of fragrant tobacco. With this would he resolutely set himself down before the fortress, and rarely failed, in the process of time, to smoke the fair enemy into a surrender upon honourable terms.

Such was the happy reign of Wouter Van Twiller, celebrated in many a long forgotten song as the real golden age, the rest being nothing but counterfeit copper-washed coin. In that delightful period a sweet and holy calm reigned over the whole province. The *burgomaster* smoked his pipe in peace; the substantial solace of his domestic cares, after her daily toils were done, sat soberly at the door, with her arms crossed over her apron of snowy white without being insulted by ribald street walkers or vagabond boys—those unlucky urchins who do so infest our streets, displaying under the roses of youth the thorns and briars of iniquity.

Then it was that the lover with ten breeches, and the damsel with petticoats of half a score, indulged in all the innocent endearments of virtuous love without fear and without reproach; for what had that virtue to fear which was defended by a shield of good linsey-woolsey, equal at least to the seven bull-hides of the invincible Ajax?

Ah! blissful and never to be forgotten age! when everything was better than it has ever been since, or ever will be again—when Buttermilk Channel was quite dry at low water—when the shad in the Hudson were all salmon, and when the moon shone with a pure and resplendent whiteness, instead of that melancholy yellow light which is the consequence of her sickening at the abominations she every night witnesses in this degenerate city!

Happy would it have been for New Amsterdam could it always have existed in this state of blissful ignorance and lowly simplicity—but, alas! the days of childhood are too sweet to last.

Cities, like men, grow out of them in time, and are doomed alike to grow into the bustle, the cares, and miseries of the world. Let no man congratulate himself when he beholds the child of his bosom, or the city of his birth, increasing in magnitude and importance—let the history of his own life teach him the dangers of the one, and this excellent little history of Manna-hata convince him of the calamities of the other.

CHAPTER 5
IN WHICH THE READER IS BEGUILED INTO A DELECTABLE WALK, WHICH ENDS VERY DIFFERENTLY FROM WHAT IT COMMENCED.

In the year of our Lord one thousand eight hundred and four, on a fine afternoon in the glowing month of September, I took my customary walk upon the battery, which is at once the pride and bulwark of this ancient and impregnable city of New York. The ground on which is I trod was hallowed by recollections of the past, and as I slowly wandered through the long alley of poplars, which, like so many birch-brooms standing on end, diffused a melancholy and lugubrious shade, my imagination drew a contrast between the surrounding scenery, and what it was in the classic days of our forefathers.

Where the government house by name, but the customhouse by occupation, proudly reared its brick walls and wooden pillars, there whilom stood the low, but substantial red-tiled mansion of the renowned Wouter Van Twiller. Around it the mighty bulwarks of Fort Amsterdam frowned defiance to every absent foe; but, like many a whiskered warrior and gallant militia captain, confined their martial deeds to frowns alone. The mud breastworks had long been levelled with the earth, and their site converted into the green lawns and leafy alleys of the battery, where the gay apprentice sported his Sunday coat, and the laborious mechanic, relieved from the dirt and drudgery of the week, poured his weekly tale of love into the half averted ear of the sentimental chambermaid.

The capacious bay still presented the same expansive sheet of water, studded with islands, sprinkled with fishing boats, and bounded by shores of picturesque beauty. But the dark forests which once clothed those shores had been violated by the savage hand of cultivation, and their tangled mazes and impenetrable thickets had degenerated into teeming orchards, and waving fields of grain. Even Governor's Island, once a smiling garden appertaining to the sovereigns of the province, was now covered with fortifications, inclosing a tremendous block house—so that this once peaceful island resembled a fierce little warrior in a big cocked hat, breathing gunpowder and defiance to the world!

For some time did I indulge in a pensive train of thought, contrasting in sober sadness the present day with the hallowed years behind the mountains, lamenting the melancholy progress of improvement, and praising the zeal with which our worthy *burghers* endeavour to preserve the wrecks of venerable customs, prejudices, and errors, from the overwhelming tide of modern innovation—when, by degrees, my ideas took a different turn, and I insensibly awakened to an enjoyment of the beauties around me.

It was one of those rich autumnal days, which heaven particularly bestows upon the beauteous island of Manna-hata and its vicinity—not a floating cloud obscured the azure firmament—the sun rolling in glorious splendour through his ethereal course, seemed to expand his honest Dutch countenance into an unusual expression of benevolence, as he smiled his evening salutation upon a city which he delights to visit with his most bounteous beams; the very winds seemed to hold in their breaths in mute attention, lest they should ruffle the tranquillity of the hour; and the waveless bosom of the bay presented a polished mirror, in which

Nature beheld herself and smiled. The standard of our city, reserved like a choice handkerchief for days of gala, hung motionless on the flag-staff which forms the handle of a gigantic churn; and even the tremulous leaves of the poplar and the aspen ceased to vibrate to the breath of heaven. Everything seemed to acquiesce in the profound repose of Nature. The formidable eighteen-pounders slept in the embrasures of the wooden batteries, seemingly gathering fresh strength to fight the battles of their country on the next fourth of July—the solitary drum on Governor's Island forgot to call the garrison to the *shovels*—the evening gun had not yet sounded its signal for all the regular well-meaning poultry throughout the country to go to roost; and the fleet of canoes at anchor between Gibbet Island and Communipaw slumbered on their rakes, and suffered the innocent oysters to lie for a while unmolested in the soft mud of their native banks.

My own feelings sympathized with the contagious tranquillity, and I should infallibly have dozed upon one of those fragments of benches which our benevolent magistrates have provided for the benefit of convalescent loungers had not the extraordinary inconvenience of the couch set all repose at defiance.

In the midst of this slumber of the soul my attention was attracted to a black speck, peering above the western horizon, just in the rear of Bergen steeple—gradually it augments and overhangs the would-be cities of Jersey, Harsimus, and Hoboken, which, like three jockeys, are starting on the course of existence, and jostling each other at the commencement of the race. Now it skirts the long shore of ancient Pavonia, spreading its wide shadows from the high settlements of Weehawk quite to the *lazaretto* and quarantine, erected by the sagacity of our police for the embarrassment of commerce—now it climbs the serene vault of heaven, cloud rolling over cloud, shrouding the orb of day, darkening the vast expanse, and bearing thunder, and hail, and tempest, in its bosom.

The earth seems agitated at the confusion of the heavens— the late waveless mirror is lashed into furious waves, that roll in hollow murmurs to the shore—the oyster boats that erst sported in the placid vicinity of Gibbet Island, now hurry affrighted to the land—the poplar writhes and twists, and whistles in the blast—torrents of drenching rain and sounding hail deluge the battery walks—the gates are thronged by apprentices, servant-maids, and little Frenchmen, with pocket-handkerchiefs over their hats, scampering from the storm—the late beauteous prospect presents one scene of anarchy and wild uproar, as though old Chaos had resumed his reign, and was hurling back into one vast turmoil the conflicting elements of Nature.

Whether I fled from the fury of the storm, or remained bodily at my post, as our gallant train-band captains, who march their soldiers through the rain without flinching, are points which I leave to the conjecture of the reader. It is possible he may be a little perplexed also to know the reason why I introduced this tremendous tempest to disturb the serenity of my work.

On this latter point I will gratuitously instruct his ignorance. The panorama view of the battery was given to gratify the reader with a correct description of that celebrated place, and the parts adjacent—secondly, the storm was played off partly to give a little bustle and life to this tranquil part of my work, and to keep my drowsy readers from falling asleep, and partly to serve as an overture to the tempestuous times which are about to assail the pacific province of Nieuw Nederlandts—and that overhang the slumbrous administration of the renowned Wouter Van Twiller.

It is thus the experienced playwright puts all the fiddles, the French-horns, the kettle drums, and trumpets of his orchestra, in requisition, to usher in one of those horrible and brimstone uproars called *melodrames*; and it is thus he discharges his thunder, his lightning, his *rosin*, and *saltpetre*, preparatory to the rising of a ghost, or the murdering of a hero.—We will now proceed with our history.

Whatever may be advanced by philosophers to the contrary, I am of opinion that, as to nations, the old maxim, that "*honesty is the best policy*," is a sheer and ruinous mistake. It might have answered well enough in the honest times when it was made; but, in these degenerate days, if a nation pretends to rely merely upon the justice of its dealings, it will fare something like the honest man who fell among thieves, and found his honesty a poor protection against bad company.

Such, at least, was the case with the guileless government of the New Netherlands; which, like a worthy, unsuspicious old *burgher*, quietly settled itself down in the city of New Amsterdam as into a snug elbow-chair—and fell into a comfortable nap—while, in the meantime, its cunning neighbours stepped in and picked his pockets. In a word, we may ascribe the commencement of all the woes of this great province and its magnificent metropolis to the tranquil security, or, to speak more accurately, to the unfortunate honesty of its government.

But as I dislike to begin an important part of my history towards the end of a chapter; and as my readers, like myself, must doubtless be exceedingly fatigued with the long walk we have taken, and the tempest we have sustained—I hold it meet we shut up the book, smoke a pipe, and having thus refreshed our spirits, take a fair start in a new chapter.

CHAPTER 6

FAITHFULLY DESCRIBING THE INGENIOUS PEOPLE OF CONNECTICUT AND THEREABOUTS—SHOWING MOREOVER, THE TRUE MEANING OF LIBERTY OF CONSCIENCE, AND A CURIOUS DEVICE AMONG THESE STURDY BARBARIANS, TO KEEP UP A HARMONY OF INTERCOURSE, AND PROMOTE POPULATION.

That my readers may the more fully comprehend the extent of the calamity at this very moment impending over the honest, unsuspecting province of Nieuw Nederlandts and its dubious governor, it is necessary that I should give some account of a horde of strange barbarians bordering upon the eastern frontier.

Now so it came to pass that, many years previous to the time of which we are treating, the sage Cabinet of England had adopted a certain national creed, a kind of public walk of faith, or rather a religious turnpike, in which every loyal subject was directed to travel to Zion—taking care to pay the *toll-gatherers* by the way.

Albeit a certain shrewd race of men, being very much given to indulge their own opinions on all manner of subjects (a propensity exceedingly offensive to your free governments of Europe), did most presumptuously dare to think for themselves in matters of religion, exercising what they considered a natural and unextinguishable right—the liberty of conscience.

As, however, they possessed that ingenuous habit of mind which always thinks aloud—which rides cock-a-hoop on the tongue, and is for ever galloping into other people's ears—it naturally followed that their liberty of conscience likewise implied *liberty of speech*, which being freely indulged, soon put the country in a hubbub, and aroused the pious indignation of the vigilant fathers of the Church.

The usual methods were adopted, to reclaim them, which in those days were considered efficacious in bringing back stray sheep to the fold; that is to say, they were coaxed, they were admonished, they were menaced, they were buffeted—line upon line, precept upon precept, lash upon lash, here a little and there a great deal, were exhausted without mercy and without success; until worthy pastors of the Church, wearied out by their unparalleled stubbornness, were driven in the excess of their tender mercy to adopt the Scripture text, and literally to "*heap live embers on their heads.*"

Nothing, however, could subdue that invincible spirit of independence which has ever distinguished this singular race of people, so that, rather than submit to such horrible tyranny, they one and all embarked for the wilderness of America, where they might enjoy, unmolested, the inestimable luxury of talking. No sooner did they land on this loquacious soil, than, as if they had caught the disease from the climate, they all lifted up their voices at once, and for the space of one whole year did keep up such a joyful clamour, that we are told they frightened every bird and beast out of the neighbourhood, and so completely dumfounded certain fish, which abound on their coast, that they have been called dumb-fish ever since.

From this simple circumstance, unimportant as it my seem, did first originate that renowned privilege so loudly boasted of throughout this country—which is so eloquently exercised in newspapers, pamphlets, ward meetings, pot-house committees, and congressional deliberations—which established the right of talking without ideas and without information—of misrepresenting public affairs—of decrying public measures—of aspersing great characters, and destroying little ones; in short, that palladium of our country, the *liberty of speech*.

The simple aborigines of the land for a while contemplated these strange folk in utter astonishment, but discovering that they wielded harmless, though noisy weapons, and were a lively, ingenious, good-humored race of men, they became very friendly and sociable, and gave them the name of *Yanokies*, which in the Mais-Tchusaeg (or Massachusett) language signifies *silent men*—a waggish appellation, since shortened into the familiar epithet of Yankees, which they retain unto the present day.

True it is, and my fidelity as an historian will not allow me to pass over in silence, that the zeal of these good people to maintain their rights and privileges unimpaired, did for a while betray them into errors, which is easier to pardon than defend. Having served a regular apprenticeship in the school of persecution, it behoved them to show that they had become proficient in the art. They accordingly employed their leisure hours in banishing, scourging, or hanging divers heretical Papists, Quakers, and Anabaptists for daring to abuse the *liberty of conscience*: which they now clearly proved to imply nothing more than that every man should think as he pleased in matters of religion—*provided* he thought *right*; for otherwise it would be giving a latitude to damnable heresies.

Now as they, the majority, were convinced that *they alone* thought right, it consequently followed that whoever thought different from them thought wrong—and whoever thought wrong, and obstinately persisted in not being convinced and converted, was a flagrant violator of the inestimable liberty of conscience, and a corrupt and infestious member of the body politic, and deserved to be lopped off and cast into the fire.

Now I'll warrant there are hosts of my readers ready at once to lift up their hands and eyes, with that virtuous indignation with which we contemplate the faults and errors of our neighbours, and to exclaim at these well-meaning, but mistaken people, for inflicting on others the injuries they had suffered themselves—

for indulging the preposterous idea of convincing the mind by tormenting the body, and establishing the doctrine of charity and forbearance by intolerant persecution.

But, in simple truth, what are we doing at this very day, and in this very enlightened nation, but acting upon the very same principle in our political controversies? Have we not, within but a few years, released ourselves from the shackles of a government which cruelly denied us the privilege of governing ourselves, and using in full latitude that invaluable member, the tongue? and are we not at this very moment striving our best to tyrannize over the opinions, tie up the tongues, and ruin the fortunes of one another?

What are our great political societies but mere political inquisitions—our pot-house committees but little tribunals of denunciation—our newspapers but mere whipping-posts and pillories, where unfortunate individuals are pelted with rotten eggs—and our council of appointment but a grand *auto-da-fe*, where culprits are annually sacrificed for their political heresies?

Where, then, is the difference in principle between our measures and those you are so ready to condemn among the people I am treating of? There is none; the difference is merely circumstantial. Thus we *denounce*, instead of banishing—we *libel*, instead of scourging—we *turn out of office*, instead of hanging—and where they burnt an offender in *propria persona*, we either tar and feather, or *burn him in effigy*—this political persecution being, somehow or other, the grand palladium of our liberties, and an incontrovertible proof that this is a *free country!*

But not withstanding the fervent zeal with which this holy war was prosecuted against the whole race of unbelievers, we do not find that the population of this new colony was in anywise hindered thereby; on the contrary, they multiplied to a degree which would be incredible to any man unacquainted with the marvellous fecundity of this growing country.

This amazing increase may, indeed, be partly ascribed to a singular custom prevalent among them, commonly known by the name of *bundling*—a superstitious rite observed by the young people of both sexes, with which they usually terminated their festivities, and which was kept up with religious strictness by the more bigoted part of the community.

This ceremony was likewise, in those primitive times, considered as an indispensable preliminary to matrimony, their courtships commencing where ours usually finish; by which means they acquired that intimate acquaintance with each other's good qualities before marriage, which has been pronounced by philosophers the sure basis of a happy union. Thus early did this cunning and ingenious people display a shrewdness of making a bargain which has ever since distinguished them—and a strict adherence to the good old vulgar maxim about "*buying a pig in a poke.*"

To this sagacious custom, therefore, do I chiefly attribute the unparalleled increase of the Yanokie or Yankee race: for it is a certain fact, well authenticated by court records and parish registers, that wherever the practice of bundling prevailed, there was an amazing number of sturdy brats annually born unto the state, without the license of the law or the benefit of clergy. Neither did the irregularity of their birth operate in the least to their disparagement. On the contrary, they grew up a long-sided, raw-boned, hardy race of whalers, wood-cutters, fishermen, and pedlars, and strapping corn-fed wenches, who, by their united efforts, tended marvellously toward peopling those notable tracts of country called Nantucket, Piscataway, and Cape Cod.

CHAPTER 7

HOW THESE SINGULAR BARBARIANS TURNED OUT TO BE NOTORIOUS SQUATTERS—HOW THEY BUILT AIR CASTLES, AND ATTEMPTED TO INITIATE THE NEDERLANDERS IN THE MYSTERY OF BUNDLING.

In the last chapter I have given a faithful and unprejudiced account of the origin of that singular race of people inhabiting the country eastward of the Nieuw Nederlandts, but I have yet to mention certain peculiar habits which rendered them exceedingly annoying to our ever-honoured Dutch ancestors.

The most prominent of these was a certain rambling propensity with which, like the sons of Ishmael, they seem to have been gifted by Heaven, and which continually goads them on to shift their residence from place to place, so that a Yankee farmer is in a constant state of migration, *tarrying* occasionally here and there, clearing lands for other people to enjoy, building houses for others to inhabit, and in a manner may be considered the wandering Arab of America.

His first thought, on coming to the years of manhood, is to *settle* himself in the world—which means nothing more nor less than to begin his rambles. To this end he takes unto himself for a wife some buxom country heiress, passing rich in red ribbons, glass beads, and mock-tortoiseshell combs, with a white gown and morocco shoes for Sunday, and deeply skilled in the mystery of making apple sweetmeats, long sauce, and pumpkin pie.

Having thus provided himself, like a pedlar, with a heavy knapsack, wherewith to regale his shoulders through the journey of life, he literally sets out on the peregrination. His whole family, household furniture, and farming utensils are hoisted into a covered cart; his own and his wife's wardrobe packed up in a firkin—which done, he shoulders his axe, takes his staff in hand, whistles "Yankee doodle," and trudges off to the woods, as confident of the protection of Providence, and relying as cheerfully upon his own resources, as did ever a patriarch of yore, when he journeyed into a strange country of the Gentiles.

Having buried himself in the wilderness, he builds himself a log hut, clears away a corn-field and potato patch, and, Providence smiling upon his labours, is soon surrounded by a snug farm and some half a score of flaxen-headed urchins, who, by their size, seem to have sprung all at once out of the earth like a crop of toadstools.

But it is not the nature of this most indefatigable of speculators to rest contented with any state of sublunary enjoyment—*improvement* is his darling passion, and having thus improved his lands, the next care is to provide a mansion worthy the residence of a landholder. A huge palace of pine boards immediately springs up in the midst of the wilderness, large enough for a parish church, and furnished with windows of all dimensions, but so rickety and flimsy withal, that every blast gives it a fit of the ague.

By the time the outside of this mighty air castle is completed, either the funds or the zeal of our adventurer are exhausted, so that he barely manages to half finish one room within, where the whole family burrow together—while the rest of the house is devoted to the curing of pumpkins, or storing of carrots and potatoes, and is decorated with fanciful festoons of dried apples and peaches. The outside, remaining unpainted, grows venerably black with time; the family wardrobe is laid under contribution for old hats, petticoats, and breeches, to stuff into the broken windows, while the four winds of heaven keep up a whistling and howling about this aerial palace, and play as many unruly gambols as they did of yore in the cave of old Æolius.

The humble log hut which whilom nestled this *improving* family snugly within its narrow but comfortable walls, stands hard by, in ignominious contrast, degraded into a cow-house or pig-sty; and the whole scene reminds one forcibly of a fable, which I am surprised has never been recorded, of an aspiring snail who abandoned his humble habitation, which he had long filled with great respectability, to crawl into the empty shell of a lobster—where he would no doubt have resided with great style and splendour, the envy and the hate of all the painstaking snails in the neighbourhood, had he not perished with cold in one corner of his stupendous mansion.

Being thus completely settled, and, to use his own words, "to rights," one would imagine that he would begin to enjoy the comforts of his situation, to read newspapers, talk politics, neglect his own business, and attend to the affairs of the nation like a useful and patriotic citizen; but now it is that his wayward disposition begins again to operate. He soon grows tired of a spot where there is no longer any room for improvement—sells his farm, air castle, petticoat windows and all, reloads his cart, shoulders his axe, puts himself at the head of his family, and wanders away in search of new lands—again to fell trees—again to clear corn-fields—again to build a shingle palace, and again to sell off and wander.

Such were the people of Connecticut, who bordered upon the eastern frontier of Nieuw Nederlandts, and my readers may easily imagine what uncomfortable neighbours this light-hearted but restless tribe must have been to our tranquil progenitors. If they cannot, I would ask them if they have ever known one of our regular, well-organized Dutch families, whom it hath pleased Heaven to afflict with the neighbourhood of a French boarding-house?

The honest old *burgher* cannot take his afternoon's pipe on the bench before his door but he is persecuted with the scraping of fiddles, the chattering of women, and the squalling of children—he cannot sleep at night for the horrible melodies of some amateur, who chooses to serenade the moon, and display his terrible proficiency in *execution* on the clarionet, *hautboy*, or some other soft-toned instrument—nor can he leave the street door open, but his house is defiled by the unsavoury visits of a troop of pug dogs, who even sometimes carry their loathsome ravages into the *sanctum sanctorum*, the parlour.

If my readers have ever witnessed the sufferings of such a family, so situated, they may form some idea how our worthy ancestors were distressed by their mercurial neighbours of Connecticut.

Gangs of these marauders, we are told, penetrated into the New-Netherland settlements, and threw whole villages into consternation by their unparalleled volubility, and their intolerable inquisitiveness—two evil habits hitherto unknown in those parts, or only known to be abhorred; for our ancestors were noted as being men of truly Spartan taciturnity, and who neither knew nor cared aught about anybody's concerns but their own. Many enormities were committed on the highways, where several unoffending *burghers* were brought to a stand, and tortured with questions and guesses, which outrages occasioned as much vexation and heart-burning as does the modern right of search on the high seas.

Great jealousy did they likewise stir up by their intermeddling and successes among the divine sex, for being a race of brisk, likely, pleasant-tongued varlets, they soon seduced the light affections of the simple damsels from their ponderous Dutch gallants.

Among other hideous customs, they attempted to introduce among them that *bundling*, which the Dutch lasses of the Nederlandts, with that eager passion for novelty and foreign fashions natural to their sex, seemed very well inclined to follow, but that their mothers, being more experienced in the world, and better acquainted with men and things, strenuously discountenanced all such outlandish innovations.

But what chiefly operated to embroil our ancestors with these strange folk was an unwarrantable liberty which they occasionally took of entering in hordes into the territories of the New Netherlands, and settling themselves down, without leave or license, to *improve* the land in the manner I have before noticed.

This unceremonious mode of taking possession of *new land* was technically termed *squatting*, and hence is derived the appellation of *squatters*, a name odious in the ears of all great landholders, and which is given to those enterprising worthies who seize upon land first, and take their chance to make good their title to it afterward.

All these grievances, and many others which were constantly accumulating, tended to form that dark and portentous cloud which, as I observed in a former chapter, was slowly gathering over the tranquil province of New Netherlands. The pacific cabinet of Van Twiller, however, as will be perceived in the sequel, bore them all with a magnanimity that redounds to their immortal credit—becoming by passive endurance inured to this increasing mass of wrongs, like that mighty man of old, who by dint of carrying about a calf from the time it was born, continued to carry it without difficulty when he had grown to be an ox.

CHAPTER 8

HOW THE FORT GOED HOOP WAS FEARFULLY BELEAGUERED—
HOW THE RENOWNED WOUTER FELL INTO A PROFOUND DOUBT,
AND HOW HE FINALLY EVAPORATED.

By this time my readers must fully perceive what an arduous task I have undertaken—collecting and collating with painful minuteness, the chronicles of past times, whose events almost defy the power of research—exploring a little kind of Herculaneum of history, which had lain nearly for ages buried under the rubbish of years, and almost totally forgotten—raking up the limbs and fragments of disjointed facts, and endeavouring to put them scrupulously together, so as to restore them to their original form and connection—now lugging forth the character of an almost forgotten hero, like a mutilated statue—now deciphering a half-defaced inscription, and now lighting upon a mouldering manuscript, which, after painful study, scarce repays the trouble of perusal.

In such cases how much has the reader to depend upon the honour and probity of his author, lest, like a cunning antiquarian, he either impose upon him some spurious fabrication of his own for a precious relic from antiquity—or else dress up the dismembered fragment with such false trappings, that it is scarcely possible to distinguish the truth from the fiction with which it is enveloped. This is a grievance which I have more than once had to lament, in the course of my wearisome researches among the works of my fellow-historians, who have strangely disguised and distorted the facts respecting this country, and particularly respecting the great province of New Netherlands, as will be perceived by any who will take the trouble to compare their romantic effusions, tricked out in the meretricious gauds of fable, with this authentic history.

I have had more vexations of the kind to encounter, in those parts of my history which treat of the transactions on the eastern border than in any other, in consequence of the troops of historians who have infested those quarters, and have shown the honest people of Nieuw Nederlands no mercy in their works.

Among the rest, Mr. Benjamin Trumbull arrogantly declares that "the Dutch were always mere intruders."

Now, to this I shall make no other reply than to proceed in the steady narration of my history, which will contain not only proofs that the Dutch had clear title and possession in the fair valleys of the Connecticut, and that they were wrongfully dispossessed thereof—but, likewise, that they have been scandalously maltreated ever since by the misrepresentations of the crafty historians of New England. And in this I shall be guided by a spirit of truth and impartiality, and a regard to immortal fame—for I would not wittingly dishonour my work by a single falsehood, misrepresentation, or prejudice, though it should gain our forefathers the whole country of New England.

It was at an early period of the province and previous to the arrival of the renowned Wouter, that the cabinet of Nieuw-Nederlandts purchased the lands about Connecticut, and established, for their superintendence and protection, a fortified post on the banks of the river, which was called Fort Goed Hoop, and was situated hard by the present fair city of Hartford. The command of this important post, together with the rank, title, and appointment of commissary, were given in charge to Jacobus Van Curlet, or as some historians will have it, Van Curlis—a most doughty soldier, of that stomachful class of which we have such numbers on parade days—who are famous for eating all they kill.

He was of a very soldierlike appearance, and would have been an exceeding tall man had his legs been in proportion to his body; but the latter being long, and the former uncommonly short, it gave him the uncouth appearance of a tall man's body mounted upon a little man's legs. He made up for this turnspit construction by striding to such an extent, that you would have sworn he had on the seven-leagued boots of Jack the Giant Killer; and so high did he tread on parade, that his soldiers were sometimes alarmed lest he should trample himself under foot.

But not withstanding the erection of this fort, and the appointment of this ugly little man of war as commander, the Yankees continued the interlopings hinted at in my last chapter, and taking advantage of the character which the cabinet of Wouter Van Twiller soon acquired, for profound and phlegmatic tranquillity—did audaciously invade the territories of the Nieuw-Nederlandts, and *squat* themselves down within the very jurisdiction of Fort Goed Hoop.

On beholding this outrage, the long-bodied Van Curlet proceeded as became a prompt and valiant officer. He immediately protested against these unwarrantable encroachments, in Low Dutch, by way of inspiring more terror, and forthwith dispatched a copy of the protest to the governor at New Amsterdam, together with a long and bitter account of the aggressions of the enemy. This done, he ordered his men, one and all, to be of good cheer—shut the gate of the fort, smoked three pipes, went to bed, and awaited the result with a resolute and intrepid tranquillity, that greatly animated his adherents, and, no doubt, struck sore dismay and affright into the hearts of the enemy.

Now it came to pass that, about this time, the renowned Wouter Van Twiller, full of years and honours, and council dinners, had reached the period of life and faculty which, according to the great Gulliver, entitles a man to admission into the ancient order of Struldbruggs. He employed his time in smoking his Turkish pipe amid an assemblage of sages equally enlightened, and nearly as venerable, as himself, and who, for their silence, their gravity, their wisdom, and their cautious averseness to coming to any conclusion in business, are only to be equalled by certain profound corporations which I have known in my time.

Upon reading the protest of the gallant Jacobus Van Curlet, therefore, His Excellency fell straightway into one of the deepest doubts that ever he was known to encounter; his capacious head gradually drooped on his chest; he closed his eyes, and inclined his ear to one side, as if listening with great attention to the discussion that was going on in his belly, and which all who knew him declared to be the huge courthouse or council chamber of his thoughts, forming to his head what the House of Representatives does to the Senate.

An inarticulate sound, very much resembling a snore, occasionally escaped him—but the nature of this internal cogitation was never known, as he never opened his lips on the subject to man, woman or child. In the meantime, the protest of Van Curlet lay quietly on the table, where it served to light the pipes of the venerable sages assembled in council; and, in the great smoke which they raised, the gallant Jacobus, his protest, and his mighty Fort Goed Hoop, were soon as completely beclouded and forgotten, as is a question of emergency swallowed up in the speeches and resolutions of a modern session of Congress.

There are certain emergencies when your profound legislators and sage deliberative councils are mightily in the way of a nation, and when an ounce of hair-brained decision is worth a pound of sage doubt and cautious discussion. Such, at least, was the case at present; for while the renowned Wouter Van Twiller was daily battling with his doubts, and his resolution growing weaker and weaker in the contest, the enemy pushed farther and farther into his territories, and assumed a most formidable appearance in the neighbourhood of the Fort Goed Hoop.

Here they founded the mighty town of *Pyquag*, or, as it has since been called, *Weathersfield*—a place which, if we may credit the assertions of that worthy historian, John Josselyn, gent., "hath been infamous by reason of the witches therein." And so daring did these men of Pyquag become, that they extended those plantations of onions, for which their town is illustrious, under the very noses of the garrison of Fort Goed Hoop—insomuch that the honest Dutchmen could not look toward that quarter without tears in their eyes.

This crying injustice was regarded with proper indignation by the gallant Jacobus Van Curlet. He absolutely trembled with the violence of this choler and the exacerbations of his valour, which were the more turbulent in their workings from the length of the body in which they were agitated. He forthwith proceeded to strengthen his redoubts, heighten his breastworks, deepen his fosse, and fortify his position with a double row of abattis; after which he dispatched a fresh courier with accounts of his perilous situation.

The courier chosen to bear the dispatches was a fat, oily little man, as being less liable to be worn out or to lose leather on the journey; and, to insure his speed, he was mounted on the fleetest wagon horse in the garrison, remarkable for length of limb, largeness of bone, and hardness of trot; and so tall, that the little messenger was obliged to climb on his back by means of his tail and crupper. Such extraordinary speed did he make, that he arrived at Fort Amsterdam in a little less than a month, though the distance was full two hundred pipes, or about one hundred and twenty miles.

With an appearance of great hurry and business, and smoking a short travelling pipe, he proceeded on a long swing trot through the muddy lanes of the metropolis, demolishing whole batches of dirt pies which the little Dutch children were making in the road, and for which kind of pastry the children of this city have ever been famous. On arriving at the governor's house, he climbed down from his steed, roused the gray-headed doorkeeper, old Skaats, who, like his lineal descendant and faithful representative, the venerable crier of our court, was nodding at his post—rattled at the door of the council chamber, and startled the members as they were dozing over a plan for establishing a public market.

At that very moment a gentle grunt, or rather a deep-drawn snore, was heard from the chair of the governor, a whiff of smoke was at the same instant observed to escape from his lips, and a light cloud to ascend from the bowl of his pipe. The council, of course, supposed him engaged in deep sleep for the good of the community, and according to custom, in all such cases established, every man bawled out "Silence!" when, of a sudden, the door flew open, and the little courier straddled into the apartment, cased to the middle in a pair of Hessian boots, which he had got into for the sake of expedition.

In his right hand he held forth the ominous dispatches, and with his left he grasped firmly the waistband of his galligaskins, which had unfortunately given way in the exertion of descending from his horse. He stumped resolutely up to the governor, and, with more hurry than perspicuity, delivered his message. But, fortunately, his ill tidings came too late to ruffle the tranquillity of this most tranquil of rulers. His venerable Excellency had just breathed and smoked his last—his lungs and his pipe having been exhausted together, and his peaceful soul having escaped in the last whiff that curled from his tobacco pipe. In a word, the renowned Walter the Doubter, who had so often slumbered with his contemporaries, now slept with his fathers, and Wilhelmus Kieft governed in his stead.

BOOK 4

CONTAINING THE CHRONICLES OF THE REIGN OF WILLIAM THE TESTY.

CHAPTER 1

SHOWING THE NATURE OF HISTORY IN GENERAL; CONTAINING FURTHERMORE THE UNIVERSAL ACQUIREMENTS OF WILLIAM THE TESTY, AND HOW A MAN MAY LEARN SO MUCH AS TO RENDER HIMSELF GOOD FOR NOTHING.

When the lofty Thucydides is about to enter upon his description of the plague that desolated Athens, one of his modern commentators assures the reader, that the history is now going to be exceeding solemn, serious, and pathetic; and hints, with that air of chuckling gratulation with which a good dame draws forth a choice morsel from a cupboard to regale a favourite, that this plague will give his history a most agreeable variety.

In like manner did my heart leap within me, when I came to the dolorous dilemma of Fort Good Hope, which I at once perceived to be the forerunner of a series of great events and entertaining disasters. Such are the true subjects for the historic pen. For what is history, in fact, but a kind of Newgate calendar, a register of the crimes and miseries that man has inflicted on his fellow man. It is a huge libel on human nature, to which we industriously add page after page, volume after volume, as if we were building up a monument to the honour, rather than the infamy of our species.

If we turn over the pages of these chronicles that man has written of himself, what are the characters dignified by the appellation of great, and held up to the admiration of posterity? Tyrants, robbers, conquerors, renowned only for the magnitude of their misdeeds, and the stupendous wrongs and miseries they have inflicted on mankind—warriors, who have hired themselves to the trade of blood, not from motives of virtuous patriotism, or to protect the injured and defenceless, but merely to gain the vaunted glory of being adroit and successful in massacring their fellow beings! What are the great events that constitute a glorious era?—The fall of empires—the desolation of happy countries—splendid cities smoking in their ruins—the proudest works of art tumbled in the dust—the shrieks and groans of whole nations ascending unto heaven!

It is thus the historians may be said to thrive on the miseries of mankind, like birds of prey that hover over the field of battle, to fatten on the mighty dead. It was observed by a great projector of inland lock navigation, that rivers, lakes, and oceans, were only formed to feed canals. In like manner I am tempted to believe, that plots, conspiracies, wars, victories, and massacres, are ordained by Providence only as food for the historian.

It is a source of great delight to the philosopher, in studying the wonderful economy of nature, to trace the mutual dependencies of things, how they are created reciprocally for each other, and bow the most noxious and apparently unnecessary animal has its uses. Thus those swarms of flies, which are so often execrated as useless vermin, are created for the sustenance of spiders— and spiders, on the other hand, are evidently made to devour flies. So those heroes who have been such scourges to the world, were bounteously provided as themes for the poet and the historian, while the poet and the historian were destined to record the achievements of heroes!

These, and many similar reflections, naturally arose in my mind, as I took up my pen to commence the reign of William Kieft: for now the stream of our history, which hitherto has rolled in a tranquil current, is about to depart for ever from its peaceful haunts, and brawl through many a turbulent and rugged scene. Like some sleek ox, which, having fed and fattened in a rich clover field lies sunk in luxurious repose, and will bear repeated taunts and blows, before it heaves its unwieldy limbs and clumsily arouses from its slumbers; so the province of the Nieuw-Nederlandts, having long thrived and grown corpulent, under the prosperous reign of the Doubter, was reluctantly awakened to a melancholy conviction, that, by patient sufferance, its grievances had become so numerous and aggravating, that it was preferable to repel than endure them.

The reader will now witness the manner in which a peaceful community advances towards a state of war; which it is too apt to approach, as a horse does a drum, with much prancing and parade, but with little progress—and too often with the wrong end foremost.

Wilhelmus Kieft, who in 1634 ascended the *gubernatorial* chair (to borrow a favourite, though clumsy appellation of modern phraseologists,) was in form, feature, and character, the very reverse of Wouter Van Twiller, his renowned predecessor. He was of very respectable descent, his father being Inspector of Windmills in the ancient town of Saardam; and our hero, we are told, made very curious investigations into the nature and operations of those machines when a boy, which is one reason why he afterwards came to be so ingenious a governor.

His name, according to the most ingenious etymologists, was a corruption of *Kyver*, that is to say, a *wrangler* or *scolder*, and expressed the hereditary disposition of his family; which for nearly two centuries had kept the windy town of Saardam in hot water, and produced more tartars and brimstones than any ten families in the place—and so truly did Wilhelmas Kieft inherit this family endowment, that he had scarcely been a year in the discharge of his government, before he was universally known by the appellation of William the Testy.

He was a brisk, waspish, little old gentleman, who had dried and withered away, partly through the natural process of years, and partly from being parched and burnt up by his fiery soul; which blazed like a vehement rush light in his bosom, constantly inciting him to most valorous broils, altercations, and misadventures. I have heard it observed by a profound and philosophical judge of human nature, that if a woman waxes fat as she grows old, the tenure of her life is very precarious, but if haply she withers, she lives forever—such likewise was the case with William the Testy, who grew tougher in proportion as he dried.

He was some such a little Dutchman as we may now and then see stumping briskly about the streets of our city, in a broad-skirted coat, with huge buttons, an old fashioned cocked hat stuck on the back of his head, and a cane as high as his chin. His visage was broad, and his features sharp, his nose turned up with a most petulant curl; his cheeks were scorched into a dusky red—doubtless in consequence of the neighbourhood of two fierce little gray eyes, through which bit torrid soul beamed with tropical fervour.

The corners of his mouth were curiously modelled into a kind of fret work, not a little resembling the wrinkled proboscis of an irritable pug dog—in a word, he was one of the most positive, restless, ugly, little men, that ever put himself in a passion about nothing. Such were the personal endowments of William the Testy, but it was the sterling riches of his mind that raised him to dignity and power. In his youth he had passed with great credit through a celebrated academy at the Hague, noted for producing finished scholars with a despatch unequalled, except by certain of our American colleges.

Here he skirmished very smartly on the frontiers of several of the sciences, and made so gallant an inroad in the dead languages, as to bring off captive a host of Greek nouns and Latin verbs, together with divers pithy saws and apophthegms, all which he constantly paraded in conversation and writing, with as much vain glory as would a triumphant general of yore display the spoils of the countries he had ravaged. He had, moreover, puzzled himself considerably with logic, in which he had advanced so far as to attain a very familiar acquaintance, by name at least, with the whole family of syllogisms and dilemmas; but what he chiefly valued himself on, was his knowledge of metaphysics, in which, having once upon a time ventured too deeply, he came well nigh being smothered in a slough of unintelligible learning—a fearful peril, from the effects of which he never perfectly recovered.

This, I must confess, was in some measure a misfortune, for he never engaged in argument, of which he was exceeding fond, but what, between logical deductions and metaphysical jargon, he soon involved himself and his subject in a fog of contradictions and perplexities, and then would get into a mighty passion with his adversary for not being convinced gratis.

It is in knowledge as in swimming; he who ostentatiously sports and flounders on the surface, makes more noise and splashing, and attracts more attention, than the industrious pearl diver, who plunges in search of treasures to the bottom. The "universal acquirements" of William Kieft were the subject of great marvel and admiration among his countrymen—he figured about at the Hague with as much vain glory as does a profound Bonze at Pekin, who has mastered half the letters of the Chinese alphabet; and, in a word, was unanimously pronounced an *universal genius!*—I have known many universal geniuses in my time, though, to speak my mind freely, I never knew one, who, for the ordinary purposes of life, was worth his weight in straw—but, for the purposes of government, a little sound judgment, and plain common sense, is worth all the sparkling genius that ever wrote poetry, or invented theories.

Strange as it may sound, therefore, the *universal acquirements* of the illustrious Wilhelmus were very much in his way, and had he been a less learned man, it is possible he would have been much greater governor. He was exceedingly fond of trying philosophical and political experiments; and having stuffed his head full of scraps and remnants of ancient republics, and oligarchies, an aristocracies, and monarchies, and the laws of Solon and Lycurgus and Charondas, and the imaginary commonwealth of Plato, and the Pandects of Justinian, and a thousand other fragments of venerable antiquity, he was forever bent upon introducing someone or other of them into use; so that between one contradictory measure an another, he entangled the government of the little province of Nieuw-Nederlandts in more knots during his administration, than half a dozen successors could have untied.

No sooner had this bustling little man been blown by a whiff of fortune into the seat of government, than he called together his council, and delivered a very animated speech on the affairs of the province. As everybody knows what a glorious opportunity a governor, a president, or even an emperor has, of drubbing his enemies in his speeches, messages, and bulletins, where he has the talk all on his own side, they may be sure the high-mettled William Kieft did not suffer so favourable an occasion to escape him, of evincing that gallantry of tongue, common to all able legislators.

Before he commenced, it is recorded that he took out his pocket-handkerchief, and gave a very sonorous blast of the nose, according to the usual custom of great orators. This, in general, I believe, is intended as a signal trumpet, to call the attention of the auditors, but with William the Testy it boasted a more classic cause, for he had read of the singular expedient of that famous demagogue, Caius Gracchus, who, when he harangued the Roman populace, modulated his tones by an oratorical flute or pitch-pipe.

This prepatory symphony being performed, he commenced by expressing a humble sense of his own want of talents—his utter unworthiness of the honour conferred upon him, and his humiliating incapacity to discharge the important duties of his new station—in short, he expressed so contemptible an opinion of himself, that many simple country members present, ignorant that these were mere words of course, always used on such occasions, were very uneasy, and even felt wroth that he should accept an office, for which he was consciously so inadequate.

He then proceeded in a manner highly classic and profoundly erudite, though nothing at all to the purpose, being nothing more than a pompous account of all the governments of ancient Greece, and the wars of Rome and Carthage, together with the rise and fall of sundry outlandish empires, about which the assembly knew no more than their great grand children yet unborn.

Thus having, after the manner of your learned orators, convinced the audience that he was a man of many words and great erudition, he at length came to the less important part of his speech, the situation of the province—and here he soon worked himself into a fearful rage against the Yankees, whom he compared to the Gauls who desolated Rome, and the Goths and Vandals who overran the fairest plains of Europe—nor did he forget to mention, in terms of adequate opprobrium, the insolence with which they had encroached upon the territories of New-Netherlands, and the unparalleled audacity with which they had commenced the town of New-Plymouth, and planted the onion patches of Weathersfield, under the very walls of Fort Goed Hoop.

Having thus artfully wrought up his tale of terror to a climax, he assumed a self-satisfied look, and declared, with a nod of knowing import, that he had taken measures to put a final stop to these encroachments—that he had been obliged to have recourse to a dreadful engine of warfare, lately invented, awful in its effects, but authorized by direful necessity. In a word, he was resolved to conquer the Yankees—by proclamation!

For this purpose he had prepared a tremendous instrument of the kind, ordering, commanding, and enjoining the intruders aforesaid, forthwith to remove, depart, and withdraw from the districts, regions, and territories aforesaid, under pain of suffering all the penalties, forfeitures, and punishments in such case made and provided. This proclamation, he assured them, would at once exterminate the enemy from the face of the country, and he pledged his valour as a governor, that within two months after it was published, not one stone should remain on another in any of the towns which they had built.

The council remained for some time silent after he had finished; whether struck dumb with admiration at the brilliancy of his project, or put to sleep by the length of his harangue, the history of the times does not mention. Suffice it to say, they at length gave a universal grunt of acquiescence—the proclamation was immediately despatched with due ceremony, having the great seal of the province, which was about the size of a buckwheat pancake, attached to it by a broad red riband. Governor Kieft having thus vented his indignation, felt greatly relieved—adjourned the council—put on his cocked hat and corduroy small clothes, and mounting a tall raw boned charger, trotted out to his country seat, which was situated in a sweet, sequestered swamp, now called Dutch-street, but more commonly known by the name of Dog's Misery.

Here, like the good Numa, he reposed from the toils of legislation, taking lessons in government, not from the nymph Egeria, but from the honoured wife of his bosom; who was one of that peculiar kind of females, sent upon earth a little after the flood, as a punishment for the sins of mankind, and commonly known by the appellation of *knowing women.*

In fact, my duty as an historian obliges me to make known a circumstance which was a great secret at the time, and consequently was not a subject of scandal at more than half the tea tables in New-Amsterdam, but which, like many other great secrets, has leaked out in the lapse of years—and this was, that the great Wilhelmus the Testy, though one of the most potent little men that ever breathed, yet submitted at home to a species of government, neither laid down in Aristotle nor Plato; in short, it partook of the nature of a pure, unmixed tyranny, and is familiarly denominated *petticoat government.*—An absolute sway, which, though exceedingly common in these modern days, was very rare among the ancients, if we may judge from the rout made about the domestic economy of honest Socrates; which is the only ancient case on record.

The great Kieft, however, warded off all the sneers and sarcasms of his particular friends, who are ever ready to joke with a man on sore points of the kind, by alleging that it was a government of his own election, to which he submitted through choice; adding at the same time a profound maxim which he had found in an ancient author, that *"he who would aspire to govern should first learn to obey."*

CHAPTER 2

IN WHICH ARE RECORDED THE SAGE PROJECTS OF A RULER OF UNI-
VERSAL GENIUS—THE ART OF FIGHTING BY PROCLAMATION—AND
HOW THAT THE VALIANT JACOBUS VAN CURLET CAME TO BE FOULLY
DISHONOURED AT FORT GOED HOOP.

Never was a more comprehensive, a more expeditious, or, what is still better, a more economical measure devised, than this of defeating the Yankees by proclamation—an expedient, like-wise, so humane, so gentle and pacific, there were ten chances to one in favour of its succeeding,—but then there was one chance to ten that it would not succeed—as the ill-natured fates would have it, that single chance carried the day! The proclamation was perfect in all its parts, well constructed, well written, well sealed, and well published—all that was wanting to insure its effect was that the Yankees should stand in awe of it; but, provoking to relate, they treated it with the most absolute contempt, applied it to an unseemly purpose, and thus did the first warlike proc-lamation come to a shameful end—a fate which I am credibly informed has befallen but too many of its successors.

It was a long time before Wilhelmus Kieft could be persuaded by the united efforts of all his counsellors, that his war measures had failed in producing any effect. On the contrary, he flew in a passion whenever any one dared to question its efficacy; and swore that, though it was slow is operating, yet when once it began to work, it would soon purge the land of these rapacious intruders. Time, however, that test of all experiments, both in philosophy and politics, at length convinced the great Kieft, that his proclamation was abortive; and that notwithstanding he had waited nearly four years in a state of constant irritation, yet he was still farther off than ever from the object of his wishes.

His implacable adversaries in the east became more and more troublesome in their encroachments, and founded the thriving colony of Hartford close upon the skirts of Fort Goed Hoop. They, moreover, commenced the fair settlement of New Haven (otherwise called the Red Hills,) within the domains of their High Mightinesses—while the onion patches of Pyquag were a continual eye-sore to the garrison of Van Curlet. Upon beholding, therefore, the inefficacy of his measure, the sage Kieft, like many a worthy practitioner of physic, laid the blame, not to the medicine, but to the quantity administered, and resolutely resolved to double the dose.

In the year 1638, therefore, that being the fourth year of his reign, he fulminated against them second proclamation, of heavier metal than the former; written in thundering long sentences, not one word of which was under five syllables. This, in fact, was a kind of non-intercourse hill, forbidding and prohibiting all commerce and connexion between any and every of the said Yankee intruders, and the said fortified post of Fort Goed Hoop, and ordering, commanding, and advising, all his trusty, loyal, and well-beloved subjects, to furnish them with no supplies of gin, gingerbread, or *sourkrout*; to buy none of their pacing horses, measly pork, apple brandy, Yankee rum, cider water, apple sweetmeats, Weathersfield onions, or wooden bowls, but to starve and exterminate them from the face of the land.

Another pause of a twelvemonth ensued, during which this last proclamation received the same attention, and experienced the same fate as the first. In truth, it was rendered of no avail by the heroic spirit of the Nederlanders themselves. No sooner were they prohibited the use of Yankee merchandise, than it immediately became indispensable to their very existence. The men who all their lives had been content to drink gin and ride Esopus switch-tails, now swore that it was sheer tyranny to deprive them of apple-brandy and Narraghaneset pacers; and as to the women, they declared there was no comfort in life without Weathersfield onions, tin kettles, and wooden bowls.

So they set to work with might and main, to carry on a smuggling trade over the borders; and the province was as full as ever of Yankee wares,—with this difference, that those who used them had to pay double price, for the trouble and risk incurred in breaking the laws.

A signal benefit arose from these measures of William the Testy. The efforts to evade them had a marvellous effect in sharpening the intellects of the people. They were no longer to be governed without laws, as in the time of Orloffe the Dreamer; nor would the jack-knife and tobacco-box of Walter the Doubter have any more served as a judicial process. The old Nederlandt maxim, that "*honesty is the best policy*," was scouted as the bane of all ingenious enterprise. To use a modern phrase, "*a great impulse has been given to the public mind;*" and from the time of this first experience in smuggling, we may perceive a vast increase in the number, intricacy, and severity of laws and statutes—a sure proof of the increasing keenness of the public intellect.

A twelvemonth having elapsed since the gallant Jacobus Van Curlet despatched his annual messenger, with his customary budget of complaints and entreaties. Whether the regular interval of a year, intervening between the arrival of Van Curtlet's couriers, was occasioned by the systematic regularity of his movements, or by the immense distance at which he was stationed from the seat of government, is a matter of uncertainty. Some have ascribed it to the slowness of his messengers, who, as I have before noticed, were chosen from the shortest and fattest of his garrison, as least likely to be worn out on the road; and who, being pursy, short winded little men, generally travelled fifteen miles a day, and then laid by a whole week to rest. All these, however, are matters of conjecture; and I rather think it may be ascribed to the immemorial maxim of this worthy country—and which has ever influenced all its public transactions—*not to do things in a hurry*.

The gallant Jacobus Van Curlet in his despatches, respectfully represented, that several years had now elapsed since his first application to his late Excellency, Wouter Van Twiller; during which interval, his garrison had been reduced nearly one-eighth, by the death of two of his most valiant and corpulent soldiers, who had accidentally overeaten themselves on some fat salmon, caught in the Varsche River. He further stated, that the enemy persisted in their inroads, taking no notice of the fort or its inhabitants; but squatting themselves down, and forming settlements all around it; so that, in a little while, he should find himself enclosed and blockaded by the enemy, and totally at their mercy.

But among the most atrocious of his grievances, I find the following still on record, which may serve to show the bloody minded outrages of these savage intruders.

In the meantime, they of Hartford have not only usurped and taken in the lands of Connecticott, although unrighteously and against the lawes of nations, but have hindered our nation in sowing theire own purchased broken up lands, but have also sowed them with corne in the night, which the Nederlanders had broken up and intended to sowe: and have beaten the servants of the high and mighty the honored companie, which were labouring upon theire master's lands, from theire lands, with sticks and plough staves in hostile manner laming, and among the rest, struck Ever Duckings[1] a hole in his head, with a stick, so that the blood ran downe very strongly downe upon his body.

But what is still more atrocious—

Those of Hartford sold a hogg, that belonged to the honored companie, under pretence that it had eaten of theire grounde grass, when they had not any foot of inheritance. They proffered the hogg for 5s. if the commissioners would have given 5s. for damage; which the commissioners denied, because noe man's own hogg (as men used to say) can trespass upon his owne master's grounde.[2]

The receipt of this melancholy intelligence incensed the whole community—there was something in it that spoke to the dull comprehension, and touched the obtuse feelings even

1. This name is no doubt misspelt. In some old Dutch MSS. of the time, we find the name of Evert Duyckingh, who is unquestionably the unfortunate hero above alludded to.
2. Haz. Col. Stat. Papers.

of the puissant vulgar, who generally require a kick in the rear to awaken their slumbering dignity. I have known my profound fellow citizens bear without murmur, a thousand essential infringements of their rights, merely because they were not immediately obvious to their senses—but the moment the unlucky Pearce was shot upon our coasts, the whole body politic was in a ferment—so the enlightened Nederlanders, though they had treated the encroachments of their eastern neighbours with but little regard, and left their quill valiant governor to bear the whole brunt of war with his single pen—yet now every individual felt his head broken in the broken head of Duckings—and the unhappy fate of their fellow citizen the hog, being impressed, carried and sold into captivity, awakened a grunt of sympathy from every bosom.

The governor and council, goaded by the clamours of the multitude, now set themselves earnestly to deliberate upon what was to be done.—Proclamations had at length fallen into temporary disrepute; some were for sending the Yankees a tribute, as we make peace offerings to the petty Barbary powers, or as the Indians sacrifice to the devil. Others were for buying them out, hut this was opposed, as it would be acknowledging their title to the land they had seized. A variety of measures were as usual in such cases, proposed, discussed and abandoned, and the council had at last to adopt the means, which being the most common and obvious, had been knowingly overlooked—for your amazing acute politicians are forever looking through telescopes, which only enable them to see such objects as are far off, and unattainable, but which incapacitate them to see such things as are in their reach, and obvious to all simple folks, who are content to look with the naked eyes heaven has given them.

The profound council, as I have said, in their pursuit after Jack-o'-lanterns, accidentally stumbled on the very measure they were in need of; which was to raise a body of troops, and despatch them to the relief and reinforcement of the garrison. This measure was carried into such prompt operation, that in less than twelve months, the whole expedition, consisting of a sergeant and twelve men, was ready to march; and was reviewed for that purpose, in the public square, now known by the name of the Bowling Green. Just at this juncture the whole community was thrown into consternation, by the sudden arrival of the gallant Jacobus Van Curlet; who came straggling into town at the head of his crew of tatterdemalions, and bringing the melancholy tidings of his own defeat, and the capture of the redoutable post of Fort Goed Hoop by the ferocious Yankees.

The fate of this important fortress is an impressive warning to all military commanders. It was neither carried by storm nor famine; no practicable breach was effected by cannon or mines; no magazines were blown up by red hot shot, nor were the barracks demolished, or the garrison demolished, by the bursting of bombshells. In fact, the place was taken by a stratagem no less singular than effectual; and one that can never fail of success, whenever an opportunity occurs of putting it in practice. Happy am I to add, for the credit of our illustrious ancestors, that it was a stratagem, which though it impeached the vigilance, yet left the bravery of the intrepid Van Curlet and his garrison perfectly free from reproach.

It appeals that the crafty Yankees, having heard of the regular habits of the garrison, watched a favourable opportunity, and silently introduced themselves into the fort, about the middle of a sultry day; when its vigilant defenders, having gorged themselves with a hearty dinner, and smoked out their pipes, were one and all snoring most obstreperously at their posts, little dreaming of so disastrous an occurrence.

The enemy most inhumanly seized Jacobus Van Curlet and his sturdy myrmidons by the nape of the neck, gallanted them to the gate of the fort, and dismissed them severally, with a kick on the crupper, as Charles the Twelfth dismissed the heavy bottomed Russians, after the battle of Narva—only taking care to give two kicks to Van Curlet, as a signal mark of distinction.

A strong garrison was immediately established in the fort, consisting of twenty long sided, hard fisted Yankees, with Weathersfield onions stuck in their hats, by way of cockades and feathers—long rusty fowling pieces for muskets—hasty pudding, dumb fish, pork and molasses for stores; and a huge pumpkin was hoisted on the end of a pole, as a standard—liberty caps not having as yet come into fashion.

Chapter 3
Containing the fearful wrath of William the Testy, and the great dolour of the New-Amsterdammers, because of the affair of Fort Goed Hoop,—And, moreover, how William the Testy did strongly fortify the city—Together with the exploits of Stoffel Brinkerhoff.

Language cannot express the prodigious fury into which the testy Wilhelmus Kieft was thrown by this provoking intelligence. For three good hours the rage of the little man was too great for words, or rather the words were too great for him; and he was nearly choked by some dozen huge, misshapen, nine cornered Dutch oaths, that crowded all at once into his gullet. Having blazed off the first broadside, he kept up a constant firing for three whole days—anathematizing the Yankees, man, woman, and child, body and soul, for a set of *dieven, schobbejaken, deugenieten, twist-zoekeren, loozen-schalken, blaes-kaken, kakken-bedden,* and a thousand other names of which, unfortunately for posterity, history does not make mention.

Finally, he swore that he would have nothing more to do with such a squatting, bundling, guessing, questioning, swapping, pumpkin-eating, molasses-daubing, shingle-splitting, cider-watering, horse-jockeying, notion-peddling crew—that they might stay at Fort Goed Hoop and rot, before he would dirty his hands by attempting to drive them away; in proof of which he ordered the new raised troops to be marched forthwith into winter quarters, although it was not as yet quite mid-summer. Governor Kieft faithfully kept his word, and his adversaries as faithfully kept their post; and thus the glorious River Connecticut, and all the gay valleys through which it rolls, together with the salmon, shad, and other fish within its waters, fell into the hands of the victorious Yankees, by whom they are held at this very day.

Great despondency seized upon the city of New Amsterdam, in consequence of these melancholy events. The name of Yankee became as terrible among our good ancestors as was that of Gaul among the ancient Romans; and all the sage old women of the province used it as a bug-bear, wherewith to frighten their unruly children into obedience.

The eyes of all the province were now turned upon their governor, to know what he would do for the protection of the commonweal, in these days of darkness and peril. Great apprehensions prevailed among the reflecting part of the community, especially the old women, that these terrible warriors of Connecticut, not content with the conquest of Fort Goed Hoop, would incontinently march on to New-Amsterdam and take it by storm—and as these old ladies, through means of the governor's spouse, who, as has been already hinted, was "the better horse," had obtained considerable influence in public affairs, keeping the province under a kind of petticoat government, it was determined that measures should be taken for the effective fortification of the city.

Now it happened that at this time there sojourned in New-Amsterdam one Anthony Van Corlear,[3] a jolly fat Dutch trumpeter, of a pleasant burly visage, famous for his long wind and his huge whiskers, and who, as the story goes, could twang so potently upon his instrument, as to produce an effect upon all within hearing, as though ten thousand bagpipes were singing right lustily i' the nose. Him did the illustrious Kieft pick out as the man of all the world most fitted to be the champion of New-Amsterdam, and to garrison its fort; making little doubt but that his instrument would be as effectual and offensive in war as was that of the Paladin Astolpho, or the more classic horn of Alecto.

It would have done one's heart good to have seen the gov-

---

3. David Pietrez De Vries, in his *Reyze naer Nieuw-Nederlandt onder het year 1640*, makes mention of one Corlear, a trumpeter in Fort Amsterdam, who gave name to Corlear's Hook, and who was doubtless this same champion, described by Mr. Knickerbocker.—Original Editor.

ernor snapping his fingers and fidgeting with delight, while his sturdy trumpeter strutted up and down the ramparts, fearlessly twanging his trumpet in the face of the whole world, like a thrice valorous editor daringly insulting all the principalities and powers—on the other side of the Atlantic.

Nor was he content with thus strongly garrisoning the fort, but he likewise added exceedingly to its strength, by furnishing it with a formidable battery of Quaker guns—rearing a stupendous flag staff in the centre, which overtopped the whole city—and, moreover, by building a great windmill on one of the bastions.[4] This last, to be sure, was somewhat of a novelty in the art of fortification, but, as I have already observed, William Kieft was notorious for innovations and experiments, and traditions do affirm that he was much given to mechanical inventions—constructing patent smoke-jacks—carts that went before the horses, and especially erecting windmills, for which machines he had acquired a singular predilection in his native town of Saardam.

All these scientific vagaries of the little governor were cried up with ecstasy by his adherents, as proof of his universal genius—but there were not wanting ill-natured grumblers, who railed at him as employing his mind in frivolous pursuits, and devoting that time to smoke-jacks and windmills which should have been occupied in the more important concerns of the province. Nay they even went so far as to hint once or twice, that his head was turned by his experiments, and that he really thought to manage his government as he did his mills—by mere wind!—such is the illiberality and slander to which enlightened rulers are ever subject.

Notwithstanding all the measures, therefore, of William the Testy, to place the city in a posture of defence, the inhabitants continued in great alarm and despondency. But fortune, who seems always careful, in the very nick of time, to throw a bone for hope to gnaw upon, that the starveling elf may be kept alive,

4. De Vries mentions that this windmill stood on the south-east bastion, and it is likewise to be seen, together with the flag-staff, in Justus Danker's View of New-Amsterdam.

did about this time crown the arms of the province with success in another quarter, and thus cheered the drooping hearts of the forlorn Nederlanders; otherwise there is no knowing to what lengths they might have gone in the excess of their sorrowing— *"for grief,"* says the profound historian of the seven champions of Christendom, *"is companion with despair, and despair a procurer of infamous death!"*

Among the numerous inroads of the Mosstroopers of Connecticut, which, for some time past had occasioned such great tribulation, I should particularly have mentioned a settlement made on the eastern part of Long Island, at a place which, from the peculiar excellence of its shell fish, was called Oyster Bay. This was attacking the province in a most sensible part, and occasioned great agitation at New-Amsterdam.

It is an incontrovertible fact, well known to skilful physiologists, that the high road to the affections is through the throat; and this may be accounted for on the same principles which I have already quoted in my strictures on fat aldermen. Nor is the fact unknown to the world at large; and hence do we observe, that the surest way to gain the hearts of the million, is to feed them well—and that a man is never so disposed to flatter, to please and serve another, as when he is feeding at his expense; which is one reason why your rich men, who give frequent dinners, have such abundance of sincere and faithful friends.

It is on this principle that our knowing leaders of parties secure the affections of their partisans, by rewarding them bountifully with loaves and fishes; and entrap the suffrages of the greasy mob, by treating them with bull feasts and roasted oxen. I have known many a man, in this same city, acquire considerable importance in society, and usurp a large share of the good will of his enlightened fellow-citizens, when the only thing that could be said in his eulogium was, that "he gave a good dinner, and kept excellent wine."

Since then the heart and the stomach are so nearly allied, it follows conclusively that what affects the one, must sympathetically affect the other. Now it is an equally incontrovertible fact, that of all offerings to the stomach, there is none more grateful than the testaceous marine animal, known commonly by the vulgar name of Oyster, And in such great reverence has it ever been held, by my gormandizing fellow-citizens, that temples have been dedicated to it, time out of mind, in every street, lane, and alley, throughout this well fed city. It is not to be expected, therefore, that the seizing of Oyster Bay, a place abounding with their favourite delicacy, would be tolerated by the inhabitants of New-Amsterdam.

An attack upon their honour they might have pardoned; even the massacre of a few citizens might have been passed over in silence; but an outrage that affected the larders of the great city of New-Amsterdam, and threatened the stomachs of its corpulent burgomasters, was too serious to pass unrevenged.—The whole council was unanimous in opinion, that the intruders should be immediately driven by force of arms from Oyster Bay and its vicinity, and a detachment was accordingly despatched for the purpose, under the command of one Stoffel Brinkerhoff, or Brinkerhoofd, (*i. e.* Stofiel, the head-breaker) so called because he was a man of mighty deeds, famous throughout the whole extent of Nieuw-Nederlandts for his skill at quarter-staff, and for size, he would have been a match for Colbrand, the Danish champion, slain by Guy of Warwick.

Stoffel Brinkerhoff was a man of few words, but prompt actions—one of your straight going officers, who march directly forward, and do their orders without making any parade. He used no extraordinary speed in his movements, but trudged steadily on, through Nineveh and Babylon, and Jericho and Patchog, and the mighty town of Quag, and various other renowned cities of yore, which, by some unaccountable witchcraft of the Yankees, have been strangely transplanted to Long-Island, until he arrived in the neighbourhood of Oyster Bay.

Here was he encountered by a tumultuous host of valiant warriors, headed by Preserved Fish, and Habbakuk Nutter, and Return Strong, and Zerubbabel Fisk, and Jonathan Doolittle, and Determined Cock!—at the sound of whose names the courageous Stoffel verily believed that the whole parliament of Praise-God Barebones had been let loose to discomfit him. Finding, however, that this formidable, body was composed merely of the "select men" of the settlement, armed with no other weapon but their tongues, and that they had issued forth with no other intent than to meet him on the field of argument—he succeeded in putting them to the rout with little difficulty, and completely broke up their settlement.

Without waiting to write an account of his victory on the spot, and thus letting the enemy slip through his fingers, while he was securing his own laurels, as a more experienced general would have done, the brave Stoffel thought of nothing but completing his enterprise, and utterly driving the Yankees from the island. This hardy enterprise he performed in much the same manner as he had been accustomed to drive his oxen; for as the Yankees fled before him, he pulled up his breeches and trudged steadily after them, and would infallibly have driven them into the sea, had they not begged for quarter, and agreed to pay tribute.

The news of this achievement was a seasonable restorative to the spirits of the citizens of New-Amsterdam. To gratify them still more, the governor resolved to astonish them with one of those gorgeous spectacles, known in the days of classic antiquity, a full account of which had been flowed into his memory, when a school-boy at the Hague. A grand triumph, therefore, was decreed to Stoffel Brinkerhoff, who made his triumphant entrance into town riding on a Naraganset pacer; five pumpkins, which, like Roman Eagles, had served the enemy for standards, were carried before him—fifty cart loads of oysters, five hundred bushels of Weathersfield onions, a hundred quintals of codfish, two hogsheads of molasses, and various other treasures, were exhibited as the spoils and tribute of the Yankees; while three notorious counterfeiters of Manhattan notes[5] were led captive

5. This is one of those trivial anachronisms, that now and then occur in the course of this otherwise authentic history. How could Manhattan notes be counterfeited, when as yet Banks were unknown in this country—and our simple progenitors had not even dreamt of those inexhaustible mines of paper opulence.—Print. Dev.

to grace the hero's triumph.

The procession was enlivened by martial music from the trumpet of Antony Van Corlear the champion, accompanied by a select band of boys and negroes, performing on the national instruments of rattle bones and clam-shells. The citizens devoured the spoils in sheer gladness of heart—every man did honour to the conqueror by getting devoutly drunk on New-England rum—and the learned Wilhelmus Kieft calling to mind, in a momentary fit of enthusiasm and generosity, that it was customary among the ancients to honour their victorious generals with public statues, passed a gracious degree, by which every tavern-keeper was permitted to paint the head of the intrepid Stoffel on his sign!

CHAPTER 4

PHILOSOPHICAL REFLECTIONS ON THE FOLLY OF BEING HAPPY IN TIMES OF PROSPERITY.—SUNDRY TROUBLES ON THE SOUTHERN FRONTIERS.—HOW WILLIAM THE TESTY HAD WELL NIGH RUINED THE PROVINCE THROUGH A CABALISTIC WORD—AS ALSO THE SECRET EXPEDITION OF JAN JANSEN ALPENDAM, AND HIS ASTONISHING REWARD.

If we could but get a peep at the tally of Dame Fortune, where, like a notable landlady, she regularly chalks up the debtor and creditor accounts of mankind, we should find that, upon the whole, good and evil are pretty nearly balanced in this world; and that though we may for a long while revel in the very lap of prosperity, the time will at length come when we must ruefully pay off the reckoning. Fortune, in fact, is a pestilent shrew, and withal a most inexorable creditor; for though she may indulge her favourites in long credits, and overwhelm them with her favours, yet sooner or later she brings up her arrears with the rigour of an experienced publican, and washes out her scores with their tears.

"Since," says good old Boetius, "no man can retain her at his pleasure, and since her flight is so deeply lamented what are her favours but sure prognostications of approaching trouble and calamity?"

There is nothing that more moves my contempt at the stupidity and want of reflection of my fellow men, than to behold them rejoicing, and indulging in security and self-confidence, in times of prosperity. To a wise man, who is blessed with the light of reason, those are the very moment of anxiety and apprehension, well knowing that according to the system of things, happiness is at best but transient—and that the higher he is elevated by the capricious breath of fortune, the lower must be his proportionate depression. Whereas, he who is overwhelmed by calamity, has the less chance of encountering fresh disasters, as a man at the bottom of a ladder runs very little risk of breaking his neck by tumbling to the top.

This is the very essence of true wisdom, which consists in knowing when we ought to be miserable; and was discovered much about the same time with that invaluable secret, that *"every thing is vanity and vexation of spirit"* is consequence of which maxim, your wise men have ever been the unhappiest of the human race; esteeming it an infallible mark of genius to be distressed without reason—since any man may be miserable in time of misfortune, but it is the philosopher alone who can discover cause for grief in the very hour of prosperity.

According to the principle I have just advanced, we find that the colony of New-Netherlands, which under the reign of the renowned Van Twiller, had flourished in such alarming and fatal serenity, is now paying for its former welfare, and discharging the enormous debt of comfort which it contracted. Foes harass it from different quarters; the city of New-Amsterdam, while yet in its infancy, is kept in constant alarm; and its valiant commander, William the Testy, answers the vulgar, but expressive idea, of *"a man in a peck of troubles."*

While busily engaged repelling his bitter enemies the Yankees on one side, we find him suddenly molested in another quarter, and by other assailants. A vagrant colony of Swedes, under the conduct of Peter Minnewits, and professing allegiance to that redoubtable *virago*, Christina, queen of Sweden, had settled themselves and erected a fort on South (or Delaware) River—within the boundaries claimed by the government of the New-Netherlands; History is mute as to the particulars of their first landing, and their real pretensions to the soil; and this is the more to be lamented, as this same colony of Swedes will hereafter be found most materially to affect not only the interests of the Nederlanders, but of the world at large!

In whatever manner, therefore, this vagabond colony of Swedes first took possession of the country, it is certain that in 1638 they established a fort, and Minnewits, according to the off-hand usage of his contemporaries, declared himself governor of all the adjacent country, under the name of the province of New-Sweden. No sooner did this reach the ears of the choleric Wilhelmus, than, like a true spirited chieftain, he immediately broke into a violent rage, and calling together his council, belaboured the Swedes most lustily in the longest speech that had ever been heard in the colony, since the memorable dispute of Ten Breeches and Tough Breeches.

Having thus given vent to the first ebullitions of his indignation, he had resort to his favourite measure of proclamation, and despatched one, piping hot, in the first year of his reign, informing Peter Minnewits that the whole territory, bordering on the South river, had, time out of mind, been in possession of the Dutch colonists, having been "beset with forts, and sealed with their blood."

The latter sanguinary sentence would convey an idea of direful war and bloodshed, were we not relieved by the information that it merely related to a fray, in which some half a dozen Dutchmen had been killed by the Indians, in their benevolent attempts to establish a colony and promote civilization. By this it will be seen that William Kieft, though a very small man, delighted in big expressions, and was much given to a praise-worthy figure, in rhetoric, generally cultivated by your little great men, called hyperbole. A figure which has been found of infinite service among many of his class, and which has helped to swell the grandeur of many a mighty, self-important, but windy chief magistrate.

Nor can I refrain in this place from observing how much my beloved country is indebted to this same figure of hyperbole, for supporting certain of her greatest characters—statesmen, orators, civilians, and divines; who, by dint of big words, inflated periods, and windy doctrines, are kept afloat on the surface of society, as ignorant swimmers are buoyed up by blown bladders.

The proclamation against Minnewits concluded by ordering the self-dubbed governor, and his gang of Swedish adventurers, immediately to leave the country under penalty of the high displeasure, and inevitable vengeance of the puissant government of the Nieuw-Nederlandts. This "strong measure," however, does not seem to have had a whit more effect than its predecessors which had been thundered against the Yankees—the Swedes resolutely held on to the territory they had taken possession of—whereupon matters for the present remained in *statu quo*.

That Wilhelmus Kieft should put up with this insolent obstinacy in the Swedes would appear incompatible with his valorous temperament; but we find that about this time the little man had his hands full, and what with one annoyance and another, was kept continually on the bounce.

There is a certain description of active legislators, who, by shrewd management, contrive always to have a hundred irons on the anvil, every one of which must be immediately attended to; who consequently are ever full of temporary shifts and expedients, patching up the public welfare, and cobbling the national affairs, so as to make nine holes where they mend one—stopping chinks and flaws with whatever comes first to hand, like the Yankees I have mentioned, stuffing old clothes in broken windows.

Of this class of statesmen was William the Testy—and had he only been blessed with powers equal to his zeal, or his zeal been disciplined by a little discretion, there is very little doubt but he would have made the greatest governor of his size on record—the renowned governor of the island of Barataria alone excepted.

The great defect of Wilhelmus Kieft's policy was, that though no man could be more ready to stand forth in an hour of emergency, yet he was so intent upon guarding the national pocket, that he suffered the enemy to break its head—in other words, whatever precaution for public safety he adopted, he was so intent upon rendering it cheap, that he invariably rendered it ineffectual.

All this was a remote consequence of his profound education at the Hague—where, having acquired a smattering of knowledge, he was ever after a great conner of indexes, continually dipping into books, without ever studying to the bottom of any subject; so that he had the scum of all kinds of authors fermenting in his *pericranium*. In some of these title-page researches he unluckily stumbled over a grand political *cabalistic word*, which, with his customary facility, he immediately incorporated into his great scheme of government, to the irretrievable injury and delusion of the honest province of Nieuw-Nederlandts, and the eternal misleading of all experimental rulers.

In vain have I pored over the *theurgia* of the Chaldeans, the *cabala* of the Jews, the *necromancy* of the Arabians, the magic of the Persians, the *hocus pocus* of the English, the witchcraft of the Yankees, or the *pow-wowing* of the Indians, to discover where the little man first laid eyes on this terrible word. Neither the Sephir Jetzirah, that famous cabalistic volume, ascribed to the patriarch Abraham; nor the pages of the Zohar, containing the mysteries of the cabala, recorded by the learned *rabbi* Simeon Jochaddes, yield any light to my inquiries—Nor am I in the least benefited by my painful researches in the Shem-ham-phorah of Benjamin, the wandering Jew, though it enabled Davidus Elm to make a ten days' journey in twenty-four hours.

Neither can I perceive the slightest affinity in the *Tetragrammaton*, or sacred name of four letters, the profoundest word of the Hebrew *cabala*; a mystery sublime, ineffable, and incommunicable—and the letters of which Jod-He-Vau-He, having been stolen by the pagans, constituted their great name Jao or Jove. In short, in all my *cabalistic, theuigic, necromantic,* magical, and astrological researches, from the Tetractys of Pythagoras to the recondite works of Breslaw and Mother Bunch, I have not discovered the least vestige of an origin of this word, nor have I discovered any word of sufficient potency to counteract it.

Not to keep my reader in any suspense, the word which had so wonderfully arrested the attention of William the Testy, and which in German character had a particularly black and ominous aspect, on being fairly translated into the English is no other than *economy*—a talismanic term, which, by constant use and frequent mention, has ceased to be formidable in our eyes, but which has as terrible potency as any in the *arcana* of *necromancy*.

When pronounced in a national assembly it has an immediate effect in closing the hearts, beclouding the intellects, drawing the purse strings, and buttoning the breeches pockets of all philosophic legislators. Nor are its effects on the eyes less wonderful. It produces a contraction of the retina, an obscurity of the crystalline lens, a viscidity of the vitreous, and an inspissation of the *aqueous humours*, an induratiion of the *tunica sclerotica*, and: a convexity of the cornea; insomuch that the organ of vision loses its strength and perspicuity, and the unfortunate patient becomes *myopes*, or in plain English, purblind, perceiving only the amount of immediate expense, without being able to look farther, and regard it in connexion with the ultimate object to be effected—"So that," to quote the words of the eloquent Burke, "*a briar at his nose is of greater magnitude than an oak at five hundred yards distance.*"

Such are its instantaneous operations, and the results and still more astonishing. By its magic influence seventy-fours shrink into frigates—frigates into ships, and sloops into gun-boats.

This all potent word, which served as his touchstone in politics, at once explains the whole system of proclamations, protests, empty threats, windmills, trumpeters, and paper war, carried on by Wilhelmus the Testy—and we may trace its operations in an armament which he fitted out in 1642 in a moment of great wrath, consisting of two sloops and thirty men, under the command of Mynheer Jan Jansen Alpendam, as admiral of the fleet, and commander in chief of the forces.

This formidable expedition, which can only be paralleled by some of the daring cruises of our infant navy about the bay and up the sound, was intended to drive the Marylanders from the Schuylkill, of which they had recently taken possession—and which was claimed as part of the province of New-Nederlandts—for it appears that at this time our infant colony was in that enviable state, so much coveted by ambitious nations, that is to say, the government had a vast extent of territory, part of which it enjoyed, and the greater part of which it had continually to quarrel about.

Admiral Jan Jansen Alpendam was a man of great mettle and prowess, and no way dismayed at the character of the enemy, who were represented as a gigantic, gunpowder race of men, who lived on hoe cakes and bacon, drank mint *juleps* and apple toddy, and were exceedingly expert at boxing, biting, gouging, tar and feathering, and a variety of other athletic accomplishments, which they had borrowed from their cousins-german and prototypes the Virginians, to whom they have ever borne considerable resemblance. Notwithstanding all these alarming representations, the admiral entered the Schuylkill most undauntedly with his fleet, and arrived without disaster or opposition at the place of destination.

Here he attacked the enemy in a vigorous speech in Low Dutch, which the wary Kieft had previously put in his pocket; wherein he courteously commenced by calling them a pack of lazy, louting, dram-drinking, cock-fighting, horse-racing, slave-driving, tavern-haunting, Sabbath-breaking, *mulatto* breeding upstarts—and concluded by ordering them to evacuate the country immediately—to which they most laconically replied in plain English, "they'd see him d———d first."

Now this was a reply for which neither Jan Jansen Alpendam nor Wilhelmus Kieft had made any calculation—and finding himself totally unprepared to answer so terrible a rebuff with suitable hostility, he concluded that his wisest course was to return home and report progress. He accordingly sailed back to

New-Amsterdam, where he was received with great honours, and considered as a pattern for all commanders, having achieved a most hazardous enterprise, at a trifling expense of treasure, and without losing a single man to the state!—He was unani-mously called the deliverer of his country, (an appellation liberally bestowed on all great men;) his two sloops having done their duty, were laid up (or dry docked) in a cove now called the Albany basin, where they, quietly rotted in the mud; and to immortalize his name, they erected, by subscription, a magnificent shingle monument on the top of Flatten Barrack Hill, which lasted three whole years; when it fell to pieces, and was burnt for firewood.

Chapter 5
How William the Testy enriched the province by a multitude of laws, and came to be the patron of lawyers and bum-bailiffs—And how the people became exceedingly enlightened and unhappy under his instructions.

Among the many wrecks and fragments of exalted wisdom which have floated down the stream of time, from venerable antiquity, and have been carefully picked up by those humble, but industrious wights, who ply along the shores of literature, we find the following sage ordinance of Charondas, the Locrian legislator.—Anxious to preserve the ancient laws of the state from the addictions and improvements of profound "country members," or officious candidates for popularity, he ordained, that whoever proposed a new law, should do it with halter about his neck; so that in case his proposition was rejected, they just strung him up—and there the matter ended.

This salutary institution had such an effect, that for more than two hundred years there was only one trifling alteration in the criminal code—and the whole race of lawyers starved to death for want of employment. The consequence of this was, that the Locrians being unprotected by an overwhelming load of excellent laws, and undefended by a standing army of pettifoggers and sheriff's officers, lived very lovingly together, and were such a happy people, that they scarce make any figure throughout the whole Grecian history—for it is well known that none but your unlucky, quarrelsome, rantipole nations make any noise in the world.

Well would it have been for William the Testy, had he haply in the course of his "universal acquirements," stumbled upon this precaution of the good Charondas. On the contrary, he conceived that the true policy of a legislator was to multiply laws, and thus secure the property, the persons, and the morals of the people, by surrounding them in a manner with men traps and spring guns, and besetting even the sweet sequestered walks of private life with quickset hedges, so that a man could scarcely turn, without the risk of encountering some of these pestiferous protectors. Thus was he continually coining petty, laws for every petty offence that occurred, until in time they became too numerous to be remembered, and remained like those of certain modern legislators, mere dead-letters—revived occasionally for the purpose of individual oppression, or to entrap ignorant offenders.

Petty courts consequently began to appear, where the law was administered with nearly as much wisdom and impartiality as in those august tribunals, the aldermen's and justices' courts of the present day. The plaintiff was generally favoured, as being a customer and bringing business to the shop, the offences of the rich were discreetly winked at—for fear of hurting the feelings of their friends;—but it could never be laid to the charge of the vigilant burgomasters, that they suffered vice to skulk unpunished, under the disgraceful rags of poverty.

About this time may we date the first introduction of capital punishments—a goodly gallows being erected on the water-side, about where Whitehall stairs are at present, a little to the east of the battery. Hard by also was erected another gibbet of a very strange, uncouth, and unmatchable description, but on which the ingenious William Kieft valued himself not a little, being a punishment entirely of his own invention.

It was for loftiness of altitude not a whit inferior to that of

Haman, so renowned in Bible history; but the marvel of the contrivance was, that the culprit, instead of being suspended by the neck, according to venerable custom, was hoisted by the waistband, and was kept for an hour together, dangling and sprawling between heaven and earth—to the infinite entertainment and doubtless great edification of the multitude of respectable citizens, who usually attend upon exhibitions of the kind.

It is incredible how the little governor chuckled at beholding *caitiff* vagrants and sturdy beggars thus swinging by the crupper, and cutting antic gambols in the air. He had a thousand pleasantries, and mirthful conceits to utter upon these occasions. He called them his dandle-lions—his wild fowl—his high flyers—his spread eagles—his goshawks—his scare crows, and finally his *gallows-birds*, which ingenious appellation, though originally confined to worthies who had taken the air in this strange manner, has since grown to be a cant name given to all candidates for legal elevation.

This punishment, moreover, if we may credit the assertions of certain grave etymologists, gave the first hint for a kind of harnessing, or strapping, by which our forefathers braced up their multifarious breeches, and which has of late years been revived, and continues to be worn at the present day.

Such were the admirable improvements of William Kieft in criminal law—nor was his civil code less a matter of wonderment, and much does it grieve me that the limits of my work will not suffer me to expatiate on both, with the prolixity they deserve. Let it suffice then to say, that in a little while the blessings of innumerable laws became notoriously apparent. It was soon found necessary to have a certain class of men to expound and confound them—divers pettifoggers accordingly made their appearance, under whose protecting care the community was soon set together by the ears.

I would not here be thought to insinuate anything derogatory to the profession of the law, or to its dignified members. Well am I aware, that we have in this ancient city innumerable worthy gentlemen who have embraced that honourable order, not for the sordid love of filthy lucre, nor the selfish cravings of renown, but through no other motives, but a fervent zeal for the correct administration of justice, and a generous and disinterested devotion to the interests of their fellow citizens!—Sooner would I throw this trusty pen into the flames, and cork up my inkbottle forever, than infringe even for a nail's breadth upon the dignity of this truly benevolent class of citizens—on the contrary I allude solely to that crew of *caitiff* scouts, who, in these latter days of evil, have become so numerous—who infest the skirts of the profession, as did the recreant Cornish knights the honourable order of chivalry—who, under its auspices, commit their depredations on society—who thrive by quibbles, quirks, and chicanery, and, like vermin, swarm most where there is most corruption.

Nothing so soon awakens the malevolent passions as the facility of gratification. The courts of law would never be so constantly crowded with petty, vexatious, and disgraceful suits, were it not for the herds of pettifogging lawyers that infest them. These tamper with the passions of the lower and more ignorant classes; who, as if poverty were not a sufficient misery in itself, are always ready to heighten it by the bitterness of litigation. They are in law what quacks are in medicine—exciting the malady for the purpose of profiting by the cure, and retarding the cure for the purpose of augmenting the fees.

Where one destroys the constitution, the other impoverishes the purse; and it may likewise be observed, that a patient, who has once been under the hands of a quack, is ever after dabbling in drugs, and poisoning himself with infallible remedies; and an ignorant man, who has once meddled with the law under the auspices of one of these empirics, is forever after embroiling himself with his neighbours, and impoverishing himself with successful law suits.—My readers will excuse this digression, into which I have been unwarily betrayed; but I could not avoid giving a cool, unprejudiced account of an abomination too prevalent in this excellent city, and with the effects of which I am unluckily acquainted to my cost; having been nearly ruined by a law suit, which was unjustly decided against me—and my ruin having been completed by another, which was decided in my favour.

It has been remarked by the observant writer of the Stuyvesant manuscript, that under the administration of Wilhelmus Kieft the disposition of the inhabitants of New-Amsterdam experienced an essential change, so that they became very meddlesome and factious. The constant exacerbations of temper into which the little governor was thrown, by the maraudings on his frontiers, and his unfortunate propensity to experiment and innovation, occasioned him to keep his council in a continual worry—and the council being to the people at large, what yeast or leaven is to a batch, they threw the whole community into a ferment—and the people at large being to the city what the mind is to the body, the unhappy commotions they underwent operated most disastrously upon New-Amsterdam—insomuch, that in certain of their paroxysms of consternation and perplexity, they begat several of the most crooked, distorted, and abominable streets, lanes, and alleys, with which this metropolis is disfigured.

But the worst of the matter was, that just about this time the mob, since called the sovereign people, like Balaam's ass, began to grow more enlightened than its rider, and exhibited a strange desire of governing itself. This was another effect of the "universal acquirements" of William the Testy. In some of his pestilent researches among the rubbish of antiquity, he was struck with admiration at the institution of public tables among the Lacedaemonians, where they discussed topics of a general and interesting nature—at the schools of the philosophers, where they engaged in profound disputes upon politics and morals—where gray beards were taught the rudiments of wisdom, and youths learned to become little men before they were boys.

"There is nothing," said the ingenious Kieft, shutting up the book, "there is nothing more essential to the well management of a country, than education among the people; the basis of a good government should be laid in the public mind."—Now this was true enough, but it was ever the wayward fate of William the Testy, that when he thought right, he was sure to go to work wrong. In the present instance he could scarcely eat or sleep until he had set on foot brawling debating societies among the simple citizens of New-Amsterdam.

This was the one thing wanting to complete his confusion. The honest Dutch *burghers*, though in truth but little given to argument or wordy altercation, yet by dint of meeting often together, fuddling themselves with strong drink, beclouding their brains with tobacco smoke, and listening to the harangues of some half a dozen oracles, soon became exceedingly wise, and— as is always the case where the mob is politically enlightened— exceedingly discontented. They found out, with wonderful quickness of discernment, the fearful error in which they had indulged, in fancying themselves the happiest people in creation—and were fortunately convinced, that, all circumstances to the contrary notwithstanding, they were a very unhappy, deluded, and consequently, ruined people.

In a short time the *quidnuncs* of New-Amsterdam formed themselves into sage *juntos* of political croakers, who daily met together to groan over political affairs, and make themselves miserable; thronging to these unhappy assemblages with the same eagerness that zealots have in all ages abandoned the milder and more peaceful paths of religion, to crowd to the howling convocations of fanaticism. We are naturally prone to discontent, and avaricious after imaginary causes of lamentation—like lubberly monks, we belabour our own shoulders, and seem to take a vast satisfaction in the music of our own groans.

Nor is this said for the sake of paradox; daily experience shows the truth of these observations. It is almost impossible to elevate the spirits of a man groaning under ideal calamities; but nothing is more easy than to render him wretched, though on the pinnacle of felicity; as it is an Herculean task to hoist a man to the top of a steeple, though the merest child can topple him off thence.

In the sage assemblages I have noticed, the reader will at once perceive the faint germs of those sapient convocations called popular meetings, prevalent at our day. Thither resorted all those idlers and "squires of low degree," who, like rags, hang loose upon the back of society, and are ready to be blown away by every wind of doctrine.

Cobblers abandoned their stalls, and hastened thither to give lessons on political economy—blacksmiths left their handicraft and suffered their own fires to go out, while they blew the bellows and stirred up the fire of faction; and even tailors, though but the shreds and patches, the ninth parts of humanity, neglected their own measures, to attend to the measures of governments—Nothing was wanting but half a dozen newspapers and patriotic editors, to have completed this public illumination, and to have thrown the whole province in an uproar!

I should not forget to mention, that these popular meetings were held at a noted tavern; for houses of that description have always been found the most fostering nurseries of politics; abounding with those genial streams which give strength and sustenance to faction.—We are told that the ancient Germans had an admirable mode of treating any question of importance; they first deliberated upon it when drunk, and afterwards reconsidered it, when sober.

The shrewder mobs of America, who dislike having two minds upon a subject, both determine and act upon it drunk; by which means a world of cold and tedious speculations is dispensed with—and as it is universally allowed, that when a man is drunk he sees double, it follows most conclusively that he sees twice as well as his sober neighbours.

CHAPTER 6

OF THE GREAT PIPE PLOT—AND OF THE DOLOROUS PERPLEXITIES INTO WHICH WILLIAM THE TESTY WAS THROWN, BY REASON OF HIS HAVING ENLIGHTENED THE MULTITUDE.

Wilhelmus Kieft, as has already been made manifest, was a great legislator upon a small scale. He was of an active, or rather a busy mind; that is to say, his was one of those small, but brisk minds, which make up by bustle and constant motion for the want of great scope and power. He had, when quite a youngling, been impressed with the advice of Solomon, *"go to the ant thou sluggard, consider her ways and be wise,"* in conformity to which, he had ever been of a restless, ant-like turn, worrying hither and thither, busying himself about little matters, with an air of great importance and anxiety—laying up wisdom by the morsel, and often toiling and puffing at a grain of mustard seed, under the full conviction that he was moving a mountain.

Thus we are told, that once upon a time, in one of his fits of mental bustle, which he termed deliberation, he framed an unlucky law, to prohibit the universal practice of smoking. This he proved, by mathematical demonstration, to be, not merely a heavy tax on the public pocket, but an incredible consumer of time, a great encourager of idleness, and, of course, a deadly bane to the prosperity and morals of the people. Ill fated Kieft! had he lived in this enlightened and libel-loving age, and attempted to subvert the inestimable liberty of the press, he could not have struck more closely on the sensibilities of the million.

The populace were in as violent a turmoil as the constitutional gravity of their deportment would permit—a mob of factious citizens had even the hardihood to assemble before the governor's house, where, setting themselves resolutely down, like a besieging army before a fortress, they one and all fell to one smoking with a determined perseverance, that seemed as though it were their intention to smoke him into terms. The testy William issued out of his mansion like a wrathful spider, and demanded to know the cause of this seditious assemblage, and this lawless fumigation; to which these sturdy rioters made no other reply, than to loll back phlegmatically in their seats, and puff away with redoubled fury; whereby they raised such a murky cloud, that the governor was fain to. take refuge in the interior of his castle.

The governor immediately perceived the object of this unusual tumult, and that it would be impossible to suppress a practice, which, by long indulgence, had become a second nature.

And here I would observe, partly to explain why I have so often made mention of this practice in my history, that it was insepara- bly connected with all the affairs, both public and private, of our revered ancestors. The pipe, in fact, was never from the mouth of the true-born Nederlander. It was his companion in solitude, the relaxation of his gayer hours, his counsellor, his consoler, his joy, his pride; in a word, he seemed to think and breathe through his pipe.

When William the Testy bethought himself of all these mat- ters, which he certainly did, although a little too late, he came to a compromise with the besieging multitude. The result was, that though he continued to permit the custom of smoking, yet did he abolish the fair long pipes which were used in the days of Wouter Van Twiller, denoting ease, tranquillity, and sobriety of deportment; and, in place thereof, did introduce little, captious, short pipes, two inches in length; which, he observed, could be stuck in one corner of the mouth, or twisted in the hat band, and would not be in the way of business. By this the multitude seemed somewhat appeased, and dispersed to their habitations. Thus ended this alarming insurrection, which was long known by the name of the *pipe plot*, and which, it has been somewhat quaintly observed, did end, like most other plots, seditions, and conspiracies, in mere smoke.

But mark. Oh reader! the deplorable consequences that did afterwards result. The smoke of these villainous little pipes, con- tinually ascending in a cloud about the nose, penetrated into, and befogged the *cerebellum*, dried up all the kindly moisture of the brain, and rendered the people that used them as vapourish and testy as their renowned little governor—nay, what is more, from a goodly, burly race of folk, they became, like our worthy Dutch farmers, who smoke short pipes, a lantern-jawed, smoke- dried, leathern-hided race of men.

Nor was this all, for from hence may we date the rise of par- ties in this province. Certain of the more wealthy and impor- tant *burghers* adhering to the ancient fashion, formed a kind of aristocracy, which went by the appellation of the *Long Pipes*,—

while the lower orders, submitting to the innovation, which they found to be more convenient in their handicraft employments, and to leave them more liberty of action, were branded with the plebeian name of *Short Pipes.*

A third party likewise sprang up, differing from both the other, headed by the descendants of the famous Robert Chewit, the companion of the great Hudson. These entirely discarded the use of pipes, and took to chewing tobacco, and hence they were called *Quids,* It is worthy of notice, that this last appellation has since come to be invariably applied to those mongrel or third parties, that will sometimes spring up between two great contending parties, as a mule is produced between a horse and an ass.

And here I would remark the great benefit of these party distinctions, by which the people at large are saved the vast trouble of thinking. Hesiod divides mankind into three classes, those who think for themselves, those who let others think for them, and those who will neither do one nor the other. The second class, however, comprises the great mass of society, and hence is the origin of *party,* by which is meant a large body of people, some few of whom think, and all the rest talk. The former, who are called the leaders, marshal out and discipline the latter, teaching them what they must approve—what they must hoot at—what they must say—whom they must support—but, above all, whom they must hate—for no man can be a right good partisan, unless he be a determined and thorough-going hater.

But when the sovereign people are thus properly broken to the harness, yoked, curbed, and reined, it is delectable to see with what docility and harmony they jog onward, through mud and mire, at the will of their drivers, dragging the dirt carts of faction at their heels. How many a patriotic member of congress have I seen, who would never have known how to make up his mind on any question, and might have run a great risk of voting right by mere accident, had he not had others to think for him, and a file leader to vote after.

Thus then the enlightened inhabitants of the Manhattoes,

being divided into parties, were enabled to organize dissension, and to oppose and hate one another more accurately. And now the great business of politics went bravely on—the parties assembling in separate beer houses, and smoking at each other with implacable animosity, to the great support of the state, and emolument of the tavern-keepers.

Some, indeed, who were more zealous than the rest, went farther, and began to bespatter one another with numerous very hard names and scandalous little words, to be found in the Dutch language; every partisan believing religiously that he was serving his country, when he traduced the character, or impoverished the pocket of a political adversary. But, however they might differ between themselves, all parties agreed on one point, to cavil at and condemn every measure of government whether right or wrong; for as the governor was by his station independent of their power, and was not elected by their choice, and as he had not decided in favour of either faction, neither of them was interested in his success, nor in the prosperity of the country, while under his administration.

"Unhappy William Kieft!" exclaims the sage writer of the Stuyvesant manuscript—"doomed to contend with enemies too knowing to be entrapped, and to reign over a people too wise to be governed!"

All his expeditions against his enemies were baffled and set at naught, and all his measures for the public safety were cavilled at by the people. Did he propose levying an efficient body of troops for internal defence—the mob, that is to say, those vagabond members of the community who have nothing to lose, immediately took the alarm, vociferated that their interests were in danger—that a standing army was a legion of moths, preying on the pockets of society; a rod of iron in the hands of government; and that a government with a military force at its command would inevitably swell into a despotism.

Did he, as was but too commonly the case, defer preparation until the moment of emergency, and then hastily collect a handful of undisciplined vagrants—the measure was hooted at as feeble and inadequate, as trifling with the public dignity and safety, and as lavishing the public funds on impotent enterprises.—Did he resort to the economic measure of proclamation—he was laughed at by the Yankees; did he back it by non-intercourse—it was evaded and counteracted by his own subjects.

Whichever way he turned himself he was beleaguered and distracted by petitions of "numerous and respectable meetings," consisting of some half a dozen brawling pot-house politicians—all of which he read, and, what is worse, all of which he attended to. The consequence was, that by incessantly changing his measures, he gave none of them a fair trial; and by listening to the clamours of the mob, and endeavouring to do everything, he, in sober truth, did nothing.

I would not have it supposed, however, that he took all these memorials and interferences good naturedly, for such an idea would do injustice to his valiant spirit; on the contrary, he never received a piece of advice in the whole course of his life, without first getting into a passion with the giver. But I have ever observed that your passionate little men, like small boats with large sails; are the easiest upset or blown out of their course; and this is demonstrated by Governor Kieft, who, though in temperament as hot as an old radish, and with a mind, the territory of which was subjected to perpetual whirlwinds and tornadoes, yet never failed to he carried away by the last piece of advice that was blown into his ear.

Lucky was it for him that his power was not dependent upon the greasy multitude, and that as yet the populace did not possess the important privilege of nominating their chief magistrate. They, however, did their best to help along public affairs; pestering their governor incessantly, by goading him on with harangues and petitions, and then thwarting his fiery spirit with reproaches and memorials, like Sunday jockeys managing an unlucky devil of a hack horse—so that Wilhelmus Kieft may be said to have been kept either on a worry or a hand gallop throughout the whole of his administration.

CHAPTER 7

CONTAINING DIVERS FEARFUL ACCOUNTS OF BORDER WARS, AND
THE FLAGRANT OUTRAGES OF THE MOSSTROOPERS OF CONNECTI-
CUT—WITH THE RISE OF THE GREAT AMPHYCTIONIC COUNCIL OF
THE EAST, AND THE DECLINE OF WILLIAM, THE TESTY.

It was asserted by the wise men of ancient times, who were
intimately acquainted with these matters, that at the gate of Jupiter's palace lay two huge tuns, the one filled with blessings,
the other with misfortunes—and it verily seems as if the latter
had been completely overturned, and left to deluge the unlucky
province of Nieuw-Nederlandts.

Among the many internal and external causes of irritation,
the incessant irruptions of the Yankees upon his frontiers were
continually adding fuel to the inflammable temper of William
the Testy. Numerous accounts of these molestations may still be
found among the records of the times; for the commanders on
the frontiers were especially careful to evince their vigilance
and zeal, by striving who should send home the most frequent
and voluminous budgets of complaints, as your faithful servant
is eternally running with complaints to the parlour, of the petty
squabbles and misdemeanours of the kitchen.

Far be it from me to insinuate, however, that our worthy
ancestors indulged in groundless alarms; on the contrary, they
were daily suffering a repetition of cruel wrongs,[1] not one of

---

1. From among a multitude of bitter grievances still on record, I select a few of the
most atrocious, and leave my readers to judge if our ancestors were not justifiable
in getting into a very valiant passion on the occasion.   *24 June,* 1641. Some of
Hartford have taken a hogg out of the *vlact* or common, and shut it up out of meer
hate or other prejudice, causing it to starve for hunger in the stye!   *26 July.* The
foremencioned English did again drive the Companies hoggs out of the *vlact* of
Sicojoke into Hartford; contending daily with reproaches, blows, beating the people
with all disgrace that they could imagine.   *May 20,* 1642. The English of Hartford
have violently cut loose a horse of the honoured Companie's, that stood bound
upon the common or *vlact*.   *May 9,* 1643. The Companie's horses pastured upon
the Companie's ground, were driven away by them of Connecticott or Hartford,
and the herdsmen lustily beaten with hatchets and sticks.   *16.* Again they sold a
young hogg belonging to the Companie which piggs had pastured on the Companie's land.—*Haz. Col. State Papers.*

which but was a sufficient reason, according to the maxims of national dignity and honour, for throwing the whole universe into hostility and confusion.

Oh ye powers! into what indignation did every one of these outrages throw the philosophic William! letter after letter, protest after protest, proclamatidn after proclamation, bad Latin, worse English, and hideous Low Dutch, were exhausted in vain upon the inexorable Yankees, and the four-and-twenty letters of the alphabet, which, excepting his champion the sturdy trumpeter Van Corlear, composed the only standing army he had at his command, were never off duty throughout the whole of his administration.

Nor was Antony, the trumpeter, a whit behind his patron in fiery zeal; but like a faithful champion of the public safety, on the arrival of every fresh article of news, he was sure to sound his trumpet from the ramparts, with most disastrous notes, throwing the people into violent alarms, and disturbing their rest at all times and seasons—which caused him to be held in very great regard, the public pampering and rewarding him, as we do brawling editors, for similar services.

I am well aware of the perils that environ me in this part of my history. While raking with curious hands but pious heart, among the mouldering remains of former days, anxious to draw therefrom the honey of wisdom, I may fare somewhat like that valiant, worthy, Samson, who in meddling with the carcass of a dead lion, drew a swarm of bees about his ears. Thus while narrating the many misdeeds of the Yanokie, or Yankee tribe, it is ten chances to one but I offend the morbid sensibilities of certain of their unreasonable descendants, who may fly out and raise such a bussing about this unlucky head of mine, that I shall need the tough hide of an Achilles, or an Orlando Furioso, to protect me from their stings.

Should such be the case, I should deeply and sincerely lament—not my misfortune in giving offence—but the wrongheaded perverseness of an ill-natured generation, in taking offence at anything I say. That their ancestors did use my ancestors ill is true, and I am very sorry for it. I would, with all my heart, the fact were otherwise; but as I am recording the sacred events of history, I'd not bate one nail's breadth of the honest truth, though I were sure the whole edition of my work should be bought up and burnt by the common hangman of Connecticut.

And in sooth, now that these testy gentlemen have drawn me out, I will make bold to go farther and observe, that this is one of the grand purposes for which we impartial historians are sent into the world—to redress wrongs and render justice on the heads of the guilty. So that, though a powerful nation may wrong its neighbours with temporary impunity, yet sooner or later an historian springs up who wreaks ample chastisement on it in return.

Thus these mosstroopers of the east, little thought, I'll warrant it, while they were harassing the inoffensive province of Nieuw-Nederlandts, and driving its unhappy governor to his wit's end, that an historian should ever arise and give them their own with interest. Since, then, I am but performing my bounden duty as an historian, in avenging the wrongs of our revered ancestors, I shall make no further apology; and indeed, when it is considered that I have all these ancient borderers of the east in my power, and at the mercy of my pen, I trust that it will be admitted I conduct myself with great humanity and moderation.

To resume then the course of my history—Appearances to the eastward began now to assume a more formidable aspect than ever—for I would have you note that hitherto the province had been chiefly molested by its immediate neighbours, the people of Connecticut, particularly of Hartford; which, if we may judge from ancient chronicles, was the strong hold of these sturdy moss troopers, from whence they sallied forth, on their daring incursions, carrying terror and devastation into the barns, the hen-roosts, and pig-styes of our revered ancestors.

Albeit about the year 1643, the people of the east country, inhabiting the colonies of Massachusetts, Connecticut, New-Plymouth, and New-Haven, gathered together into a mighty conclave, and after buzzing and debating for many days, like a political hive of bees in swarming time, at length settled themselves into a formidable confederation, under the title of the United Colonies of New-England.

By this union they pledged themselves to stand by one another in all perils and assaults, and to co-operate in all measures, offensive and defensive, against the surrounding savages, among which were doubtlessly included our honoured ancestors of the Manhattoes; and to give more strength and system to this confederation, a general assembly or grand council was to be annually held, composed of representatives from each of the provinces.

On receiving accounts of this combination, Wilhelmus Kieft was struck with consternation, and, for the first time in his whole life, forgot to bounce, at hearing an unwelcome piece of intelligence—which a venerable historian of the times observes, was especially noticed among the politicians of New-Amsterdam. The truth was, on turning over in his mind all that he had read at the Hague, about leagues and combinations, he found that this was an exact imitation of the Amphyctionic council, by which the states of Greece were enabled to attain to such power and supremacy, and the very idea made his heart to quake for the safety of his empire at the Manhattoes.

He strenuously insisted, that the whole object of this confederation was to drive the Nederlanders out of their fair domains; and always flew into a great rage if any one presumed to doubt the probability of his conjecture. Nor was he wholly unwarranted in such a suspicion; for at the very first annual meeting of the grand council, held at Boston (which governor Kieft denominated the Delphos of this truly classic league,) strong representations were made against the Nederlanders, forasmuch as that in their dealings with the Indians, they carried on a traffic in "guns, powther, and shott—a trade damnable and injurious to the colonists."[2]

Not but what certain of the Connecticut traders did like-

2. *Haz. Col. State Papers.*

wise dabble a little in this "damnable traffick"—but then they always sold the Indians such scurvy guns, that they burst at the first discharge—and consequently hurt no one but these pagan savages.

The rise of this potent confederacy was a death blow to the glory of William the Testy, for from that day forward, it was remarked by many, he never held up his head, but appeared quite crest fallen. His subsequent reign, therefore, affords but scanty food for the historic pen—we find the grand council continually augmenting in power, and threatening to overwhelm the province of Nieuw-Nederlandts; while Wilhelmus Kieft kept constantly fulminating proclamations and protests, like a shrewd sea captain firing off carronades and swivels, in order to break and disperse a water spout—but alas! they had no more effect than if they had been so many blank cartridges.

The last document on record of this learned, philosophic, but unfortunate little man, is a long letter to the council of the Amphyctions, wherein, in the bitterness of his heart, he rails at the people of New-Haven, or Red Hills, for their uncourteous contempt of his protest, levelled at them for squatting within the province of their High Mightinesses. From this letter, which is a model of epistolory writing, abounding with pithy apophthegms and classic figures, my limits will barely allow me to extract the following recondite passage:—

Certainly when we heare the Inhabitants of New-Hartford complayninge of us, we seem to heare Esop's wolfe complayninge of the lamb, or the admonition of the younge man, who cryed out to his mother, chideing with her neighboures, 'Oh Mother revile her, lest she first take up that practice against you.' But being taught by precedent passages, we received such an answer to our protest from the inhabitants of New-Haven as we expected; *the Eagle always despiseth the Beetle Fly*; yet notwithstanding we doe undauntedly continue on our purpose of pursuing our own right, by just arms and righteous means, and doe hope without scruple to execute the express commands of our superiors.[3]

To show that this last sentence was not a mere empty menace, he concluded his letter, by intrepidly protesting against the whole council, as a horde of *squatters* and interlopers, inasmuch as they held their meeting at New-Haven, or the Red Hills, which he claimed as being within the province of the New-Netherlands.

Thus end the authenticated chronicles of the reign of William the Testy—for henceforth, in the troubles, the perplexities and the confusion of the times, he seems to have been totally overlooked and to have slipped for ever through the fingers of scrupulous history. Indeed, for some cause or other which I cannot divine, there appears to have been a combination among historians to sink his very name into oblivion, in consequence of which they have one and all forborne even to speak of his exploits. This shows how important it is for great men to cultivate the favour of the learned, if they are ambitious of honour and renown.

"Insult not the dervise," said a wise *caliph* to his son, "lest thou offend thine historian," and many a mighty man of the olden time, had he observed so obvious a maxim, might have escaped divers cruel wipes of the pen, which have been drawn across his character.

It has been a matter of deep concern to me, that such darkness and obscurity should hang over the latter days of the illustrious Kieft—for he was a mighty and great little man, worthy of being utterly renowned, seeing that he was the first potentate that introduced into this land the art of fighting by proclamation, and defending a country by trumpeters and windmills—an economic and humane mode of warfare, since revived with great applause, and which promises, if it can ever be carried into full effect, to save great trouble and treasure, and spare infinitely more bloodshed than either the discovery of gunpowder, or the invention of torpedoes.

It is true, that certain of the early provincial poets, of whom

3. *Vide* Haz. Col. State Papers.

there were great numbers in the Nieuw-Nederlandts taking advantage of the mysterious exit of William the Testy, have fabled, that like Romulus, he was translated to the skies, and forms a very fiery little star, somewhere on the left claw of the crab; while others equally fanciful, declare that he had experienced a fate similar to that of the good king Arthur; who, we are assured by ancient bards, was carried away to the delicious abodes of fairy land, where he still exists, in pristine worth and vigour, and will one day or another return to restore the gallantry, the honour, and the immaculate probity, which prevailed in the glorious days of the Round Table.[4]

All these, however, are but pleasing fantasies, the cobweb visions of those dreaming varlets, the poets, to which I would not have my judicious reader attach any credibility. Neither am I disposed to yield any credit to the assertion of an ancient and rather apocryphal historian, who alleges that the ingenious Wilhelmus was annihilated by the blowing down of one of his windmills— nor to that of a writer of later times, who affirms that he fell a victim to a philosophical experiment, which he had for many years been vainly striving to accomplish; having the misfortune to break his neck from the garret window of the *stadt* house, in an ineffectual attempt to catch swallows, by sprinkling fresh salt upon their tails.

The most probable account, and to which I am inclined to give my implicit faith, is contained in a very obscure tradition, which declares, that what with the constant troubles on his frontiers—the incessant schemings and projects going on in his own pericranium—the memorials, petitions, remonstrances, and sage pieces of advice from divers respectable meetings of the sovereign people—together with the refractory disposition of his council, who were sure to differ from him on every point,

---

4. The old Welsh bards believed that King Arthur was not dead, but *carried awaie by the faries into some pleasant place, where he shold remaine for a time, and then returne againe and reigne in as great authority as ever.—Hollingshed.* The Britons suppose that he *shall come yet and conquere all Britaigne, for certes, this is the prophicye of Merlyn—He say'd that his deth shall be doubteous; and said soth, for men thereof yet have doubte and shullen for ever more—for men wyt not whether that he lyveth or is dede.—De Leew. Chron.*

and uniformly to be in the wrong—all these, I say, did eternally operate to keep his mind in a kind of furnace heat, until he at length became as completely burnt out as a Dutch family pipe which has passed through three generations of hard smokers. In this manner did the choleric but magnanimous William the Testy undergo a kind of animal combustion, consuming away like a farthing rush-light—so that, when grim Death finally snuffed him out, there was scarce left enough of him to bury.

BOOK 5

CONTAINING THE FIRST PART OF THE REIGN OF PETER STUYVESANT, AND HIS TROUBLES WITH THE AMPHYCTIONIC COUNCIL.

CHAPTER 1

IN WHICH THE DEATH OF A GREAT MAN IS SHOWN TO NO VERY INCONSOLABLE MATTER OF SORROW AND HOW PETER STUYVESANT ACQUIRED A GREAT NAME FROM THE UNCOMMON STRENGTH OF HIS HEAD.

To a profound philosopher like myself, who am apt to see clear through a subject, where the penetration of ordinary people extends but half way, there is no fact more simple and manifest than that the death of a great man is a matter of very little importance. Much as we may think of ourselves, and much as we may excite the empty plaudits of the million, it is certain that the greatest among us do actually fill but an exceedingly small space in the world; and it is equally certain, that even that small space is quickly supplied when we leave it vacant.

"Of what consequence is it," said Pliny, "that individuals appear, or make their exit? the world is a theatre whose scenes and actors are continually changing."

Never did philosopher speak more correctly, and I only wonder that so wise a remark could have existed so many ages, and mankind not have laid it more to heart. Sage follows on in the footsteps of sage; one hero just steps out of his triumphal car, to make way for the hero who comes after him; and of the proudest monarch it is merely said that—"he slept with his fathers, and his successor reigned in his stead."

The world, to tell the private truth, cares but little for their loss, and, if left to itself, would soon forget to grieve; and though a nation has often been figuratively drowned in tears on the death of a great man, yet it is ten to one if an individual tear has been shed on the occasion, excepting from the forlorn pen of some hungry author. It is the historian, the biographer, and the poet, who have the whole burden of grief to sustain; who— kind souls!—like undertakers in England, act the part of chief mourners; who inflate a nation with sighs it never heaved, and deluge it with tears it never dreamt of shedding.

Thus, while the patriotic author is weeping and howling in prose, in blank verse, and in rhyme, and collecting the drops of public sorrow into his volume, as into a lachrymal vase, it is more than probable his fellow-citizens are eating and drinking, fiddling and dancing, as utterly ignorant of the bitter lamentations made in their name as are those men of straw, John Doe and Richard Roe, of the plaintiffs for whom they are generously pleased to become sureties.

The most glorious and praiseworthy hero that ever desolated nations might have mouldered into oblivion among the rubbish of his own monument, did not some historian take him into favour, and benevolently transmit his name to posterity— and much as the valiant William Kieft worried, and bustled, and turmoiled, while he had the destinies of a whole colony in his hand, I question seriously whether he will not be obliged to this authentic history for all his future celebrity.

His exit occasioned no convulsion in the city of New Amsterdam nor its vicinity; the earth trembled not, neither did any stars shoot from their spheres—the heavens were not shrouded in black, as poets would fain persuade us they have been, on the death of a hero—the rocks (hard-hearted varlets!) melted not into tears, nor did the trees hang their heads in silent sorrow; and as to the sun, he lay abed the next night just as long, and showed as jolly a face when he rose, as he ever did, on the same day of the month in any year, either before or since.

The good people of New Amsterdam, one and all, declared

that he had been a very busy, active, bustling little governor; that he was "the father of his country;"—that he was "the noblest work of God;"—that "he was a man, take him for all in all, they ne'er should look upon his like again;"—together with sundry other civil and affectionate speeches, regularly said on the death of all great men; after which they smoked their pipes, thought no more about him, and Peter Stuyvesant succeeded to his station.

Peter Stuyvesant was the last, and, like the renowned Wouter Van Twiller, the best of our ancient Dutch governors; Wouter having surpassed all who preceded him, and Pieter, or Piet, as he was sociably called by the old Dutch *burghers*, who were ever prone to familiarize names, having never been equalled by any successor. He was, in fact, the very man fitted by Nature to retrieve the desperate fortunes of her beloved province, had not the Fates, those most potent and unrelenting of all ancient spinsters, destined them to inextricable confusion.

To say merely that he was a hero would be doing him great injustice; he was, in truth, a combination of heroes—for he was of a sturdy, raw-boned make, like Ajax Telamon, with a pair of round shoulders that Hercules would have given his hide for (meaning his lion's hide) when he undertook to ease old Atlas of his load. He was, moreover, as Plutarch describes Coriolanus, not only terrible for the force of his arm, but likewise for his voice, which sounded as though it came out of a barrel; and, like the self-same warrior, he possessed a sovereign contempt for the sovereign people, and an iron aspect, which was enough of itself to make the very bowels of his adversaries quake with terror and dismay. All this martial excellency of appearance was inexpressibly heightened by an accidental advantage, with which I am surprised that neither Homer nor Virgil have graced any of their heroes.

This was nothing less than a wooden leg, which was the only prize he had gained in bravely fighting the battles of his country, but of which he was so proud, that he was often heard to declare he valued it more than all his other limbs put together; indeed, so highly did he esteem it, that he had it gallantly enchased and relieved with silver devices, which caused it to be related in divers histories and legends that he wore a silver leg.

Like that choleric warrior Achilles, he was somewhat subject to extempore bursts of passion, which were rather unpleasant to his favourites and attendants, whose perceptions he was apt to quicken after the manner of his illustrious imitator, Peter the Great, by anointing their shoulders with his walking staff.

Though I cannot find that he had read Plato, or Aristotle, or Hobbes, or Bacon, or Algernon Sydney, or Tom Paine, yet did he sometimes manifest a shrewdness and sagacity in his measures that one would hardly expect from a man who did not know Greek and had never studied the ancients. True it is, and I confess it with sorrow, that he had an unreasonable aversion to experiments, and was fond of governing his province after the simplest manner—but then he contrived to keep it in better order than did the erudite Kieft, though he had all the philosophers, ancient and modern, to assist and perplex him. I must likewise own that he made but very few laws, but then again he took care that those few were rigidly and impartially enforced—and I do not know but justice, on the whole, was as well administered as if there had been volumes of sage acts and statutes yearly made, and daily neglected and forgotten.

He was, in fact, the very reverse of his predecessors, being neither tranquil and inert, like Walter the Doubter, nor restless and fidgeting, like William the Testy; but a man, or rather a governor, of such uncommon activity and decision of mind, that he never sought nor accepted the advice of others, depending bravely upon his single head, as would a hero of yore upon his single arm, to carry him through all difficulties and dangers. To tell the simple truth, he wanted nothing more to complete him as a statesman than to think always right, for no one can say but that he always acted as he thought; and if he wanted in correctness, he made up for it in perseverance—an excellent quality!

Since it is surely more dignified for a ruler to be persevering and consistent in error than wavering and contradictory, in endeavouring to do what is right. This much is certain—and it is a maxim worthy the attention of all legislators, both great and small, who stand shaking in the wind, without knowing which way to steer—a ruler who acts according to his own will is sure of pleasing himself, while he who seeks to satisfy the wishes and whims of others runs great risk of pleasing nobody. The clock that stands still and points steadfastly in one direction, is certain of being right twice in the four-and-twenty hours,—while others may keep going continually, and be continually going wrong.

Nor did this magnanimous quality escape the discernment of the good people of Nieuw Nederlandts; on the contrary, so much were they struck with the independent will and vigorous resolution displayed on all occasions by their new governor, that they universally called him *Hardkoppig Piet*, or Peter the Headstrong, a great compliment to the strength of his understanding.

If, from all that I have said, thou dost not gather, worthy reader, that Peter Stuyvesant was a tough, sturdy, valiant, weather-beaten, mettlesome, obstinate, leathern-sided, lion-hearted, generous-spirited old governor, either I have written to but little purpose, or thou art very dull at drawing conclusions.

This most excellent governor commenced his administration on the 29th of May, 1647; a remarkably stormy day, distinguished in all the almanacs of the time which have come down to us by the name of "*Windy Friday*." As he was very jealous of his personal and official dignity, he was inaugurated into office with great ceremony, the goodly oaken chair of the renowned Wouter Van Twiller being carefully preserved for such occasions, in like manner as the chair and stone were reverentially preserved at Schone, in Scotland, for the coronation of the Caledonian monarchs.

I must not omit to mention that the tempestuous state of the elements, together with its being that unlucky day of the week termed "hanging day," did not fail to excite much grave speculation and divers very reasonable apprehensions among the more ancient and enlightened inhabitants; and several of the sager sex, who were reputed to be not a little skilled in the mysteries of astrology and fortune-telling, did declare outright that they were omens of a disastrous administration—an event that came to be lamentably verified, and which proves beyond dispute the wisdom of attending to those preternatural intimations furnished by dreams and visions, the flying of birds, falling of stones, and cackling of geese, on which the sages and rulers of ancient times placed such reliance—or to those shootings of stars, eclipses of the moon, howlings of dogs, and flarings of candles, carefully noted and interpreted by the oracular Sibyls of our day, who, in my humble opinion, are the legitimate inheritors and preservers of the ancient science of divination.

This much is certain, that Governor Stuyvesant succeeded to the chair of state at a turbulent period, when foes thronged and threatened from without, when anarchy and stiff-necked opposition reigned rampant within; when the authority of their High Mightinesses the Lords States General, though founded on the broad Dutch bottom of unoffending imbelicity; though supported by economy, and defended by speeches, protests, and proclamations, yet tottered to its very centre; and when the great city of New Amsterdam, though fortified by flag-staffs, trumpeters, and windmills, seemed, like some fair lady of easy virtue, to lie open to attack, and ready to yield to the first invader.

CHAPTER 2

SHOWING HOW PETER THE HEADSTRONG BESTIRRED HIMSELF
AMONG THE RATS AND COBWEBS, ON ENTERING INTO OFFICE—AND
THE PERILOUS MISTAKE HE WAS GUILTY OF, IN HIS DEALINGS WITH
THE AMPHYCTIONS.

The very first movements of the great Peter, on taking the reins of government, displayed his magnanimity, though they occasioned not a little marvel and uneasiness among the people of the Manhattoes. Finding himself constantly interrupted by the opposition, and annoyed by the advice of his privy council, the members of which had acquired the unreasonable habit of thinking and speaking to themselves during the preceding reign, he determined at once to put a stop to such grievous abominations. Scarcely, therefore, had he entered upon his authority, than he turned out of office all the meddlesome spirits of the factious cabinet of William the Testy; in place of whom he chose unto himself councillors from those fat, somniferous, respectable burghers who had flourished and slumbered under the easy reign of Walter the Doubter

All these he caused to be furnished with abundance of fair long pipes, and to be regaled with frequent corporation dinners, admonishing them to smoke, and eat, and sleep for the good of the nation, while he took the burden of government upon his own shoulders—an arrangement to which they all gave hearty acquiescence.

Nor did he stop here, but made a hideous rout among the inventions and expedients of his learned predecessor—rooting up his patent gallows, where *caitiff* vagabonds were suspended by the waistband; demolishing his flag-staffs and windmills, which, like mighty giants, guarded the ramparts of New Amsterdam—pitching to the *duyvel* whole batteries of Quaker guns—and, in a word, turning topsy-turvy the whole philosophic, economic, and windmill system of the immortal sage of Saardam.

The honest folk of New Amsterdam began to quake now for the fate of their matchless champion, Antony the Trumpeter, who had acquired prodigious favour in the eyes of the women by means of his whiskers and his trumpet. Him did Peter the Headstrong cause to be brought into his presence, and eyeing him for a moment from head to foot, with a countenance that would have appalled anything else than a sounder of brass—"Prythee, who and what art thou?" said he.

"Sire," replied the other, in no wise dismayed,—"for my name, it is Antony Van Corlear—for my parentage, I am the son of my mother—for my profession, I am champion and garrison of this great city of New Amsterdam."

"I doubt me much," said Peter Stuyvesant, "that thou art some scurvy costardmonger knave: how didst thou acquire this paramount honour and dignity? "Marry, sir," replied the other, "like many a great man before me, simply *by sounding my own trumpet.*"

"Ay, is it so?" quoth the governor; "why, then, let us have a relish of thy art."

Whereupon the good Antony put his instrument to his lips, and sounded a charge with such tremendous outset, such a delectable quaver, and such a triumphant cadence, that it was enough to make one's heart leap out of one's mouth only to be within a mile of it. Like as a war-worn charger, grazing in peaceful plains, starts at a strain of martial music, pricks up his ears, and snorts, and paws, and kindles at the noise, so did the heroic Peter joy to hear the clangour of the trumpet; for of him might truly be said, what was recorded of the renowned St. George of England, "there was nothing in all the world that more rejoiced his heart than to hear the pleasant sound of war, and see the soldiers brandish forth their steeled weapons."

Casting his eye more kindly, therefore, upon the sturdy Van Corlear, and finding him to be a jovial varlet, shrewd in his discourse, yet of great discretion and immeasurable wind, he straightway conceived a vast kindness for him, and discharging him from the troublesome duty of garrisoning, defending, and alarming the city, ever after retained him about his person, as his chief favourite, confidential envoy, and trusty squire. Instead of disturbing the city with disastrous notes, he was instructed to play so as to delight the governor while at his repasts, as did the minstrels of yore in the days of glorious chivalry—and on all public occasions to rejoice the ears of the people with warlike melody—thereby keeping alive a noble and martial spirit.

Many other alterations and reformations, both for the better and for the worse, did the governor make, of which my time will not serve me to record the particulars; suffice it to say, he soon contrived to make the province feel that he was its master, and treated the sovereign people with such tyrannical rigour, that they were all fain to hold their tongues, stay at home, and attend to their business; insomuch that party feuds and distinctions were almost forgotten, and many thriving keepers of taverns and dram-shops were utterly ruined for want of business.

Indeed, the critical state of public affairs at this time demanded the utmost vigilance and promptitude. The formidable council of the Amphyctions, which had caused so much tribulation to the unfortunate Kieft, still continued augmenting its forces, and threatened to link within its union all the mighty principalities and powers of the east. In the very year following the inauguration of Governor Stuyvesant, a grand deputation departed from the city of Providence (famous for its dusty streets and beauteous women,) in behalf of the *puissant* plantation of Rhode Island, praying to be admitted into the league.

The following mention is made of this application, in certain records of that assemblage of worthies, which are still extant.[1]

"Mr. Will Cottington and captain Partridg of Rhoode-Iland presented this insewing request to the commissioners in wrighting—

"Our request and motion is in behalfe of Rhoode-Iland, that wee the Ilanders of Rhoode-Iland may be rescauied into combination with all the united colonyes of New-England in a firme and perpetuall league of friendship and amity of ofence and defence, mutuall advice and succour upon all just occasions for our mutuall safety and wellfaire, &c.

Will Cottington,
Alicxsander Partridg."

There is certainly something in the very physiognomy of this document, that might well inspire apprehension. The name of Alexander, however misspelt, has been warlike in every age; and though its fierceness is in some measure softened by being coupled with the gentle cognomen of Partridge, still, like the colour of scarlet, it bears an exceeding great resemblance to the sound of a trumpet. From the style of the letter moreover, and the soldier-like ignorance of orthography displayed by the noble captain Alicxsander Partridg in spelling his own name, we may

---

1. Haz. Col. State Papers.

picture to ourselves this mighty man of Rhodes, strong in arms, potent in the field, and as great a scholar as though he had been educated among that learned people of Thrace, who, Aristotle assures us, could not count beyond the number four.

But, whatever might be the threatening aspect of this famous confederation, Peter Stuyvesant was not a man to be kept in a state of incertitude and vague apprehension; he liked nothing so much as to meet danger face to face, and take it by the beard. Determined, therefore, to put an end to all these petty maraudings on the borders, he wrote two or three categorical letters to the grand council; which, though neither couched in bad Latin, nor yet graced by rhetorical tropes about wolves and lambs, and beetle-flies, yet had more effect than all the elaborate epistle protests, and proclamations of his learned predecessor put together. In consequence of his urgent propositions, the great confederacy of the east agreed to enter into a final adjustment of grievances and settlement of boundaries, to the end that a perpetual and happy peace might take place between the two powers.

For this purpose Governor Stuyvesant deputed two ambassador to negotiate with commissioners from the grand council of the league; and a treaty was solemnly concluded at Hartford. On receiving intelligence of this event, the whole community was in an uproar of exultation. The trumpet of the sturdy Van Corlear sounded all day with joyful clangour from the ramparts of Fort Amsterdam, and at night the city was magnificently illuminated with two hundred and fifty tallow candles; besides a barrel of tar, which was burnt before the governor's house, on the cheering aspect of public affairs.

And now my worthy reader is, doubtless, like the great and good Peter, congratulating himself with the idea, that his feelings will no longer be molested by afflicting details of stolen horses, broken heads, impounded hogs, and all the other catalogue of heartrending cruelties that disgraced these border wars. But if he should induce in such expectations, it is a proof that he is but little versed in the paradoxical ways of cabinets; to convince him of which, I solicit his serious attention to my next chapter, wherein I will show that Peter Stuyvesant has already committed a great error in politics; and by effecting a peace, has materially hazarded the tranquillity of the province;

CHAPTER 3

CONTAINING DIVERS SPECULATIONS ON WAR AND NEGOTIATIONS— SHOWING THAT A TREATY OF PEACE IS A GREAT NATIONAL EVIL.

It was the opinion of that poetical philosopher, Lucretius, that war was the original state of man, whom he described as being primitively a savage beast of prey, engaged in a constant state of hostility with his own species; and that this ferocious spirit was tamed and meliorated by society. The same opinion has been advocated by Hobbes; nor have there been wanting many other philosophers, to admit and defend it

For my part, though prodigiously fond of these valuable speculations, so complimentary to human nature, yet, in this instance, I am inclined to take the proposition by halves, believing, with Horace, that though war may have been originally the favourite amusement and industrious employment of our progenitors, yet, like many other excellent habits, so far from being meliorated, it has been cultivated and confirmed by refinement and civilization, and increases in exact proportion as we approach towards that state of perfection which is the *ne plus ultra* of modern philosophy.

The first conflict between man and man was the mere exertion of physical force, unaided by auxiliary weapons—his arm was his buckler, his fist was his mace, and a broken head the catastrophe of his encounters. The battle of unassisted strength was succeeded by the more rugged one of stones and clubs, and war assumed a sanguinary aspect. As man advanced in refinement, as his faculties expanded, and his sensibilities became more exquisite, he grew rapidly more ingenious and experienced in the art of murdering his fellow-beings. He invented a thousand, devices to defend and to assault—the helmet, the *cuirass*, and the buckler, the sword, the dart, and the javelin, prepared him to elude the

185

wound, as well as to launch the blow.

Still urging on, in the brilliant and philanthropic career of invention, he enlarges and heightens his powers of defence and injury—the Aries, the Scorpio, the Balista, and the Catapulta, give a horror and sublimity to war, and magnify its glory by increasing its desolation. Still insatiable, though armed with machinery that seemed to reach the limits of destructive invention, and to yield a power of injury commensurate even with the desires of revenge—still deeper researches must be made in the diabolical *arcana*. With furious zeal, he dive into the bowels of the earth; he toils midst poisonous minerals and deadly salts—the sublime discover of gunpowder blazes upon the world—and finally, the dreadful art of fighting by proclamation, seems to endow the demon of war with ubiquity and omnipotence!

This, indeed, is grand!—this, indeed, marks the powers of mind, and bespeaks that divine endowment of reason, which distinguishes us from the animals, our inferiors. The unenlightened brutes content themselves with the native force which Providence has assigned them. The angry bull butts with his horns, as did his progenitors before him—the lion, the leopard, and the tiger, seek only with their talons and their fangs to gratify their sanguinary fury; and even the subtle serpent darts the same venom, and uses the same wiles, as did his sire before the flood. Man alone, blessed with the inventive mind, goes on from discovery to discovery—enlarges and multiplies his powers of destruction; arrogates the tremendous weapons of Deity itself, and tasks creation to assist him in murdering his brother worm!

In proportion as. the art of war has increased in improvement, has the art of preserving peace advanced in equal ratio; and, as we have discovered, in this age of wonders and inventions, that a proclamation is the most formidable engine in war, so have we discovered the no less ingenious mode of maintaining peace by perpetual negotiations.

A treaty, or to speak more correctly, a negotiation,, therefore, according to the acceptation of experienced statesmen, learned in these matters, is no longer an attempt to accommodate differences, to ascertain rights, and to establish an equitable exchange of kind offices; but a contest of skill between two powers, which shall overreach and take in the other. It is a cunning endeavour to obtain, by peaceable manoeuvre, and the chicanery of cabinets, those advantages which a nation would otherwise have wrested by force of arms: in the same manner that a conscientious highwayman reforms, and becomes an excellent and praiseworthy citizen, contenting himself with cheating his neighbour out of that property he would formerly have seized with open violence.

In fact, the only time when two nations can be said to be in a state of perfect amity, is, when a negotiation is open, and a treaty pending. Then, as there are no stipulations entered into, no bonds to restrain the will, no specific limits to awaken the captious jealousy of right implanted in our nature, as each party has some advantage to hope and expect from the other, then it is that the two nations are so gracious and friendly to each other; their ministers professing the highest mutual regard, exchanging *billets-doux*, making fine speeches, and indulging in all those diplomatic flirtations, *coquetries*, and fondlings, that do so marvellously tickle the good-humour of the respective nations. Thus it may paradoxically be said, that there is never so good an understanding between two nations, as when there is a little misunderstanding—and that so long as there are no terms, they are on the best terms in the world!

I do not by any means pretend to claim the merit of having made the above political discovery. It has in fact long been secretly acted upon by certain enlightened cabinets, and is, together with divers other notable theories, privately copied out of the common-place book of an illustrious gentleman, who has been member of Congress, and enjoyed the unlimited confidence of heads of departments. To this principle may be ascribed the wonderful ingenuity that has been shown of late years in protracting and interrupting negotiations.

Hence the cunning measure of appointing as ambassador

some political pettifogger skilled in delays, sophisms, and misapprehensions, and dexterous in the art of baffling argument—or some blundering statesman, whose errors and misconstructions may be a plea for refusing to ratify his engagements. And hence too that most notable expedient, so popular with our government, of sending out a brace of ambassadors; who having each an individual will to consult, character to establish, and interest to promote, you may as well look for unanimity and concord between two lovers with one mistress, two dogs with one bone, or two naked rogues with one pair of breeches.

This disagreement, therefore, is continually breeding delays and impediments, in consequence of which the negotiation goes on swimmingly—insomuch as there is no prospect of its ever coming to a close. Nothing is lost by these delays and obstacles but time, and in a negotiation, according to the theory I have exposed, all time lost is in reality so much time gained—with what delightful paradoxes does modern political economy abound! Now all that I have here advanced is so notoriously true, that I almost blush to take up the time of my readers with treating of matters which must many a time have stared them in the face. But the proposition to which I would most earnestly call their attention, is this—that though a negotiation be the most harmonizing of all national transactions, yet a treaty of peace is a great political evil, and one of the most fruitful sources of war.

I have rarely seen an instance of any special contract between individuals, that did not produce jealousies, bickerings, and often downright ruptures between them; nor did I ever know of a treaty between two nations, that did not occasion continual misunderstandings. How many worthy country neighbours have I known, who, after living in peace , and good-fellowship for years, have been thrown into a state of distrust, cavilling, and animosity, by some ill-starred agreement about fences, runs of water, and stray cattle. And how many well-meaning nations, who would otherwise have remained in the most amicable disposition towards each other, have been brought to swords' points about the infringement or misconstruction of some treaty, which in an evil hour they had concluded by way of making their amity more sure!

Treaties, at best, are but complied with so long as interest requires their fulfilment; consequently, they are virtually binding on the weaker party only, or, in plain truth, they are not binding at all. No nation will wantonly go to war with another, if, it has nothing to gain thereby, and therefore needs no treaty to restrain it from violence; and if it have anything to gain, I much question, from what I have witnessed of the righteous conduct of nations, whether any treaty could be made so strong that it could not thrust the sword through—nay, I would hold ten to one, the treaty itself would be the very source to which resort would be had, to find a pretext for hostilities.

Thus therefore I conclude—that though it is the best of all policies for a nation to keep up a constant negotiation with its neighbours, yet it is the summit of folly for it ever to be beguiled into a treaty; for then comes on the non-fulfilment and infraction, then remonstrance, then altercation, then retaliation, then recrimination, and finally open war. In a word, negotiation is like courtship, a time of sweet words, gallant speeches, soft looks, and endearing caresses; but the marriage ceremony is the signal for hostilities.

Chapter 4

How Peter Stuyvesant was greatly belied by his adersaries the Mosstroopers—and his conduct thereupon.

If my pains-taking reader be not somewhat perplexed, in the course of the ratiocination of my last chapter, he will doubtless at one glance perceive, that the great Peter, in concluding a treaty with his eastern neighbours, was guilty of a lamentable error and heterodoxy in politics. To this unlucky agreement may justly be ascribed a world of little infringements, altercations, negotiations, and bickerings, which afterwards took place between the irreproachable Stuyvesant, and the evil-disposed council of Amphyctions. All these did not a little disturb the constitutional serenity of the good *burghers* of Manna-hata; but in sooth they were so very pitiful in their nature. and effects, that a grave historian, who grudges the time spent in anything less than recording the fall of empires, and the revolution of worlds, would think them unworthy to be inscribed on his sacred page.

The reader is therefore to take it for granted, though I scorn to waste in the detail that time which my furrowed brow and trembling hand inform me is invaluable, that all the while the great Peter was occupied in those tremendous and bloody contests that I shall shortly rehearse, there was a continued series of little, dirty, snivelling skirmishes, scourings, broils, and maraudings, made on the eastern frontiers, by the mosstroopers of Connecticut. But, like that mirror of chivalry, the sage and valorous Don Quixote, I leave these petty contests for some future Sancho Panza of a historian, while I reserve my prowess and my pen for achievements of higher dignity.

Now did the great Peter conclude, that his labours had come to a close in the east, and that he had nothing to do but apply himself to the internal prosperity of his beloved Manhattoes. Though a man of great modesty, he could not help boasting that he had at length shut the temple of Janus, and that, were all rulers like a certain person who should be nameless, it would never be opened again. But the exultation of the worthy governor was put to a speedy check; for scarce was the treaty concluded, and hardly was the ink dried on the paper, before the crafty and discourteous council of the league sought a new pretence for re-illuming the flames of discord.

It seems to be the nature of confederacies, republics, and such like powers, that want the true masculine character, to indulge exceedingly in certain feminine panics and suspicions. Like some good lady of delicate and sickly virtue, who is in constant dread of having her vestal purity contaminated or seduced, and who, if a man do but take her by the hand, or look her in the face, is ready to cry out, rape! and ruin!—so these squeamish governments are perpetually on the alarm for the virtue of the country; every manly measure is a violation of the constitution —every monarchy or other masculine government around them is laying snares for their seduction; and they are forever detecting infernal plots, by which they were to be betrayed, dishonoured, and "brought upon the town."

If any proof were wanting of the truth of these opinions, I would instance the conduct of a certain republic of our day; who, good dame, has already withstood so many plots and conspiracies against her virtue, and has so often come near being made "no better than she should be." I would notice her constant jealousies of poor old England, who, by her own account, has been incessantly trying to sap her honour; though, from my soul, I never could believe the honest old gentleman meant her any rudeness.

Whereas, on the contrary, I think I have several times caught her squeezing hands and indulging in certain amorous oglings with that sad fellow Buonaparte—who all the world knows to be a great despoiler of national virtue, to have ruined all the empires in his neighbourhood, and to have debauched every republic that came in his way—but so it is, these rakes seem always to gain singular favour with the ladies.

But I crave pardon of my reader for thus wandering, and will endeavour in some measure to apply the foregoing remarks; for in the year 1651, we are told, the great confederacy of the east accused the immaculate Peter—the soul of honour and heart of steel—that by divers gifts and promises he had been secretly endeavouring to instigate the Nanrohigansett, (or Narraganset) Mohaque, and Pequot Indians, to surprise and massacre the Yankee settlements.

"For," as the council slanderously observed, "the Indians round about for divers hundred miles cercute, seemeto have drunke deep of an intoxicating cupp, att or from the Manhatoes against the English, whoe have sought their good, both in bodily and spirituall respects."

History does not make mention how the great council of the Amphyctions came by this precious plot; whether it was honestly bought at a fair market price, or discovered by sheer good fortune—it is certain, however, that they examined divers Indians, who all swore to the fact as sturdily as though they had been so many Christian troopers: and to be more sure of their veracity, the sage council previously made every mother's son of them devoutly drunk, remembering an old and trite proverb, which it is not necessary for me to repeat

Though descended from a family which suffered much injury from the losel Yankees of those times—my great-grandfather having had a yoke of oxen and his best pacer stolen, and having received a pair of black eyes and a bloody nose in one of these border wars; and my grandfather, when a very little boy tending pigs, having been kidnapped and severely flowed by a long-sided Connecticut schoolmaster—yet I should have passed over all these wrongs with forgiveness and oblivion—I could even have suffered them to have broken Evert Ducking's head, to have kicked the doughty Jacobus Van Curlet and his ragged regiment out of doors, carried every hog into captivity, and depopulated every hen-roost on the face of the earth, with perfect impunity—But this wanton attack upon one of the most gallant and irreproachable heroes of modern times is too much even for me to digest, and has overset, with a single puff, the patience of the historian, and the forbearance of the Dutchman.

Oh reader, it was false!—I swear to thee, it was false! if thou hast any respect to my word—if the undeviating character for veracity, which I have endeavoured to maintain throughout this work, has its due weight with thee, thou wilt not give thy faith to this tale of slander; for I pledge my honour and my immortal fame to thee, that the gallant Peter Stuyyesant was not only innocent of this foul conspiracy, but would have suffered his right arm, or even his wooden leg, to consume with slow and everlasting flames, rather than attempt to destroy his enemies in any other way than open generous warfare—beshrew those *caitiff* scouts, that conspired to sully his honest name by such an imputation!

Peter Stuyvesant, though he perhaps had never heard of a knight-errant, yet had he as true a heart of chivalry as ever beat at the round table of King Arthur. There was a spirit of native gallantry, a noble and generous hardihood diffused through his rugged manners, which altogether gave unquestionable tokens of a heroic mind. He was, in truth, a hero of chivalry, struck off by the hand of Nature at a single heat, and though she had taken no farther care to polish and refine her workmanship, he stood forth a miracle of her skill.

But, not to be figurative, (a fault in historic writing which I particularly eschew,) the great Peter possessed in an eminent degree, the seven renowned and noble virtues of knighthood, which, as he had never consulted authors in the disciplining and cultivating of his mind, I verily believe must have been implanted in the corner of his heart by Dame Nature herself— where they flourished among his hardy qualities like so many sweet wild flowers, shooting forth and thriving with redundant luxuriance among stubborn rocks.

Such was the mind of Peter the Headstrong, and if my admiration for it has, on this occasion, transported my style beyond the sober gravity which becomes the laborious scribe of historic events, I can plead as an apology, that though a little gray-headed Dutchman arrived almost at the bottom of the downhill of life, I still retain some portion of that celestial fire which sparkles in the eye of youth, when contemplating the virtues and achievements of ancient worthies. Blessed, thrice and nine times blessed be the good St. Nicholas—that I have escaped the inluence of that chilling apathy, which too often freezes the sympathies of age; which, like a churlish spirit, sits at the portals of the heart, repulsing every genial sentiment, and paralyzing every spontaneous glow of enthusiasm!

No sooner then did this scoundrel imputation on his honour reach the ear of Peter Stuyvesant, than he proceeded in a manner which would have redounded to his credit, even though he had studied for years in the library of Don Quixote himself. He immediately despatched his valiant trumpeter and squire, Antony Van Corlear, with orders to ride night and day, as herald, to the Amphyctionic council, reproaching them, in terms of noble indignation, for giving ear to the slanders of heathen infidels, against the character of a Christian, a gentleman, and a soldier—and declaring, that as to the treacherous and bloody plot alleged against him, whoever affirmed it to be true, lied in his teeth!—to prove which, he defied the president of the council and all his compeers, or, if they pleased, their *puissant* champion, Captain Alicxsander Partridg, that mighty man of Rhodes, to meet him in single combat, where he would trust the vindication of his innocence to the prowess of his arm.

This challenge being delivered with due ceremony, Antony Van Corlear sounded a trumpet of defiance before the whole council, ending with a most horrific and nasal twang, full in the face of Captain Partridg, who almost jumped out of his skin in an ecstasy of astonishment at the noise. This done, he mounted a tall Flanders mare, which he always rode, and trotted merrily towards the Manhattoes—passing through Hartford, and Piquag, and Middletown, and all the other border towns—twanging his trumpet like a very devil, so that the sweet valleys and banks of the Connecticut resounded with the warlike melody—and stopping occasionally to eat pumpkin pies, dance at country frolics, and bundle with the beauteous lasses of those parts—whom be rejoiced exceedingly with his soul-stirring instrument.

But the grand council, being composed of considerate men, had no idea of running a tilting with such a fiery hero as the hardy Peter—on the contrary, they sent him an answer couched in the meekest, the most mild, and provoking terms, in which they assured him that his guilt was proved to their perfect satisfaction, by the testimony of divers sober and respectable Indians, and concluding with this truly amiable paragraph—

> For youre confidant denialls of the Barbarous plott charged will waigh little in balance against such evidence, soe that we must still require and seeke due satisfaction and cecurite, so we rest, Sir,
>
> Youres in wayes of Righteousness, &c.

I am aware that the above transaction has been differently

recorded by certain historians of the east, and elsewhere; who seem to have inherited the bitter enmity of their ancestors to the brave Peter—and much good may their inheritance do them. These declare, that Peter Stuyvesant requested to have the charges against him inquired into, by commissioners to be appointed for the purpose; and yet, that when such commissioners were appointed, he refused to submit to their examination.

In this artful account, there is but the semblance of truth—he did, indeed, most gallantly offer, when that he found a deaf ear was turned to his challenge, to submit his conduct to the rigorous inspection of a court of honours—but then he expected to find it an august tribunal, composed of courteous gentlemen, the governors and nobility of the confederate plantations, and of the province of New-Netherlands; where he might be tried by his peers, in a manner worthy of his rank and dignity—whereas, let me perish, if they did not send to the Manhattoes two lean-sided hungry pettifoggers, mounted on Narraganset pacers, with saddle-bags under their bottoms, and green satchels under their arms, as though they were about to beat the hoof from one county court to another in search of a lawsuit

The chivalric Peter, as might be expected, took no notice of these cunning varlets; who, with professional industry, fell to prying and sifting about, in quest of *ex parte* evidence; perplexing divers simple Indians and old women, with their cross-questioning, until they contradicted and forswore themselves most horribly. Thus having fulfilled their errand to their own satisfaction, they returned to the grand council with their satchels and saddle-bags stuffed full of villainous rumours, apocryphal stories, and outrageous calumnies,—for all which the great Peter did not care a tobacco-stopper; but, I warrant me, had they attempted to play off the same trick upon William the Testy, he would have treated them both to an aerial gambol on his patent gallows.

The grand council of the east held a very solemn meeting, on the return of their envoys; and after they had pondered a long time on the situation of affairs, were upon the point of adjourning without being able to agree upon anything.

At this critical moment, one of those meddlesome, indefatigable spirits, who endeavour to establish a character for patriotism by blowing the bellows of party, until the whole furnace of politics is red-hot with sparks and cinders—and who have just cunning enough to know that there is no time so favourable for getting on the people's backs as when they are in a state of turmoil, and attending to every body's business but their own—this aspiring imp of faction, who was called a great politician, because he had secured a seat in council by calumniating all his opponents—he, I say, conceived this a fit opportunity to strike a blow that should secure his popularity among his constituents who lived on the borders of Nieuw-Nederlandt, and were the greatest poachers in Christendom, excepting the Scotch border nobles. Like a second Peter the Hermit, therefore, he stood forth and preached up a crusade against Peter Stuyvesant, and his devoted city.

He made a speech which lasted six hours, according to the ancient custom in these parts, in which he represented the Dutch as a race of impious heretics, who neither believed in witchcraft, nor the sovereign virtues of horse-shoes—who left their country for the lucre of gain, not like themselves, for the enjoyment of *liberty of conscience*—who, in short, were a race of mere cannibals and *anthropophagi*, inasmuch as they never eat cod-fish on Saturday, devoured swine's flesh without molasses, and held pumpkins in utter contempt

This speech had the desired effect, for the council, being awakened by the sergeant-at-arms, rubbed their eyes, and declared that it was just and politic, to declare instant war against these unchristian anti-pumpkinites. But it was necessary that the people at large should first be prepared for, this measure; and for this purpose the arguments of the orator were preached from the pulpit for several Sundays subsequent, and earnestly recommended to the consideration of every good Christian, who professed, as well as practised the doctrines of meekness, charity, and the forgiveness of injuries.

This is the first time we hear of the "drum ecclesiastic" beating up for political recruits in our country; and it proved of such signal efficacy, that it has since been called into frequent service throughout our Union. A cunning politician is often found skulking under the clerical robe, with an outside all religion, and an inside all political rancour. Things spiritual and things temporal are strangely jumbled together, like poisons and antidotes on an apothecary's shelf; and instead of a devout sermon, the simple church-going folk have often a political pamphlet thrust down their throats, labelled with a pious text from Scripture.

CHAPTER 5

HOW THE NEW-AMSTERDAMMERS BECAME GREAT IN ARMS AND OF THE DIREFUL CATASTROPHE OF A MIGHTY ARMY—TOGETHER WITH PETER STVYVESANT'S MEASURES TO FORTIFY THE CITY—AND HOW HE WAS THE ORIGINAL FOUNDER OF THE BATTERY.

But, notwithstanding that the grand council, as I have already shown, were amazingly discreet in their proceedings respecting the New-Netherlands, and conducted the whole with almost as much silence and mystery as docs the sage British cabinet one of its ill-starred *secret expeditions*—yet did the ever-watchful Peter receive as full and accurate information of every movement as does the court of France of all the notable enterprises I have mentioned. He accordingly sat himself to work, to render the machinations of his bitter adversaries abortive.

I know that many will censure the precipitation of this stout-hearted old governor, in that he hurried into the expenses of fortification, without ascertaining whether they were necessary, by prudently waiting until the enemy was at the door. But they should recollect that Peter Stuyvesant had not the benefit of an insight into the modern *arcana* of politics, and was strangely bigoted to certain obsolete maxims of the old school; among which he firmly believed, that to render a country respected abroad, it was necessary to make it formidable at home—and that a nation should place its reliance for peace and security more upon its own strength, than on the justice or good-will of its neighbours.

He proceeded, therefore, with all diligence, to put the province and metropolis in a strong posture of defence.

Among the few remnants of ingenious inventions which remained from the days of William the Testy, were those impregnable bulwarks of public safety, militia laws; by which the inhabitants were obliged to turn out twice a year, with such military equipments—as it pleased God; and were put under the command of very valiant tailors, and man-milliners, who though on ordinary occasions the meekest, pippin-hearted little men in the world, were very devils at parades and courts-martial, when they had cocked hats on their heads, and swords by their sides.

Under the instructions of these periodical warriors, the gallant train-bands made marvellous proficiency in the mystery of gunpowder. They were taught to face to the right, to wheel to the left, to snap off empty fire-locks without winking, to turn a comer without any great uproar or irregularity, and to march through sun and rain from one end of the town to the other without flinching—until in the end they became so valorous, that they fired off blank cartridges, without so much as turning away their heads—could hear the largest field-piece discharged, without stopping their ears, or falling into much confusion—and would even go through all the fatigues and perils of a summer day's parade, without having their ranks much thinned by desertion!

True it is, the genius of this truly pacific people was so little given to war, that during the interval which occurred between field days, they generally contrived to forget all the military tuition they had received; so that when they reappeared on parade, they scarcely knew the butt-end of the musket from the muzzle, and invariably mistook the right shoulder for the left—a mistake which, however, was soon obviated by chalking their left arms. But whatever might be their blunders and awkwardness, the sagacious Kieft declared them to be of but little importance—since, as he judiciously observed, one campaign would be of more instruction to them than a hundred parades; for though two-thirds of them might be food for powder, yet such of the other third as did not run away would become most experienced veterans.

The great Stuyvesant had no particular veneration for the ingenious experiments and institutions of his shrewd predecessor, and among other things held the militia system in very considerable contempt, which he was often heard to call in joke—for he was sometimes fond of a joke—governor Kieft's broken reed. As, however, the present emergency was pressing, he was obliged to avail himself of such means of defence as were next at hand, and accordingly appointed a general inspection and parade of the train-bands.

But oh! Mars and Bellona, and all ye other powers of war, both great and small, what a turning out was here!—Here came men without officers, and officers without men—long fowling-pieces, and short blunderbusses—muskets of all sorts and sizes, some without bayonets, others without locks, others without stocks, and many without either lock, stock, or barrel—cartridge-boxes, shot-belts, powder-horns, swords, hatchets, snicker-snees, crowbars, and broomsticks, all mingled higgledy piggledy—like one of our continental armies at the breaking out of the revolution. This sudden transformation of a pacific community into a band of warriors, is doubtless what is meant, in modern days, by "putting a nation in armour," and "fixing it in an attitude"—in which armour and attitude it makes as martial a figure, and as likely to acquit itself with as much prowess, as the renowned Sancho Panza, when suddenly equipped to defend his island of Barataria.

The sturdy Peter eyed this ragged regiment with some such rueful aspect as a man would eye the devil; but knowing, like a wise man, that all he had to do was to make the best out of a bad bargain, he determined to give his heroes a seasoning. Having, therefore, drilled them through the manual exercise over and over again, he ordered the fifes to strike up a quick march, and trudged his sturdy troops backwards and forwards about the streets of New-Amsterdam, and the fields adjacent, until their short legs ached, and their fat sides sweated again. But this was not all; the martial spirit of the old governor caught fire from the uprightly music of the fife, and he resolved to try the mettle of his troops, and give them a taste of the hardships of iron war.

To this end he encamped them, as the shades of evening fell, upon a hill formerly called Bunker's Hill, at some distance from the town, with a full intention of initiating them into the discipline of camps, and of renewing, the next day, the toils and perils of the field.

But so it came to pass, that in the night there fell a great and heavy rain, which descended in torrents upon the camp, and the mighty army strangely melted away before it; so that when Gaffer Phoebus came to shed his morning beams upon the place, saving Peter Stuyvesant and his trumpeter, Van Corlear, scarce one was to be found of all the multitude that had encamped there the night before.

This awful dissolution of his army would have appalled a commander of less nerve than Peter Stuyvesant; but he considered it as a matter of but small importance, though he thenceforward regarded the militia system with ten times greater contempt than ever, and took care to provide himself with a good garrison of chosen men, whom he kept in pay, of whom he boasted that they at least possessed the quality, indispensable in soldiers, of being waterproof.

The next care of the vigilant Stuyvesant was to strengthen and fortify New-Amsterdam. For this purpose, he caused to be built a strong picket fence, that reached across the island, from river to river, being intended to protect the city not merely from the sudden invasions of foreign enemies, but likewise from the incursions of the neighbouring savages.[1]

Some traditions, it is true, have ascribed the building of this

---

1. In an antique view of New-Amsterdam, taken some years after the above period, is a representation of this wall, which stretched along the course of Wall-street, so called in commemoration of this great bulwark. One gate, called the Land Poort, opened upon Broadway, hard by where at present stands the Trinity Church; and another, called the Water-Poort stood about where the Tontine Coffee-House is at present—opening upon Smits Vleye, or as it is commonly called, Smith Fly, then a marshy valley, with a creek or inlet extending up what we call Maiden-lane.

wall to a later period, but they are wholly incorrect; for a memorandum in the Stuyvesant manuscript, dated towards the middle of the governor's reign, mentions this wall particularly, as a very strong and curious piece of workmanship, and the admiration of all the savages in the neighbourhood. And it mentions, moreover, the alarming circumstance of a drove of stray cows breaking through the grand wall of a dark night; by which the whole community of New-Amsterdam was thrown into a terrible panic.

In addition to this great wall, he cast up several outworks to Fort Amsterdam, to protect the sea-board, at the point of the island. These consisted of formidable mud batteries, solidly faced, after the manner of the Dutch ovens, common in those days, with clam-shells.

These frowning bulwarks, in process of time, came to be pleasantly overrun by a verdant carpet of grass and clover, and their high embankments overshadowed by wide-spreading sycamores, among whose foliage the little birds sported about, rejoicing the ear with their melodious notes. The old *burghers* would repair of an afternoon to smoke their pipes under the shade of their branches, contemplating the golden sun as he gradually sunk into the west, an emblem of that tranquil end toward which themselves were hastening—while the young men and the damsels of the town would take many a moonlight stroll among these favourite haunts, watching the silver beams of chaste Cynthia tremble along the calm bosom of the bay, or light up the white sail of some gliding *bark*, and interchanging the honest vows, of constant affection.

Such was the origin of that renowned walk, The *battery*, which, though ostensibly devoted to the purpose of war, has ever been consecrated to the sweet delights of peace. The favourite walk of declining age—the healthful resort of the feeble invalid—the Sunday refreshment of the dusty tradesman—the scene of many a boyish gambol—the rendezvous of many a tender assignation—the comfort of the citizen—the ornament of New-York, and the pride of the lovely island of Manna-hata.

CHAPTER 6

HOW THE PEOPLE OF THE EAST COUNTRY WERE SUDDENLY AFFLICTED WITH A DIABOLICAL EVIL—AND THEIR JUDICIOUS MEASURES FOR THE EXTIRPATION THEREOF

Having thus provided for the temporary security of New-Amsterdam, and guarded it against any sudden surprise, the gallant Peter took a hearty pinch of snuff, and, snapping his fingers, set the great council of Amphyctions, and their champion, the doughty Alicxsander Partridg, at defiance. It is impossible to say, notwithstanding, what might have been the issue of this affair, had not the council been all at once involved in sad perplexity, and as much dissension sown among its members, as of yore was stirred up in the camp of the brawling warriors of Greece.

The council of the league, as I have shown in my last chapter, had already announced its hostile determinations, and already was the mighty colony of New-Haven, and the *puissant* town of Piquag, otherwise called Weathersfield—famous for its onions and its witches—and the great trading house of Hartford, and all the other redoubtable border towns, in a prodigious turmoil, furbishing up their rusty fowling-pieces, and shouting aloud for war; by which they anticipated easy conquests, and gorgeous spoils, from the little fat Dutch villages.

But this joyous brawling was soon silenced by the conduct of the colony of Massachusetts. Struck with the gallant spirit of the brave old Peter, and convinced by the chivalric frankness and heroic warmth of his vindication, they refused to believe him guilty of the infamous plot most wrongfully laid at his door. With a generosity for which I would yield them immortal honour, they declared that no determination of the grand council of the league should bind the general court of Massachusetts to join in an offensive war which should appear to such general court to be unjust.[1]

This refusal immediately involved the colony of Massachusetts and the other combined colonies in very serious difficulties

---

1. Haz. Col. State Papers.

and disputes, and would no doubt have produced a dissolution of the confederacy, but that the council of Amphyctions, finding that they could not stand alone, if mutilated by the loss of so important a member as Massachusetts, were fain to abandon for the present their hostile machinations against the Manhattoes. Such is the marvellous energy and the puissance of those confederacies, composed of a number of sturdy, self-willed, discordant parts, loosely banded together by a puny general government.

As it was, however, the war-like towns of Connecticut had no cause to deplore this disappointment of their martial ardour; for by my faith—though the combined powers of the league might have been too potent, in the end, for the robustious warriors of the Manhattoes—yet in the interim would the lion-hearted Peter and his myrmidons have choked the stomachful heroes of Piquag with their own onions, and have given the other little border towns such a scouring, that I warrant they would have had no stomach to squat on the land, or invade the hen-roost of a New-Nederlander, for a century to come.

Indeed, there was more than one cause to divert the attention of the good people of the east, from their hostile purposes; for just about this time were they horribly beleaguered and harassed by the inroads of the prince of darkness, divers of whose liege subjects they detected, lurking within their camp, all of whom they incontinently roasted as so many spies and dangerous enemies. Not to speak in parables, we are informed, that at this juncture the New-England provinces were exceedingly troubled by multitudes of losel witches, who wrought strange devices to beguile and distress the multitude; and notwithstanding numerous judicious and bloody laws had been enacted against all "solemn conversing or compacting with the divil, by way of conjuracon or the like,"[2] yet did the dark crime of witchcraft continue to increase to an alarming degree, that would almost transcend belief, were not the fact too well authenticated to be even doubted for an instant.

What is particularly worthy of admiration is, that this terrible

2. New-Plymouth Record.

art, which so long has baffled the painful researches and abstruse studies of philosophers, astrologers, alchymists, theurgists, and other sages, was chiefly confined to the most ignorant, decrepit, and ugly old women in the community, who had scarcely more brains than the broomsticks they rode upon.

When once an alarm is sounded, the public, who love dearly to be in a panic, are not long in want of proofs to support it—raise but the cry of yellow fever, and immediately every headache, and indigestion, and overflowing of the bile, is pronounced the terrible epidemic. In like manner, in the present instance, whoever was troubled with colic or lumbago, was sure to be bewitched; and woe to any unlucky old woman that lived in his neighbourhood.

Such a howling abomination could not be suffered to remain long unnoticed, and it, accordingly soon attracted the fiery indignation of the sober and reflective part of the community—more especially of those, who, whilom, had evinced so much active benevolence in the conversion of Quakers and Anabaptists. The grand council of the Amphyctions publicly set their faces against so deadly and dangerous a sin; and a severe scrutiny took place after those nefarious witches, who were easily detected by devil's pinches, black cats, broomsticks, and the circumstance of their only being able to weep three tears, and those out of the left eye.

It is incredible the number of offences that were detected, "for every one of which," says the profound and reverend Cotton Mather, in that excellent work, the *History of New-England*—"we have such a sufficient evidence, that no reasonable man in this whole country ever did question them; *and it will be unreasonable to do it in any other.*"

Indeed, that authentic and judicious historian, John Josselyn, gent. furnishes us with unquestionable facts on this subject "There are none," observes he, "that beg in this country, but. there be witches too many—bottle-bellied witches and others, that produce many strange apparitions, if you will believe report, of a *shallop* at sea manned with women—and of a ship, and great red horse standing by the mainmast; the ship being in small cove to the eastward, vanished of a sudden," &c.

The number of delinquents, however, and their magical devices, were not more remarkable than their diabolical obstinacy. Though exhorted in the most solemn, persuasive, and affectionate manner, to confess themselves guilty, and be burnt for the good of religion, and the entertainment of the public; yet did they most pertinaciously persist in asserting their innocence. Such incredible obstinacy was in itself deserving of immediate punishment, and was sufficient proof, if proof were necessary, that they were in league with the devil, who is perverseness itself.

But their judges were just and merciful, and were determined to punish none that were not convicted on the best of testimony; not that they needed any evidence to satisfy their own minds, for, like true and experienced judges, their minds were perfectly made up, and they were thoroughly satisfied of the guilt of the prisoners, before they proceeded to try them; but still something was necessary to convince the community at large—to quiet those prying *quidnuncs* who should come after them—in short, the world must be satisfied.

Oh the world—the world!—all the world knows the world of trouble the world is eternally occasioning!—The worthy judges, therefore, were driven to the necessity of sifting, detecting, and making evident as noon-day, matters which were at the commencement all clearly understood and firmly decided upon in their own pericraniums—so that it may truly be said, that the witches were burnt to gratify the populace of the day—but were tried for the satisfaction of the whole world that should, come after them.

Finding, therefore, that neither exhortation, sound reason, nor friendly entreaty, had any avail on these hardened offenders, they resorted to the more urgent arguments of the torture, and having thus absolutely wrung the truth from their stubborn lips—they condenmed them to undergo the roasting due unto the heinous crimes they had confessed. Some even carried their perverseness so far as to expire under the torture, protesting their innocence to the last; but these were looked upon as thoroughly and absolutely possessed by the devil, and the pious, bystanders only lamented that they had not lived a little longer, to have perished in the flames.

In the city of Ephesus, we are told, that the plague was expelled by stoning a ragged old beggar to death, whom Appolonius pointed out as being the evil spirit that caused it, and who actually showed himself to be a demon, by changing into a shagged dog. In like manner, and by measures equally sagacious, a salutary check was given to this growing evil. The witches were all burnt, banished, or panic-struck and in a little while there was not an ugly old woman to be found throughout New-England—which is doubtless one reason why all the young women there are so handsome.

Those honest folk who had suffered from their incantations gradually recovered, excepting such as had been afflicted with twitches and aches, which, however, assumed the less alarming aspect of rheumatisms, sciatics and lumbagos—and the good people of New-England, abandoning the study of the occult sciences, turned their attention to the more profitable *hocuspocus* of trade, and soon became expert in the legerdemain art of turning a penny. Still, however, a tinge of the old leaven is discernible, even unto this day, in their characters—witches occasionally start up among them in different disguises, as physicians, civilians, and divines. The people at large show a keenness, a cleverness, and a profundity of wisdom, that savours strongly of witchcraft—and it has been remarked, that whenever any stones fall from the moon, the greater part, of them are sure to tumble into New-England!

CHAPTER 7
WHICH RECORDS THE RISE AND RENOWN OF A VALIANT COMMANDER, SHOWING THAT A MAN, LIKE A BLADDER, MAY HE PUFFED UP TO GREATNESS AND IMPORTANCE BY MERE WIND.

When treating of these tempestuous times, the unknown

writer of the Stuyvesant manuscript breaks out into a vehement apostrophe, in praise of the good St. Nicholas; to whose protecting care he entirely ascribes the strange dissensions that broke out in the council of the Amphyctions, and the direful witchcraft that prevailed in the east country—where- by the hostile machinations against the Nederlanders were for a time frustrated, and his favourite city of New-Amsterdam preserved from imminent peril and deadly warfare.

Darkness and lowering superstition hung over the fair valleys of the east; the pleasant banks of the Connecticut no longer echoed with the sounds of rustic gayety; direful phantoms and portentous apparitions were seen in the air—gliding spectrums haunted every wild brook and dreary glen—strange voices, made by viewless forms, were heard in desert solitudes—and the border towns were so occupied in detecting and punishing the knowing old women who had produced these alarming appearances, that for a while the province of Nieuw-Nederlandt and its inhabitants were totally forgotten.

The great Peter, therefore, finding that nothing was to be immediately apprehended from his eastern neighbours, turned himself about, with a praiseworthy vigilance that ever distinguished him, to put a stop to the insults of the Swedes. These freebooters, my attentive reader will recollect, had begun to be very troublesome towards the latter part of the reign of William the Testy, having set the proclamations of that doughty little governor at nought, and put the intrepid Jan Jansen Alpendam to a perfect *nonplus!*

Peter Stuyvesant, however, as has already been shown, was a governor of different habits and turn of mind—without more ado, he immediately issued orders for raising a corps of troops to be stationed on the southern frontier, under the command of Brigadier-General Jacobus Van Poffenbargh. This illustrious warrior had risen to great importance during the reign of Wilhelmus Kieft, and if histories speak true, was second in command to the hapless Van Curlet, when he and his ragged regiment. were inhumanly kicked out of Port Good Hope by the Yankees.

In consequence of having been in such a "memorable affair," and of having received more wounds on a certain honourable part that shall be nameless than any of his comrades, he was ever after considered as a hero, who had "seen some service." Certain it is, he enjoyed the unlimited confidence and friendship of William the Testy; who would sit for hours, and listen with wonder to his gunpowder narratives of surprising victories—he had never gained; and dreadful battles—from which he had run away.

It was tropically observed by honest old Socrates, that heaven had infused into some men at their birth a portion of intellectual gold; into others of intellectual silver; while others were bounteously furnished out with abundance of brass and iron—now of this last class was undoubtedly the great General Van Poffenburgh; and from the display he continually made thereof, I am inclined to think that Dame Nature, who will sometimes be partial, had blessed him with enough of those valuable materials to have fitted up a dozen ordinary braziers.

But what is most to be admired is, that he contrived to pass off all his brass and copper upon Wilhelmus Kieft, who was no great judge of base coin, as pure and genuine gold. The consequence was, that upon the resignation of Jacobus Van Curlet, who, after the loss of Fort Good Hope, retired, like a veteran general, to live under the shade of his laurels, the mighty "copper captain," was promoted to his station. This he filled with great importance, always styling himself "commander-in-chief of the armies of New-Netherlands;" though, to tell the truth, the armies, or rather army, consisted of a handful of hen-stealing, bottle-bruising ragamuffins.

Such was the character of the warrior appointed by Peter Stuyvesant to defend his southern frontier; nor may it be uninteresting to my reader to have a glimpse of his person. He was not very tall, but notwithstanding, a huge, full-bodied man, whose bulk did not so much arise from his being fat, as windy; being so completely inflated with his own importance, that he resembled one of those bags of wind which Æolus, in an incredible fit of generosity, gave to that wandering warrior Ulysses.

His dress comported with his character, for he had almost as much brass and copper without, as nature had stored away within—his coat was crossed and slashed, and carbonadoed with stripes of copper lace, and swathed round the body with a crimson sash, of the size and texture of a fishing-net, doubtless to keep his valiant heart from bursting through his ribs. His head and whiskers were profusely powdered, from the midst of which his full-blooded face glowed like a fiery furnace; and his magnanimous soul seemed ready to bounce out at a pair of large glassy blinking eyes, which projected like those of a lobster.

I swear to thee, worthy reader, if report belie not this warrior, I would give all the money in my pocket to have seen him accoutred *cap-a-pie,* in martial array—booted to the middle—sashed to the chin—collared to the ears—whiskered to the teeth—crowned with an overshadowing cocked hat, and girded with a leathern belt ten inches broad, from which trailed a falchion, of a length that I dare not mention. Thus equipped, he strutted about, as bitter-looking a man of war as the far-famed More of More Hall, when he sallied forth, armed at all points, to slay the Dragon of Wantley.[3]

Notwithstanding all these great endowments and transcendent qualities of this renowned general, I must confess he was not exactly the kind of man that the gallant Peter would have chosen to command his troops—but the truth is, that in those days the province did not abound, as at present, in great military characters; who, like so many Cincinnatuses, people every little village—marshalling out cabbages instead of soldiers, and signalizing themselves in the cornfield, instead of the field of battle;—who have surrendered the toils of war, for the more useful but inglorious arts of peace; and so blended the laurel with the olive, that you may have a general for a landlord, a colonel for a stage-driver, and your horse shod by a valiant "captain of volunteers."

3. *Had you but seen him in, his dress How fierce he look'd and how big; You would have thought him for to be Some Egyptian Porcupig. He frighted all, cats, dogs, and all, Each cow, each horse, and each hog; For fear they did flee, for they took him to be Some strange outlandish hedgehog.*   *Ballad of Drag. of Want.*

The redoubtable General Van Poffenburgh, therefore, was appointed to the command of the new-levied troops, chiefly because there were no competitors for the station, and partly because it would have been a breach of military etiquette, to have appointed a younger officer over his head—an injustice, which the great Peter would have rather died than have committed.

No sooner did this thrice-valiant copper captain receive marching orders, than he conducted his army undauntedly to the southern frontier; through wild

lands and savage deserts; over insurmountable mountains, across impassable floods, and through impenetrable forests; subduing a vast tract of uninhabited country, and encountering more perils, according to his own account, than did ever the great Xenophon in his far-famed retreat with his ten thousand Grecians. All this accomplished, he established on the South (or Delaware) River, a redoubtable redoubt, named Fort Casimir, in honour of a favourite pair of brimstone-coloured trunk breeches of the governor.

As this fort will be found to give rise to very important and interesting events, it may be worthwhile to notice that it was afterwards called Nieuw-Amstel, and was the original germ of the present flourishing town of New-Castle, an appellation erroneously substituted for *No Castle*, there neither being, nor ever having been, a castle, or anything of the kind, upon the premises.

The Swedes did not suffer tamely this menacing movement of the Nederlanders; on the contrary, Jan Printz, at that time governor of New-Sweden, issued a protest against what he termed an encroachment upon his jurisdiction. But Van Poffenburgh had become too well versed in the nature of proclamations and protests, while he served under William the Testy, to be in any wise daunted by such paper warfare. His fortress being finished, it would have done any man's heart good to behold into what a magnitude he immediately swelled. He would stride in and out a dozen times a day, surveying it in front and in rear; on this side and on that.

Then would he dress himself in full regimentals, and strut backwards and forwards, for hours together, on the top of his little rampart—like a vain-glorious cock-pigeon vapouring on the top of his coop. In a word, unless my readers have noticed, with curious eye, the petty commander of one of our little, snivelling, military posts, swelling with all the vanity of new regimentals, and the pomposity derived from commanding a handful of tatterdemalions, I despair of giving them any adequate idea of the prodigious dignity of General Van Poffenburgh.

It is recorded, in the delectable romance of Pierce Forest, that a young knight being dubbed by King Alexander, did incontinently gallop into an adjoining forest, and belaboured the trees with such might and main, that the whole court was convinced that he was the most potent and courageous gentleman on the face of the earth. In like manner the great Van Poffenburgh would ease off that valorous spleen, which like wind is so apt to grow unruly in the stomachs of new-made soldiers, impelling them to box-lobby brawls, and broken-headed quarrels.

For at such times, when he found his martial spirit waxing hot within him, he would prudently sally forth into the fields, and lugging out his trusty sabre, would lay about him most lustily, decapitating cabbages by platoons; hewing down whole phalanxes of sunflowers, which he termed gigantic Swedes; and if, peradventure, he espied a colony of honest, big-bellied pumpkins quietly basking themselves in the sun, "Ah, *caitiff* Yankees," would he roar, " have I caught ye at last?"—so saying, with one sweep of his sword, he would cleave the unhappy vegetables from their chins to their waistbands; by which warlike havoc his choler being in some sort allayed, he would return to his garrison with a full conviction that he was a very miracle of military prowess.

The next ambition of General Van Poffenburgh was to be thought a strict disciplinarian. Well knowing that discipline is the soul of all military enterprise, he enforced it with the most rigorous precision; obliging every man to turn out his toes and hold up his head on parade, and prescribing the breadth of their ruffles to all such as had any shirts to their backs.

Having one day, in the course of his devout researches in the Bible, (for the pious Eneas himself could not exceed him in outward religion,) encountered the history of Absalom and his melancholy end, the general, in an evil hour, issued orders for cropping the hair of both officers and men throughout the garrison. Now it came to pass, that among his officers was one Kildermeester, a sturdy veteran, who had cherished, through the course of a long life, a rugged mop of hair, not a little resembling the shag of a Newfoundland dog, terminating with an immoderate queue like the handle of a frying-pan; and queued so tightly to his head, that his eyes and mouth generally stood ajar, and his eye-brows were drawn up to the top of his forehead. It may naturally be supposed that the possessor of so goodly an appendage would resist with abhorrence an order condemning it to the shears.

On hearing the general orders, he discharged a tempest of veteran, soldier-like oaths, and dunder and blixums—swore he would break any man's head who attempted to meddle with his tail—queued it stiffer than ever, and whisked it about the garrison as fiercely as the tail of a crocodile.

The eel-skin queue of old Kildermeester became instantly an affair of the utmost importance. The commander-in-chief was too enlightened an officer not to perceive that the discipline of the garrison, the subordination and good order of the *armies* of the Nieuw-Nederlandts, the consequent safety of the whole province, and ultimately the dignity and prosperity of their High Mightinesses, the Lords States General, but above all, the dignity of the great General Van Poffenburgh, all imperiously demanded the docking of that stubborn queue.

He therefore determined that old Kildermeester should be publicly shorn of his glories in the presence of the whole garrison—the old man as resolutely stood on the defensive—whereupon the general, as became a great man, was highly exasperated, and the offender was arrested and tried by a court-martial for mutiny, desertion, and all the other list of offences noticed in the articles of war, ending with a "videlicet, in wearing an eel-skin queue, three feet long, contrary to orders."—Then came on arraignments, and trials, and pleadings; and the whole country was in a ferment about this unfortunate queue.

As it is well known that the commander of a distant frontier post has the power of acting pretty much after his own will, there is little doubt that the veteran would have been hanged or shot at least, had he not luckily fallen ill of a fever, through mere chagrin and mortification—and most flagitiously deserted from all earthly command, with his beloved locks unviolated. His obstinacy remained unshaken to the very last moment, when he directed that he should be carried to his grave with his eel-skin queue sticking out of a hole in his coffin.

This magnanimous affair obtained the general great credit as an excellent disciplinarian, but it is hinted that he was ever after subject to bad dreams and fearful visitations in the night—when the grizzly spectrum of old Kildermeester would stand sentinel by his bedside, erect as a pump, his enormous queue strutting out like the handle.

BOOK 6

CONTAINING THE SECOND PART OF THE REIGN OF PETER THE HEADSTRONG, AND HIS GALLANT ACHIEVEMENTS ON THE DELAWARE.

CHAPTER 1

IN WHICH IS EXHIBITED A WARLIKE PORTRAIT OF THE GREAT PETER—AND HOW GENERAL VAN POFFENBURGH DISTINGUISHED HIMSELF AT FORT CASIMIR.

Hitherto, most venerable and courteous reader, have I shown thee the administration of the valorous Stuyvesant, under the mild moonshine of peace, or rather the grim tranquillity of awful expectation; but now the war-drum rumbles from afar, the brazen trumpet brays its thrilling note, and the rude clash of hostile arms speaks fearful prophecies of coming troubles. The gallant warrior starts from soft repose, from golden visions, and voluptuous ease; where, in the dulcet, "piping time of peace," he sought sweet Solace after all his toils. No more in beauty's syren lap reclined, he weaves fair garlands for his lady's brows; no more entwines with flowers his shining sword, nor through the live-long lazy summer's day chants forth his lovesick soul in madrigals.

To manhood, roused, he spurns the amorous flute; doffs from his brawny back the robe of peace, and clothes his pampered limbs in panoply of steel. O'er his dark braw, where late the myrtle waved, where wanton roses breathed enervate love, he rears the beaming *casque* and nodding plume; grasps the bright shield and shakes the ponderous lance; or mounts with eager pride his fiery steed, and burns for deeds of glorious chivalry!

But soft, worthy reader! I would not have you imagine, that any *preux chevalier*, thus hideously begirt with iron, existed in the city of New-Amsterdam. This is but a lofty and gigantic mode in which heroic writers always talk of war, thereby to give it a noble and imposing aspect; equipping our warriors with bucklers, helms, and lances, and such like outlandish and obsolete weapons, the like of which perchance they had never seen or heard of; in the same manner that a cunning statuary arrays a modern general or an admiral in the accoutrements of a Caesar or an Alexander. The simple truth, then, of all this oratorical flourish is this—that the valiant Peter Stuyvesant all of a sudden found it necessary to scour his trusty blade, which too long had rusted in its scabbard, and prepare himself to undergo those hardy toils of war, in which his mighty soul so much delighted.

Methinks I at this moment behold him in my imagination— or rather, I behold his goodly portrait, which still hangs up in the family mansion of the Stuyvesants—arrayed in all the terrors of a true Dutch general. His regimental coat of German blue, gorgeously decorated with a goodly show of large brass buttons, reaching from his waistband to his chin. The voluminous skirts turned up at the corners, and separating gallantly behind, so as to display the seat of a sumptuous pair of brimstone-coloured trunk breeches—a graceful style still prevalent among the warriors of our day, and which is in conformity to the custom of

ancient heroes, who scorned to defend themselves in the rear.—
His face rendered exceedingly terrible and warlike by a pair
of black *mustachios*; his hair strutting out on each side in stiffly
pomatumed ear-locks, and descending in a rat-tail queue below
his waist; a shining stock of black leather supporting his chin,
and a little but tierce cocked hat stuck with a gallant and fiery
air over his left eye.

Such was the chivalric port of Peter the Headstrong; and
when he made a sudden halt, planted himself firmly on his solid
supporter, with his wooden leg inlaid with silver, a little in advance, in order to strengthen his position, his right hand grasping a gold-headed cane, his left resting upon the pummel of his
sword; his head dressing spiritedly to the right, with a most appalling and hard-favoured frown upon his brow—he presented
altogether one of the most commanding, bitter looking, and
soldier-like figures that ever strutted upon canvas. Proceed we
now to inquire the cause of this warlike preparation.

The encroaching disposition of the Swedes, on the South, or
Delaware River, has been duly recorded in the chronicles of the
reign of William the Testy. These encroachments having been
endured with that heroic magnanimity, which is the cornerstone
of true courage, had been repeatedly and wickedly aggravated.

The Swedes, who were of that class of cunning pretenders to
Christianity, who read the Bible upsidedown, whenever it inter-
feres with their interests, inverted the golden maxim, and when
their neighbour suffered them to smite him on the one cheek,
they generally smote him on the other also, whether turned to
them or not

Their repeated aggressions had been among the numerous
sources of vexation, that conspired to keep the irritable sensibilities of Wilhelmus Kieft in a constant fever, and it was only
owing to the unfortunate circumstance, that he had always a
hundred things to do at once, that he did not take such unrelenting vengeance as their offences merited. But they had now
a chieftain of a different character to deal with; and they were
soon guilty of a piece of treachery, that threw his honest blood

into a ferment, and precluded all further sufferance.

Printz, the governor of the province of New-Sweden, being either deceased or removed, for of this fact some uncertainty exists, was succeeded by Jan Risingh, a gigantic Swede, and who, had he not been rather knock-kneed and splay-footed, might have served for the model of a Samson, or a Hercules. He was no less rapacious than mighty, and withal as crafty as he was rapacious; so that, in fact, there h very little doubt, had he lived some four or five centuries before, he would have been one of those wicked giants, who took such a cruel pleasure in pocketing distressed damsels, when gadding about the world, and locking them up in enchanted castles, without a toilet, a change of linen, or any other convenience—in consequence of which enormities, they fell under the high displeasure of chivalry, and all true, loyal, and gallant knights were instructed to attack and slay outright any miscreant they might happen to find, above six feet high; which is doubtless one reason that the race of large men is nearly extinct, and the generations of latter ages so exceeding small.

No sooner did Governor Risingh enter upon his office, than he immediately cast his eyes upon the important post of Fort Casimir, and formed the righteous resolution of taking it into his possession. The only thing that remained to consider, was the mode of carrying his resolution into effect; and here I must do him the justice to say, that he exhibited a humanity rarely to be met with among leaders, and which I have never seen equalled in modern times, excepting among the English, in their glorious affair at Copenhagen. Willing to spare the effusion of blood, and the miseries of open warfare, he benevolently shunned everything like avowed hostility or regular siege, and resorted to the less glorious, but more merciful expedient of treachery.

Under pretence, therefore, of paying a neighbourly visit to General Van Poffenburgh, at his new post of Fort Casimir, he made requisite preparation, sailed in great state up the Delaware, displayed his flag with the most ceremonious *punctilio*, and honoured the fortress with a royal salute, previous to dropping anchor. The unusual noise awakened a veteran Dutch sentinel, who was napping faithfully at his post, and who, having suffered his match to go out, contrived to return the compliment, by discharging his rusty musket with the spark of a pipe, which he borrowed from one of his comrades.

The salute indeed would have been answered by the guns of the fort, had they not unfortunately been out of order, and the magazine deficient in ammunition—accidents to which forts have in all ages been liable, and which were the more excusable in the present instance, as Fort Casimir had only been erected about two years, and General Van Poffenburgh, its mighty commander, had been fully occupied with matters of much greater importance.

Risingh, highly satisfied with this courteous reply to his salute, treated the first to a second, for he well knew its commander was marvellously delighted with these little ceremonials, which he considered as so many acts of homage paid unto his greatness. He then landed in great state, attended by a suite of thirty men—a prodigious and vain-glorious retinue, for a petty governor of a petty settlement, in those days of primitive simplicity; and to the full as great an army as generally swells the pomp and marches in the rear of our frontier commanders, at the present day.

The number, in fact, might have awakened suspicion, had not the mind of the great Van Poffenburgh been so completely engrossed with an all-pervading idea of himself, that he had not room to admit a thought besides. In fact, he considered the concourse of Risingh's followers as a compliment to himself—so apt are great men to stand between themselves and the sun, and completely eclipse the truth by their own shadow.

It may readily be imagined how much General Van Poffenburgh was flattered by a visit from so august a personage; his only embarrassment was, how he should receive him in such a manner as to appear, to the greatest advantage, and make the most advantageous impression. The main guard was ordered immediately to turn out, and the arms and regimentals (of which the garrison possessed full half-a-dozen suits) were equally distributed among the soldiers. One tall lank fellow appeared in a coat intended for a small man, the skirts of which reached a little below his waist, the buttons were between his shoulders, and the sleeves half-way to his wrists, so that his hands looked like a couple of huge spades—and the coat, not being large enough to meet in front, was linked together by loops, made of a pair of red worsted garters.

Another had an old cocked hat stuck on the back of his head, and decorated with a bunch of cocks' tails—a third had a pair of rusty garters hanging about his heels—while a fourth, who was short and duck-legged, was equipped in a huge pair of the general's cast-off breeches, which he held up with one hand, while he grasped his firelock with the other. The rest were accoutred ist similar style, excepting three graceless ragamuffins, who had no shirts, and but a pair and a half of breeches between them, wherefore they were sent to the black hole to keep them out of view.

There is nothing in which the talents of a prudent commander are more completely testified, than in thus setting matters off to the greatest advantage; and it is for this reason that our frontier posts at the present day (that of Niagara for example) display their best suit of regimentals on the back of the sentinel who stands in sight of travellers.

His men being thus gallantly arrayed—those who lacked muskets shouldering spades and pickaxes, and every man being ordered to tuck in his shirt-tail and pull up his brogues, General Van Poffenburgh first took a sturdy draught of foaming ale, which like the magnanimous More of Morehall[1] was his invariable practice on all great occasions—which done, he put himself at their head, ordered the pine planks, which served as a drawbridge, to be laid down, and issued forth from his castle, like a mighty giant, just refreshed with wine.

But when the two heroes met, then began a, scene of warlike

1. —— *as soon as he rose. To make him strong and mighty, He drank by the tale, six pots of ale, And a quart of aqua-vitae.*

parade and chivalric courtesy, that beggars all description—Risingh, who, as I before hinted, was a shrewd, cunning politician, and had grown gray much before his time, in consequence of his craftiness, saw at one glance the ruling passion of the great Van Poffenburgh, and humoured him in all his valorous fantasies.

Their detachments were accordingly drawn up in front of each other; they carried arms, and they presented arms; they gave the standing salute and the passing salute—they rolled their drums, and flourished their fifes, and they waved their colours— They faced to the left, and they faced to the right, and they faced to the right about—They wheeled forward, and they wheeled backward, and they wheeled into *echellon*.

They marched, and they counter-marched, by grand divisions, by single divisions, and by sub-divisions—by platoons, by sections, and by files—in quick time, in slow time, and in no time at all; for, having gone through all the evolutions of two great armies, including the eighteen manoeuvres of Dundas, having exhausted all that they could recollect or imagine of military tactics, including sun-dry strange and irregular evolutions, the like of which was never seen before nor since, excepting among certain of our newly-raised militia, the two great commanders and their respective troops, came at length to a dead halt, completely exhausted by the toils of war.

Never did two, valiant train-band captains, or two buskined theatric heroes, in the renowned tragedies of Pizarro, Tom Thumb, or any other heroical and, fighting tragedy, marshal their gallows-looking, duck-legged, heavy-heeled myrmidons with more glory and self-admiration.

These military compliments being finished, General Van Poffenburgh escorted his illustrious visitor, with great ceremony, into the fort; attended him throughout the fortifications; showed him the horn-works, crown-works, half-moons, and various other outworks; or rather the places where they ought to be erected, and where they might be erected if he pleased; plainly demonstrating that it was a place of "great capability," and though at present but a little redoubt, yet that it evidently was a formidable fortress, in embryo.

This survey over, he next had the whole garrison put under arms, exercised and reviewed, and concluded by ordering the three Bridewell birds to be hauled out of the black hole, brought up to the halberts, and soundly flogged, for the amusement of his visitor, and to convince him that he was a great disciplinarian.

The cunning Risingh, while he pretended to be struck dumb outright, with the *puissance* of the great Van Poffenburgh, took silent note of the incompetency of his garrison, of which he gave a hint to his trusty followers, who tipped each other the wink, and laughed most obstreperously—in their sleeves.

The inspection, review, and flogging, being concluded, the party adjourned to the table; for among his other great qualities, the general was remarkably addicted to huge entertainments, or rather carousals, and in one afternoon's campaign would leave more dead men on the field, than he ever did in the whole course of his military career.

Many bulletins of these bloodless victories do still remain on record; and the whole province was once thrown in amaze, by the return of one of his campaigns; wherein it was stated, that though, like Captain Bobadil, he had only twenty men to back him, yet in the short space of six months he had conquered and utterly annihilated sixty oxen, ninety hogs, one hundred sheep, ten thousand cabbages, one thousand bushels of potatoes one hundred and fifty kilderkins of small-beer, two thousand seven hundred and thirty-five pipes, seventy-eight pounds of sugar-plumbs, and forty bars of iron, besides sundry small meats, game, poultry, and garden stuff:—An achievement unparalleled since the days of Pantagruel and his all-devouring army, and which showed that it was only necessary to let belli-potent Van Poffenburgh and his garrison loose in an enemy's Country, and in a little while they would breed a famine, and starve all the inhabitants.

No sooner, therefore, had the general received the first intimation of the visit of Governor Risingh, than he ordered a great dinner to be prepared; and privately sent out a detachment of his most experienced veterans, to rob all the hen-roosts in the neighbourhood, and lay the pig-sties under contribution; a service to which they had been long inured, and which they discharged with such incredible zeal and promptitude, that the garrison table groaned under the weight of their spoils.

I wish, with all my heart, my readers could see the Valiant Van Poffenburgh, as he presided at the head of the banquet; it was a sight worth beholding:—there he. sat, in his greatest glory, surrounded by his soldiers, like that famous wine-bibber, Alexander, whose thirsty virtues he did most ably imitate—telling astounding stories of his hair-breadth adventures and heroic exploits, at which, though all his auditors knew them to be most incontinent and outrageous *gasconadoes*, yet did they cast up their eyes in admiration, and utter many interjections of astonishment.

Nor could the general pronounce anything that bore the remotest semblance to a joke, but the stout Risingh would strike his brawny fist upon the table till every glass rattled again, throwing himself back in the chair, and uttering gigantic peals of laughter, swearing most horribly it was the best joke he ever heard in his life.—Thus all was rout and revelry and hideous carousal within Fort Casimir, and so lustily did Van Poffenburgh ply the bottle, that in less than four short hours he made himself, and his whole garrison, who all sedulously emulated the deeds of their chieftain, dead drunk, and singing songs, quaffing bumpers, and drinking patriotic toasts, none of which but was as long as a Welsh pedigree, or a plea in chancery.

No sooner did things come to this pass, than the crafty Risingh and his Swedes, who had cunningly kept themselves sober, rose on their entertainers, tied them neck and heels, and took formal possession of the fort, and all its dependencies, in the name of Queen Christina of Sweden: administering at the same time an oath of allegiance to all the Dutch soldiers who could be made sober enough to swallow it.

Risingh then put the fortification in order, appointed his discreet and vigilant friend, Suen Scutz, a tall, wind-dried, water-drinking Swede, to the command, and departed, bearing with him this truly amiable garrison, and their puissant commander; who, when brought to himself by a sound drubbing, bore no little resemblance to a "deboshed fish," or bloated sea-monster, caught upon dry land.

The transportation of the garrison was done to prevent the transmission of intelligence to New-Amsterdam; for, much as the cunning Risingh exulted in his stratagem, he dreaded the vengeance of the sturdy Peter Stuyvesant; whose name spread as much terror in the neighbourhood as did whilom that of the unconquerable Scanderberg among his scurvy enemies the Turks.

CHAPTER 2
SHOWING HOW PROFOUND SECRETS ARE OFTEN BROUGHT TO LIGHT; WITH THE PROCEEDINGS OF PETER THE HEADSTRONG, WHEN HE HEARD OF THE MISFORTUNES OF GENERAL VAN POFFENBURGH.

Whoever first described common fame, or rumour, as belonging to the sager sex, was a very owl for shrewdness. She has, in truth, certain feminine qualities to an astonishing degree; particularly that benevolent anxiety to take care of the affairs of others, which keeps her continually hunting after secrets, and gadding about proclaiming them. Whatever is done openly and in the face of the world, she takes but transient notice of; but whenever a transaction is done in a corner, and attempted to be shrouded in mystery, then her goddess-ship is at her wit's end to find it out, and takes a most mischievous and lady-like pleasure in publishing it to the world.

It is this truly feminine propensity that induces her continually to be prying into cabinets of princes, listening at the key-holes of senate chambers, and peering through chinks and crannies, when our worthy Congress are sitting with closed doors, deliberating between a dozen excellent modes of raining the nation. It is this which makes her so obnoxious to all wary statesmen and intriguing commanders—such a stumbling-block to private negotiations and secret expeditions; which she often betrays, by means and instruments which never would have been thought of by any but a female head.

Thus it was in the case of the affair of Fort Casimir. No doubt the cunning Risingh imagined, that by securing the garrison he should for a long time prevent the history of its fate from reaching the ears of the gallant Stuyvesant; but his exploit was blown to the world when he least expected it, and by one of the last beings he would ever have suspected of enlisting as trumpeter to the wide-mouthed deity.

This was one Dirk Schuiler, (or Skulker,) a kind of hanger-on to the garrison; who seemed to belong to nobody, and in a manner to be self-outlawed. He was one of those vagabond cosmopolites, who shark, about the world as if they had no right or business in it, and who infest the skirts of society like poachers and interlopers. Every garrison and country village has one or more scapegoats of this kind, whose life is a kind of enigma, whose existence is without motive, who comes from the Lord knows where, who lives the Lord knows how, and seems to be made for no other earthly purpose but to keep up the ancient and honourable order of idleness.

This vagrant philosopher was supposed to have some Indian blood in his veins, which was manifested by a certain Indian complexion and cast of countenance; but more especially by his propensities and habits. He was a tall, lank fellow, swift of foot and long-winded: He was generally equipped in a half Indian dress, with belt, leggings, and *moccasins*. His hair hung in straight gallows locks about his ears, and added not a little to his sharking demeanour. It is an old remark, that persons of Indian mixture are half civilized, half savage, and half devil, a third half being expressly provided for their particular convenience.

It is for similar reasons, and probably with equal truth, that the back-wood-men of Kentucky are styled half man, half horse, and half alligator, by the settlers on the Mississippi, and held accordingly in great respect and abhorrence.

The above character may have presented itself to the garrison as applicable to Dirk Schuiler, whom they familiarly dubbed Gallows Dirk. Certain it is, he acknowledged allegiance to no one—was an utter enemy to work, holding it in no manner of estimation—but lounged about the fort, depending upon chance for a subsistence, getting drunk whenever he could get liquor, and stealing whatever he could lay his hands on. Every day or two he was sure to get a sound rib-roasting for some of his misdemeanours, which, however, as it broke no bones, he made very light of, and scrupled not to repeat the offence, whenever another opportunity presented.

Sometimes, in consequence of some flagrant villainy, he would abscond from the garrison, and be absent for a month at a time; skulking about the woods and swamps, with a long fowling-piece on his shoulder, laying in ambush for game—or squatting himself down on the edge of a pond catching fish for hours together, and bearing no little resemblance to that potable bird ycleped the mudpoke. When he thought his crimes had been forgotten or forgiven, he would sneak back to the fort with a bundle of skins, or a bunch of poultry, which perchance he had stolen, and would exchange them for liquor, with which, having well soaked his carcass, he would lay in the sun and enjoy all the luxurious indolence of that swinish philosopher Diogenes.

He was the terror of all the farmyards in the country, into which he made fearful inroads; and sometimes he would make his sudden appearance at the garrison at daybreak, with the whole neighbourhood at his heels, like a scoundrel thief of a fox, detected in his maraudings and hunted to his hole. Such was this Dirk Schuiler; and from the total indifference he showed to the world or its concerns, and from his truly Indian stoicism and taciturnity, no one would ever have dreamt that he would have been the publisher of the treachery of Risingh.

When the carousal was going on, which proved so fatal to the brave Van Poffenburgh and his watchful garrison, Dirk skulked about from room to room, being a kind of privileged vagrant, or useless hound, whom nobody noticed. But though a fellow of few words, yet, like your taciturn people, his eyes and ears were always open, and in the course of his prowlings he overheard the whole plot of the Swedes. Dirk immediately settled in his own mind how he should turn the matter to his own advantage. He played the perfect jack-of-both-sides—that is to say, he made a prize of everything that came in his reach, robbed both parties, stuck the copper-bound cocked hat of the *puissant* Van Poffenburgh on his head, whipped a huge pair of Risingh's jack-boots under his arms, and took to his heels, just before the catastrophe and confusion at the garrison.

Finding himself completely dislodged from his haunt in this quarter, he directed his flight towards his native place, New-Amsterdam, from whence he had formerly been obliged to abscond precipitately, in consequence of misfortune in business—that is to say, having been detected in the act of sheep-stealing. After wandering many days in the woods, toiling through swamps, fording brooks, swimming various rivers, and encountering a world of hardships, that would have killed any other being but an Indian, a back-wood-man, or the devil, he at length arrived, half famished, and lank as a starved weasel, at Communipaw, where he stole a canoe and paddled over to New Amsterdam. Immediately on landing, he repaired to Governor Stuyvesant, and in more words than he had ever spoken before in the whole course of his life, gave an account of the disastrous affair.

On receiving these direful tidings, the valiant Peter started from his seat—dashed the pipe he was smoking against the back of the chimney—thrust a prodigious quid of tobacco into his left cheek—pulled up his galligaskins, and strode up and down the room, humming, as was customary with him when in a passion, a hideous north-west ditty. But as I have before shown, he was not a man to vent his spleen in idle vapouring. His first measure after the paroxysm of wrath had subsided, was to stump upstairs, to a huge wooden chest, which served as his armoury, from whence he drew forth that identical suit of regimentals described in the preceding chapter.

In these portentous *habiliments* he arrayed himself, like Achilles, in the armour of Vulcan, maintaining all the while a most appalling silence, knitting his brows, and drawing his breath through his clenched teeth. Being hastily equipped, he strode down into the parlour, jerked down his trusty sword from over the fireplace, where it was usually suspended; but before he girded it on his thigh, he drew it from its scabbard, and as his eye coursed along the rusty blade, a grim smile stole over his iron visage—It was the first smile that had visited his countenance for five long weeks; but everyone who beheld it, prophesied that there would soon be warm work in the province!

Thus armed at all points, with grizzly war depictured in each feature, his very cocked hat assuming an air of uncommon defiance, he instantly put himself upon the alert, and despatched Antony Van Corlear hither and thither, this way and that way, through all the muddy streets and crooked lanes of the city, summoning by sound of trumpet his trusty peers to assemble in instant council. This done, by way of expediting matters, according to the custom of people in a hurry, he kept in continual bustle, shifting from chair to chair, popping his head out of every window, and stumping up and down stairs with his wooden leg in such brisk and incessant motion, that, as we are informed by an authentic historian of the times, the continual clatter bore no small resemblance to the music of a cooper hooping a flour-barrel.

A summons so peremptory, and from a man of the governor's mettle, was not to be trifled with; the sages forthwith repaired to the council chamber, seated themselves with the utmost tranquillity, and lighting their long pipes, gazed with unruffled composure on his Excellency and his regimentals; being, as all counsellors should be, not easily flustered, or taken by surprise. The governor, looking around for a moment with a lofty and soldier-like air, and resting one hand on the pummel of his sword, and flinging the other forth in a free and spirited manner, addressed them in a short, but soul-stirring harangue.

I am extremely sorry that I have not the advantages of Livy, Thucydides, Plutarch, and others of my predecessors, who are furnished, as I am told, with the speeches of all their great emperors, generals, and orators, taken down in shorthand, by the most accurate stenographers of the time; whereby they were enabled wonderfully to enrich their histories, and delight their readers with sublime strains of eloquence. Not having such important auxiliaries, I cannot possibly pronounce what was the tenor of Governor Stuyvesant's speech.

I am bold, however, to say, from the tenor of his character, that he did not wrap his rugged subject in silks and ermines, and other sickly trickeries of phrase; but spoke forth, like a man of nerve and vigour, who scorned to shrink in words, from those dangers which he stood ready to encounter in very deed. This much is certain, that he concluded by announcing his determination of leading on his troops in person, and routing these costardmonger Swedes from their usurped quarters, at Fort Casimir. To this hardy resolution such of his council as were awake gave their usual signal of concurrence, and as to the rest who had fallen asleep about the middle of the harangue, (their "usual custom in the afternoon")—they made not the least objection.

And now was seen in the fair city of New-Amsterdam, a prodigious bustle and preparation for iron war. Recruiting parties marched hither and thither, calling lustily upon all the scrubs, the runagates, and tatterdemalions of the Manhattoes and its vicinity, who had any ambition of sixpence a day, and immortal fame into the bargain, to enlist in the cause of glory. For I would have you note that your warlike heroes who trudge in the rear of conquerors, are generally of that illustrious class of gentlemen, who are equal candidates for the army or the Bridewell—the halberts or the whipping-post—for whom dame Fortune has cast an even die, whether they shall make their exit by the sword or the halter—and whose deaths shall, at all events, be a lofty example to their countrymen.

But notwithstanding all this martial rout and invitation, the ranks of honour were but scantily supplied; so averse were the peaceful *burghers* of New-Amsterdam from enlisting in foreign broils, or stirring beyond that home which rounded all their earthly ideas. Upon beholding this, the great Peter, whose noble heart was all on fire with war and sweet revenge, determined to wait no longer for the tardy assistance of these oily citizens, but to muster up his merry men of the Hudson; who, brought up among woods and wilds and savage beasts, like our yeomen of Kentucky, delighted in nothing so much as desperate adventures and perilous expeditions through the wilderness.

Thus resolving, he ordered his trusty 'squire, Antony Van Corlear, to have his state galley prepared and duly victualled; which being performed, he attended public service at the great church of St. Nicholas, like a true and pious governor, and then leaving peremptory orders with his council to have the chivalry of the Manhattoes marshalled out and appointed against his return, departed upon his recruiiting voyage, up the waters of the Hudson.

Chapter 3
Containing Peter Stuyvesant's voyage up the Hudson, and the wonders and delights of that renowned river.

Now did the soft breezes of the south steal sweetly over the beauteous face of nature, tempering the panting heats of summer into genial and prolific warmth—when that miracle of hardihood and chivalric virtue, the dauntless Peter Stuyvesant, spread his canvas to the wind, and departed from the fair island of Manna-hata. The galley in which he embarked was sumptuously adorned with pendants and streamers of gorgeous dyes, which fluttered gayly in the wind, or drooped their ends in the bosom of the stream.

The bow and poop of this majestic vessel were gallantly bedight, after the rarest Dutch fashion, with figures of little pursy Cupids with periwigs on their heads, and bearing in their hands garlands of flowers, the like of which are not to be found in any book of botany; being the matchless flowers which flourished in the golden age, and exist no longer, unless it be in the imaginations of ingenious carvers of wood and discolourers of canvas.

Thus rarely decorated, in style befitting the state of the *puissant* potentate of the Manhattoes, did the galley of Peter Stuyvesant launch forth upon the bosom of the lordly Hudson; which, as it rolled its broad waves to the ocean, seemed to pause for a while, and swell with pride, as if conscious of the illustrious burthen it sustained.

But trust me, gentlefolk, far other was the scene presented to the contemplation of the crew, from that which may be witnessed at this degenerate day. Wildness and savage majesty reigned on the borders of this mighty river—the hand of cultivation had not as yet laid down the dark forests, and tamed the features of the landscape—nor had the frequent sail of commerce yet broken in upon the profound and awful solitude of ages.

Here and there might be seen a rude *wigwam* perched among the cliffs of the mountains, with its curling column of smoke mounting in the transparent atmosphere—but so loftily situated, that the whoopings of the savage children, gambolling on the margin of the dizzy heights, fell almost as faintly on the ear, as do the notes of the lark, when lost in the azure vault of heaven. Now and then, from the beetling brow of some rocky precipice, the wild deer would look timidly down upon the splendid pageant as it passed below; and then, tossing his branching antlers in the air, would bound away into the thickets of the forest.

Through such scenes did the stately vessel of Peter Stuyvesant pass. Now did they skirt the bases of the rocky heights of Jersey, which spring up like everlasting walls, reaching from the waves unto the heavens; and were fashioned, if traditions may be believed, in times long past, by the mighty spirit Manetho, to protect his favourite abodes from the unhallowed eyes of mortals.

Now did they career it gaily across the vast expanse of Tappan Bay, whose wide extended shores present a vast variety of delectable scenery—here the bold promontory, crowned with embowering trees, advancing into the bay—there the long woodland slope, sweeping up from the shore in rich luxuriance, and terminating in the upland precipice—while at a distance a long waving line of rocky heights threw their gigantic shades across the water.

Now would they pass where some modest little interval, opening among these stupendous scenes, yet retreating as it were for protection into the embraces of the neighbouring mountains, displayed a rural paradise, fraught with sweet and pastoral beauties; the velvet-tufted lawn—the bushy copse—the tinkling rivulet, stealing through the fresh and vivid verdure—on whose banks was situated some little Indian village, or, peradventure, the rude cabin of some solitary hunter.

The different periods of the revolving day seemed each, with cunning magic, to diffuse a different charm over the scene. Now would the jovial sun break gloriously from the east, blazing from the summits of the hills, and sparkling the landscape with a thousand dewy gems; while along the borders of the river were seen heavy masses of mist, which like midnight *caitiffs*, disturbed at his approach, made a sluggish retreat, rolling in sullen reluctance up the mountains.

At such times, all was brightness and life and gayety—the atmosphere seemed of an indescribable pureness and transparency—the birds broke forth in wanton madrigals, and the freshening breezes wafted the vessel merrily on her course. But when the sun sunk amid a flood of glory in the west, mantling the heavens and the earth with a thousand gorgeous dyes—then all was calm, and silent, and magnificent. The late swelling sail hung lifelessly against the mast—the seamen with folded arms leaned against the shrouds, lost in that involuntary musing which the sober grandeur of nature commands in the rudest of her children.

The vast bosom of the Hudson, was like an unruffled mirror, reflecting the golden splendour of the heavens, excepting that now and then a bark canoe would steal across its surface, filled with painted savages, whose gay feathers glared brightly, as perchance a lingering ray of the setting sun gleamed upon them from the western mountains.

But when the hour of twilight spread its magic mists around, then did the face of nature assume a thousand fugitive charms, which, to the worthy heart that seeks enjoyment in the glorious works of its Maker, are inexpressibly captivating. The mellow dubious light that prevailed, just served to tinge with illusive colours, the softened features of the scenery. The deceived but delighted eye sought vainly to discern, in the broad masses of shade, the separating line between the land and water; or to distinguish the fading objects that seemed sinking into chaos.

Now did the busy fancy supply the feebleness of vision, producing with industrious craft a fairy creation of her own. Under her plastic wand, the barren rocks frowned upon the watery waste, in the semblance of lofty towers and high embattled castles—trees assumed the direful forms of mighty giants; and the inaccessible summits of the mountains seemed peopled with a thousand shadowy beings.

Now broke forth from the shores the notes of an innumerable variety of insects, which filled the air with a strange but not inharmonious concert—while ever and *anon* was heard the melancholy plaint of the whip-poor-will, who, perched on some lone tree, wearied the ear of night with his incessant moanings. The mind, soothed into a hallowed melancholy, listened with pensive stillness to catch and distinguish each sound that vaguely echoed from the shore—now and then startled perchance by the whoop of some straggling savage, or the dreary howl of a wolf, stealing forth upon his nightly prowlings.

Thus happily did they pursue their course, until they entered upon those awful defiles denominated *The Highlands*, where it would seem that the gigantic Titans had erst waged their impious war with heaven, piling up cliffs on cliffs, and hurling vast masses of rock in wild confusion. But in sooth, very different is the history of these cloud-capped mountains.—These in ancient days, before the Hudson poured his waters from the lakes, formed one vast prison, within whose rocky bosom the omnipotent Manetho confined the rebellious spirits who repined at his control. Here, bound in adamantine chains, or jammed in rifted pines, or crushed by ponderous rocks, they groaned for many an age. At length the conquering Hudson, in his irresistible career towards the ocean, burst open their prison-house, rolling his tide triumphantly through its stupendous ruins.

Still, however, do many of them lurk about their old abodes;

and these it is, according to venerable legends, that cause the echoes which resound throughout these awful solitudes; which are nothing but their angry clamours, when any noise disturbs the profoundness of their repose. For when the elements are agitated by tempest, when the winds are up and the thunder rolls, then horrible is the yelling and howling of these troubled spirits, making the mountains to rebellow with their hideous uproar; for at such times, it is said, they think the great Manetho is returning once more to plunge them in gloomy caverns, and renew their intolerable captivity.

But all these fair and glorious scenes were lost upon the gallant Stuyvesant; nought occupied his mind but thoughts of iron war, and proud anticipations of hardy deeds of arms. Neither did his honest crew trouble their vacant heads with any romantic speculations of the kind. The pilot at the helm quietly smoked his pipe, thinking of nothing either past, present, or to come— those of his comrades who were not industriously snoring under the hatches were listening with open mouths to Antony Van Corlear; who, seated on the windlass, was relating to them the marvellous history of those myriads of fire-flies, that sparkled like gems and spangles upon the dusky robe of night.

These, according to tradition, were originally a race of pestilent *sempiternous beldames*, who peopled these parts long before the memory of man; being of that abominated race emphatically called *brimstones*; and who, for their innumerable sins against the children of men, and to furnish an awful warning to the beauteous sex, were doomed to infest the earth in the shape of these threatening and terrible little bugs; enduring the internal torments of that fire, which they formerly carried in their hearts and breathed forth in their words; but now are sentenced to bear about forever—in their tails.

And now am I going to tell a fact, which I doubt much my readers will hesitate to believe; but if they do, they are welcome not to believe a word in this whole history, for nothing which it contains is more true. It must be known then that the nose of Antony the trumpeter was of a very lusty size, strutting boldly from his countenance like a mountain of Golconda; being sumptuously bedecked with rubies and other precious stones—the true regalia of a king of good fellows, which jolly Bacchus grants to all who bouse it heartily at the flagon.

Now thus it happened, that bright and early in the morning, the good Antony having washed his burly visage, was leaning over the quarter-railing of the galley, contemplating it in the glassy wave below—just at this moment, the illustrious sun, breaking in all his splendour from behind one of .the high bluffs of the Highlands, did dart one of his most potent beams full upon the refulgent nose of the sounder of brass—the reflection of which shot straightway down, hissing hot, into the water, and killed a mighty sturgeon that was sporting beside the vessel!

This huge monster being with infinite labour hoisted on board, furnished a luxurious repast to all the crew, being accounted of excellent flavour, excepting about the wound, where it smacked a little of brimstone—and this, on my veracity, was the first time that ever sturgeon was eaten in these parts by Christian people.[1]

When this astonishing miracle came to be made known to Peter Stuyvesant, and that he tasted of the unknown fish, he, as may well be supposed, marvelled exceedingly; and as a monument thereof, he gave the name of *Antony's Nose* to a stout promontory in the neighbourhood—and it has continued to be called Antony's Nose ever since that time.

But hold—Whither am I wandering?—By the mass, if I attempt to accompany the good Peter Stuyvesant on this voyage, I shall never make an end, for never was there a voyage so fraught with marvellous incidents, nor a river so abounding with transcendent beauties, worthy of being severally recorded. Even now I have it on the point of my pen to relate, how his crew were most horribly frightened, on going on shore above the highlands, by a gang of merry, roistering devils, frisking and curvet-

---

1. The learned Hans Megapolensis, treating of the country about Albany, in a letter which was written some time after the settlement thereof, says, "There is in the river great plenty of Sturgeon, which we Christians do not make use of; but the Indians eat them greedilie."

ting on a huge flat rock, which projected into the river—and which is called the Duyviel's Dans-Kamer to this very day.— But no! Diedrich Knickerbocker—it becomes thee not to idle thus in thy historic wayfaring.

Recollect that while dwelling with the fond garrulity of age over these fairy scenes, endeared to thee by the recollections of thy youth, and the charms of a thousand legendary tales which beguiled the simple ear of thy childhood; recollect that thou art trifling with those fleeting moments which should be devoted to loftier themes.—Is not Time—relentless Time!—shaking, with palsied hand, his almost exhausted hourglass before thee?— hasten then to pursue thy weary task, lest the last sands be run, ere thou hast finished thy history of the Manhattoes.

Let us then commit the dauntless Peter, his brave galley, and his loyal crew, to the protection of the blessed St. Nicholas; who I have no doubt will prosper him in his voyage, while we await his return at the great city of New-Amsterdam.

CHAPTER 4
DESCRIBING THE POWERFUL ARMY THAT ASSEMBLED AT THE CITY OF NEW-AMSTERDAM—TOGETHER WITH THE INTERVIEW BETWEEN PETER THE HEADSTRONG AND GENERAL VAN POFFENBURGH, AND PETER'S SENTIMENTS TOUCHING UNFORTUNATE GREAT MEN.

While thus the enterprising Peter was coasting, with flowing sail, up the shores of the lordly Hudson, and arousing all the phlegmatic little Dutch settlements upon its herders, a great and *puissant* concourse of warriors was assembling at the city of New-Amsterdam. And here that invaluable fragment of antiquity, the Stuyvesant manuscript, is more than commonly particular; by which means I am enabled to record the illustrious host that encamped itself in the public square in front of the fort, at present denominated the Bowling-Green.

In the centre, then, was pitched the tent of the men of battle of the Manhattoes, who being the inmates of the metropolis, composed the life-guards of the governor. These were commanded by the valiant Stoffel Brinkerhoff, who whilom had acquired such immortal fame at Oyster Bay—they displayed as a standard, a beaver *rampant* on a field of orange being the arms of the province, and denoting the persevering industry and the amphibious origin of the Nederianders.[1]

On their right hand might be seen the vassals of that renowned *Mynheer*, Michael Paw,[2] who lorded it over the fair regions of ancient Pavonia, and the lands away south, even unto the Navesink mountains,[3] and was moreover *patroon* of Gibbet Island. His standard was borne by his trusty squire, Cornelius Van Vorst; consisting of a huge oyster *recumbent* upon a sea-green field; being the armorial bearings of his favourite metropolis, Communipaw. He brought to the camp a stout force of warriors, heavily armed, being each clad in ten pair of linsey-woolsey breeches, and overshadowed by broad-brimmed beavers, with short pipes twisted in their hat-bands. These were the men who vegetated in the mud along the shores of Pavonia; being of the race of genuine copper-heads, and were fabled to have sprung from oysters.

At a little distance was encamped the tribe of warriors who came from the neighbourhood of Hell-Gate. These were commanded by the Suy Dams, and the Van Dams, incontinent hard swearers, as their names betoken—they were terrible-looking fellows, clad in broad-skirted gabardines, of that curious coloured cloth called thunder and lightning—and bore as a standard three Devil's-darning-needles, *Volant,* in a flame-coloured field.

Hard by was the tent of the men of battle from the marshy

---

1. This was likewise the great seal of the New-Netherlands, as may still be seen in ancient records.
2. Besides what is related in the Stuyvesant MS., I have found mention made of this illustrious *Patroon* in another manuscript, which says: "De Heer (or the squire) Michael Paw, a Dutch subject, about 10th Aug, 1630, by deed purchased Staten Island. N. B. The same Michael Paw had what the Dutch call a colonic at Pavonia, on the Jersey shore, opposite New-York, and his overseer, in 1636, was named Corns. Van Vorst—a person of the same name in 1769 owned Powles Hook, and a large farm at Pavonia, and is a lineal descendant from Van Vorst."
3. So called from the Navesink tribe of Indians that inhabited these parts—at present they are erroneously denominated the Neversink, or Neversunk mountains.

borders of the Waale-Boght[4] and the country thereabouts—these were of a sour aspect by reason that they lived on crabs, which abound in these parts. They were the first institutors of that honourable order of knighthood, called *Fly market shirks*, and, if tradition speak true, did likewise introduce the far-famed step in dancing, called "double trouble." They were commanded by the fearless Jacobus Varra Vanger, and had moreover a jolly band of Breuckelen[5] ferry-men, who performed a brave concerto on conch-shells.

But I refrain from pursuing this minute description, which goes on to describe the warriors of Bloemendael, and Weehawk, and Hoboken, and sundry other places, well known in history and song—for now does the sound of martial music alarm the people of New-Amsterdam, sounding afar from beyond the walls of the city. But this alarm was in a little while relieved; for lo, from the midst of a vast cloud of dust, they recognised the brimstone-coloured breeches, and splendid silver leg, of Peter Stuyvesant, glaring in the sunbeams; and beheld him approaching at the head of a formidable army, which he had mastered along the banks of the Hudson.

And here the excellent, but anonymous writer of the Stuyvesant manuscript, breaks out into a brave and glorious description of the forces, as they defiled through the principal gate of the city, that stood by the head of Wall-street.

First of all came the Van Bummels, who inhabit the pleasant borders of the Bronx—these were short fat men, wearing exceeding large trunk breeches, and are renowned for feats of the trencher—they were the first inventors of suppawn or mush-and-milk—Close in their rear marched the Van Vlotens, of Kaatskill, most horrible quaffers of new cider, and arrant braggarts in their liquor—After them came the Van Pelts, of Groodt Esopus, dexterous horsemen, mounted upon goodly switch-tailed steeds of the Esopus breed—these were mighty hunters of minks and musk-rats, whence came the word *Peltry*—Then the Van Nests,

---

4. Since corrupted into the *Wallabout*; the bay where the Navy-Yard is situated.
5. Now spelt Brooklyn.

of Kinderhook, valiant robbers of birds' nests, as their name denotes; to these, if report may be believed, are we indebted for the invention of slap-jacks, or buckwheat cakes.

Then the Van Higginbottoms, of Wapping's creek; these came armed with ferules and birchen rods, being a race of schoolmasters, who first discovered the marvellous sympathy between the seat of honour and the seat of intellect, and that the shortest way to get knowledge into the head, was to hammer it into the bottoms.—Then the Van Grolls of Antony's Nose, who carried their liquor in fair round little pottles, by reason they could not bouse it out of their canteens, having such rare long noses— Then the Gardeniers, of Hudson and thereabouts, distinguished by many triumphant feats, such as robbing watermelon patches, smoking rabbits out of their holes, and the like; and by being great lovers of roasted pig's tails; these were the ancestors of the renowned congressman of that name.

Then the Van Hoesens, of Sing-Sing, great choristers and players upon the Jews-harp; these marched two and two, singing the great song of St. Nicholas—Then the Couenhovens, of Sleepy Hollow; these gave birth to a jolly race of publicans, who first discovered the magic artifice of conjuring a quart of wine into a pint bottle—Then the Van Kortlandts, who lived on the wild banks of the Croton, and were great killers of wild ducks, being much spoken of for their skill in shooting with the long bow—Then the Van Bunschotens, of Nyack and Kakiat, who were the first that did ever kick with the left foot; they were gallant bush-whackers and hunters of raccoons by moonlight.

Then the Van Winkles, of Haerlem, potent suckers of eggs, and noted for running of horses, and running up of scores at taverns; they were the first that ever winked with both eyes at once— Lastly came the *Knickerbockers*, of the great town of Schaghticoke, where the folk lay stones upon the houses in windy weather, lest they should be blown away. These derive their name, as some say, from *Knicker*, to shake, and *Beker*, a goblet, indicating thereby that they were sturdy toss-pots of yore; but, in truth, it was derived from *Knicker*, to nod, and *Boeken*, books; plainly meaning that they were great nodders or dozers over books—from them did descend the writer of this history.

Such was the legion of sturdy bush-beaters that poured in at the grand gate of New-Amsterdam; the Stuyvesant manuscript indeed speaks of many more, whose names I omit to mention, seeing that it behoves me to hasten to matters of greater moment Nothing could surpass the joy and martial pride of the lion-hearted Peter, as he reviewed this mighty host of warriors, and he determined no longer to defer the gratification of his much-wished-for revenge upon the scoundrel Swedes at Fort Casimir.

But before I hasten to record those unmatchable events, which will be found in the sequel of this faithful history, let me pause to notice the fate of Jacobus Van Poffenburgh, the discomfited commander-in-chief of the armies of the New-Netherlands. Such is the inherent uncharitableness of human nature, that scarcely did the news become public of his deplorable discomfiture at Fort Casimir, than a thousand scurvy rumours were set afloat in New-Amsterdam, wherein it was insinuated, that he had in reality a treacherous understanding with the Swedish commander; that he had long been in the practice of privately communicating with the Swedes; together with divers hints about "secret service money:"—to all which deadly charges I do not give a jot more credit than I think they deserve.

Certain it is, that the general vindicated his character by the most vehement oaths and protestations and put every man out of the ranks of honour who dared to doubt his integrity. Moreover, on returning to New-Amsterdam, he paraded up and down the streets with a crew of hard swearers at his heels—sturdy bottle companions, whom he gorged and fattened, and who were ready to bolster him through all the courts of justice—heroes of his own kidney, fierce-whiskered, broad-shouldered, colbrand-looking swaggerer's—not one of whom but looked as though he could eat up an ox, and pick his teeth with the horns.

These life-guard men quarrelled all his quarrels, were ready to fight all his battles, and scowled at every man that turned up his nose at the general, as though they would devour him alive. Their conversation was interspersed with oaths like minute-guns, and every bombastic *rodomontado* was rounded off by a thundering execration, like a patriotic toast honoured with a discharge of artillery.

All these valorous vapourings had a considerable effect in convincing certain profound sages, many of whom began to think the general a hero of unutterable loftiness and magnanimity of soul, particularly as he was continually protesting *on the honour of a soldier*—a marvellously high-sounding asseveration. Nay, one of the members of the council went as far as to propose they should immortalize him by an imperishable statue of plaster of Paris.

But the vigilant Peter the Headstrong was not thus to be deceived.—Sending privately for the commander-in-chief of all the armies, and having heard all his story, garnished with the customary pious oaths, protestations, and ejaculations—"Harken, comrade," cried he, "though by your own account you are the most brave, upright, and honourable man in the whole province, yet do you lie under the misfortune of being damnably traduced, and immeasurably despised. Now, though it is certainly hard to punish a man for his misfortunes, and though it is very possible you are totally innocent of the crimes laid to your charge, yet as Heaven, at present, doubtless for some wise purpose, sees fit to withhold all proofs of your innocence, far be it from me to counteract its sovereign will.

"Besides, I cannot consent to venture my armies with a commander whom they despise, or to trust the welfare of my people to a champion whom they distrust. Retire, therefore, my friend, from the irksome toils and cares of public life, with this comforting reflection—that if guilty, you are but enjoying your just reward—and if innocent, you are not the first great and good man who has most wrongfully been slandered and maltreated in this wicked world—doubtless to be better treated in a better world, where there shall be neither error, calumny, nor persecution. In the meantime let me never see your face again, for I have a horrible antipathy to the countenances of unfortunate great men like yourself."

CHAPTER 5
IN WHICH THE AUTHOR DISCOURSES VERY INGENUOUSLY OF HIM-SELF—AFTER WHICH IS TO BE FOUND MUCH INTERESTING HISTORY ABOUT PETER THE HEADSTRONG AND HIS FOLLOWERS.

As my readers and myself are about entering on as many perils as ever a confederacy of meddlesome knights-errant wilfully ran their heads into, it is meet that, like those hardy adventurers, we should join hands, bury all differences, and swear to stand by one another, in weal or woe, to the end of the enterprise. My readers must doubtless perceive, how completely I have altered my tone and deportment, since we first set out together. I warrant they then thought me a crabbed, cynical, impertinent little son of a Dutchman; for I scarcely ever gave them a civil word, nor so much as touched my beaver, when I had occasion to address them.

But as we jogged along together, in the high-road of my history, I gradually began to relax, to grow more courteous, and occasionally to enter into familiar discourse, until at length I came to conceive a most social, companionable, kind regard for them. This is just my way—I am always a little cold and reserved at first, particularly to people whom I neither know nor care for, and am only to be completely won by long intimacy.

Besides, why should I have been sociable to the crowd of how-d'ye-do acquaintances, that flocked around me at my first appearance? Many were merely attracted by a new face; and having stared me full in the title-page, walked off without saying a word while others lingered yawningly through the preface and having gratified their short-lived curiosity, soon dropped off one by one. But more especially to try their mettle, I had recourse to an expedient, similar to one which we are told was used by that peerless flower of chivalry.

King Arthur; who, before he admitted any knight to his intimacy, first required that he should show himself superior to danger or hardships, by encountering unheard-of mishaps, slaying some dozen giants, vanquishing wicked enchanters, not to say a word of dwarfs, hippogriffs, and fiery dragons. On a similar principle, I cunningly led my readers, at the first sally, into two or three knotty chapters, where they were most woefully belaboured and buffeted, by a host of pagan philosophers and *infidel* writers.

Though naturally a very grave man, yet could I scarce refrain from smiling outright at seeing the utter confusion and dismay of my valiant cavaliers—some dropped down dead (asleep) on the field; others threw down my book in the middle of the first chapter, took to their heels, and never ceased scampering until they had fairly run it out of sight; when they stopped to take breath, to tell their friends what troubles they had undergone, and to warn all others from venturing on so thankless an expedition. Every page thinned my ranks more and more; and of the vast multitude that first set out, but a comparatively few made shift to survive, in exceedingly battered condition, through the five introductory chapters.

What, then I would you have had me take such sunshine, faint-hearted recreants to my bosom at our first acquaintance? No—no; I reserved my friendship for those who deserved it, for those who undauntedly bore me company, in despite of difficulties, dangers, and fatigues. And now, as to those who adhere to me at present, I take them affectionately by the hand—Worthy and thrice beloved readers! brave and well-tried comrades! who have faithfully followed my footsteps through all my wanderings—I salute you from my heart—I pledge myself to stand by you to the last; and to conduct you (so Heaven speed this trusty weapon which I now hold between my fingers) triumphantly to the end of this our stupendous undertaking.

But hark! while we are thus talking, the city of New-Amsterdam is in a bustle. The host of warriors encamped in the Bowling-Green are striking their tents; the brazen trumpet of Antony Van Corlear makes the welkin to resound with portentous clangour—the drums beat—the standards of the Manhattoes, of Hell-Gate, and of Michael Paw, wave proudly in the air. And now behold where the mariners are busily employed hoisting the sails of yon topsail schooner, and those clump-built sloops, which are to waft the army of the Nederlanders to gather immortal honours on the Delaware!

The entire population of the city, man, woman, and child, turned out to behold the chivalry of New-Amsterdam, as it paraded the streets previous to embarkation. Many a handkerchief was waved out at the windows; many a fair nose was blown in melodious sorrow, on the mournful occasion. The grief of the fair dames and beauteous damsels of Grenada could not have been more vociferous on the banishment of the gallant tribe of Abencerrages, than was that of the kind-hearted fair ones of New-Amsterdam on the departure of their intrepid warriors.

Every love-sick maiden fondly crammed the pockets of her hero with gingerbread and doughnuts—many a copper ring was exchanged and crooked sixpence broken, in pledge of eternal constancy—and there remain extant to this day some love verses written on that occasion, sufficiently crabbed and incomprehensible to confound the whole universe.

But it was a moving sight to see the buxom lasses, how they hung about the doughty Antony Van Corlear—for he was a jolly, rosy-faced, lusty bachelor, fond of his joke, and withal a desperate rogue among the women. Fain would they have kept him to comfort them while the army was away; for besides what I have said of him, it is no more than justice to add, that he was a kind-hearted soul, noted for his benevolent attentions in comforting disconsolate wives during the absence of their husbands—and this made him to be very much regarded by the honest *burghers* of the city.

But nothing could keep the valiant Antony from following the heels of the old governor, whom he loved as he did his very soul—so, embracing all the young *vrouws*, and giving every one of them that had good teeth and rosy lips, a dozen hearty smacks, he departed loaded with their kind wishes.

Nor was the departure of the gallant Peter among the least

causes of public distress. Though the old governor was by no means indulgent to the follies and waywardness of his subjects, yet somehow or other he had become strangely popular among the people. There is something so captivating in personal bravery, that, with the common mass of mankind, it takes the lead of most other merits. The simple folk of New-Amsterdam looked upon Peter Stuyvesant as a prodigy of valour. His wooden leg, that trophy of his martial encounter, was regarded with reverence and admiration.

Every old *burgher* had a budget of miraculous stories to tell about the exploits of Hardkopping Piet, wherewith he regaled his children of a long winter night; and on which be dwelt with as much delist and exaggeration, as do our honest country yeomen on the hardy adventures of old General Putnam (or as he is familiarly termed. *Old Put*) during our glorious revolution. Not an individual but verily believed the old governor was a match for Belzebub himself; and there was even a story told, with great mystery, and under the rose, of his having shot the devil with a silver ballet, one dark, stormy night, as he was sailing in a canoe through Hell-Gate—But this I do not record as being an absolute fact—perish the man who would let fall a drop to discolour the pure stream of history!

Certain it is, not an old woman in New-Amsterdam but considered Peter Stuyyesant as a tower of strength, and rested satisfied that the public welfare was secure so long as he was in the city. It is not surprising, then that they looked upon his departure as a sore affliction. With heavy hearts they dragged at the heels of his troop, as they marched down to the riverside to embark. The governor, from the stern of his schooner, gave a short, but truly patriarchal address to his citizens; wherein he recommended them to comport like loyal and peaceable subjects—to go to church regularly on Sundays, and to mind their business all the week besides.

That the women should be dutiful and affectionate to their husbands—looking after nobody's concerns but their own: eschewing all gossipings and morning gaddings—and carrying short tongues and long petticoats—That the men should abstain from intermeddling in public concerns, intrusting the cares of government to the officers appointed to support them—staying at home like good citizens, making money for themselves, and getting children for the benefit of their country. That the *burgomasters* should look well to the public interest—not oppressing the poor, nor indulging the rich— not tasking their sagacity to devise new laws, but faithfully enforcing those which were already made—rather bending their attention to prevent evil than to punish it; ever recollecting that civil magistrates should consider themselves more as guardians of public morals, than rat-catchers employed to entrap public delinquents.

Finally, he exhorted them, one and all, high and low, rich and poor, to conduct themselves *as well as they could*; assuring them that if they faithfully and conscientiously complied with this golden rule, there was no danger but that they would all conduct themselves well enough.—This done, he gave them a paternal benediction; the sturdy Antony sounded a most loving farewell with his trumpet, the jolly crews put up a shout of triumph, and the invincible *armada* swept off proudly down the bay.

The good people of New-Amsterdam crowded down to the battery—that blest resort, from whence so many a tender prayer has been wafted, so many a fair hand waved, so many a tearful look been cast by love-sick damsels, after the lessening bark, bearing her adventurous swain to distant climes. Here the populace watched with straining eyes the gallant squadron, as it slowly floated down the bay, and when the intervening land at the Narrows shut it from their sight, gradually dispersed with silent tongues and downcast countenances.

A heavy gloom hung over; the late bustling city—The honest *burghers* smoked their pipes in profound thoughtfulness, casting many a wistful look to the weathercock, on the church of Saint Nicholas; and all the old women, having no longer the presence of Peter Stuyvesant to hearten them, gathered their children home, and *barricadoed* the doors and windows every evening at sundown.

In the meanwhile, the *armada* of the sturdy Peter proceeded prosperously on its voyage, and after encountering about as many storms, and waterspouts, and whales, and other horrors and phenomena, as generally befall adventurous landsmen, in perilous voyages of the kind; and after undergoing a severe scouring from that deplorable and unpitied malady called seasickness, the whole squadron arrived safely in the Delaware. .

Without so much as dropping anchor and giving his weaned ships time to breathe after labouring so long in the ocean, the intrepid Peter pursued his course up the Delaware, and made a sudden appearance before Fort Casimir.—Having summoned the astonished garrison by a terrific blast from the trumpet of the long-winded Van Corlear, he demanded in a tone of thunder an instant surrender of the fort. To this demand, Suen Scutz, the wind-dried commandant, replied in a shrill, whiffling voice; which, by reason of his extreme spareness, sounded like the wind whistling through a broken bellows—"that he had no very strong reasons for refusing, except that the demand was particularly disagreeable, as he had been ordered to maintain his post to the last extremity." He requested time, therefore, to consult with Governor Risingh, and proposed a truce for that purpose.

The choleric Peter, indignant at having his rightful fort so treacherously taken from him, and thus pertinaciously withheld, refused the proposed armistice, and swore by the pipe of St Nicholas, which like the sacred fire was never extinguished, that unless the fort were surrendered in ten minutes, he would incontinently storm the works, make all the garrison run the gauntlet, and split their scoundrel of a commander like a pickled shad.

To give this menace the greater effect, he drew forth his trusty sword, and shook it at them with such a fierce and vigorous motion, that doubtless if it had not been exceeding rusty, it would have lightened terror into the eyes and hearts of the enemy. He then ordered his men to bring a broadside to bear upon the fort, consisting of two swivels, three muskets, a long duck fowling-piece, and two brace of horse-pistols.

In the meantime, the sturdy Van Corlear marshalled all his forces, and commenced his warlike operations. Distending his cheeks like a very Boreas, he kept up a most horrific twanging of his trumpet—the lusty choristers of Sing-Sing broke forth into a hideous song of battle—the warriors of Breuckelen and the Wallabout blew a potent and astounding blast on their conch-shells, altogether forming as outrageous a *concerto* as though five thousand French orchestras were displaying their skill in a modern overture.

Whether the formidable front of war thus suddenly presented, smote the garrison with sore dismay—or whether the concluding terms of the summons, which mentioned that he should surrender "at discretion" were mistaken by Suen Scutz, who, though a Swede, was a very considerate easy-tempered man—as a compliment to his discretion, I will not take upon me to say; certain it is, he found it impossible to resist so courteous a demand.

Accordingly, in the very nick of time, just as the cabin-boy had gone after a coal of fire, to discharge the swivel, a chamade was beat on the rampart, by the only drum in the garrison, to the no small satisfaction of both parties; who, notwithstanding their great stomach for fighting, had full as good an inclination to eat a quiet dinner, as to exchange black eyes and bloody noses.

Thus did this impregnable fortress once more return to the domination of their High Mightinesses; Scutz and his garrison of twenty men were allowed to march out with the honours of war, and the victorious Peter, who was as generous as brave, permitted them to keep possession of all their arms and ammunition—the same on inspection being found totally unfit for service, having long rusted in the magazine of the fortress, even before it was wrested by the Swedes from the magnanimous, but windy Van Poffenburgh.

But I must not omit to mention, that the governor was so well pleased with the services of his faithful squire Van Corlear, in the reduction of this great fortress, that he made him on the spot lord of a goodly domain in the vicinity of New-Amsterdam—which goes by the name Corlear's Hook unto this very day.

The unexampled liberality of the valiant Stuyvesant towards the Swedes, occasioned great surprise in the city of New-Amsterdam—nay, certain of these factious individuals, who had been enlightened by the political meetings that prevailed during the days of William the Testy, but who had not dared to indulge their meddlesome habits, under the eye of their present ruler, now emboldened by his absence, dared even to give vent to their censures in the street.

Murmurs were heard in the very council chamber of New-Amsterdam; and there is no knowing whether they would not have broken out into downright speeches and invectives, had not Peter Stuyvesant privately sent home his walking-staff, to be laid as a mace on the table of the council chamber, in the midst of his counsellors; who, like wise men, took the hint, and for ever after held their peace.

CHAPTER 6
SHOWING THE GREAT ADVANTAGE THAT THE AUTHOR HAS OVER HIS READER IN TIME OF BATTLE—TOGETHER WITH DIVERS PORTENTOUS MOVEMENTS, WHICH BETOKEN THAT SOMETHING TERRIBLE IS ABOUT TO HAPPEN.

Like as a mighty alderman, when at a corporation feast the first spoonful of turtle soup salutes his palate, feels his impatient appetite but tenfold quickened, and redoubles his vigorous attacks upon the tureen, while his voracious eyes, projecting from his head, roll greedily round, devouring everything at table—so did the mettlesome Peter Stuyvesant feel that intolerable hunger for martial glory, which raged within his very bowels, inflamed by the capture of Fort Casimir, and nothing could allay it but the conquest of all New-Sweden. No sooner, therefore, had he secured his conquest, than he stumped resolutely on, flushed with success, to gather fresh laurels at Fort Christina.[1]

This was the grand Swedish post, established on a small river

---

1. This is at present a flourishing town, called Christiana, or Christeen, about thirty-seven miles from Philadelphia, on the post-road to Baltimore.

(or as it is improperly termed, creek) of the same name; and here that crafty Governor Jan Risingh lay grimly drawn up, like a gray-bearded spider in the citadel of his web.

But before we hurry into the direful scenes that must attend the meeting of two such potent chieftains, it is advisable that we pause for a moment, and hold a kind of warlike council. Battles should not be rushed into precipitately by the historian and by readers, any more than by the general and his soldiers. The great commanders of antiquity never engaged the enemy, without previously preparing the minds of their followers by animating harangues; spiriting them up to heroic feelings, assuring them of the protection of the gods, and inspiring them with a confidence in the prowess of their leaders. So the historian should awaken the attention and enlist the passions of his readers, and having set them all on fire with the importance of his subject, he should put himself at their head, flourish his pen, and lead them on to the thickest of the fight.

An illustrious example of this rule may be seen in that mirror of historians, the immortal Thucydides. Having arrived at the breaking out of the Peloponnesian war, one of his commentators observes, that "he sounds the charge in all the disposition and spirit of Homer. He catalogues the allies on both sides. He awakens our expectations, and fast engages our attention.

"All mankind are concerned in the important point now going to be decided. Endeavours are made to disclose futurity. Heaven itself is interested in the dispute. The earth totters, and nature seems to labour with the great event This is his solemn sublime manner of getting out. Thus he magnifies a war between two, as Rapin styles them, petty states; and thus artfully he supports a little subject, by treating it in a great and noble method."

In like manner, having conducted my readers into the very teeth of peril—having followed the adventurous Peter and his band into foreign regions—surrounded by foes, and stunned by the horrid din of arms—at this important moment, while darkness and doubt hang over each coming chapter, I hold it meet to harangue them, and prepare them for the events that are to follow.

And here I would premise one great advantage which, as the historian, I possess over my reader; and this it is, that though I cannot save the life of my favourite hero, nor absolutely contradict the event of a battle, (both which liberties, though often taken by the French writers of the present reign, I hold to be utterly unworthy of a scrupulous historian,) yet I can now and then make him to bestow on his enemy a sturdy back-stroke sufficient to fell a giant; though, in honest truth, he may never have done anything of the kind—or I can drive his antagonist clear round and round the field; as did Homer make that fine fellow Hector scamper like a *poltroon* round the walls of Troy; for which, if ever they have encountered one another in the Elysisn fields, I'll warrant the prince of poets has had to make the most humble apology.

I am aware that many conscientious readers will be ready to cry out "foul play!" whenever I render a little assistance to my hero—but I consider it one of those privileges exercised by historians of all ages, and one which has never been disputed. In fact, a historian is, as it were, bound in honour to stand by his hero—the fame of the latter is intrusted to his hands, and it is his duty to do the best by it he can. Never was there a general, an admiral, or any other commander, who, in giving an account of any battle he had fought, did not sorely belabour the enemy; and I have no doubt that, had my heroes written the history of their own achievements, they would have dealt much harder blows than any that I shall recount.

Standing forth, therefore, as the guardian of their fame, it behoves me to do them the same justice they would have done themselves; and if I happen to be a little hard upon the Swedes, I give free leave to any of their descendants, who may write a history of the State of Delaware, to take fair retaliation, and belabour Peter Stuyvesant as hard as they please.

Therefore stand by for broken heads and bloody noses!—my pen hath long pitched for a battle—siege after siege have I carried on without blows or bloodshed; but now I have at length got a chance, and I vow to Heaven and St. Nicholas, that, let the chronicles of the time say what they please, neither Sallust, Livy, Tacitus, Polybius, nor any other historian, did ever record a fiercer fight than that in which my valiant chieftains are now about to engage.

And you, oh most excellent readers, whom, for your faithful adherence, I could cherish in the warmest corner of my heart—be not uneasy—trust the fate of our favourite Stuyvesant to me—for by the rood, come what may, I'll stick by Hardkopping Piet to the last; I'll make him drive about these losels vile, as did the renowned Launcelot of the lake, a herd of recreant Cornish knights——and if he does fall, let me never draw my pen to fight another battle, in behalf of a brave man, if I don't make these lubberly Swedes pay for it

No sooner had Peter Stuyvesant arrived before Fort Christina than he proceeded without delay to intrench himself, and immediately, on running his first parallel, despatched Antony Van Corlear to summon the fortress to surrender. Van Corlear was received with all due formality, hoodwinked at the portal, and conducted through a pestiferous smell of salt fish and onions, to the citadel, a substantial hut, built of pine logs.

His eyes were here uncovered, and he found himself in the august presence of Governor Risingh. This chieftain, as I have before noted, was a very giantly man; and was clad in a coarse blue coat, strapped round the waist with a leathern belt, which caused the enormous skirts and pockets to set off with a very warlike sweep. His ponderous legs were cased in a pair of foxy-coloured jack-boots, and he was straddling in the attitude of the Colossus of Rhodes, before a bit of broken looking-glass, shaving himself with a villainously dull razor. This afflicting operation caused him to make a series of horrible grimaces, that heightened exceedingly the grizzly terrors of his visage.

On Antony Van Corlear's being announced, the grim commander paused for a moment, in the midst of one of his most hard-favoured contortions, and after eying him askance over the shoulder, with a kind of snarling grin on his countenance, resumed his labours at the glass.

This iron harvest being reaped, he turned once more to the trumpeter, and demanded the purport of his errand. Antony Van Corlear delivered in a few words, being a kind of short-hand speaker, a long message from his Excellency, recounting the whole history of the province, with a recapitulation of grievances, and enumeration of claims, and concluding with a peremptory demand of instant surrender; which done, he turned aside, took his nose between his thumb and finger, and blew a tremendous blast, not unlike the flourish of a trumpet of defiance—which it had doubtless learned from a long and intimate neighbourhood with that melodious instrument.

Governor Risingh heard him through, trumpet and all, but with infinite impatience; leaning at times, as was his usual custom, on the pommel of his sword, and at times twirling a huge steel watch-chain, or snapping his fingers. Van Corlear having finished, he bluntly replied, that Peter Stuyvesant and his summons might go to the d——l, whither he hoped to send him and his crew of ragamuffins before supper time. Then unsheathing his brass-hilted sword, and throwing away the scabbard—"'Fore gad," quod he, "but I will not sheathe thee again, until I make a scabbard of the smoke-dried, leathern hide of this runagate Dutchman."

Then having flung a fierce defiance in the teeth of his adversary, by the lips of his messenger, the latter was reconducted to the portal, with all the ceremonious civility due to the trumpeter, 'squire and ambassador of so great a commander; and being again unblinded, was courteously dismissed with a tweak of the nose, to assist him in recollecting his message.

No sooner did the gallant Peter receive this insolent reply, than he let fly a tremendous volley of red-hot execrations, that would infallibly have battered down the fortifications, and blown up the powder-magazine about the ears of the fiery Swede, had not the ramparts been remarkably strong, and the magazine bomb-proof. Perceiving that the works withstood this terrific blast, and that it was utterly impossible (as it really was in those unphilosophic days) to carry on a war with words, he ordered his merry men all to prepare for an immediate assault.

But here a strange murmur broke out among his troops, beginning with the tribe of the Van Bummels, those valiant-trencher-men of the Bronx, and spreading from man to man, accompanied with certain mutinous looks and discontented murmurs. For once in his life, and only for once, did the great Peter turn pale, for he verily thought his warriors were going to falter in this hour of perilous trial, and thus tarnish forever the fame of the province of New-Nederlands.

But soon did he discover, to his great joy, that in this suspicion he deeply wronged this most undaunted army; for the cause of this agitation and uneasiness simply was, that the hour of dinner was at hand, and it would have almost broken the hearts of these regular Dutch Warriors, to have broken in upon the invariable routine of their habits. Besides, it was an established rule among our valiant ancestors, always to fight upon a full stomach, and to this may be doubtless attributed the circumstance that they came to be so renowned in arms.

And now are the hearty men of the Manhattoes, and their no less hearty comrades, all lustily engaged under the trees, buffeting stoutly with the contents of their wallets, and taking such affectionate embraces of their canteens and pottles, as though they verily believed they were to be the last And as I foresee we shall have hot work in a page or two, I advise my readers to do the same, for which purpose I will bring this chapter to a close; giving them my word of honour, that no advantage shall be taken of this armistice, to surprise, or in any wise molest, the honest Nederlanders, while at their vigorous repast

CHAPTER 7
CONTAINING THE MOST HORRIBLE BATTLE EVER RECORDED IN POETRY OR PROSE—WITH THE ADMIRABLE EXPLOITS OF PETER THE HEADSTRONG.

"Now had the Dutchmen snatched a huge repast," and finding themselves wonderfully encouraged and animated thereby, prepared to take the field. Expectation, says the writer of the Stuyvesant manuscript—Expectation now stood on stilts. The world forgot to turn round, or rather stood still, that it might witness the affray; like a fat round-bellied alderman, watching the combat of two chivalric flies upon his jerkin.

The eyes of all mankind, as usual in such cases, were turned upon Fort Christina. The sun, like a little man in a crowd, at a puppet-show, scampered about the heavens, popping his head here and there, and endeavouring to get a peep between the unmannerly clouds that obtruded themselves in his way. The historians filled their ink-horns—the poets went without their dinners, either that they might buy paper and goose-quills, or because they could not get anything to eat—antiquity scowled sulkily out of its grave, to see itself outdone—while even posterity stood mute, gazing in gaping ecstasy of retrospection, on the eventful field.

The immortal deities, who whilom had seen service at the "affair" of Troy—now mounted their feather-bed clouds, and sailed over the plain or mingled among the combatants in different disguises, all itching to have a finger in the pie. Jupiter sent off his thunderbolt to a noted coppersmith, to have it furbished up for the direful occasion. Venus swore by her chastity she'd patronize the Swedes, and in semblance of a blear-eyed trull, paraded the battlements of Fort Christina, accompanied by Diana as a sergeant's widow, of cracked reputation.—The noted bully, Mars, stuck two horse-pistols into his belt, shouldered a rusty firelock, and gallantly swaggered at their elbow as a drunken corporal—while Apollo trudged in their rear, as a bandy-legged fifer, playing most villainously out of tune.

On the other side, the ox-eyed Juno, who had gained a pair of black eyes over night, in one of her curtain lectures with old Jupiter, displayed her haughty beauties on a baggage-wagon—Minerva, as a brawny gin suttler, tucked up her skirts, brandished her fists, and swore most heroically, in exceeding bad Dutch, (having but lately studied the language,) by way of keeping up the spirits of the soldiers; while Vulcan halted as a club-footed blacksmith, lately promoted to be a captain of militia. All was silent horror, or bustling preparation; war reared his horrid front, gnashed loud his iron fangs, and shook his direful crest of bristling bayonets.

And now the mighty chieftains marshalled out their hosts. Here stood stout Risingh, firm as a thousand rocks—incrusted with stockades, and entrenched to the chin in mud batteries. His valiant soldiery lined the breastwork in grim array, each having his *mustachios* fiercely greased, and his hair *pomatumed* back, and queued so stiffly, that he grinned above the ramparts like a grizzly death's head.

There came on the intrepid Peter—his brows knit, his teeth set, his fists clenched, almost breathing forth volumes of smoke, so fierce was the fire that raged within his bosom. His faithful 'squire, Van Corlear, trudged valiantly at his heels, with his trumpet gorgeously bedecked with red and yellow ribands, the remembrances of his fair mistresses at the Manhattoes. Then came waddling on the sturdy chivalry of the Hudson. There were the Van Wycks, and the Van Dycks, and the Ten Eycks— the Van Nesses, the Van Tassels, the Van Grolls, the Van Hoesens, the Van Giesons, and the Van Blarcoms—The Van Warts, the Van Winkles, the Van Dams, the Van Pelts, the Van Rippers, and the Van Brunts.

There were the Van Hornes, the Van Hooks, the Van Bunschotens; the Van Gelders, the Van Arsdales, and the Van Bummels—The Vander Belts, the Vander Hoofs, the Vander Voorts, the Vander Lyns, the Vander Pools, and the Vander Spiegels.— There came the Hoffmans, the Hooghlands, the Hoppers, the Cloppers, the Ryckmans, the Dyckmans, the Hogebooms, the Rosebooms, the Oothouts, the Quackenbosses, the Roerbacks, the Garrebrantzs, the Bensons, the Brouwers, the Waldrons, the Onderdonks, the Varra Vangers, the Schermerhornes, the Stoutenburghs, the Brinkerhoffs, the Bontecous, the Knickerbockers, the Hockstfassers, the Ten Breecheses, and the Tough Breecheses, with a host more of worthies, whose names are too crabbed to be written, or if they could be written, it would be impossible for man to utter—all fortified with a mighty dinner, and to use the words of a great Dutch poet,

Brimful of wrath and cabbage!

For an instant the mighty Peter paused in the midst of his career, and mounting on a stump, addressed his troops in eloquent Low Dutch, exhorting them to fight like *duyvels*, and assuring them that if they conquered, they should get plenty of booty— if they fell, they should be allowed the unparalleled satisfaction, while dying, of reflecting that it was in the service of their country—and after they were dead, of seeing their names inscribed in the temple of renown, and handed down, in company with all the other great men of the year, for the admiration of posterity.

Finally, he swore to them, on the word of a governor, (and they knew him too well to doubt it for a moment) that if he caught any mother's son of them looking pale, or playing craven, he'd curry his hide till he made him run out of it like a snake in spring time.—Then lugging out his trusty sabre, he brandished it three times over his head, ordered Van Corlear to sound a tremendous chaise, and shouting the word "St. Nicholas and the Manhattoes!" courageously dashed forwards. His warlike followers, who had employed the interval in lighting their pipes, instantly stuck them in their mouths, gave a furious puff, and charged gallantly, under cover of the smoke.

The Swedish garrison, ordered by the cunning Risingh not to fire until they could distinguish the whites of their assailants' eyes, stood in horrid silence on the covert-way, until the eager Dutchmen had ascended the glacis. Then did they pour into them such a tremendous volley, that the very hills quaked around, and were terrified even unto an incontinence of water, insomuch that certain springs, burst forth from their sides, which continue to run unto the present day. Not a Dutchman but would have bitten the dust, beneath that dreadful fire, had not the protecting Minerva kindly taken care that the Swedes should, one and all, observe their usual custom of shutting their eyes and turning away their heads, at the moment of discharge.

The Swedes followed up their fire by leaping the counterscarp, and falling tooth and nail upon the foe, with furious outcries. And now might be seen prodigies of valour, of which neither history nor song has ever recorded a parallel. Here was beheld the sturdy Stoffel Brinkerhoff, brandishing his lusty quarter-staff, like the terrible giant Blanderon his oak tree, (for he scorned to carry any other weapon,) and drumming a horrific tune upon the heads of whole squadrons of Swedes.

There were the crafty Van Kortlandts, posted at a distance, like the Locrian archers of yore, and plying it most potently with the long bow, for which they were so justly renowned. At another place were collected on a rising knoll the valiant men of Sing-Sing, who assisted marvellously in the fight, by chanting forth the great song of St Nicholas, but as to the Gardeniers of Hodson, they were absent from its battle, having been sent out on a marauding party, to lay waste the neighbouring water-melon patches.

In a different part of the field might be seen the Van Grolls of Antony's Nose; but they were horribly perplexed in a defile between two little hills, by reason of the length of their noses. There were the Van Bunschotens of Nyack and Kakiat, so renowned for kicking with the left foot, but their skill availed them little at present, being short of wind in consequence of the hearty dinner they had eaten, and they would irretrievably have been put to rout, had they not been re-enforced by a gallant corps of *Voltigeures*, composed of the Hoppers, who advanced to their assistance nimbly on one foot

Nor must I omit to mention the incomparable achievements of Antony Van Corlear, who, for a good quarter of an hour, waged stubborn fight with a little pursy Swedish drummer, whose hide he drummed most magnificently; and had he not come into the battle with no other weapon but his trumpet, would infallibly have put him to an untimely end.

But now the combat thickened—on came the mighty Jacobus Varra Vanger, and the fighting men of the Wallabout; after them thundered the Van Pelts of Esopus, together with the Van Rippers and the Van Brunts, bearing down all before them—then the Suy Dams and the Van Dams, pressing forward with many a blustering oath, at the head of the warriors of Hell-Gate, clad in their thunder and lightning gabardines; and lastly, the standard-bearers and body-guards of Peter Stuyvesant, bearing the great beaver of the Manhattoes.

And now commenced the horrid din, the desperate struggle, the maddening ferocity, the frantic desperation, the confusion and self-abandonment of war. Dutchman and Swede commingled, tugged, panted, and blowed. The heavens were darkened with a tempest of missives. Bang! went the guns—whack! struck the broad-swords—thump! went the cudgels—crash! went the musket stocks—blows—kicks—cuffs—scratches—black eyes and bloody noses, swelling the horrors of the scene!

Thick-thwack, cut and hack, helter-skelter, higgledy-piggledy, hurly-burly, head over heels, rough and tumble!—Dunder and blixum! swore the Dutchmen—splitter and splutter! cried the Swedes—Storm the works! shouted Hardkoppig Peter—fire the mine! roared stout Risingh—Tanta-ra-ra-ra! twanged the trumpet of Antony Van Corlear—until all voice and sound became unintelligible—grunts of pain, yells of fury, and shouts of triumph commingling in one hideous clamour. The earth shook as if struck with a paralytic stroke—trees shrunk aghast, and withered at the sight—rocks burrowed in the ground like rabbits, and even Christina Creek turned from its course, and ran up a mountain in breathless terror!

Long hung the contest doubtful; for, though a heavy shower of rain, sent by the "cloud-compelling Jove," in some measure cooled their ardour, as doth a bucket of water thrown on a group of fighting mastiffs, yet did they but pause for a moment, to return with tenfold fury to the charge, belabouring each other with black and bloody bruises. Just at this juncture was seen a vast and dense column of smoke, slowly rolling towards the scene of battle, which for a while made even the furious combatants to stay their arms in mute astonishment—but the wind for a moment dispersing the murky cloud, from the midst thereof emerged the flaunting banner of the immortal Michael Paw.

This noble chieftain came fearlessly on, leading a solid pha-lanx of oyster-fed Pavonians, who had remained behind, partly as a *corps de reserve*, and partly to digest the enormous dinner they had eaten. These sturdy yeomen, nothing daunted, did trudge manfully forward, smoking their pipes with outrageous vigour, so as to raise the awful cloud that has been mentioned; but marching exceedingly slow, being short of leg, and of great rotundity in the belt

And now the protecting deities of the army of New-Amster-dam, having unthinkingly left the field and stept into a neigh-bouring tavern to refresh themselves with a pot of beer, a direful catastrophe had well-nigh chanced to befall the Nederlanders. Scarcely had the myrmidons of the *puissant* Paw attained the front of battle, before the Swedes, instructed by the cunning Risingh, levelled a shower of blows foil at their tobacco-pipes.

Astounded at this unexpected assault, and totally discomfited at seeing their pipes broken, the valiant Dutchmen fell in vast confusion—already they begin to fly—like a frightened drove of unwieldy elephants they throw their own army in an uproar, bearing down a whole legion of little Hoppers—the sacred ban-ner on which is blazoned the gigantic oyster of Communipaw is trampled in the dirt—the Swedes pluck up new spirits, and pressing on their rear, apply their feet a *parte poste*, with a vigour that prodigiously accelerates their motions—nor doth the re-nowned Paw himself fail to receive divers grievous and dishon-ourable visitations of shoe-leather!

But what, Oh muse? was the rage of the gallant Peter, when from afar he saw his army yield? With a voice of thunder did he roar after his recreant warriors. The men of the Manhat-toes plucked up new courage when they heard their leader—or rather they dreaded his fierce displeasure, of which they stood in more awe than of all the Swedes in Christendom—but the dar-ing Peter, not waiting for their aid, plunged, sword in hand, into the thickest of the foe. Then did he display some such incredible achievements as have never been known since the miraculous days of the giants.

Wherever he went, the enemy shrunk before him—with fierce impetuosity he pushed forward, driving the Swedes, like dogs, into their own ditch—but as he fearlessly advanced, the foe thronged in his rear, and hung upon his flank with fearful peril. One crafty Swede, advancing warily on one side, drove his dastard sword full at the hero's heart; but the protecting power that watches over the safety of all great and good men, turned aside the hostile blade, and directed it to a side pocket, where reposed an enormous iron tobacco-box, endowed, like the shield of Achilles, with supernatural powers—no doubt in consequence of its being piously decorated with a portrait of the blessed St Nicholas. Thus was the dreadful blow repelled, but not without occasioning to the great Peter a fearful loss of wind.

Like as a furious bear, when gored by curs, turns fiercely round, gnashes his teeth, and springs upon the foe, so did our hero turn upon the treacherous Swede. The miserable varlet sought in flight for safety—but the active Peter, seizing him by an immeasurable queue, that dangled from his head—"Ah, whoreson-caterpillar!" roared he, "here is what shall make dog's meat of thee!" So saying, he whirled his trusty sword, and made a blow that would have decapitated him, but that the pitying steel struck short, and shaved the queue for ever from his crown.

At this very moment a cunning *arquebusier*, perched on the summit of a neighbouring mound, levelled his deadly instrument, and would have sent the gallant Stuyvesant a wailing ghost to haunt the Stygian shore—had not the watchful Minerva, who had just stopped to tie up her garter, seen the great peril of her favourite chief, and despatched old Boreas with his bellows; who, in the very nick of time, just as the match descended to the pan, gave such a kicky blast, as blew all the priming from the touch-hole!

Thus waged the horrid fight—when the stout Risingh, surveying the battle from the top of a little ravelin, perceived his faithful troops banged, beaten, and kicked by the invincible Peter. Language cannot describe the choler with which he was seized at the sight—he only stopped for a moment to disburthen himself of five thousand anathemas; and then drawing his immeasurable falchion, straddled down to the field of combat, with some such thundering strides as Jupiter is said by Hesiod to have taken when he strode down the spheres, to hurl his thunderbolts at the Titans.

No sooner did these two rival heroes come face to face, than they each made a prodigious start, such as is made by your most experienced stage champions Then did they regard each other for a moment, with bitter aspect, like two furious ram-cats, on the very point of a clapper-clawing. Then did they throw themselves in one attitude, then in another, striking their swords on the ground, first on the right side, then on the left—at last, at it they went with incredible ferocity. Words cannot tell the prodigies of strength and valour displayed in this direful encounter—an encounter, compared to which the far-famed battles of Ajax with Hector, of Eneas with Turnus, Orlando with Rodomont, Guy of Warwick with Colbrand the Dane, or that renowned Welsh knight, Sir Owen of the Mountains with the giant Guylon, were all gentle sports and holyday recreations.

At length the valiant Peter, watching his opportunity, aimed a fearful blow, with the full intention of cleaving his adversary to the very chine; but Risingh, nimbly raising his sword, warded it off so narrowly, that glancing on one side, it shaved away a huge canteen that he always carried swung on one side; thence pursuing its trenchant course, it severed off a deep coat-pocket, stored with bread and cheese—all which dainties rolling among the armies, occasioned a fearful scrambling between the Swedes and Dutchmen, and made the general battle to wax ten times more furious than ever.

Enraged to see his military stores thus woefully laid waste, the stout Risingh, collecting all his forces, aimed a mighty blow full at the hero's crest. In vain did his fierce little cocked hat oppose its course; the biting steel clove through the stubborn rambeaver, and would infallibly have cracked his crown, but that the skull was of such adamantine hardness, that the brittle weapon shivered into pieces, shedding a thousand sparks, like beams of glory, round his grizzly visage.

Stunned with the blow, the valiant Peter reeled, turned up his eyes, and beheld fifty thousand suns, besides moons and stars, dancing about the firmament—at length, missing his footing, by reason of his wooden leg, down he came, on his seat of honour, with a crash that shook the surrounding hills, and would infallibly have wrecked his anatomical system, had he not been received into a cushion softer than velvet, which Providence, or Minerva, or St. Nicholas, or some kindly cow, had benevolently prepared for his reception.

The furious Risingh, in despite of that noble maxim, cherished by all true knights, that *"fair play is a jewel,"* hastened to take advantage of the hero's fall; but just as he was stooping to give the fatal blow, the ever-vigilant Peter bestowed him a sturdy thwack over the sconce with his wooden leg, that set some dozen chimes of bells ringing triple bob-majors in his *cerebellum.*

The bewildered Swede staggered with the blow, and in the meantime the wary Peter, espying a pocket-pistol lying hard by, (which had dropped from the wallet of his faithful 'squire and trumpeter, Van Corlear, during his furious encounter with the drummer,) discharged it full at the head of the reeling Risingh—Let not my reader mistake—it was not a murderous weapon loaded with powder and ball, but a little sturdy stone pottle, charged to the muzzle with a double dram of true Dutch courage, which the knowing Van Corlear always carried about him by way of replenishing his valour. The hideous missive sung through the air, and true to its course, as was the mighty fragment of a rock discharged at Hector by bully Ajax, encountered the huge head of the gigantic Swede with matchless violence.

This heaven-directed blow decided the eventful battle. The ponderous *pericranium* of General Jan Risingh sunk upon his breast; his knees tottered under him; a deathlike torpor seized upon his giant frame, and he tumbled to the earth with such tremendous violence, that old Pluto started with affright, lest he should have broken through the roof of his infernal palace.

His fall was the signal of defeat and victory—The Swedes gave way—the Dutch pressed forward; the former took to their heels, the latter hotly pursued—some entered with them, pell-mell, through the sally-port—others stormed the bastion, and others scrambled over the curtain. Thus, in a little while, the impregnable fortress of Fort Christina, which like another Troy had stood a siege of full ten hours, was finally carried by assault, without the loss of a single man on either side. Victory, in the likeness of a gigantic ox fly, sat perched upon the cocked hat of the gallant Stuyvesant; and it was universally declared, by all the writers whom he hired to write the history of his expedition, that on this memorable day he gained a sufficient quantity of glory to immortalize a dozen of the greatest heroes in Christendom!

Chapter 8
In which the author and the reader, while reposing after the battle, fall into a very grave discourse—after which is recorded the conduct of Peter Stuyvesant after his victory.

Thanks to St Nicholas, we have safely finished this tremendous battle: let us sit down, my worthy reader, and cool ourselves, for I am in a prodigious sweat and agitation—Truly this fighting of battles is hot work! and if your great commanders did but know what trouble they give their historians, they would not have the conscience to achieve so many horrible victories. But methinks I hear my reader complain, that throughout this boasted battle, there is not the least slaughter, nor a single individual maimed, if we except the unhappy Swede, who was shorne of his queue by the trenchant blade of Peter Stuyvesant; all which, he observes, is a great outrage on probability, and highly injurious to the interest of the narration.

This is certainly an objection of no little moment; but it arises entirely from the obscurity that envelops the remote periods of time, about which I have undertaken to write. Thus, though, doubtless, from the importance of the object, and the prowess of the parties concerned, there must have been terrible carnage, and prodigies of valour displayed, before the walls of Christina, yet, notwithstanding that I have consulted every history, manuscript, and tradition, touching this memorable, though long-forgotten battle, I cannot find mention made of a single man killed or wounded in the whole affair.

This is, without doubt, owing to the extreme modesty of our forefathers, who, like their descendants, were never prone to vaunt of their achievements; but it is a virtue that places their historian in a most embarrassing predicament; for, having promised my readers a hideous and unparalleled battle, and having worked them up into a warlike and bloodthirsty state of mind, to put them off without any havoc and slaughter, was as bitter a disappointment as to summon a multitude of good people to attend an execution, and then cruelly balk by a reprieve.

Had the inexorable fates only allowed me some half a score of dead men, I had been content; for I would have made them such heroes as abounded in the olden time, but whose race is now unfortunately extinct— any one of whom, if we may believe those authentic writers, the poets, could drive great armies like sheep before him, and conquer and desolate whole cities by his single arm.

But seeing that I had not a single life at my disposal, all that was left me was to make the most I could of my battle, by means of kicks, and cuffs, and bruises, and such like ignoble wounds. And here I cannot but compare my dilemma, in some sort, to that of the divine Milton, who, having arrayed with sublime preparation his immortal hosts against each other, is sadly put to it how to manage them, and how he shall make the end of his battle answer to the beginning; inasmuch as, being mere spirits, he cannot deal a mortal blow, nor even give a flesh wound to any of his combatants.

For my part, the greatest difficulty I found, was, when I had once put my warriors in a passion, and let them loose into the midst of the enemy, to keep them from doing mischief. Many a time had I to restrain the sturdy Peter from cleaving a gigantic Swede to the very waistband, or spitting half-a-dozen little fellows on his sword, like so many sparrows: and when I had set some hundreds of missives flying in the air, I did not dare to suffer one of them to reach the ground, lest it should have put an end to some unlucky Dutchman.

The reader cannot conceive how mortifying it is to a writer, thus in a manner to have his hands tied, and how many tempting opportunities I had to wink at, where I might have made as fine a death-blow as any recorded in history or song.

From my own experience, I begin to doubt most potently of the authenticity of many of Homer's stories. I verily believe, that when he had once lanched one of his favourite heroes among a crowd of the enemy, he cut down many an honest fellow, without any authority for so doing, excepting that he presented a fair mark—and that often a poor devil was sent to grim Pluto's domains, merely because he had a name that would give a sounding turn to a period.

But I disclaim all such unprincipled liberties—let me but have truth and the law on my side, and no man would fight harder than myself: but since the various records I consulted did not warrant it, I had too much conscience to kill a single soldier. By St. Nicholas, but it would have been a pretty piece of business! My enemies, the critics, who I foresee will be ready enough to lay any crime they can discover at my door, might have charged me with murder outright—and I should have esteemed myself lucky to escape with no harsher verdict than manslaughter!

And now, gentle reader, that we are tranquilly sitting down here, smoking our pipes, permit me to indulge in a melancholy reflection, which at this moment passes across my mind.—How vain, how fleeting, how uncertain are all those gaudy bubbles after which we are panting and toiling in this world of fair delusion! The wealth which the miser has amassed with so many weary days, so many sleepless nights, a spendthrift heir may squander away in joyless prodigality. The noblest monuments which pride has ever reared to perpetuate a name, the hand of time will shortly tumble into ruins—and even the brightest laurels, gained by feats of arms, may wither and be forever blighted by the chilling neglect of mankind.

"How many illustrious heroes," says the good Boetius, "who were once the pride and glory of the age, hath the silence of historians buried in eternal oblivion!"

And this it was that induced the Spartans, when they went to battle, solemnly to sacrifice to the muses, supplicating that their achievements, should be worthily recorded. Had not Homer tuned his lofty lyre, observes the elegant Cicero, the valour of Achilles had remained unsung. And such too, after all the toils and perils he had braved, after all the gallant actions he had achieved, such too had nearly been the fate of the chivalric Peter Stuyvesant, but that I fortunately stepped in and engraved his name on the indelible tablet of history, just as the *caitiff* Time was silently brushing it away forever.

The more I reflect, the more am I astonished at the important character of the historian. He is the sovereign censor, to decide upon the renown or infamy of his fellowmen—he is the patron of kings and conquerors, on whom it depends whether they shall live in after ages, or be forgotten, as were their ancestors before them. The tyrant may oppress while the object of his tyranny exists, but the historian possesses superior might, for his power extends even beyond the grave. The shades of departed and long-forgotten heroes anxiously bend down from above, while he writes, watching each movement of his pen, whether it shall pass by their names with neglect, or inscribe them on the deathless pages of renown.

Even the drop of ink that hangs trembling on his pen, which he may either dash upon the floor or waste in idle scrawlings—that very drop, which to him is not worth the twentieth part of a farthing, may be of incalculable value to some departed worthy—may elevate half a score, in one moment, to immortality, who would have given worlds, had they possessed them, to insure the glorious meed.

Let not my readers imagine, however, that I am indulging

in vain-glorious boastings, or am anxious to blazon forth the importance of my tribe. On the contrary, I shrink when I reflect on the awful responsibility we historians assume—I shudder to think what direful commotions and calamities we occasion in the world—I swear to thee, honest reader, as I am a man, I weep at the very idea!

Why, let me ask, are so many illustrious men daily tearing themselves away from the embraces of their families—slighting the smiles of beauty—despising the allurements of fortune, and exposing themselves to the miseries of war?—Why are kings desolating empires, and depopulating whole countries? In short, what induces all great men, of all ages and countries, to commit so many victories and misdeeds, and inflict so many miseries upon mankind and on themselves, but the mere hope that some historian will kindly take them into notice, and admit them into a corner of his volume.

For, in short, the mighty object of all their toils, their hard-ships, and privations, is nothing but *immortal fame*—and what is immortal fame?—why, half a page of dirty paper!—Alas! alas! how humiliating the idea—that the renown of so great a man as Peter Stuyvesant should depend upon the pen of so little a man as Diedrich Knickerbocker!

And now, having refreshed ourselves after the fatigues and perils of the field, it behoves us to return once more to the scene of conflict, and inquire what were the results of this renowned conquest The fortress of Christina being the fair metropolis, and in a manner the key to New-Sweden its capture was speedily followed by the entire subjugation of the province. This was not a little promoted by the gallant and courteous deportment of the chivalric Peter.

Though a man terrible in battle, yet in the hour of victory was he endued with a spirit generous, merciful, and humane— he vaunted not over his enemies, nor did he make defeat more galling by unmanly insults; for like that mirror of knightly virtue, the renowned Paladin Orlando, he was more anxious to do great actions than to talk of them after they were done. He put no man to death; ordered no houses to be burnt down; permitted no ravages to be perpetrated on the property of the vanquished, and even gave one of his bravest officers a severe admonishment with his walking-staff, for having been detected in the act of sacking a hen-roost.

He moreover issued a proclamation, inviting the inhabitants to submit to the authority of their His Mightinesses; but declaring, with unexampled clemency, that whoever refused should be lodged, at the public expense, in a goodly castle provided for the purpose, and have an armed retinue to wait on them in the bargain. In consequence of these beneficent terms, about thirty Swedes stepped manfully forward and took the oath of allegiance; in reward for which, they were graciously permitted to remain on the banks of the Delaware, where their descendants reside at this very day. But I am told by divers observant travellers, that they have never been able to get over the chapfallen looks of their ancestors, and do still unaccountably transmit from father to son manifest marks of the sound drubbing given them by the sturdy Amsterdammers.

The whole country of New-Sweden, having thus yielded to the arms of the triumphant Peter, was reduced to a colony, called South River, and placed under the superintendence of a lieutenant-governor; subject to the control of the supreme government at New-Amsterdam. This great dignitary was called Mynher William Beekman, or rather *Beck*man, who derived his surname, as did Ovidius Naso of yore, from the lordly dimensions of his nose, which projected from the centre of his countenance like the beak of a parrot. He was the great progenitor of the tribe of the Beekmans, one of the most ancient and honourable families of the province, the members of which do gratefully commemorate the origin of their dignity, not as your noble families, in England would do, by having a glowing proboscis emblazoned in their *escutcheon*, but by one and all wearing a right goodly nose stuck in the very middle of their faces.

Thus was this perilous enterprise gloriously terminated with the loss of only two men—Wolfert Van Horne, a tall spare man, who was knocked overboard by the boom of a sloop, in a flaw of wind; and fat Brom Van Bummel, who was suddenly carried off by an indigestion; both, however, were immortalized as having bravely fallen in the service of their country. True it is, Peter Stuyvesant had one of his limbs terribly fractured, being shattered to pieces in the act of storming the fortress; but as it was fortunately his wooden leg, the wound was promptly and effectually healed.

And now nothing remains to this branch of my history, but to mention that this immaculate hero, and his victorious army, returned joyously to the Manhattoes, where they made a solemn and triumphant entry, bearing with them the conquered Risingh, and the remnant of his battered crew, who had refused allegiance: for it appears that the gigantic Swede had only fallen into a swoon at the end of the battle, from whence he was speedily restored by a wholesome tweak of the nose.

These captive heroes were lodged, according to the promise of the governor, at the public expense, in a fair and spacious castle; being the prison of state, of which Stoffel Brinkerhoff, the immortal conqueror of Oyster Bay, was appointed governor; and which has ever since remained in the possession of his descendants.[1] It was a pleasant and goodly sight to witness the joy of the people of New-Amsterdam, at beholding their warriors once more return from this war in the wilderness.

The old women thronged round Antony Van Corlear, who gave the whole history of the campaign with matchless accuracy; saving that he took the credit of fighting the whole battle himself, and especially of vanishing the stout Risingh, which he considered himself as clearly entitled to, seeing that it was effected by his own stone pottle. The schoolmasters throughout the town gave holy-day to their little urchins, who followed in droves after the drums, with paper caps on their heads, and sticks in their breeches, thus taking the first lesson in the art of war. As to the sturdy rabble, they thronged at the heels of Peter

---

1. This castle, though very much altered and modernized, is still in being, and stands at the comer of Pearl-street, facing Coenties' slip.

Stuyvesant wherever he went, waving their greasy hats in the air, and shouting "Hard-koppig Piet forever!"

It was, indeed, a day of roaring rout and jubilee. A huge dinner was prepared at the *Stadt*-house in honour of the conquerors, where were assembled, in one glorious constellation, the great and the little luminaries of New-Amsterdam. There were the lordly Schout and his obsequious deputy—the *burgomasters* with their officious *schepens* at their elbows—the subaltern officers at the elbows of the *schepens*, and so on to the lowest hanger-on of police; every Tag having his Rag at his side, to finish his pipe, drink off his heel-taps, and laugh at his flights of immortal dullness. In short—for a city feast is a city feast all the world over, and has been a city feast ever since the creation—the dinner went off much the same as do our great corporation junketings and fourth of July banquets. Loads of fish, flesh, and fowl were devoured, oceans of liquor drunk, thousands of pipes smoked, and many a dull joke honoured with much obstreperous fat-sided laughter.

I must not omit to mention, that to this far-famed victory Peter Stuyvesant was indebted to another of his many titles—for so hugely delighted were the honest *burghers* with his achievements, that they unanimously honoured him with the name of *Pietre de Groodt*, that is to say, Peter the Great, or, as it was translated by the people of New-Amsterdam, *Piet de Pig*—an appellation which he maintained even unto the day of his death.

Book 7

Containing The Third Part of the Reign of Peter the Headstrong—His Troubles with the British Nation, and the Decline and fall of the Dutch Dynasty.

Chapter 1

How Peter Stuyvesant relieved the sovereign people from the burthen of taking care of the nation—with sundry particulars of his conduct in time of peace.

The history of the reign of Peter Stuyvesant furnishes a melancholy picture of the incessant cares and vexations inseparable from government; and may serve as a solemn warning to all who are ambitious of attaining the seat of power. Though crowned with victory, enriched by conquest, and returning in triumph to his metropolis, his exultation was checked by beholding the sad abuses that had taken place during the short interval of his absence.

The populace, unfortunately for their own comfort, had taken a deep draught of the intoxicating cup of power, during the reign of William the Testy; and though upon the accession of Peter Stuyvesant, they, felt, with a certain instinctive perception, which mobs as well as cattle possess, that the reins of government had passed into stronger hands, yet could they not help fretting and chafing and champing upon the bit, in restive silence.

It seems, by some strange and inscrutable fatality, to be the destiny of most countries, (and more especially of your enlightened republics,) always to be governed by the most incompetent man in the nation—so that you will scarcely find an individual, throughout the whole community, who cannot point out innumerable errors in administration, and convince you, in the end, that had he been at the head of affairs, matters would have gone on a thousand times more prosperously. Strange! that government, which seems to be so generally understood, should invariably be so erroneously administered—estrange, that the talent of legislation, so prodigally bestowed, should be denied to the only man in the nation to whose station it is requisite!

Thus it was in the present instance; not a man of all the herd of pseudo politicians in New-Amsterdam, but was an oracle on topics of state, and could have directed public affairs incomparably better than Peter Stuyvesant But so severe was the old governor, in his disposition, that he would never suffer one of the multitude of able counsellors by whom he was surrounded, to intrude his advice, and save the country from destruction.

Scarcely, therefore, had he departed on his expedition against the Swedes, than the old factions of William Kieft's reign began to thrust their heads above water, and to gather together in political meetings, to discuss "the state of the nation." At these assemblages, the busy *burgomasters* and their officious *schepens* made a very considerable figure. These worthy dignitaries were no longer the fat, well-fed, tranquil magistrates that presided in the peaceful days of Wouter Van Twiller—on the contrary, being elected by the people, they formed in a manner a sturdy bulwark between the mob and the administration. They were great candidates for popularity, and strenuous advocates for the rights of the rabble; resembling in disinterested zeal the wide-mouthed tribunes of ancient Rome, or those virtuous patriots of modern days, emphatically denominated "the friends of the people."

Under the tuition of these profound politicians, it is astonishing how suddenly enlightened the swinish multitude became, in matters above their comprehension. Cobblers, tinkers, and tailors, all at once felt themselves inspired, like those religious idiots, in the glorious times of monkish illumination; and, without any previous study or experience, became instantly capable of directing all the movements of government.

Nor must I neglect to mention a number of superannuated, wrong-headed old *burghers*, who had come over, when boys, in the crew of the *Goede Vrauw*, and were held up as infallible oracles by the enlightened mob. To suppose that a man who had helped to discover a country, did not know how it ought to be governed, was preposterous in the extreme. It would have been deemed as much a heresy, as at the present day to question the political talents and universal infallibility of our old "heroes of '76"— and to doubt that he who had fought for a government, however stupid he might naturally be, was not competent to fill any station under it

But as Peter Stuyvesant had a singular inclination to govern his province without the assistance of his subjects, he felt highly incensed on his return to find the factious appearance they had assumed during his absence. His first measure, therefore, was to restore perfect order, by prostrating the dignity of the sovereign people.

He accordingly watched his opportunity, and one evening, when the enlightened mob was gathered together, listening to a patriotic speech from an inspired cobbler, the intrepid Peter all at once appeared among them, with a countenance sufficient to petrify a mill-stone. The whole meeting was thrown into consternation—the orator seemed to have received a paralytic stroke in the very middle of a sublime sentence, and stood aghast with open mouth, and trembling knees, while the words horror! tyranny! liberty! rights! taxes! death! destruction! and a deluge of other patriotic phrases, came roaring from his throat, before he had power to close his lips.

The shrewd Peter took no notice of the skulking throng around him, but advancing to the brawling bully-ruffian, and drawing out a huge silver watch which might have served in times of yore as a town clock, and which is still retained by his descendants as a family curiosity, requested the orator to mend it, and set it going. The orator humbly confessed it was utterly out of his power, as he was unacquainted with the nature of its construction.

"Nay, but," said Peter, "try your ingenuity, man; you see all the springs and wheels, and how easily the clumsiest hand may stop it, and pull it to pieces; and why should it not be equally easy to regulate as to stop it?"

The orator declared that his trade was wholly different—that he was a poor cobbler, and had never meddled with a watch in his life—that there were men skilled in the art, whose business it was to attend to those matters, but for his part, he should only mar the workmanship, and put the whole in confusion.

"Why harkee, master of mine," cried Peter, turning suddenly upon him, with a countenance that almost petrified the patcher of shoes into a perfect lapstone—"dost thou pretend to meddle with the movements of government—to regulate, and correct, and patch, and cobble a complicated machine, the principles of which are above thy comprehension, and its simplest operations too subtle for thy understanding; when thou canst not correct a trifling error in a common piece of mechanism, the whole mystery of which is open to thy inspection?—Hence with thee to the leather and stone, which are emblems of thy head; cobble thy shoes, and confine thyself to the vocation for which Heaven has fitted thee—But," elevating his voice until it made the welkin ring, "if ever I catch thee, or any of thy tribe, meddling again with affairs of government, by St Nicholas, but I'll have every mother's bastard of ye flay'd alive, and your hides stretched for drum-heads, that ye may thenceforth make a noise to some purpose!"

This threat, and the tremendous voice in which it was uttered, caused the whole multitude to quake with fear. The hair of the orator arose on his head like his own swine's bristles, and not a knight of the thimble present but his heart died within him, and he felt as though he could have verily escaped through the eye of a needle.

But though this measure produced the desired effect in reducing the community to order, yet it tended to injure the popularity of the great Peter among the enlightened vulgar. Many accused him of entertaining highly aristocratic sentiments, and of lining too much in favour of the patricians. Indeed, there appeared to be some ground for such an accusation, as he always carried himself with a very lofty, soldier-like port, and was somewhat particular in his dress; dressing himself, when not in uniform, in simple, but rich apparel, and was especially noted for having his sound leg (which was a very comely one) always arrayed in a red stocking, and high-heeled shoe. Though a man of great simplicity of manners, yet there was something about him that repelled rude familiarity, while it encouraged frank, and even social intercourse.

He likewise observed some appearance of court ceremony and etiquette. He received the common class of visitors on the *stoop*[1] before his door, according to the custom of our Dutch ancestors. But when visitors were formally received in his parlour, it was expected they would appear in clean linen; by no means to be bare-footed, and always to take their hats off. On public occasions, he appeared with great pomp of equipage, (for, in

---

1. Properly spelled *stoeb*— the porch commonly built in front of Dutch houses, with benches on each side.

truth, his station required a little show and dignity,) and always rode to church in a yellow wagon with flaming red wheels.

These symptoms of state and ceremony occasioned considerable discontent among the vulgar. They had been accustomed to find easy access to their former governors, and in particular had lived on terms of extreme familiarity with William the Testy. They therefore were very impatient of these dignified precautions, which discouraged intrusion. But Peter Stuyvesant had his own way of thinking in these matters, and was a staunch upholder of the dignity of office.

He always maintained that government to be the least popular which is most open to popular access and control; and that the very brawlers against court ceremony, and the reserve of men in power, would soon despise rulers among whom they found even themselves to be of consequence. Such, at least, had been the case with the administration of William the Testy; who, bent on making himself popular, had listened to every man's advice, suffered everybody to have admittance to his person at all hours, and, in a word, treated every one as his thorough equal.

By this means, every scrub politician, and public busy body, was enabled to measure wits with him, and to find out the true dimensions, not only of his person, but his mind—And what great man can stand such scrutiny?—It is the mystery that envelops great men that gives (hem half their greatness. We are always inclined to think highly of those who hold themselves aloof from our examination. There is likewise a kind of superstitious reverence for office, which leads us to exaggerate the merits and abilities of men in power, and to suppose that they must be constituted different from other men.

And, indeed, faith is as necessary in politics as in religion. It certainly is of the first importance, that a country should be governed by wise men; but when it is almost equally important, that the people should believe than to be wise; for this belief alone can produce willing subordination.

To keep up, therefore, this desirable confidence in rulers, the people should be allowed to see as little of them as possible. He who gains access to cabinets soon finds out by what foolishness the world is governed. He discovers that there is quackery in legislation, as well as in everything else; that many a measure, which is supposed by the million to be the result of great wisdom and deep deliberation, is the effect of mere chance, or, perhaps, of harebrained experiment—that rulers have their whims and errors as well as other men, and after all are not so wonderfully superior to their fellow-creatures as he at first imagined; since he finds that even his own opinions have had some weight with them.

Thus awe subsides into confidence, confidence inspires familiarity, and familiarity produces contempt Peter Stuyvesant, on the contrary, by conducting himself with dignity and loftiness, was looked up to with great reverence. As he never gave his reasons for any thing he did, the public always gave him credit for very profound ones—every movement, however intrinsically unimportant, was a matter of speculation, and his very red stockings excited some respect, as being different from the stockings of other men.

To these times may we refer the rise of family pride and aristocratic distinctions;[2] and indeed, I cannot but look back with reverence to the early planting of those mighty Dutch families, which have taken such vigorous root, and branched out so luxuriantly in our state. The blood which has flowed down uncontaminated through a succession of steady, virtuous generations since the times of the patriarchs of Communipaw, must certainly be pure and worthy. And if so, then are the Van Rensselaers, the Van Zandts, the Van Homes, the Rutgers, the Bensons, the Brinkerhoffs, the Schermehornes, and all the true descendants of the ancient Pavonians, the only legitimate nobility and real lords of the soil.

I have been led to mention thus particularly the well-authenticated claims of our genuine Dutch families, because I have

2. In a work published many years alter the time here treated of, (in 1701, by C. W. A. M.) it is mentioned that Frederick Philipse was counted the richest *Mynher* in New-York, and was said to have *whole hogsheads of Indian money or wampum*, and had a son and daughter, who, according to the Dutch custom, should divide it equally.

noticed with great sorrow and vexation, that they have been somewhat elbowed aside in latter days by foreign intruders. It is really astonishing to behold how many great families have sprung up of late years, who pride themselves excessively on the score of ancestry. Thus he who can look up to his father without humiliation assumes not a little importance—he who can safely talk of his grandfather, is still more vain-glorious—but he who can look back to his great-grandfather without blushing, is absolutely intolerable in his pretensions to family—bless us! what a piece of work is here, between these mushrooms of an hour, and these mushrooms of a day!

But from what I have recounted in the former part of this chapter, I would not have my reader imagine that the great Peter was a tyrannical governor, ruling his subjects with a rod of iron—on the contrary, where the dignity of authority was not implicated, he abounded with generosity and courteous condescension. In fact, he really believed, though I fear my more enlightened republican readers will consider it a proof of his ignorance and illiberality, that in preventing the cup of social life from being dashed with the intoxicating ingredient of politics, he promoted the tranquillity and happiness of the people—and by detaching their minds from subjects which they could not understand, and which only tended to inflame their passions, he enabled them to attend more faithfully and industriously to their proper callings; becoming more useful citizens, and more attentive to their families and fortunes.

So far from having any unreasonable austerity, he delighted to see the poor and the labouring man rejoice, and for this purpose was a great promoter of holydays and public amusements. Under his reign was first introduced the custom of cracking eggs at Paas, or Easter. New-year's day was also observed with extravagant festivity, and ushered in by the ringing of bells and firing of guns. Every house was a temple to the jolly god—oceans of cherry brandy, true Hollands, and mulled cider, were set afloat on the occasion; and not a poor man in town, but made it a point to get drunk, out of a principle of pure economy—taking in liquor enough to serve him for half a year afterwards.

It would have done one's heart good, also, to have seen the valiant Peter, seated among the old *burghers* and their wives of a Saturday afternoon, under the great trees that spread their shade over the battery, watching the young men and women, as they danced on the green. Here he would smoke his pipe, crack his joke, and forget the rugged toils of war in the sweet oblivious festivities of peace. He would occasionally give a nod of approbation to those of the young men who shuffled and lacked most vigorously, and now. and then give a hearty smack, in all honesty of soul, to the buxom lass that held out longest, and tired down all her competitors, which he considered as infallible proofs of her being the best dancer.

Once, it is true, the harmony of the meeting was rather interrupted. A young *vrouw*, of great figure in the gay worlds and who, having lately come from Holland, of course led the fashions, in the city, made her appearance in not more than half-a-dozen petticoats, and these too of most alarming shortness An universal whisper ran through the assembly, the old ladies all felt shocked in the extreme, the young ladies blushed, and felt excessively for the "poor thing," and even the governor himself was observed to be a little troubled in mind. To complete the astonishment of the good folks, she undertook, in the course of a jig, to describe some astonishing figures in algebra, which she had learned from a dancing-master at Rotterdam.

Whether she was too animated in flourishing her feet, or whether some vagabond zephyr took the liberty of obtruding his services, certain it is that in the course of a grand evolution, which would not have disgraced a modern ball-room, she made a most unexpected display—whereat the whole assembly was thrown into great admiration, several grave country members were not a little moved, and the good Peter himself, who was a man of unparalleled modesty, felt himself grievously scandalized.

The shortness of the female dresses, which had continued in fashion ever since the days of William Kieft, had long offended his eye, and though extremely averse to meddling with the petticoats of the ladies, yet he immediately recommended that every one should be furnished with a flounce to the bottom. He likewise ordered that the ladies, and indeed the gentlemen, should use no other step in dancing, than shuffle-and-turn, and double-trouble; and forbade, under pain of his high displeasure, any young lady thenceforth to attempt what was termed "exhibiting the graces."

These were the only restrictions he ever imposed upon the sex, and these were considered by them as tyrannical oppressions, and resisted with that becoming spirit, always manifested by the gentle sex, whenever their privileges are invaded.—In fact, Peter Stuyvesant plainly perceived, that if he attempted to push the matter any further, there was danger of their leaving off petticoats altogether; so like a wise man, experienced in the ways of women, he held his peace, and suffered them ever after to wear their petticoats and cut their capers as high as they pleased.

CHAPTER 2

HORN PETER STUYVESANT WAS MUCH MOLESTED BY THE MOSSTROOPERS OF THE EAST, AND THE GIANTS OF MERRYLAND—AND HOW A DARK AND HORRID CONSPIRACY WAS CARRIED ON IN THE BRITISH CABINET AGAINST THE PROSPERITY OF THE MANHATTOES,

We are now approaching towards the crisis of our work, and if I be not mistaken in my forebodings, we shall have a world of business to despatch in the ensuing chapters.

It is with some communities, as it is with certain meddlesome individuals, they have a wonderful facility at getting into scrapes; and I have always remarked, that those are most liable to get in, who have the least talent at getting out again. This is, doubtless, owing to the excessive valour of those states; for I have likewise noticed that this rampant and ungovernable quality is always most unruly where most confined; which accounts for its vapouring so amazingly in little states, little men, and ugly little women especially.

Thus, when one reflects, that the province of the Manhattoes, though of prodigious importance in the eyes of its inhabitants and its historian, was really of no very great consequence in the eyes of the rest of the world; that it had but little wealth or other spoils to reward the trouble of assailing it, and that it had nothing to expect from running wantonly into war, save an exceeding good beating—On pondering these things, I say, one would utterly despair of finding in its history either battles or bloodshed, or any other of those calamities which give importance to a nation, and entertainment to the reader.

But, on the contrary, we find, so valiant is this province, that it has already drawn upon itself a host of enemies; has had as many buffetings as would gratify the ambition of the most warlike nation; and is, in sober sadness, a very forlorn, distressed, and woebegone little province!—all which was, no doubt, kindly ordered by Providence, to give interest and sublimity to this pathetic history.

But I forbear to enter into a detail of the pitiful maraudings and harassments, that, for a long while after its victory on the Delaware, continued to insult the dignity, and disturb the repose, of the Nederlanders. Suffice it in brevity to say that the implacable hostility of the people of the east, which had so miraculously been prevented from breaking out, as my readers must remember, by the sudden prevalence of witchcraft, and the dissensions in the council of Amphyctions, now again displayed itself in a thousand grievous and bitter scourings upon the borders.

Scarcely a month passed but what the Dutch settlements on the frontiers were alarmed by the sudden appearance of an invading army from Connecticut. This would advance resolutely through the country, like a *puissant* caravan of the deserts, the women and children mounted in carts loaded with pots and kettles, as though they meant to boil the honest Dutchmen alive, and devour them like so many lobsters.

At the tails of these carts would stalk a crew of long-limbed, lank-sided varlets, with axes on their shoulders and packs on their backs, resolutely bent upon improving the country in despite of its proprietors. These, settling themselves down, would in a short time completely dislodge the unfortunate Nederlanders; elbowing them out of those rich bottoms and fertile valleys, in which our Dutch yeomanry are so famous for nestling themselves. For it is notorious, that wherever these shrewd men of the east get a footing, the honest Dutchmen do gradually disappear, retiring slowly, like the Indians before the whites; being totally discomfited by the talking, chaffering, swapping, bargaining disposition of their new neighbours.

All these audacious infringements on the territories of their High Mightinesses were accompanied, as has before been hinted, by a world of rascally brawls, ribroastings, and bundlings, which would doubtless have incensed the valiant Peter to wreak immediate chastisement, had he not at the very same time been perplexed by distressing accounts from Mynheer Beckman, who commanded the territories at South River.

The restless Swedes, who had so graciously been suffered to remain about the Delaware, already began to show signs of mutiny and disaffection. But what was worse, a peremptory claim was laid to the whole territory, as the rightful property of Lord Baltimore, by Fendal, a chieftain who ruled over the colony of Maryland, or Merry-land, as it was anciently called, because that the inhabitants, not having the fear of the Lord before their eyes; were notoriously prone to get fuddled, and make merry with mint-julep and apple-toddy.

Nay, so hostile was this bully Fendal, that he threatened, unless his claim was instantly complied with, to march incontinently at the head of a potent force of the roaring boys of Merry-land, together with a great and mighty train of giants, who infested the banks of the Susquehanna[1]—and to lay waste and depopu-

1. We find very curious and wonderful accounts of these strange people (who were doubtless the ancestors of the present Marylanders) made by Master Hariot, in his interesting history. "The Susquesahanocks," observes he, "are a giantly people strange in proportion, behaviour, and attire—their voice sounding from them as if out of a cave. Their tobacco-pipes were three quarters of a yard long, carved at the great end with a bird, beare, or other device, sufficient to beat (cont. next page.)

late the whole country of South River.

By this it is manifest, that this boasted colony, like all great acquisitions of territory, soon became a greater evil to the conqueror than the loss if it was to the conquered; and caused greater uneasiness and trouble than all the territory of the New-Netherlands besides. Thus Providence wisely orders that one evil shall balance another. The conqueror who wrests the property of his neighbour, who wrongs a nation and desolates a country, though he may acquire increase of empire and immortal fame, yet insures his own inevitable punishment He takes to himself a cause of endless anxiety—he incorporates with his late sound domain a loose part—a rotten disaffected member; which is an exhaustless source of internal treason and disunion, and external altercation and hostility.

Happy is that nation, which, compact, united, loyal in all its parts, and concentrated in its strength, seeks no idle acquisition of unprofitable and ungovernable territory—which, content to be prosperous and happy, has no ambition to be great It is like a man well organized in his system, sound in health, and full of vigour; unencumbered by useless trappings, and fixed in an unshaken attitude. But the nation, insatiable of territory, whose domains are scattered, feebly united and weakly organized, is like a senseless miser sprawling among golden stores, open to every attack, and unable to defend the riches he vainly endeavours to overshadow.

At the time of receiving the alarming despatches from South river, the great Peter was busily employed in quelling certain Indian troubles that had broken out about Esopus, and was moreover meditating bow to relieve his eastern borders on the Connecticut. He, however, sent word to Mynheer Beckman to be of good heart, to maintain incessant vigilance, and to let him know if matters wore a more threatening appearance; in which case he would incontinently repair with his warriors of the Hudson,

out the braines of a horse, (and how many asses braines are beaten out, or rather men's braines smoked out, and asses braines haled in, by our lesser pipes at home.) The calfe of one of their legges measured three quarters of a yard about, the rest of his limbs proportionable."—*Master Hariot's Journ. Purch. Pil.*

to spoil the merriment of these Merry-landers; for he coveted exceedingly to have a bout, hand to hand, with some half a score of these giants—Slaving never encountered a giant in his whole life, unless we may so call the stout Risingh, and he was but a little one.

Nothing farther, however, occurred to molest the tranquillity of Mynheer Beckman and his colony. Fendal and his myrmidons remained at home, carousing it soundly upon hoe-cakes, bacon, and mint-*julep*, and running horses, and fighting cocks, for which they were greatly renowned.—At hearing of this, Peter Stuyvesant was very well pleased, for notwithstanding his inclination to measure weapons with these monstrous men of the Susquehanna, yet he had already as much employment nearer home as he could turn his hands to. Little did he think, worthy soul, that this southern calm was but the deceitful prelude to a most terrible and fatal storm, then brewings which was soon to burst forth and overwhelm the unsuspecting city of New-Amsterdam!

Now so it was, that while this excellent governor was giving his little senate laws, and not only giving them, but enforcing them too—while he was incessantly travelling the rounds of his beloved province—posting from place to place to redress grievances, and while busy at one corner of his dominions, all the rest getting into an uproar—at this very time, I say, a dark and direful plot was hatching against him, in that nursery of monstrous projects, the British cabinet The news of his achievements on the Delaware, according to a sage old historian of New-Amsterdam, had occasioned not a little talk and marvel in the courts of Europe. And the same profound writer assures us, that the cabinet of England began to entertain great jealousy and uneasiness at the increasing power of the Manhattoes, and the valour of its sturdy yeomanry.

Agents, the same historian observes, were sent by the Amphyctionic council of the east to entreat the assistance of the British cabinet in subjugating this mighty province. Lord Sterling also asserted his right to Long Island, and, at the same time.

Lord Baltimore, whose agent, as has before been mentioned, had so alarmed Mynheer Beckman, laid his claim before the cabinet to the lands of South River, which he complained were unjustly and forcibly detained from him, by these daring usurpers of the New-Nederlandts.

Thus did the unlucky empire of the Manhattoes stand in imminent danger of experiencing the fate of Poland, and being torn limb from limb to be shared among its savage neighbours. But while these rapacious powers were whetting their fangs, and waiting for the signal to fall tooth and nail upon this delicious little fat Dutch empire, the lordly lion, who sat as umpire, all at once settled the claims of all parties, by laying his own paw upon the spoil. For we are told, that His Majesty, Charles the Second, not to be perplexed by adjusting these several pretensions, made a present of a large tract of North America, including the province of New-Netherlands, to his brother, the Duke of York—a donation truly royal, since none but great monarchs have a right to give away what does not belong to them.

That this munificent gift might not be merely nominal, His Majesty, on the 12th of March, 1664, ordered that an armament should be forthwith prepared, to invade the city of New-Amsterdam by land and water, and put his brother in complete possession of the premises.

Thus critically are situated the affairs of the New-Netherlanders. The honest *burghers*, so far from thinking of the jeopardy in which their interests are placed, are soberly smoking their pipes, and thinking of nothing at all—the privy counsellors of the province are at this moment snoring in full quorum, while the active Peter, who takes all the labour of thinking and acting upon himself is busily devising some method of bringing the grand council of Amphyctions to terms. In the meanwhile, an angry cloud is darkly scowling on the horizon—soon shall it rattle about the ears of these dozing Nederlanders and put the mettle of their stout-hearted governor completely to the trial.

But come what may, I here pledge my veracity that in all warlike conflicts and subtle perplexities, he shall still acquit himself with the gallant bearing and spotless honour of a noble-minded obstinate old cavalier.—Forward then to the charge!—shine out, propitious stars, on the renowned city of the Manhattoes; and may the blessing of St Nicholas go with thee—honest Peter Stuyvesant!

Chapter 3
Of Peter Stuyvesan's expedition into the East Country, showing that though an old bird he did not understand trap.

Great nations resemble great men in this particular, that their greatness is seldom known until they get in trouble; adversity, therefore, has been wisely denominated the ordeal of true greatness, which, like gold, can never receive its real estimation, until it has passed through the furnace. In proportion, therefore, as a nation, a community, or an individual (possessing the inherent quality of greatness) is involved in perils and misfortunes, in proportion does it rise in grandeur—and even when sinking under calamity, makes, like a house on fire, a more glorious display than ever it did in the fairest period of its prosperity.

The vast empire of China, though teeming with population and imbibing and concentrating the wealth of nations, has vegetated through a succession of drowsy ages; and were it not for its internal revolution, and the subversion of its ancient government by the Tartars, might have presented nothing but an uninteresting detail of dull, monotonous prosperity. Pompeii and Herculaneum might have passed into oblivion, with a herd of their contemporaries, if they had not been fortunately overwhelmed by a volcano.

The renowned city of Troy has acquired celebrity only from its ten years' distress, and final conflagration—Paris rises in importance by the plots and massacres which have ended in the exaltation of the illustrious Napoleon—and even the mighty London itself has skulked through the records of time, celebrated for nothing of moment, excepting the plague, the great fire, and Guy Faux's gunpowder plot!—Thus cities and empires seem to creep along, enlarging in silent obscurity under the pen of the historian, until at length they burst forth in some tremendous calamity—and snatch, as it were, immortality from the explosion!

The above principle being admitted, my reader will plainly perceive that the city of New-Amsterdam, and its dependent province are on the high road to greatness. Dangers and hostilities threaten from every side, and it is really a matter of astonishment to me, how so small a state has been able, in so short a time, to entangle itself in so many difficulties. Ever since the province was first taken by the nose, at the Fort of Good Hope in the tranquil days of Wouter Van Twiller, has it been gradually increasing in historic importance; and never could it have had a more appropriate chieftain to conduct it to the pinnacle of grandeur, than Peter Stuyvesant.

In the fiery heart of this iron-headed old warrior sat enthroned all those five kinds of courage described by Aristotle, and had the philosopher mentioned five hundred more to the back of them, I verily believe he would have been found master of them all. The only misfortune was, that he was deficient in the better part of valour called discretion, a cold- blooded virtue which could not exist in the tropical climate of his mighty soul. Hence it was, he was continually hurrying into those unheard-of enterprises, that give an air of chivalric romance to all his history, and hence it was that he now conceived a project worthy of the hero of La Mancha himself.

This was no other than to repair in person to the great council of the Amphyctions, bearing the sword in one hand, and the olive-branch in the other—to require immediate reparation for the innumerable violations of that treaty which in an evil hour he had formed—to put a stop to those repeated maraudings on the eastern borders—or else to throw his gauntlet and appeal to arms for satisfaction.

On declaring this resolution in his privy council, the venerable members were seized with vast astonishment; for once in their lives they ventured to remonstrate, setting forth the rashness of exposing his sacred person in the midst of a strange and barbarous people, with sundry other weighty remonstrances—all which had about as much influence upon the determination of the headstrong Peter, as though you were to endeavour to turn a rusty weathercock with a broken-winded bellows.

Summoning, therefore, to his presence, his trusty follower, Antony Van Corlear, he commanded him to hold himself in readiness to accompany him, the following morning, on this his hazardous enterprise. Now Antony the trumpeter was a little stricken in years, yet by dint of keeping up a good heart, and having never known care or sorrow, (having never been married,) he was still a hearty, jocund, rubicund, gamesome wag, and of great capacity in the doublet This last was ascribed to his living a jolly life on those domains at the Hook, which Peter Stuyvesant had granted to him for his gallantry at Fort Casimir.

Be this as it may, there was nothing that more delighted Antony than this command of the great Peter, for he could have followed the stout-hearted old governor to the world's end with love and loyalty—and he moreover still remembered the frolicking, and dancing, and bundling, and other disports of the east country, and entertained dainty recollection of numerous kind and buxom lasses, whom he longed exceedingly again to encounter.

Thus then did this mirror of hardihood set forth, with no other attendant but his trumpeter, upon one of the most perilous enterprises ever recorded in the annals of knight-errantry. For a single warrior to venture openly among a whole nation of foes; but, above all, for a plain downright Dutchman to think of negotiating with the whole council of New-England—never was there known a more desperate undertaking!—Ever since I have entered upon the chronicles of this peerless but hitherto uncelebrated chieftain, has he kept me in a state of incessant action and anxiety with the toils and dangers he is constantly encountering—Oh! for a chapter of the tranquil reign of Wouter Van Twiller, that I might repose on it as on a feather bed!

Is it not enough, Peter Stuyvesant, that I have once already rescued thee from the machinations of these terrible Amphyctions, by bringing the whole powers of witchcraft to thine aid?—Is it not enough, that I have followed thee undaunted, like a guardian spirit, into the midst of the horrid battle of Fort Christina?—That I have been put incessantly to my trumps to keep thee safe and sound—now warding off with my single pen the shower of dastard blows that fell upon thy rear—now narrowly shielding thee from a deadly thrust, by a mere tobacco-box—now casing thy dauntless skull with adamant, when even thy stubborn ram-beaver failed to resist the sword of the stout Risingh—and now, not merely bringing thee off alive, but triumphant, from the clutches of the gigantic Swede, by the desperate means of a paltry stone pottle?—Is not all this enough, but must thou still be plunging into new difficulties, and jeopardizing in headlong enterprises, thyself, thy trumpeter, and thy historian?

And now the ruddy-faced Aurora, like a buxom chambermaid, draws aside the sable curtains of the night, and out bounces from his bed the jolly red-haired Phoebus, startled at being caught so late in the embraces of Dame Thetis. With many a sable oath, he harnesses his brazen-footed steeds, and whips and lashes, and splashes up the firmament, like a loitering postboy, half an hour behind his time. And now behold that imp of fame and prowess, the headstrong Peter, bestriding a raw-boned, switch-tailed charger, gallantly arrayed in full regimentals, and bracing on his thigh that trusty brass-hilted sword, which had wrought such fearful deeds on the banks of the Delaware.

Behold, hard after him, his doughty trumpeter Van Corlear, mounted on a broken-winded, wall-eyed, calico mare; his stone pottle, which had laid low the mighty Risingh, slung under his arm, and his trumpet, displayed vauntingly in his right hand, decorated with a gorgeous banner, on which is emblazoned the great beaver of the Manhattoes. See them proudly issuing out of the city gate like an iron-clad hero of yore, with his faithful 'squire at his heels, the populace following them with their eyes, and shouting many a parting wish and hearty cheering—Farewell, Hardkoppig Piet! Farewell, honest Antony!—Pleasant be your wayfaring—prosperous your return! The stoutest hero that ever drew a sword, and the worthiest trumpeter that ever trod shoe-leather!

Legends are lamentably silent about the events that befell our adventurers in this their adventurous travel, excepting the Stuyvesant manuscript, which gives the substance of a pleasant little heroic poem, written on the occasion by Domini Ægidius Luyck,[1] who appears to have been the poet laureate of New-Amsterdam, This inestimable manuscript assures us, that it was a rare spectacle to behold the great Peter and his loyal follower, hailing the morning sun, and rejoicing in the clear countenance of nature, as they pranced it through the pastoral scenes of Bloemen Dael;[2] which in those days was a sweet and rural valley, beautified with many a bright wild flower, refreshed by many a pure streamlet, and enlivened here and there by a delectable little Dutch cottage, sheltered under some sloping hill, and almost buried in embowering trees.

Now did they enter upon the confines of Connecticut, where they encountered many grievous difficulties and perils. At one place they were assailed by a troop of country 'squires and militia colonels, who, mounted on goodly steeds, hung upon their rear for several miles, harassing them exceedingly with guesses and questions, more especially the worthy Peter, whose silver-chased leg excited not a little marvel.

At another place, hard by the renowned town of Stamford, they were set upon by a great and mighty legion of church deacons, who imperiously demanded of them five shillings, for travelling on Sunday, and threatened to carry them captive to a neighbouring church, whose steeple peered above the trees; but these the valiant Peter put to rout with little difficulty, insomuch that they bestrode their canes and galloped off in horrible confusion, leaving their cocked hats behind in the hurry of their flight But not so easily did he escape from the hands of

1. This Luyck was, moreover, rector of the Latin School in Nieuw-Nederlandt, 1663. There are two pieces addressed to Ægidius Luyck, in D. Selyn's MSS. of poesies, upon his marriage with Judith Isendoorn. Old MS.
2. Now called Blooming Dale, about four miles from New-York.

a crafty man of Piquag; who, with undaunted perseverance, and repeated onsets, fairly bargained him out of his goodly switch-tailed charger, leaving in place thereof a villainous foundered Narraganset pacer.

But, maugre all these hardships, they pursued their journey cheerily along the course of the soft flowing Connecticut, whose gentle wave, says the song, roll through many a fertile vale and sunny plain; now reflecting the lofty spires of the bustling city, and now the rural beauties of the humble hamlet; now echoing with the busy hum of commerce, and now with the cheerful song of the peasant.

At every town would Peter Stuyvesant, who was, noted for warlike punctilio, order the sturdy Antony to sound a courteous salutation; though the manuscript observes, that the inhabitants were thrown into great dismay when they heard of his approach. For the fame of his incomparable achievements on the Delaware had spread throughout the east country and they dreaded lest he had come to take vengeance on their manifold transgressions.

But the good Peter rode through these towns with a smiling aspect; waving his hand with inexpressible majesty and conde-scension; for he verily believed that the old clothes which these ingenious people had thrust into their broken windows, and the festoons of dried apples and peaches which ornamented the fronts of their houses, were so many decorations in honour of his approach; as it was the custom, in the days of chivalry, to compliment renowned heroes, by sumptuous displays of tapes-try and gorgeous furniture.

The women crowded to the doors to gaze upon him as he passed, so much does prowess in arms delight the gentle sex. The little children too, ran after him. in troops, staring with wonder at his regimentals, his brimstone breeches, and the silver garniture of his wooden leg. Nor must I omit to mention the joy which many strapping wenches betrayed at beholding the jovial Van Corlear, who had whilom delighted them so much with his trumpet, when he bore the great Peter's challenge to the Amphyctions.

The kind-hearted Antony alighted from his calico mare, and kissed them all with, infinite loving kindness—and was right pleased to see a crew of little trumpeters crowding around him for his blessing; each of whom he patted on the head, bade him be a good boy, and gave him a penny to buy molasses candy.

The Stuyvesant manuscript makes but little farther mention of the governor's adventures upon this expedition, excepting that he was received with extravagant courtesy and respect by the great council of the Amphyctions, who almost talked him to death with complimentary and congratulatory harangues. I will not detain my readers by dwelling on his negotiations with the grand council.

Suffice it to mention, it was like all other negotiations—a great deal was said, and very little done: one conversation led to another—one conference begat misunderstandings which it took a dozen conferences to explain; at the end of which, the parties found themselves just where they were at first; excepting that they had entangled themselves in a host of questions of etiquette, and conceived a cordial distrust of each other, that rendered their future negotiations ten times more difficult than ever.[3]

In the midst of all these perplexities, which bewildered the brain and incensed the ire of the sturdy Peter, who was perhaps of all men in the world, least fitted for diplomatic wiles, he privately received the first intimation of the dark conspiracy which had been matured in the Cabinet of England. To this was added the astounding intelligence that a hostile squadron had already sailed from England, destined to reduce the province of New-Netherlands, and that the grand council of Amphyctions had engaged to co-operate, by sending a great army to invade New-Amsterdam by land.

Unfortunate Peter! did I not enter with sad foreboding upon this, ill-starred expedition? did I not tremble when I saw thee,

---

3. For certain of the particulars of this ancient negotiation, see Haz. Col. State Papers. It is singular that Smith is entirely silent with respect to this memorable expedition of Peter Stuyvesant.

with no other counsellor but thine own head, with no other armour but an honest tongue, a spotless conscience, and a rusty sword! with no other protector but St. Nicholas—and no other attendant but a trumpeter—did I not tremble when I beheld thee thus sally forth to contend with all the knowing powers of New-England?

Oh, how did the sturdy old warrior rage and roar, when he found himself thus entrapped, like a lion in the hunter's toil! Now did he determine to draw his trusty sword, and manfully to fight his way through all the countries of the east Now did he resolve to break in upon the council of the Amphyctions, and put every mother's son of them to death. At length, as his direful wrath subsided, he resorted to safer though less glorious expedients.

Concealing from the council his knowledge of their machinations, he privately despatched a trusty messenger, with missives to his counsellors at New-Amsterdam, apprising them of the impending danger, commanding them immediately to put the city in a posture of defence, while in the meantime he would endeavour to elude his enemies and come to their assistance. This done, he felt himself marvellously relieved, rose slowly, shook himself like a rhinoceros, and issued forth from his den, in much the same manner as Giant Despair is described to have issued from Doubting Castle, in the chivalric history of the Pilgrim's Progress.

And now, much does it grieve me that I must leave the gallant Peter in this imminent jeopardy: but it behoves us to hurry back and see what is going on at New-Amsterdam, for greatly do I fear that city is already in a turmoil. Such was ever the fate of Peter Stuyvesant; while doing one thing with heart and soul, he was too apt to leave everything else at sixes and sevens. While, like a potentate of yore, he was absent, attending to those things in person, which in modern days are trusted to generals and ambassadors, his little territory at home was sore to get in an uproar—All which was owing to that uncommon strength of intellect which induced him to trust to nobody but himself, and which had acquired him the renowned appellation of Peter the Headstrong.

CHAPTER 4

HOW THE PEOPLE OF NEW-AMSTERDAM WERE THROWN INTO A GREAT PANIC, BY THE NEWS OF A THREATENED INVASION, AND THE MANNER IN WHICH THEY FORTIFIED THEMSELVES.

There is do sight more truly interesting to a philosopher, than to contemplate a community, where every individual has a voice in public affairs, where every individual thinks himself the Atlas of the nation, and where every individual thinks it his duty to bestir himself for the good of his country—I say, there is nothing more interesting to a philosopher, than to see such a community in a sudden hustle of war. Such a clamour of tongues—such a bawling of patriotism—such running hither and thither—everybody in a hurry—everybody up to the ears in trouble—everybody in the way, and everybody interrupting his industrious neighbour—who is busily employed in doing nothing!

It is like witnessing a great fire, where every man is at work like a hero—some dragging about empty engines—others scampering with full buckets, and spilling the contents into the boots of their neighbours—and others ringing the church bells all night, by way of putting out the fire. Little firemen, like sturdy little knights storming a breach, clambering up and down scaling ladders, and bawling through tin trumpets, by way of directing the attack—Here one busy fellow, in his great zeal to save the property of the unfortunate, catches up an anonymous chamber utensil, and gallants it off with an air of as much self-importance, as if he had rescued a pot of money—another throws looking-glasses and china out of the window, to save them from the flames, whilst those who can do nothing else, to assist the great calamity, run up and down the streets with open throats, keeping up an incessant cry of *Fire! Fire! Fire!*

"When the news arrived at Sinope," says the grave and profound Lucian—though I own the story is rather trite, "that

Philip was about to attack them, the inhabitants were thrown into violent alarm. Some ran to furbish up their arms; others rolled stones to build up the walls—everybody, in short, was employed, and everybody was in the way of his neighbour. Diogenes alone was the only man who could find nothing to do—whereupon, determining not to be idle when the welfare of his country was at stake, he tucked up his robe, and fell to rolling his tub with might and main up and down the Gymnasium."

In like manner ay every mother's son, in the patriotic community of New-Amsterdam on receiving the missives of Peter Stuyvesant, busy himself most mightily in putting things in contusion, and assisting the general uproar. "Every man"—saith the Stuyvesant manuscript—"flew to arms!"—by which is meant, that not one of our honest Dutch citizens would venture to church or to market, without an old-fashioned spit of a sword dangling at his side, and a long Dutch fowling-piece on his shoulder—nor would he go out of a night without a lantern; nor turn a comer without first peeping cautiously round, lest he should come unawares upon a British army—And we are informed that Stoffel Brinkerhoff, who was considered by the old women almost as brave a man as the governor himself—actually had two one-pound swivels mounted in his entry, one pointing out at the front door, and the other at the back.

But the most strenuous measure resorted to on this awful occasion, and one which has since been found of wonderful efficacy, was to assemble popular meetings. These brawling convocations, I have already shown, were extremely offensive to Peter Stuyvesant, but as this was a moment of unusual agitation, and as the old governor was not present to repress them, they broke out with intolerable violence. Hither, therefore, the orators and politicians repaired, and there seemed to be a competition among them who should bawl the loudest, and exceed the others in hyperbolical bursts of patriotism, and in resolutions to uphold and defend the government.

In these sage and all-powerful meetings, it was determined, *nem, con.* that they were the most enlightened, the most dignified, the most formidable, and the most ancient community upon the face of the earth. Finding that this resolution was so universally and readily carried, another was immediately proposed—whether it were not possible and politic to exterminate Great Britain? upon which sixty-nine members spoke most eloquently in the affirmative, and only one arose to suggest some doubts—who, as a punishment for his treasonable presumption, was immediately seized by the mob, and tarred and feathered—which punishment being equivalent to the Tarpeian Rock, he was afterwards considered as an outcast from society, and his opinion went for nothing.

The question, therefore, being unanimously carried in the affirmative, it was recommended to the grand council to pass it into a law; which was accordingly done.—By this measure, the hearts of the people at large were wonderfully encouraged, and they waxed exceeding choleric and valorous. Indeed, the first paroxysm of alarm having in some measure subsided; the old women having buried all the money they could lay their hands on, and their husbands daily getting fuddled with what was left—the community began even to stand on the offensive.

Songs were manufactured in Low Dutch, and sung about the streets, wherein the English were most woefully beaten, and shown no quarter; and popular addresses were made, wherein it was proved to a certainty that the fate of Old England depended upon the will of the New-Amsterdammers.

Finally, to strike a violent blow at the very vitals of Great Britain, a multitude of the wiser inhabitants assembled, and having purchased all the British manufactures they could find, they made thereof a huge bonfire; and in the patriotic glow of the moment, every man present, who had a hat or breeches of English workmanship, pulled it off, and threw it most undauntedly into the flames—to the irreparable detriment, loss, and ruin, of the English manufacturers.

In commemoration of this great exploit, they erected a pole on the spot, with a device on the top intended to represent the province of Nieuw-Nederlandts destroying Great Britain, under the similitude of an eagle picking the little island of Old England out of the globe; but either through the unskilfulness of the sculptor, or his ill-timed waggery, it bore a striking resemblance to a goose, vainly striving to get hold of a dumpling.

CHAPTER 5
SHOWING HOW THE GRAND COUNCIL OF THE NEW-NETHERLANDS CAME TO BE MIRACULOUSLY GIFTED WITH LONG TONGUES—TOGETHER WITH A GREAT TRIUMPH OF ECONOMY.

It will need but very little penetration in any one acquainted with the character and habits of that most potent and blustering monarch, the sovereign people, to discover, that, notwithstanding all the bustle and talk of war that stunned him in the last chapter, the renowned city of New-Amsterdam is, in sad reality, not a whit better prepared for defence than before.

Now, though the people, having gotten over the first alarm, and finding no enemy immediately at hand, had, with that valour of tongue, for which your illustrious rabble is so famous, run into the opposite extreme, and by dint of gallant vapouring and *rodomontado*, had actually talked themselves into the opinion that they were the bravest and most powerful people under the sun, yet were the privy counsellors of Peter Stuyvesant somewhat dubious on that point. They dreaded moreover lest that stern hero should return, and find, that instead of obeying his peremptory orders, they had wasted their time in listening to the hectorings of the mob, than which, they well knew, there was nothing he held in more exalted contempt.

To make up, therefore, as speedily as possible, for lost time, a grand divan of the counsellors and *burgomasters* was convened, to talk over the critical state of the province, and devise measures for its safety. Two things were unanimously agreed upon in this venerable assembly:—first, that the city required to be put in a state of defence; and, secondly, that as the danger was imminent, there should be no time lost—which points being settled, they immediately fell to making long speeches, and belabouring one another in endless and intemperate disputes.

For about this time was this unhappy city first visited by that talking endemic, so universally prevalent in this country, and which so invariably evinces itself wherever a number of wise men assemble together; breaking out in long, windy speeches, caused, as physicians suppose, by the foul air which is ever generated in a crowd. Now it was, moreover, that they first introduced the ingenious method of measuring the merits of a harangue by the hour-glass; he being considered the ablest orator, who spoke longest on a question. For which excellent invention, it is recorded, we are indebted to the same profound Dutch critic who judged of books by their size.

This sudden passion for endless harangues, so little consonant with the customary gravity and taciturnity of our sage forefathers, was supposed by certain learned philosophers, to have been imbibed, together with divers other barbarous propensities, from their savage neighbours; who were peculiarly noted for their *long talks* and *council fires*—who would never undertake any affair of the least importance, without previous debates and harangues among their chiefs and *old men*.

But the real cause was, that the people, in electing their representatives to the grand council, were particular in choosing them for their talents at talking, without inquiring whether they possessed the more rare, difficult, and oft-times important talent of holding their tongues. The consequence was, that this deliberative body was composed of the most loquacious men in the community.

As they considered themselves placed there to talk, every man concluded that his duty to his constituents, and, what is more, his popularity with them, required that he should harangue on every subject, whether he understood it or not. There was an ancient mode of burying a chieftain, by every soldier throwing his shield full of earth on the corpse, until a mighty mound was formed; so, whenever a question was brought forward in this assembly, every member pressing forward to throw on his quantum of wisdom, the subject was quickly buried under a huge mass of words.

We are told, that when disciples were admitted into the school of Pythagoras, they were for two years enjoined silence, and were neither permitted to ask questions nor make remarks. After they had thus acquired the inestimable art of holding their tongues, they were gradually permitted to make inquiries, and finally to communicate their own opinions.

What a pity is it, that, while superstitiously hoarding up the rubbish and rags of antiquity, we should suffer these precious gems to lie unnoticed! What a beneficial effect would this wise regulation of Pythagoras have, if introduced in legislative bodies—and how wonderfully would it have tended to expedite business in the grand council of the Manhattoes!

Thus, however, did dame Wisdom, (whom the wags of antiquity have humorously personified as a woman,) seem to take mischievous pleasure in jilting the venerable counsellors of New-Amsterdam. The old factions of Long Pipes and Short Pipes, which had been almost strangled by the herculean grasp of Peter Stuyvesant, now sprung up with tenfold violence. Not that the original cause of difference still existed,—but, it has ever been the fate of party names and party rancour to remain, long after the principles that gave rise to them have been forgotten.

To complete the public confusion and bewilderment, the fatal word *Economy*, which one would have thought was dead and buried with William the Testy, was once more set afloat, like the apple of discord, in the grand council of Nieuw-Nederlandts— according to which sound principle of policy, it was deemed more expedient to throw away twenty thousand *guilders* upon an inefficacious plan of defence, than thirty thousand on a good and substantial one—the province thus making a clear saving of ten thousand *guilders*.

But when they came to discuss the mode of defence, then began a war of words that baffles all description. The members being, as I observed, enlisted in opposite parties, were enabled to proceed with amazing system and regularity in the discussion of the questions before them. Whatever was proposed by a Long Pipe, was opposed by the whole tribe of Short Pipes, who, like

297

true politicians, considered it their first duty to effect the downfall of the Long Pipes—their second, to elevate themselves—and their third, to consult the welfare of the country. This at least was the creed of the most upright among the party; for as to the great mass, they left the third consideration out of the question altogether.

In this great collision of hard heads, it is astonishing the number of projects for defence that were struck out, not one of which had ever been heard of before, nor has been heard of since, unless it be in very modern days—projects that threw the windmill system of the ingenious Kieft completely in the back ground. Still, however, nothing could be decided on; for so soon as a formidable host of air castles were reared by one party, they were demolished by the other. The simple populace, stood gazing in anxious expectation of the mighty egg that was to be hatched with all this cackling; but they gazed in vain, for it appeared that the grand council was determined to protect the province as did the noble and gigantic Pantagruel his army—by covering it with his tongue.

Indeed, there was a portion of the members, consisting of fat, self-important old *burghers*, who smoked their pipes and said nothing, excepting to negative every plan of defence that was offered. These were of that class of wealthy old citizens, who, having amassed a fortune, button up their pockets, shut their mouths, look rich, and are good for nothing all the rest of their lives. Like some phlegmatic oyster, which having swallowed a pearl, closes its shell, settles down in the mud, and parts with its life sooner than its treasure.

Every plan of defence seemed to these worthy old gentlemen pregnant with ruin. An armed force was a legion of locusts, preying upon the public property—to fit out a naval armament, was to throw their money into the sea—to build fortifications, was to bury it in the dirt. In short, they settled it as a sovereign maxim, so long as their pockets were full, no matter how much they were drubbed—A kick left no scar a broken head cured itself—but an empty purse was of all maladies the slowest to heal, and one in which nature did nothing for the patient

Thus did this venerable assembly of *sages* lavish away that time which the urgency of affairs rendered invaluable, in empty brawls and long-winded speeches, without ever agreeing, except on the point with which they started, namely, that there was no time to be lost, and delay was ruinous.

At length St. Nicholas, taking compassion on their distracted situation, and anxious to preserve them from anarchy, so ordered, that in the midst of one of their most noisy debates on the subject of fortification and defence, when they had nearly fallen to loggerheads in consequence of not being able to convince each other, the question was happily settled by a messenger, who bounced into the chamber and informed them that the hostile fleet had arrived, and was actually advancing up the bay!

Thus was all farther necessity of either fortifying or disputing completely obviated, and thus was the grand council saved a world of words, and the province a world of expense—a most absolute and glorious triumph of economy!

CHAPTER 6
IN WHICH THE TROUBLES OF NEW-AMSTERDAM APPEAR TO THICK-EN—SHOWING THE BRAVERY, IN TIME OF PERILS OF A PEOPLE WHO DEFEND THEMSELVES BY RESOLUTIONS.

Like as an assemblage of politic cats, engaged in clamorous gibberings, and caterwaulings, eyeing one another with hideous grimaces, spitting in each other's faces, and on the point of breaking forth into a general clapper-clawing, are suddenly put to scampering rout and confusion, by the startling appearance of a house-dog—so was the no less vociferous council of New-Amsterdam, amazed, astounded, and totally dispersed, by the sudden arrival of the enemy. Every member made the best of his way home, waddling along as fast as his short legs could fag under their heavy burden, and wheezing as he went with corpulency and terror. When he arrived at his castle, he *barricadoed* the street door, and buried himself in the cider cellar, without daring to peep out, lest he should have his head carried off by a cannon-ball.

The sovereign people all crowded into the market-place, herding together with the instinct of sheep, who seek for safety in each other's company, when the shepherd and his dog are absent, and the wolf is prowling round the fold. Far from finding relief, however, they only increased each other's terrors. Each man looked ruefully in his neighbour's face, in search of encouragement, but only found in its woebegone lineaments, a confirmation of his own dismay.

Not a word now was to be heard of conquering Great Britain, not a whisper about the sovereign virtues of economy—while the old women heightened the general gloom by clamorously bewailing their fate, and incessantly calling for protection on Saint Nicholas and Peter Stuyvesant.

Oh, how did they bewail the absence of the lion-hearted Peter!—and how did they long for the comforting presence of Antony Van Corlear! Indeed, a gloomy uncertainty hung over the fate of these adventurous heroes. Day after day had elapsed since the alarming message from the governor, without bringing any farther tidings of his safety. Many a fearful conjecture was hazarded as to what had befallen him and his loyal 'squire. Had they not been devoured alive by the cannibals of Marblehead and Cape Cod?—were they not put to the question by the great council of Amphyctions?—were they not smothered in onions by the terrible men of Piquag?

In the midst of this consternation and perplexity when horror, like a mighty nightmare, sat brooding upon the little, fat, plethoric city of New-Amsterdam, the ears of the multitude were suddenly startled by a strange and distant sound—it approached—it grew louder and louder—and now it resounded at the city gate. The public could not be mistaken in the well-known sound—a shout of joy burst from their lips, as the gallant Peter, covered with dust, and followed by his faithful trumpeter, came galloping into the market-place.

The first transports of the populace having subsided, they gathered round the honest Antony, as he dismounted from his horse, overwhelming him with greetings and congratulations. In breathless accents he related to them the marvellous adventures through which the old governor and himself had gone, in making their escape from the clutches of the terrible Amphyctions. But though the Stuyvesant manuscript, with its customary minuteness where anything touching the great Peter is concerned, is very particular as to the incidents of this masterly retreat, yet the particular state of the public affairs will not allow me to indulge in a full recital thereof.

Let it suffice to say, that while Peter Stuyvesant was anxiously revolving in his mind how he could make good his escape with honour and dignity, certain of the ships sent out for the conquest of the Manhattoes touched at the eastern ports, to obtain needful supplies, and to call on the grand council of the league for its promised co-operation. Upon hearing of this, the vigilant Peter, perceiving that a moment's delay were fatal, made a secret and precipitate decampment, though much did it grieve his lofty soul to be obliged to turn his back even upon a nation of foes.

Many hair-breadth 'scapes and divers perilous mishaps did they sustain, as they scoured, without sound of trumpet, through the fair regions of the east. Already was the country in an uproar with hostile preparation, and they were obliged to take a large circuit in their flight, lurking along through the woody mountains of the Devil's Backbone; from whence the valiant Peter sallied forth one day, like a lion, and put to rout a whole legion of squatters, consisting of three generations of a prolific family, who were already on their way to take possession of some corner of the New-Netherlands.

Nay, the faithful Antony had great difficulty at sundry times to prevent him, in the excess of his wrath, from descending down from the mountains, and falling, sword in hand, upon certain of the border towns, who were marshalling forth their draggletailed militia.

The first movements of the governor, on reaching his dwelling, was to mount the roof, from whence he contemplated with rueful aspect the hostile squadron. This had already come to anchor in the bay, and consisted of two stout frigates, having on board, as John Josselyn, gent. informs us, "three hundred valiant red-coats." Having taken this survey, he sat himself down, and wrote an epistle to the commander, demanding the reason of his anchoring in the harbour without obtaining previous permission so to do.

This letter was couched in the most dignified and courteous terms, though I have it from undoubted authority, that his teeth were clinched, and he had a bitter sardonic grin upon his visage all the while he wrote. Having despatched his letter, the grim Peter stumped to and fro about the town, with a most war-betokening countenance, his hands thrust into his breeches pockets, and whistling a Low Dutch psalm tune, which bore no small resemblance to the music, of a north-east wind, when a storm is brewing. The very dogs, as they eyed him, skulked away in dismay—while all the old and ugly women of New-Amsterdam ran howling at his heels, imploring him to save them from murder, robbery, and pitiless ravishment!

The reply of Col. Nichols, who commanded the invaders, was couched in terms of equal courtesy with the letter of the governor—declaring the right and title of his British Majesty to the province, where he affirmed the Dutch to be mere interlopers; and demanding that the town, forts, &c. should be forthwith rendered into his majesty's obedience and protection—promising at the same time, life, liberty, estate, and free trade, to every Dutch *denizen* who should readily submit to his majesty's government

Peter Stuyvesant read over this friendly epistle with some such harmony of aspect as we may suppose a crusty farmer, who has long been fattening upon his neighbour's soil, reads the loving letter of John Stiles, that warns him of an action of ejectment The old governor, however, was not to be taken by surprise, but thrusting the summons into his breeches pocket, he stalked three times across the room, took a pinch of snuff with great vehemence, and then loftily waving his hand, promised to send an answer the next morning.

In the meantime, he called a general council of war of his privy counsellors and *burgomasters*, not for the purpose of asking their advice, for that, as has been already shown, he valued not a rush; but to make known unto them his sovereign determination, and require their prompt adherence.

Before, however, he convened his council, he resolved upon three important points; *first*, never to give up the city without a little hard fighting, for he deemed it highly derogatory to the dignity of so renowned a city, to suffer itself to be captured and stripped, without receiving a few kicks into the bargain—*secondly*, that the majority of his grand council was composed of arrant poltroons, utterly destitute of true bottom—and, *thirdly*, that he would not therefore suffer them to see the summons of Col. Nichols, lest the easy terms it held out might induce them to clamour for a surrender.

His orders being duly promulgated, it was a piteous sight to behold the late valiant *burgomasters*, who had demolished the whole British empire in their harangues, peeping ruefully out of their hiding-places, and then crawling cautiously forth; dodging through narrow lanes and alleys; starting at every little dog that barked, as though it had been a discharge of artillery—mistaking lamp-posts for British grenadiers, and, in the excess of their panic, metamorphosing pumps into formidable soldiers, levelling blunderbusses at their bosoms!

Having, however, in despite of numerous perils and difficulties of the kind, arrived safe, without the loss of a single man, at the hall of assembly, they took their seats, and awaited in fearful silence the arrival of the governor. In a few moments, the wooden leg of the intrepid Peter was heard in regular and stouthearted thumps upon the staircase. He entered the chamber, arrayed in a full suit of regimentals, and carrying his trusty *toledo*, not girded on his thigh, but tucked under his arm. As the governor never equipped himself in this portentous manner, unless something of a martial nature were working within his fearless *pericranium*, his council regarded him ruefully, as if they saw fire and sword in his iron countenance, and forgot to light their pipes in breathless suspense.

The great Peter was as eloquent as he was valorous—indeed, these two rare qualities seemed to go hand in hand in his composition; and, unlike most great statesmen, whose victories are only confined to the bloodless field of argument, he was always ready to enforce his hardy words by no less hardy deeds. His speeches were generally marked by a simplicity, approaching to bluntness, and by a truly categorical decision. Addressing the grand council, he touched briefly upon the perils and hardships he had sustained in escaping from his crafty foes.

He next reproached the council, for wasting, in idle debate and party feuds, that time which should have been devoted to their country. He was particularly indignant at those brawlers, who, conscious of individual security, had disgraced the councils of the province by impotent hectorings and scurrilous invectives, against a noble and powerful enemy—those cowardly curs, who were incessant in their barkings and yelpings at the lion, while distant or asleep, but, the moment he approached, were the first to skulk away.

He now called on those who had been so valiant in their threats against Great Britain, to stand forth and support their vauntings by their actions—for it was *deeds*, not *words*, that bespoke the spirit of a nation. He proceeded to recall the golden days of former prosperity, which were only to be regained by manfully withstanding their enemies; for the peace, he observed, which is effected by force of arms, is always more sure and durable than that which is patched up by temporary accommodations. He endeavoured, moreover, to arouse their martial fire, by reminding them of the time when, before the frowning walls of Fort Christina, he had led them on to victory.

He strove likewise to awaken their confidence, by assuring them of the protection of St. Nicholas, who had hitherto maintained them in safety, amid all the savages of the wilderness, the witches and squatters of the east, and the giants of Merry-land. Finally, he informed them of the insolent summons he had received to surrender, but concluded by swearing to defend the province as long as Heaven was on his side, and he had a wooden leg to stand upon—which noble sentence he emphasized by a tremendous thwack with the broadside of his sword upon the table, that totally electrified his auditors.

The privy counsellors, who had long been accustomed to the governor's way, and in fact had been brought into as perfect discipline as were ever the soldiers of the great Frederick, saw that there was no use in saying a word—so lighted their pipes and smoked away in silence, like fat and discreet counsellors. But the *burgomasters*, being less under the governor's control, considering themselves as representatives of the sovereign people, and being moreover inflated with considerable importance and self-sufficiency, which they had acquired at those notable schools of wisdom and morality, the popular meetings, were not so easily satisfied.

Mustering up fresh spirit, when they found there was some change of escaping from their present jeopardy, without the disagreeable alternative of fighting, they requested a copy of the summons to surrender, that they might show it to a general meeting of the people.

So insolent and mutinous a request would have been enough to have roused the gorge of the tranquil Van Twiller himself—what then must have been its effect upon the great Stuyvesant, who was not only a Dutchman, a governor, and a valiant wooden-legged soldier to boot, but withal a man of the most stomachful and gunpowder disposition? He burst forth into a blaze of noble indignation,—swore not a mother's son of them should see a syllable of it—that they deserved, every one of them, to be hanged, drawn and quartered, for traitorously daring to question the infallibility of government—that as to their advice or concurrence, he did not care a whiff of tobacco for either—that he had long been harassed and thwarted by their cowardly counsels; but that they might thenceforth go home, and go to bed like old women; for he was determined to defend the colony himself, without the assistance of them or their adherents!

So saying, he tucked his sword under his arm, cocked his hat upon his head, and girding up his loins, stumped indignantly out of the council chamber—everybody making room for him as he passed.

No sooner had he gone, than the busy *burgomasters* called a public meeting in front of the *Stadt*-house, where they appointed as chairman one Dofue Roerback, a mighty gingerbread-baker in the land, and formerly of the cabinet of William the Testy. He was looked up to with great reverence by the populace, who considered him a man of dark knowledge, seeing he was the first that imprinted new-year cakes with the mysterious hieroglyphics of the Cock and Breeches, and such like magical devices.

This great *burgomaster*, who still chewed the cud of ill-will against the valiant Stuyvesant, in consequence of having been ignominiously kicked out of his cabinet at the time of his taking the reins of government—addressed the greasy multitude in what is called a patriotic speech, in which he informed them of the courteous summons to surrender—of the governor's refusal to comply therewith—of his denying the public a sight of the summons, which, he had no doubt, contained conditions highly to the honour and advantage of the province.

He then proceeded to speak of his Excellency in high-sounding terms, suitable to the dignity and grandeur of his station, comparing him to Nero, Caligula, and those other great men of yore, who are generally quoted by popular orators on similar occasions; assuring the people, that the history of the world did not contain a despotic outrage to equal the present, for atrocity, cruelty, tyranny, and blood-thirstiness—that it would be recorded in letters of fire, on the blood-stained tablet of history! that ages would roll back with sudden horror when they came to view it! that the womb of time—(by the way, your orators and writers take strange liberties with the womb of time, though some would fain have us believe that time is an old gentleman)—that the womb of time, pregnant as it was with direful horrors, would never produce a parallel enormity!

With a variety of other heart-rending, soul-stirring tropes

and figures, which I cannot enumerate—neither, indeed, need I, for they were exactly the same that are used in all popular harangues and patriotic orations at the present day, and may be classed in rhetoric under the general title of *Rigmarole*.

The speech of this inspired *burgomaster* being finished, the meeting fell into a kind of popular fermentation, which produced not only a string of right wise resolutions, but likewise a most resolute memorial, addressed to the governor, remonstrating at his conduct—which was no sooner handed to him, than he handed it into the fire; and thus deprived posterity of an invaluable document, that might have served as a precedent to the enlightened cobblers and tailors of the present day, in their sage intermeddlings with politics.

CHAPTER 7
CONTAINING A DOLEFUL DISASTER OF ANTONY THE TRUMPETER— AND HOW PETER STUYVESANT, LIKE A SECOND CROMWELL, SUDDENLY DISSOLVED A RUMP PARLIAMENT.

Now did the high-minded Pieter de Groodt shower down a pannier-load of benedictions upon his *burgomasters*, for a set of self-willed, obstinate, headstrong varlets, who would neither be convinced nor persuaded; and determined thenceforth to have nothing more to do with them, but to consult merely the opinion of his privy counsellors, which he knew from experience to be the best in the world—inasmuch as it never differed from his own.

Nor did he omit, now that his hand was up, to bestow some thousand left-handed compliments upon the sovereign people; whom he railed at for a herd of poltroons, who had no relish for the glorious hardships and illustrious misadventures of battle— but would rather stay at home, and eat and sleep in ignoble ease, than gain immortality and a broken head by valiantly fighting in a ditch.

Resolutely bent, however, upon defending his beloved city, in despite even of itself, he called unto him his trusty Van Corlear, who was his right-hand man in all times of emergency. Him did he adjure to take his war-denouncing trumpet, and mounting his horse, to beat up the country, night and day. Sounding the alarm along the pastoral borders of the Bronx—starting the wild solitudes of Croton—arousing the rugged yeomanry of Weehawk and Hoboeken—the mighty men of battle of Tappan Bay[1]—and the brave boys of Tarry Town and Sleepy Hollow—together with all the other warriors of the country round about; charging them one and all to sling their powder-horns, shoulder their fowling-pieces, and march merrily down to the Manhattoes.

Now there was nothing in all the world, the divine sex excepted, that Antony Van Corlear loved better than errands of this kind. So, just stopping to take a lusty dinner, and bracing to his side his junk bottle, well charged with heart-inspiring Hollands, he issued jollily from the city gate, that looked out upon what is at present called Broadway; sounding as usual a farewell strain, that rung in sprightly echoes through the winding streets of New-Amsterdam—Alas! never more were they to be gladdened by the melody of their favourite trumpeter!

It was a dark and stormy night, when the good Antony arrived at the famous creek (sagely denominated Haerlem *River*) which separates the island of Manna-hata from the mainland. The wind was high, the elements were in an uproar, and no Charon could he found to ferry the adventurous sounder of brass across the water. For a short time he vapoured like an impatient ghost upon the brink, and then, bethinking himself of the urgency of his errand, took a hearty embrace of his stone bottle, swore most valorously that he would swim across, *en spijt den Duyel*, (in spite of the devil!) and daringly plunged into the stream.—Luckless Antony! scarce had he buffeted half-way over, when he was observed to struggle violently, as if battling with the spirit of the waters—instinctively he put his trumpet to his mouth, and giving a vehement blast sunk forever to the bottom!

---

1. A corruption of Top-paun; so called from a tribe of Indians, which boasted a hundred and fifty fighting men. See Ogilby's *History*.

The potent clangour of his trumpet, like the ivory horn of the renowned Paladin Orlando, when expiring in the glorious field of Roncesvalles, rung far and wide through the country, alarming the neighbours round, who hurried in amazement to the spot. Here an old Dutch *burgher*, famed for his veracity, and who had been a witness of the fact, related to them the melancholy affair; with the fearful addition (to which I am slow of giving belief) that he saw the *duyvel*, in the shape of a huge moss-bonker, seize the sturdy Antony by the leg, and drag him beneath the waves.

Certain it is, the place, with the adjoining promontory, which projects into the Hudson, has been called *Spijt den duyvel*, or *Spiking Devil*, ever since;—the restless ghost of the unfortunate Antony still haunts the surrounding solitudes, and his trumpet has often been heard by the neighbours, of a stormy night, mingling with the howling of the blast. Nobody ever attempts to swim over the creek, after dark; on the contrary, a bridge has been built, to guard against such melancholy accidents in future—and as to moss-bonkers, they are held in such abhorrence, that no true Dutchman will admit them to his table, who loves good fish and hates the devil.

Such was the end of Antony Van Corlear—a man deserving of a better fate. He lived roundly and soundly, like a true and jolly bachelor, until the day of his death; but though he was never married, yet did he leave behind some two or three dozen children, in different parts of the country—fine, chubby, brawling, flatulent little urchins, from whom, if legends speak true, (and they are not apt to lie,) did descend the innumerable race of editors who people and defend this country, and who are bountifully paid by the people for keeping up a constant alarm—and making them miserable. Would that they inherited the worth, as they do the wind, of their renowned progenitor!

The tidings of this lamentable catastrophe imparted a severer pang to the bosom of Peter Stuyvesant, than did even the invasion of his beloved Amsterdam. It came ruthlessly home to those sweet affections that grow close around the heart, and are nourished by its warmest current As some lorn pilgrim, while the tempest whistles through his locks, and dreary night is gathering around, sees stretched, cold and lifeless, his faithful dog—the sole companion of his journeying, who had shared his solitary meal, and so often licked his hand in humble gratitude—so did the generous-hearted hero of the Manhattoes contemplate the untimely end of his faithful Antony.

He had been the humble, attendant of his footsteps—he had cheered him in many a heavy hour by his honest gayety, and had followed him in loyalty and affection through many a scene of direful peril and mishap; he was gone forever—and that too at a moment when every mongrel cur seemed skulking from his side. This—Peter Stuyvesant—this was the moment to try thy fortitude; and this was the moment when thou didst indeed shine forth—*Peter the Headstrong!*

The glare of day had long dispelled the horrors of the last stormy night; still all was dull and gloomy. The late jovial Apollo hid his face behind lugubrious clouds, peeping out now and then, for an instant, as if anxious, yet fearful, to see what was going on in his favourite city. This was the eventful morning, when the great Peter was to give his reply to the summons of the invaders. Already was he closeted with his privy council, sitting in grim state, brooding over the fate of his favourite trumpeter, and anon boiling with indignation as the insolence of his recreant *burgomasters* flashed upon his mind. While in this state of irritation, a courier arrived in all haste from Winthrop, the subtle governor of Connecticut, counselling him in the most affectionate and disinterested manner to surrender the province, and magnifying the dangers and calamities to which a refusal would subject him.

What a moment was this to intrude officious advice upon a man who never took advice in his whole life!—The fiery old governor strode up and down the chamber, with a vehemence that made the bosoms of his counsellors to quake with awe—railing at his unlucky fate, that thus made him the constant butt of factious subjects and Jesuitical advisers.

Just at this ill-chosen juncture, the officious *burgomasters*, who were now completely on the watch, and had heard of the arrival of mysterious despatches, came marching in a resolute body into the room, with a legion of *schepens* and toad-eaters at their heels, and abruptly demanded a perusal of the letter. Thus to be broken in upon by what he esteemed a "rascal rabble," and that, too, at the very moment he was grinding under an irritation from abroad, was too much for the spleen of the choleric Peter. He tore the letter in a thousand pieces[2]—threw it in the face of the nearest *burgomaster*—broke his pipe over the head of the next—hurled his spitting-box at an unlucky *schepen*, who was just making a masterly retreat out at the door, and finally prorogued the whole meeting *sine die*, by kicking them downstairs with his wooden leg.

As soon as the *burgomasters* could recover from the confusion into which their sudden exit had thrown them, and had taken a little time to breathe, they protested against the conduct of the governor, which they did not hesitate to pronounce tyrannical, unconstitutional, highly indecent, and somewhat disrespectful. They then called a public meeting, where they read the protest, and addressing the assembly in a set speech, related at full length, and with appropriate colouring and exaggeration, the despotic and vindictive deportment of the governor; declaring that, for their own parts, they did not value a straw the being kicked, cuffed, and mauled by the timber toe of His Excellency, but they felt for the dignity of the sovereign people, thus rudely insulted by the outrage committed on the seat of honour of their representatives.

The latter part of the harangue had a violent effect upon the sensibility of the people, as it came home at once to that delicacy of feeling and jealous pride of character, vested in all true mobs; who, though they may bear injuries without a murmur, yet are marvellously jealous of their sovereign dignity—and there is no knowing to what act of resentment they might have been provoked against the redoubtable Peter, had not the greasy rogues

2. Smith's *History of New-York.*

been somewhat more afraid of their sturdy old governor, than they were of St Nicholas, the English—or the D——l himself.

CHAPTER 8

HOW PETER STUYVESANT DEFENDED THE CITY OF NEW-AMSTERDAM, FOR SEVERAL DAYS, BY DINT OF THE STRENGTH OF HIS HEAD.

There is something exceedingly sublime and melancholy, in the spectacle which the present crisis of our history presents. An illustrious and venerable little city—the metropolis of an immense extent of uninhabited country—garrisoned by a doughty host of orators, chairmen, committee-men, *burgomasters*, *schepens*, and old women—governed by a determined and strong-headed warrior, and fortified by mud batteries, *pallisadoes*, and resolution—blockaded by sea, beleaguered by land, and threatened with direful desolation from without; while its very vitals are torn with internal faction and commotion!

Never did historic pen record a page of more complicated distress, unless it be the strife that distracted the Israelites during the siege of Jerusalem—where discordant parties were cutting each other's throats, at the moment when the victorious legions of Titus had toppled down their bulwarks, and were carrying fire and sword into the very *sanctum sanctorum* of the temple.

Governor Stuyvesant, having triumphantly, as has been recorded, put his grand council to the rout, and thus delivered himself from a multitude of impertinent advisers, despatched a categorical reply to the commanders of the invading squadron; wherein he asserted the right and title of their High Mightinesses the Lords States General to the province of New-Netherlands, and, trusting in the righteousness of his cause, set the whole British nation at defiance! My anxiety to extricate my readers and myself from these disastrous scenes, prevents me from giving the whole of this gallant letter, which concluded in these manly and affectionate terms:

As touching the threats in your conclusion, we have nothing to answer, only that we fear nothing but what God (who is as just as merciful) shall lay upon us; all things being in his gracious disposal, and we may as well be pre-served by him with small forces, as by a great army; which makes us to wish you all happiness and prosperity, and recommend you to his protection.—My lords, your thrice humble and affectionate servant and friend,

P. Stuyvesant.

Thus having resolutely thrown his gauntlet, the brave Peter stuck a pair of horse-pistols in his belt, girded an immense powder-horn on his side—thrust his sound leg into a Hessian boot, and clapping his fierce little war hat on the top of his head—paraded up and down in front of his house, determined to defend his beloved city to the last.

While all these woeful struggles and dissentions were prevailing in the unhappy city of New-Amsterdam, and while its worthy, but ill-starred governor was framing the above-quoted letter, the English commanders did not remain idle. They had agents secretly employed to foment the fears and clamours of the populace; and moreover circulated far and wide, through the adjacent country, a proclamation, repeating the terms they had already held out in their summons to surrender, and beguiling the simple Nederlanders with the most crafty and conciliating professions.

They promised that every man who voluntarily submitted to the authority of his British Majesty, should retain peaceable possession of his house, his *vrouw*, and his cabbage-garden. That he should be suffered to smoke his pipe, speak Dutch, wear as many breeches as he pleased, and import bricks, tiles, and stone jugs from Holland, instead of manufacturing them on the spot. That he should on no account be compelled to learn the English language, or keep accounts in any other way than by casting them up on his fingers, and chalking them down upon the crown of his hat; as is still observed among the Dutch yeomanry at the present day.

That every man should be allowed quietly to inherit his father's hat, coat, shoe-buckles, pipe, and every other personal appendage, and that no man should be obliged to conform to any improvements, inventions, or any other modern innovations; but, on the contrary, should be permitted to build his house, follow his trade, manage his farm, rear his hogs, and educate his children, precisely as his ancestors did before him since time immemorial. Finally, that he should have all the benefits of free trade, and should not be required to acknowledge any other saint in the calendar than St Nicholas, who should thenceforward, as before, be considered the tutelar saint of the city.

These terms, as may be supposed, appeared very satisfactory to the people, who had a great disposition to enjoy their property unmolested, and a most singular aversion to engage in a contest, where they could gain little more than honour and broken heads—the first of which they held in philosophic indifference, the latter in utter detestation. By these insidious means, therefore, did the English succeed in alienating the confidence and affections of the populace from their gallant old governor, whom they considered as obstinately bent upon running them into hideous misadventures; and did not hesitate to speak their minds freely, and abuse him most heartily—behind his back.

Like as a mighty grampus, who, though assailed and buffeted by roaring waves and brawling surges, still keeps on an undeviating course; and though overwhelmed by boisterous billows, still emerges from the troubled deep, spouting and blowing with tenfold violence—so did the inflexible Peter pursue, unwavering, his determined career, and rise, contemptuous, above the clamours of the rabble.

But when the British warriors found, by the tenor of his reply, that he set their power at defiance, they forthwith despatched recruiting officers to Jamaica, and Jericho, and Nineveh, and Quag, and Patchog, and all those towns on Long Island which had been subdued of yore by the immortal Stoffel Brinkerhoff; stirring up the valiant progeny of Preserved Fish, and Determined Cock, and those other illustrious squatters, to assail the city of New-Amsterdam by land. In the meanwhile, the hostile ships made awful preparation to commence an assault by water.

The streets of New-Amsterdam now presented a scene of

wild dismay and consternation. In vain did the gallant Stuyvesant order the citizens to arm, and assemble in the public square or market-place. The whole party of Short Pipes in the course of a single night had changed into arrant old women—a metamorphosis only to be paralleled by the prodigies recorded by Livy as having happened at Rome on the approach of Hannibal, when statues sweated in pure affright, goats were converted into sheep, and cocks turning into hens ran cackling about the streets.

The harassed Peter, thus menaced from without, and tormented from within—baited by the *burgomasters*, and hooted at by the rabble, chafed and growled and raged like a furious bear, tied to a stake and worried by a legion of scoundrel curs. Finding, however, that all further attempts to defend the city were in vain, and hearing that an irruption of borderers and mosstroopers was ready to deluge him from the east, he was at length compelled, in spite of his proud heart, which swelled in his throat until it had nearly choked him, to consent to a treaty of surrender.

Words cannot express the transports of the people, on receiving this agreeable intelligence; had they obtained a conquest over their enemies, they could not have indulged greater delight The streets resounded with their congratulations—they extolled their governor, as the father and deliverer of his country—they crowded to his house to testify their gratitude, and were ten times more noisy in their plaudits, that when he returned, with victory perched upon his beaver, from the glorious capture of Fort Christina. But the indignant Peter shut his doors and windows, and took refuge in the innermost recesses of his mansion,. that he might not hear the ignoble rejoicings of the rabble.

In consequence of this consent of the governor, a parley was demanded of the besieging forces to treat of the terms of surrender. Accordingly, a deputation of six commissioners was appointed on both sides; and on the 27th August, 1664, a capitulation highly favourable to the province, and honourable to Peter Stuyvesant, was agreed to by the enemy, who had conceived a high opinion of the valour of the Manhattoes, and the magnanimity and unbounded discretion of their governor.

One thing alone remained, which was, that the articles of surrender should be ratified, and signed by the governor. When the commissioners respectfully waited upon him for this purpose, they were received by the hardy old warrior with the most grim and bitter courtesy. His warlike accoutrements were laid aside—an old India nightgown was wrapped about his rugged limbs, a red night-cap overshadowed his frowning brow, and an iron gray beard, of three day's growth, gave additional grimness to his visage.

Thrice did he seize a little worn-out stump of a pen, and essay to sign the loathsome paper—thrice did he clinch his teeth, and make a most horrible countenance, as though a pestiferous dose of rhubarb, senna, and *ipecacuanha*, had been offered to his lips; at length, dashing it from him, he seized his brass-hilted sword, and jerking it from the scabbard, swore by St Nicholas, he'd sooner die than yield to any power under heaven.

In vain was every attempt to shake this sturdy resolution— menaces, remonstrances, revilings, were exhausted to no purpose—for two whole days was the house of the valiant Peter besieged by the clamorous rabble, and for two whole days did he partake himself to his arms, and persist in a magnanimous refusal to ratify the capitulation.

At length the populace, fining that boisterous measures did but incense more determined opposition, bethought themselves of an humble expedient, by which, happily, the governor's ire might be soothed, and his resolution undermined. And now a solemn and mournful procession, headed by the *burgomasters* and *schepens*, and followed by the populace, moves slowly to the governor's dwelling, bearing the capitulation. Here they found the stout old hero, drawn up like a giant in his castle, the doors strongly *barricadoed*, and himself in full regimentals, with his cocked hat on his head, firmly posted with a blunderbuss at the garret-window.

There was something in this formidable position, that struck even the ignoble vulgar with awe and admiration. The brawling multitude could not but reflect with self-abasement upon their own pusillanimous conduct, when they beheld their hardy but deserted old governor, thus faithful to his post, like a forlorn hope, and fully prepared to defend his on grateful city to the last These compunctions, however, were soon overwhelmed by the recurring tide of public apprehension.

The populace arranged themselves before the house, taking off their hats with most respectful humility.—Burgomaster Roerback, who was of that popular class of orators described by Sallust, as being "talkative rather than eloquent," stepped forth and addressed the governor in a speech of three hours' length; detailing in the most pathetic terms the calamitous situation of the province, and urging him in a constant repetition of the same arguments and words to sign the capitulation.

The mighty Peter eyed him from his little garret-window in grim silence—now and then his eye would glance over the surrounding rabble, and an indignant grin, like that of an angry mastiff, would mark his iron visage. But though he was a man of most undaunted mettle—though he had a heart as big as an ox, and a head that would have set adamant to scorn—yet after all he was a mere mortal:—wearied out by these repeated oppositions and this eternal haranguing, and perceiving that unless be complied, the inhabitants would follow their own inclinations, or rather their fears, without waiting for his consent, he testily ordered them to hand up the paper.

It was accordingly hoisted to him on the end of a pole, and having scrawled his name at the bottom of it, he anathematized them all for a set of cowardly, mutinous, degenerate poltroons— threw the capitulation at their heads, slammed, down the window, and was heard stumping downstairs with the most vehement indignation. The rabble incontinently took to their heels; even the *burgomasters* were not slow in evacuating the premises, fearing lest the sturdy Peter might issue from his den, and greet them with some unwelcome testimonial of his displeasure.

Within three hours after the surrender, a legion of British beef-fed warriors poured into New-Amsterdam, taking possession of the fort and batteries. And now might be heard, from all quarters, the sound of hammers, made by the old Dutch *burghers*, who were busily employed in nailing up their doors and windows, to protect their *vrouws* from these fierce barbarians, whom they contemplated in silent sullenness from the garret-windows, as they paraded through the streets.

Thus did Col. Richard Nichols, the commander of the British forces, enter into quiet possession of the conquered realm, as *locum tenens* for the Duke of York. The victory was attended with no other outrage than that of changing the name of the province and its metropolis, which thenceforth were denominated *New-York*, and so have continued to be called unto the present day. The inhabitants, according to treaty, were allowed to maintain quiet possession of their property; but so inveterately did they retain their abhorrence of the British nation, that in a private meeting of the leading citizens, it was unanimously determined, never to ask any of their conquerors to dinner.

CHAPTER 9
CONTAINING THE DIGNIFIED RETIREMENT AND MORTAL SURRENDER OF PETER THE HEADSTRONG.

Thus, then, have I concluded this great historical enterprise; but before I lay aside my weary pen, there yet remains to be performed one pious duty. If among the variety of readers that may peruse this book, there should haply be found any of those souls of true nobility, which glow with celestial fire at the history of the generous and the brave, they will doubtless be anxious to know the fate of the gallant Peter Stuyvesant To gratify one such sterling heart of gold, I would go more lengths than to instruct the cold-blooded curiosity of a whole fraternity of philosophers.

No sooner had that high-mettled cavalier signed the articles of capitulation, than, determined not to witness the humiliation of his favourite city, he turned his back on its walls, and made a growling retreat to his *Bouwery*, or country-seat, which was situated about two miles off, where he passed the remainder of his days in patriarchal retirement. There he enjoyed that tranquillity of mind, which he had never known amid the distracting cares of government, and tasted the sweets of absolute and uncontrolled authority, which his factious subjects had so often dashed with the bitterness of opposition.

No persuasions could ever induce him to revisit the city—on the contrary, he would always have his great armchair placed with its back to the window: which looked in that direction; until a thick grove of trees, planted by his own hand, grew up and formed a screen that effectually excluded it from the prospect He railed continually at the degenerate innovations und improvements introduced by the conquerors—forbade a word of their detested language to be spoken in his family, a prohibition readily obeyed, since none of the household could speak anything but Dutch—and even ordered a fine avenue to be cut down in front of his house, because it consisted of English cherry-trees.

The same incessant vigilance that blazed forth when he had a vast province under his care, now showed itself with equal vigour, though in narrower limits. He patrolled with unceasing watchfulness Ground the boundaries of his little territory; repelled every encroachment with intrepid promptness; punished every vagrant depredation upon his orchard or his farmyard, with inflexible severity—and conducted every stray hog or cow in triumph to the pound. But to the indigent neighbour, the friendless stranger, or the weary wanderer, his spacious doors were ever open, and his capacious fireplace, that emblem of his own warm and generous heart, had always a corner to receive and cherish them.

There was an exception to this, I must confess, in case the ill-starred applicant was an Englishman or a Yankee, to whom, though he might extend the hand of assistance, he never could be brought to yield the rites of hospitality. Nay, if peradventure some straggling merchant of the east should stop at his door, with his cart-load of tin ware or wooden bowls, the fiery Peter would issue forth like a giant from his castle, and make such a furious clattering among his pots and kettles, that the vender of "*notions*" was fain to betake himself to instant flight

His handsome suit of regimentals, worn threadbare by the brush, was carefully hung up in the state bedchamber, and regularly aired on the first fair day of every month—and his cocked hat and trusty sword were suspended in grim repose over the parlour mantelpiece, forming supporters to a full-length portrait of the renowned Admiral Van Tromp. In his domestic empire he maintained strict discipline, and a well-organized, despotic government; but, though his own will was the supreme law, yet the good of his subjects was his constant object He watched over, not merely their immediate comforts, but their morals and their ultimate welfare; for he gave them abundance of excellent admonition, nor could any of them complain, that, when occasion required, he was by any means niggardly in bestowing wholesome correction.

The good old Dutch festivals, those periodical demonstrations of an overflowing heart and a thankful spirit, which are falling into sad disuse among my fellow-citizens, were faithfully observed in the mansion of Governor Stuyvesant. New-year was truly a day of open-handed liberality, of jocund revelry, and warm-hearted congratulation—when the bosom seemed to swell with genial good-fellowship—and the plenteous table was attended with an unceremonious freedom, and honest broad-mouthed merriment, unknown in these days of degeneracy and refinement. Pas and Pinxter were scrupulously observed, throughout his dominions; nor was the day of St Nicholas suffered to pass by, without making presents, hanging the stocking in the chimney, and complying with all its other ceremonies.

Once a year, on the first day of April, he used to array himself in full regimentals, being the anniversary of his triumphal entry into New-Amsterdam, after the conquest of New-Sweden. This was always a kind of *saturnalia* among the domestics, when they considered themselves at liberty, in some measure, to say and do what they pleased; for on this day, their master was always observed to unbend, and become exceeding pleasant and jocose, sending the old gray-headed negroes on April fool's errands for pigeon's milk; not one of whom but allowed himself to be taken in, and humoured his old master's jokes, as became a faithful and well-disciplined dependant

Thus did he reign, happily and peacefully, on his own land— injuring no man—envying no man—molested by no outward strifes—perplexed by no internal commotions; and the mighty monarchs of the earth, who were vainly seeking to maintain peace, and promote the welfare of mankind, by war and desola- tion, would have done well to have made a voyage to the little island of Manna-hata, and learned a lesson in government from the domestic economy of Peter Stuyvesant.

In process of time, however, the old governor, like all other children of mortality, began to exhibit tokens of decay. Like an aged oak, which, though it long has braved the fury of the ele- ments, and still retains its gigantic proportions, yet begins to shake and groan with every blast—so was it with the gallant Peter; for though he still bore the port and semblance of what he was in the days of his hardihood and chivalry, yet did age and infirmity begin to sap the vigour of his frame—but his heart, that most unconquerable citadel, still triumphed unsubdued.

With matchless avidity would he listen to every article of intelligence concerning the battles between the English and Dutch—still would his pulse beat high, whenever he heard of the victories of De Ruyter—and his countenance lower, and his eye-brows knit, when fortune turned in favour of the English. At length, as on a certain day he had just smoked his fifth pipe, and was napping after dinner, in his armchair, conquering the whole British nation in his dreams, he was suddenly aroused by a fearful ringing of bells, rattling of drums, and roaring of can- non, that put all his blood in a ferment.

But when he learnt that these, rejoicings were in honour of a great victory obtained by the combined English and French fleets over the brave De Ruyter and the younger Van Tromp, it went, so much to his heart, that he took to his bed, and, in less than three days, was brought to death's door by a violent cholera *morbus*! But, even in this extremity, he still displayed the unconquerable spirit of Peter *the Headstrong*; holding out, to the last gasp, with the roost inflexible obstinacy, against a whole army of old women, who were bent upon driving the enemy out of his bowels, after a true Dutch mode of defence, by inundating the seat of war with catnip and pennyroyal.

While he thus lay, lingering on the verge of dissolution, news was brought him, that the brave De Ruyter had suffered but little loss—had made good his retreat—and meant once more to meet the enemy in battle. The closing eye of the old warrior kindled at the words—he partly raised himself in bed—a flash of martial fire beamed across his visage—he clinched his withered hand, as if he felt within his gripe that sword which waved in triumph before the walls of Fort Christina, and, giving a grim smile of exultation, sunk back upon his pillow and expired.

Thus died Peter Stuyvesant, a valiant soldier—a loyal subject—an upright governor, and an honest Dutchman—who wanted only a few empires to desolate to have been immortalized as a hero!

His funeral obsequies were celebrated with the utmost grandeur and solemnity. The town was perfectly emptied of its inhabitants, who crowded in throngs to pay the last sad honours to their good old governor. All his sterling qualities rushed in full tide upon their recollections, while the memory of his foibles and his faults had expired with him. The ancient *burghers* contended who should have the privilege of bearing, the pall; the populace strove who should walk nearest to the bier—and the melancholy procession was closed by a number of gray-headed negroes, who had wintered and summered in the household of their departed master, for the greater part of a century.

With sad and gloomy countenances, the multitude gathered around the grave. They dwelt with mournful hearts on the sturdy virtues, the signal services, and the gallant exploits of the brave old worthy. They recalled, with secret upbraidings, their own factious opposition to his government—and many an ancient *burgher*, whose phlegmatic features had never been known to relax, nor his eyes to moisten, was now observed to puff a pensive pipe, and the big drop to steal down his cheek—while he muttered, with affectionate accent, and melancholy shake of the head—"Well den!—Hardkoppig Peter ben gone at last!"

His remains were deposited in the family vault, under a chapel, which he had piously erected on his estate, and dedicated to St. Nicholas—and which stood on the identical spot at present occupied by St. Mark's church, where his tombstone is still to be seen. His estate, or *Bouwery*, as it was called, has ever continued in the possession of his descendants, who, by the uniform integrity of their conduct, and their strict adherence to the customs and manners that prevailed in the "*good old times*," have proved themselves worthy of their illustrious ancestor.

Many a time and oft has the farm been haunted, at night, by enterprising money-diggers, in quest of pots of gold, said to have been buried by the old governor—though I cannot learn that any of them have ever been enriched by their researches: and who is there, among my native-born fellow-citizens, that does not remember, when, in the mischievous days of his boyhood, he conceived it a great exploit to rob "Stuyvesant's orchard" on a holyday afternoon?

At this strong hold of the family, may still be seen certain memorials of the immortal Peter, His full-length portrait frowns in martial terrors from the parlour wall—his cocked hat and sword still hang up in the best bedroom—his brimstone-coloured breeches were for a long while suspended in the hall, until some years since they occasioned a dispute between a new married couple—and his silver-mounted wooden leg is still treasured up in the storeroom, as an invaluable relic.

Chapter 10
The Author's reflections upon what has been said.

Among the numerous events, which are each in their turn the most direful and melancholy of all possible occurrences, in your interesting and authentic history, there is none that occasions such deep arid heart-rending grief as the decline and fall of your renowned and mighty empires. Where is the reader who can contemplate, without emotion, the disastrous events by which the great dynasties of the world have been extinguished? While wandering, in imagination, among the gigantic ruins of states and empires, and marking the tremendous convulsions that wrought their overthrow, the bosom of the melancholy inquirer, swells with sympathy commensurate to the surrounding desolation.

Kingdoms, principalities, and powers, have each had their rise, their progress, and their downfall—each in its turn has swayed a potent sceptre—each has returned to its primeval nothingness. And thus did it fare with the empire of their High Mightinesses, at the Manhattoes, under the peaceful reign of Walter the Doubter—the fretful reign of William the Testy—and the chivalric reign of Peter the Headstrong.

Its history is fruitful instruction, and worthy of being pondered over attentively; for it is by thus raking among the ashes of departed greatness, that the sparks of true knowledge are found, and the lamp of wisdom illumined. Let then the reign of Walter the Doubter warn against yielding to that sleek, contented security, that overweening fondness for comfort and repose, that are produced by a state of prosperity and peace. These tend to unnerve a nation; to destroy its pride of character; to render it patient of insult, deaf to the calls of honour and of justice; and cause it to cling to peace, like the sluggard to his pillow, at the expense of every valuable duty and consideration.

Such supineness insures the very evil from which it shrinks. One right, yielded up, produces the usurpation of a second; one encroachment, passively suffered, makes way for another; and the nation that thus, through a doting love of peace, has sacrificed honour and interest, will at length have to fight for existence.

Let the disastrous reign of William the Testy serve as a salutary warning against that fitful, feverish mode of legislation, that acts without system; depends on shifts and projects, and trusts to lucky contingencies; that hesitates, and wavers, and at length decides with the rashness of ignorance and imbecility; that stoops for popularity, by courting the prejudices and flattering the arrogance, rather than commanding the respect, of the rabble; that seeks safety in a multitude of counsellors, and distracts itself by a variety of contradictory schemes and opinions; that mistakes procrastination for deliberate wariness—hurry for decision—starveling parsimony for wholesome economy—bustle for business, and vapouring for valour; that is violent; in council, sanguine in expectation, precipitate in action, and feeble in execution; that undertakes enterprises without forethought, enters upon them without preparation, conducts them without energy, and ends them in confusion and defeat

Let the reign of the good Stuyvesant show the effects of vigour and decision, even when destitute of cool judgement, and surrounded by perplexities. Let it show how frankness, probity, and high-souled courage, will command respect and secure honour, even where success is unattainable. But, at the same time, let it caution against a too ready reliance on the good faith of others, and a too honest confidence in the loving professions of powerful neighbours, who are most friendly when they most mean to betray. Let it teach a judicious attention to the opinions and wishes of the many, who, in times of peril, must be soothed and led, or apprehension will overpower the deference to authority.

Let the empty wordiness of his factious subjects; their intemperate harangues; their violent "resolutions;" their hectorings against an absent enemy, and their pusillanimity on his approach, teach us to distrust and despise those clamorous patriots, whose courage dwells but in the tongue. Let them serve as a lesson to repress that insolence of speech, destitute of real force, which too often breaks forth in popular bodies, and bespeaks the vanity, rather than the spirit of a nation. Let them caution us against vaunting too much of our own power and prowess, and reviling a noble enemy. True gallantry of soul would always lead us to treat a foe with courtesy and proud *punctilio*; a contrary conduct but takes from the merit of victory, and renders defeat doubly disgraceful.

But I cease to dwell on the stores of excellent examples to be drawn from the ancient chronicles of the Manhattoes. He who reads attentively will discover the threads of gold, which run throughout the web of history, and are invisible to the dull eye of ignorance. But, before I conclude, let me point out a solemn warning, furnished in the subtle chain of events by which the capture of Fort Casimir has produced the present convulsions of our globe.

Attend then, gentle reader, to this plain deduction, which, if thou art a king, an emperor, or other powerful potentate, I advise thee to treasure up in thy heart—though little expectation have I that my work will fall into such hands, for well I know the care of crafty ministers, to keep all grave and edifying books of the kind out of the way of unhappy monarchs—lest peradventure they should read them and learn wisdom.

By the treacherous surprisal of Fort Casimir, then, did the crafty Swedes enjoy a transient triumph; but drew upon their heads the vengeance of Peter Stuyvesant, who wrested all New-Sweden from their hands. By the conquest of New-Sweden, Peter Stuyvesant aroused the claims of Lord Baltimore; who appealed to the Cabinet of Great Britain; who subdued the whole province of New-Netherlands.

By this great achievement, the whole extent of North America, from Nova Scotia to the Floridas, was rendered one entire dependency upon the British crown—but mark the consequence:—The hitherto scattered colonies being thus consolidated, and having no rival colonies to check or keep them in awe, waxed great and powerful, and finally becoming too strong for the mother country, were enabled to shake off its bonds, and by a glorious revolution became an independent empire.

But the chain of effects stopped not here; the successful revolution in America produced the sanguinary revolution in France, which produced the *puissant* Buonaparte, who produced the French despotism. Which has thrown the whole world in confusion!—Thus have these great powers been successively punished for their ill-starred conquests—and thus, as I asserted, have all the present convulsions, revolutions, and disasters that overwhelm mankind, originated in the capture of the little Fort Casimir, as recorded in this eventful history.

And now, worthy reader, ere I take a sad farewell—which, alas! must be forever—willingly would I part, in cordial fellowship, and bespeak thy kind hearted remembrance. That I have not written a better history of the days of the patriarchs, is not my fault—had any other person written one as good, I should not have attempted it at all. That many will hereafter spring up and surpass me in excellence, I have very little doubt, and still less care; well knowing, when the great Christovallo Colon (who is vulgarly called Columbus) had once stood his egg upon its end, everyone at table could stand his up a thousand times more dexterously.

Should any reader find matter of offence in this history, I should heartily grieve, though I would on no account question his penetration by telling him he is mistaken—his good nature, by telling him be is captious—or his pure conscience, by telling him he is startled at a shadow. Surely if he is so ingenious in finding offence where none is intended, it were a thousand pities he should not be suffered to enjoy the benefit of his discovery.

I have too high an opinion of the understanding of my fellow-citizens, to think of yielding them my instruction; and I covet too much their good will, to forfeit it by giving them good advice. I am none of those cynics who despise the world because it despises them—on the contrary, though but low in its regard, I look up to it with the most perfect good nature, and my only sorrow is, that it does not prove itself more worthy of the unbounded love I bear it

If, however, in this my historic production—the scanty fruit of a long and laborious life—I have failed to gratify the dainty palate of the age, I can only lament my misfortune—for it is too late in the season for me even to hope to repair it. Already has withering age showered his sterile snows upon my brow; in a little while, and this genial warmth, which still lingers around my heart, and throbs—worthy reader—throbs kindly towards thyself, will be chilled forever.

Haply this frail compound of dust, which while alive may have given birth to nought but unprofitable weeds, may form an humble sod of the valley, from whence may spring many a sweet wild flower, to adorn my beloved island of Manna-hata!

A Tale From *Wolfert's Roost*

Origin of the White, the Red and the Black Men

A Seminole Tradition

When the Floridas were erected into a territory of the United States, one of the earliest cares of the Governor, William P. Duval, was directed to the instruction and civilization of the natives. For this purpose he called a meeting of the chiefs, in which he informed them of the wish of their Great Father at Washington that they should have schools and teachers among them, and that their children should be instructed like the children of white men. The chiefs listened with their customary silence and decorum to a long speech, setting forth the advantages that would accrue to them from this measure, and when he had concluded, begged the interval of a day, to deliberate on it.

On the following day a solemn convocation was held, at which one of the chiefs addressed the Governor in the name of all the rest.

"My brother," said he, "we have been thinking over the proposition of our Great Father at Washington, to send teachers and set up schools among us. We are very thankful for the interest he takes in our welfare; but after much deliberation have concluded to decline his offer. What will do very well for white men, will not do for red men. I know you white men say we all come from the same father and mother, but you are mistaken.

"We have a tradition handed down from our forefathers, and we believe it, that the Great Spirit, when he undertook to make

329

men, made the black man; it was his first attempt, and pretty well for a beginning; but he soon saw he had bungled; so he determined to try his hand again. He did so, and made the red man. He liked him much better than the black man, but still *he* was not exactly what he wanted. So he tried once more, and made the white man; and then he was satisfied. You see, therefore, that you were made last, and that is the reason I call you my youngest brother.

"When the Great Spirit had made the three men, he called them together and showed them three boxes. The first was filled with books, and maps, and papers; the second with bows and arrows, knives and tomahawks; the third with spades, axes, hoes, and hammers. 'These, my sons,' said he, 'are the means by which you are to live; choose among them according to your fancy.'

"The white man, being the favourite, had the first choice. He passed by the box of working-tools without notice; but when he came to the weapons for war and hunting, he stopped and looked hard at them. The red man trembled, for he had set his heart upon that box. The white man, however, after looking upon it for a moment, passed on, and chose the box of books and papers. The red man's turn came next, and you may be sure he seized with joy upon the bows and arrows and tomahawks. As to the black man, he had no choice left, but to put up with the box of tools.

"From this it is clear that the Great Spirit intended the white man should learn to read and write, to understand all about the moon and stars, and to make everything, even rum and whiskey. That the red man should be a first-rate hunter, and a mighty warrior, but he was not to learn anything from books, as the Great Spirit had not given him any; nor was he to make rum and whiskey, lest he should kill himself with drinking. As to the black man, as he had nothing but working-tools, it was clear he was to work for the white and red man, which he has continued to do.

"We must go according to the wishes of the Great Spirit, or we shall get into trouble. To know how to read and write is very good for white men, but very bad for red men. It makes white men better, but red men worse. Some of the Creeks and Cherokees learnt to read and write, and they are the greatest rascals among all the Indians. They went on to Washington, and said they were going to see their Great Father, to talk about the good of the nation. And when they got there, they all wrote upon a little piece of paper, without the nation at home knowing anything about it. And the first thing the nation at home knew of the matter, they were called together by the Indian agent, who showed them a little piece of paper, which he told them was a treaty which their brethren had made in their name with their Great Father at Washington.

"And as they knew not what a treaty was, he held up the little piece of paper, and they looked under it, and lo! it covered a great extent of country, and they found that their brethren, by knowing how to read and write, had sold their houses, and their lands, and the graves of their fathers; and that the white man, by knowing how to read and write, had gained them. Tell our Great Father at Washington, therefore, that we are very sorry we cannot receive teachers among us; for reading and writing, though very good for white men, is very bad for Indians."

A Tale From *Wolfert's Roost*

Guests From Gibbet Island

Whoever has visited the ancient and renowned village of Communipaw, may have noticed an old stone building, of most ruinous and sinister appearance. The doors and window-shutters are ready to drop from their hinges; old clothes are stuffed in the broken panes of glass, while legions of half-starved dogs prowl about the premises, and rush out and bark at every passer-by; for your beggarly house in a village is most apt to swarm with profligate and ill-conditioned dogs. What adds to the sinister appearance of this mansion, is a tall frame in front, not a little resembling a gallows, and which looks as if waiting to accommodate some of the inhabitants with a well-merited airing.

It is not a gallows, however, but an ancient sign-post; for this dwelling, in the golden days of Communipaw, was one of the most orderly and peaceful of village taverns, where all the public affairs of Communipaw were talked and smoked over. In fact, it was in this very building that Oloffe the Dreamer, and his companions, concerted that great voyage of discovery and colonization, in which they explored Buttermilk Channel, were nearly shipwrecked in the strait of Hell-Gate, and finally landed on the Island of Manhattan, and founded the great city of New-Amsterdam.

Even after the province had been cruelly wrested from the sway of their High Mightinesses, by the combined forces of the British and Yankees, this tavern continued its ancient loyalty. It is true, the head of the Prince of Orange disappeared from the sign; a strange bird being painted over it, with the explanatory legend of "*Die Wilde Gans*," or The Wild Goose; but this all the world knew to be a sly riddle of the landlord, the worthy Teunis Van Gieson, a knowing man in a small way, who laid his finger beside his nose and winked, when any one studied the signification of his sign, and observed that his goose was hatching, but would join the flock whenever they flew over the water; an enigma which was the perpetual recreation and delight of the loyal but fat-headed *burghers* of Communipaw.

Under the sway of this patriotic, though discreet and quiet publican, the tavern continued to flourish in primeval tranquillity, and was the resort of all true-hearted Nederlanders, from all parts of Pavonia; who met here quietly and secretly, to smoke and drink the downfall of Briton and Yankee, and success to Admiral Van Tromp.

The only drawback on the comfort of the establishment, was a nephew of mine host, a sister's son, Yan Yost Vanderscamp by name, and a real scamp by nature. This unlucky whipster showed an early propensity to mischief, which he gratified in a small way, by playing tricks upon the frequenters of the Wild Goose; putting gunpowder in their pipes, or squibs in their pockets, and astonishing them with an explosion, while they sat nodding round the fireplace in the bar-room; and if perchance a worthy *burgher* from some distant part of Pavonia had lingered until dark over his potation, it was odds but that young Vanderscamp would slip a briar under his horse's tail, as he mounted, and send him clattering along the road, in neck-or-nothing style, to his infinite astonishment and discomfiture.

It may be wondered at, that mine host of the Wild Goose did not turn such a graceless varlet out of doors; but Teunis Van Gieson was an easy-tempered man, and, having no child of his own, looked upon his nephew with almost parental indulgence. His patience and good-nature were doomed to be tried by another inmate of his mansion. This was a cross-grained curmudgeon of a negro, named Pluto, who was a kind of enigma in Communipaw. Where he came from, nobody knew. He was found one morning, after a storm, cast like a sea-monster on the strand, in front of the Wild Goose, and lay there, more dead than alive.

The neighbours gathered round, and speculated on this production of the deep; whether it were fish or flesh, or a compound of both, commonly yclept a merman. The kind-hearted Teunis Van Gieson, seeing that he wore the human form, took him into his house, and warmed him into life. By degrees, he showed signs of intelligence, and even uttered sounds very much like language, but which no one in Communipaw could understand. Some thought him a negro just from Guinea, who had either fallen overboard, or escaped from a slave-ship. Nothing, however, could ever draw from him any account of his origin. When questioned on the subject, he merely pointed to Gibbet-Island, a small rocky islet, which lies in the open bay, just opposite to Communipaw, as if that were his native place, though everybody knew it had never been inhabited.

In the process of time, he acquired something of the Dutch language, that is to say, he learnt all its vocabulary of oaths and maledictions, with just words sufficient to string them together. *"Donder en blicksen!"* (thunder and lightning,) was the gentlest of his ejaculations. For years he kept about the Wild Goose, more like one of those familiar spirits, or household goblins, that we read of, than like a human being. He acknowledged allegiance to no one, but performed various domestic offices, when it suited his humour; waiting occasionally on the guests; grooming the horses, cutting wood, drawing water; and all this without being ordered.

Lay any command on him, and the stubborn sea-urchin was sure to rebel. He was never so much at home, however, as when on the water, plying about in skiff or canoe, entirely alone, fishing, crabbing, or grabbing for oysters, and would bring home quantities for the larder of the Wild Goose, which he would throw down at the kitchen door, with a growl. No wind nor weather deterred him from launching forth on his favourite element: indeed, the wilder the weather, the more he seemed to enjoy it. If a storm was brewing, he was sure to put off from

shore; and would be seen far out in the bay, his light skiff dancing like a feather on the waves, when sea and sky were all in a
turmoil, and the stoutest ships were fain to lower their sails.

Sometimes, on such occasions, he would be absent for days
together. How he weathered the tempest, and how and where
he subsisted, no one could divine, nor did any one venture to
ask, for all had an almost superstitious awe of him. Some of the
Communipaw oystermen declared that they had more than once
seen him suddenly disappear, canoe and all, as if they plunged
beneath the waves, and after a while come up again, in quite a
different part of the bay; whence they concluded that he could
live under water like that notable species of wild duck, commonly called the Hell-diver. All began to consider him in the
light of a foul-weather bird, like the Mother Carey's Chicken, or
Stormy Petrel; and whenever they saw him putting far out in his
skiff, in cloudy weather, made up their minds for a storm.

The only being for whom he seemed to have any liking, was
Yan Yost Vanderscamp, and him he liked for his very wickedness.
He in a manner took the boy under his tutelage, prompted him
to all kinds of mischief, aided him in every wild, harum-scarum
freak, until the lad became the complete scapegrace of the village; a pest to his uncle, and to everyone else. Nor were his
pranks confined to the land; he soon learned to accompany old
Pluto on the water.

Together these worthies would cruise about the broad bay,
and all the neighbouring straits and rivers; poking around in
skiffs and canoes; robbing the set-nets of the fishermen; landing
on remote coasts, and laying waste orchards and water-melon
patches; in short, carrying on a complete system of piracy, on
a small scale, Piloted by Pluto, the youthful Vanderscamp soon
became acquainted with all the bays, rivers, creeks, and inlets of
the watery world around him; could navigate from the Hook to
Spiting-devil on the darkest night, and learned to set even the
terrors of Hell-Gate at defiance.

At length, negro and boy suddenly disappeared, and days and
weeks elapsed, but without tidings of them. Some said they must

have run away and gone to sea; others jocosely hinted, that old Pluto, being no other than his namesake in disguise, had spirited away the boy to the nether regions. All, however, agreed in one thing—that the village was well rid of them.

In the process of time, the good Teunis Van Gieson slept with his fathers, and the tavern remained shut up, waiting for a claimant, for the next heir was Yan Yost Vanderscamp, and he had not been heard of for years. At length, one day, a boat was seen pulling for the shore, from a long, black, rakish-looking schooner, that lay at anchor in the bay. The boat's crew seemed worthy of the craft from which they debarked. Never had such a set of noisy, roistering, swaggering varlets landed in peaceful Communipaw.

They were outlandish in garb and demeanour, and were headed by a rough, burly, bully ruffian, with fiery whiskers, a copper nose, a scar across his face, and a great Flaunderish beaver slouched on one side of his head, in whom, to their dismay, the quiet inhabitants were made to recognize their early pest, Yan Yost Vanderscamp. The rear of this hopeful gang was brought up by old Pluto, who had lost an eye, grown grizzly-headed, and looked more like a devil than ever. Vanderscamp renewed his acquaintance with the old *burghers*, much against their will, and in a manner not at all to their taste. He slapped them familiarly on the back, gave them an iron grip of the hand, and was hail fellow well met. According to his own account, he had been all the world over; had made money by bags full; had ships in every sea, and now meant to turn the Wild Goose into a country seat, where he and his comrades—all rich merchants from foreign parts—might enjoy themselves in the interval of their voyages.

Sure enough, in a little while there was a complete metamorphose of the Wild Goose. From being a quiet, peaceful Dutch public house, it became a most riotous, uproarious private dwelling; a complete rendezvous for boisterous men of the seas, who came here to have what they called a "blow out" on dry land, and might be seen at all hours, lounging about the door, or lolling out of the windows; swearing among themselves, and cracking rough jokes on every passer-by.

The house was fitted up, too, in so strange a manner: hammocks slung to the walls, instead of bedsteads; odd kinds of furniture, of foreign fashion; bamboo couches, Spanish chairs; pistols, cutlasses, and blunderbusses, suspended on every peg; silver crucifixes on the mantel-pieces, silver candle-sticks and porringers on the tables, contrasting oddly with the pewter and Delf ware of the original establishment. And then the strange amusements of these sea-monsters! Pitching Spanish dollars, instead of quoits; firing blunderbusses out of the window; shooting at a mark, or at any unhappy dog, or cat, or pig, or barn-door fowl, that might happen to come within reach.

The only being who seemed to relish their rough waggery, was old Pluto; and yet he led but a dog's life of it; for they practised all kinds of manual jokes upon him; kicked him about like a football; shook him by his grizzly mop of wool, and never spoke to him without coupling a curse by way of adjective to his name, and consigning him to the infernal regions. The old fellow, however, seemed to like them the better, the more they cursed him, though his utmost expression of pleasure never amounted to more than the growl of a petted bear, when his ears are rubbed.

Old Pluto was the ministering spirit at the orgies of the Wild Goose; and such orgies as took place there! Such drinking, singing, whooping, swearing; with an occasional interlude of quarrelling and fighting. The noisier grew the revel, the more old Pluto plied the potations, until the guests would become frantic in their merriment, smashing everything to pieces, and throwing the house out of the windows. Sometimes, after a drinking bout, they sallied forth and scoured the village, to the dismay of the worthy *burghers*, who gathered their women within doors, and would have shut up the house.

Vanderscamp, however, was not to be rebuffed. He insisted on renewing acquaintance with his old neighbours, and on introducing his friends, the merchants, to their families; swore he was on the look-out for a wife, and meant, before he stopped, to find husbands for all their daughters. So, will-ye, nil-ye, sociable he was; swaggered about their best parlours, with his hat on one side of his head; sat on the good wife's nicely-waxed mahogany table, kicking his heels against the carved and polished legs; kissed and tousled the young *vrouws*; and, if they frowned and pouted, gave them a gold rosary, or a sparkling cross, to put them in good humour again.

Sometimes nothing would satisfy him, but he must have some of his old neighbours to dinner at the Wild Goose. There was no refusing him, for he had got the complete upper-hand of the community, and the peaceful *burghers* all stood in awe of him. But what a time would the quiet, worthy men have, among these rake-hells, who would delight to astound them with the most extravagant gunpowder tales, embroidered with all kinds of foreign oaths; clink the can with them; pledge them in deep potations; bawl drinking songs in their ears; and occasionally fire pistols over their heads, or under the table, and then laugh in their faces, and ask them how they liked the smell of gunpowder.

Thus was the little village of Communipaw for a time like the unfortunate wight possessed with devils; until Vanderscamp and his brother merchants would sail on another trading voyage, when the Wild Goose would be shut up, and everything relapse into quiet, only to be disturbed by his next visitation.

The mystery of all these proceedings gradually dawned upon the tardy intellects of Communipaw. These were the times of the notorious Captain Kidd, when the American harbours were the resorts of piratical adventurers of all kinds, who, under pretext of mercantile voyages, scoured the West Indies, made plundering descents upon the Spanish Main, visited even the remote Indian Seas, and then came to dispose of their booty, have their revels, and fit out new expeditions, in the English colonies.

Vanderscamp had served in this hopeful school, and having risen to importance among the *buccaneers*, had pitched upon his native village and early home, as a quiet, out-of-the-way, unsuspected place, where he and his comrades, while anchored at New York, might have their feasts, and concert their plans, without molestation.

At length the attention of the British government was called to these piratical enterprises, that were becoming so frequent and outrageous. Vigorous measures were taken to check and punish them. Several of the most noted freebooters were caught and executed, and three of Vanderscamp's chosen comrades, the most riotous swash-bucklers of the Wild Goose, were hanged in chains on Gibbet-Island, in full sight of their favourite resort. As to Vanderscamp himself, he and his man Pluto again disappeared, and it was hoped by the people of Communipaw that he had fallen in some foreign brawl, or been swung on some foreign gallows.

For a time, therefore, the tranquillity of the village was restored; the worthy Dutchmen once more smoked their pipes in peace, eying, with peculiar complacency, their old pests and terrors, the pirates, dangling and drying in the sun, on Gibbet-Island.

This perfect calm was doomed at length to be ruffled. The fiery persecution of the pirates gradually subsided. Justice was satisfied with the examples that had been made, and there was no more talk of Kidd, and the other heroes of like kidney. On a calm summer evening, a boat, somewhat heavily laden, was seen pulling into Communipaw. What was the surprise and disquiet of the inhabitants, to see Yan Yost Vanderscamp seated at the helm, and his man Pluto tugging at the oars! Vanderscamp, however, was apparently an altered man. He brought home with him a wife, who seemed to be a shrew, and to have the upper-hand of him. He no longer was the swaggering, bully ruffian, but affected the regular merchant, and talked of retiring from business, and settling down quietly, to pass the rest of his days in his native place.

The Wild Goose mansion was again opened, but with diminished splendour, and no riot. It is true, Vanderscamp had frequent nautical visitors, and the sound of revelry was occasionally overheard in his house; but everything seemed to be done under the rose; and old Pluto was the only servant that officiated at these orgies. The visitors, indeed, were by no means of the turbulent stamp of their predecessors; but quiet, mysterious traders, full of nods, and winks, and hieroglyphic signs, with whom, to use their cant phrase, "everything was smug." Their ships came to anchor at night in the lower bay; and, on a private signal, Vanderscamp would launch his boat, and accompanied solely by his man Pluto, would make them mysterious visits.

Sometimes boats pulled in at night, in front of the Wild Goose, and various articles of merchandise were landed in the dark, and spirited away, nobody knew whither. One of the more curious of the inhabitants kept watch, and caught a glimpse of the features of some of these night visitors, by the casual glance of a lantern, and declared that he recognized more than one of the freebooting frequenters of the Wild Goose, in former times; from whence he concluded that Vanderscamp was at his old game, and that this mysterious merchandise was nothing more nor less than piratical plunder. The more charitable opinion, however, was, that Vanderscamp and his comrades, having been driven from their old line of business, by the "oppressions of government," had resorted to smuggling to make both ends meet.

Be that as it may: I come now to the extraordinary fact, which is the butt-end of this story. It happened late one night, that Yan Yost Vanderscamp was returning across the broad bay, in his light skiff, rowed by his man Pluto. He had been carousing on board of a vessel, newly arrived, and was somewhat obfuscated in intellect, by the liquor he had imbibed. It was a still, sultry night; a heavy mass of lurid clouds was rising in the west, with the low muttering of distant thunder. Vanderscamp called on Pluto to pull lustily, that they might get home before the gathering storm. The old negro made no reply, but shaped his course so as to skirt the rocky shores of Gibbet-Island.

A faint creaking overhead caused Vanderscamp to cast up his eyes, when, to his horror, he beheld the bodies of his three pot companions and brothers in iniquity dangling in the moonlight, their rags fluttering, and their chains creaking, as they were slowly swung backward and forward by the rising breeze.

"What do you mean, you blockhead!" cried Vanderscamp, "by pulling so close to the island?"

"I thought you'd be glad to see your old friends once more," growled the negro; "you were never afraid of a living man, what do you fear from the dead?"

"Who's afraid?" hiccupped Vanderscamp, partly heated by liquor, partly nettled by the jeer of the negro; "who's afraid! Hang me, but I would be glad to see them once more, alive or dead, at the Wild Goose. Come, my lads in the wind!" continued he, taking a draught, and flourishing the bottle above his head, "here's fair weather to you in the other world; and if you should be walking the rounds tonight, odds fish! but I'll be happy if you will drop in to supper."

A dismal creaking was the only reply. The wind blew loud and shrill, and as it whistled round the gallows, and among the bones, sounded as if there were laughing and gibbering in the air. Old Pluto chuckled to himself, and now pulled for home. The storm burst over the voyagers, while they were yet far from shore. The rain fell in torrents, the thunder crashed and pealed, and the lightning kept up an incessant blaze. It was stark midnight, before they landed at Communipaw.

Dripping and shivering, Vanderscamp crawled homeward. He was completely sobered by the storm; the water soaked from without, having diluted and cooled the liquor within. Arrived at the Wild Goose, he knocked timidly and dubiously at the door, for he dreaded the reception he was to experience from his wife. He had reason to do so. She met him at the threshold, in a precious ill humour.

"Is this a time," said she, "to keep people out of their beds, and to bring home company, to turn the house upside down?"

"Company?" said Vanderscamp, meekly; "I have brought no company with me, wife."

"No, indeed! they have got here before you, but by your invitation; and blessed-looking company they are, truly!"

Vanderscamp's knees smote together. "For the love of heaven, where are they, wife?"

"Where?—why, in the blue-room, upstairs, making themselves as much at home as if the house were their own."

Vanderscamp made a desperate effort, scrambled up to the room, and threw open the door. Sure enough, there at a table, on which burned a light as blue as brimstone, sat the three guests from Gibbet-Island, with halters round their necks, and bobbing their cups together, as if they were hob-or-nobbing, and trolling the old Dutch freebooter's glee, since translated into English:—

For three merry lads be we,
And three merry lads be we;
I on the land, and thou on the sand,
And Jack on the gallows-tree.

Vanderscamp saw and heard no more. Starting back with horror, he missed his footing on the landing-place, and fell from the top of the stairs to the bottom. He was taken up speechless, and, either from the fall or the fright, was buried in the yard of the little Dutch church at Bergen, on the following Sunday.

From that day forward, the fate of the Wild Goose was sealed. It was pronounced a *haunted house,* and avoided accordingly. No one inhabited it but Vanderscamp's shrew of a widow, and old Pluto, and they were considered but little better than its hobgoblin visitors. Pluto grew more and more haggard and morose, and looked more like an imp of darkness than a human being. He spoke to no one, but went about muttering to himself; or, as some hinted, talking with the devil, who, though unseen, was ever at his elbow.

Now and then he was seen pulling about the bay alone, in his skiff, in dark weather, or at the approach of night-fall; nobody could tell why, unless on an errand to invite more guests from the gallows. Indeed it was affirmed that the Wild Goose still continued to be a house of entertainment for such guests, and that on stormy nights, the blue chamber was occasionally illuminated, and sounds of diabolical merriment were overheard, mingling with the howling of the tempest.

Some treated these as idle stories, until on one such night—it was about the time of the equinox—there was a horrible uproar in the Wild Goose, that could not be mistaken. It was not so much the sound of revelry, however, as strife, with two or three piercing shrieks, that pervaded every part of the village. Nevertheless, no one thought of hastening to the spot. On the contrary, the honest *burghers* of Communipaw drew their night-caps over their ears, and buried their heads under the bedclothes, at the thoughts of Vanderscamp and his gallows companions.

The next morning, some of the bolder and more curious undertook to reconnoitre. All was quiet and lifeless at the Wild Goose. The door yawned wide open, and had evidently been open all night, for the storm had beaten into the house. Gathering more courage from the silence and apparent desertion, they gradually ventured over the threshold.

The house had indeed the air of having been possessed by devils. Everything was topsy-turvy; trunks had been broken open, and chests of drawers and corner cupboards turned inside out, as in a time of general sack and pillage; but the most woeful sight was the widow of Yan Yost Vanderscamp, extended a corpse on the floor of the blue-chamber, with the marks of a deadly gripe on the wind-pipe.

All now was conjecture and dismay at Communipaw; and the disappearance of old Pluto, who was nowhere to be found, gave rise to all kinds of wild surmises. Some suggested that the negro had betrayed the house to some of Vanderscamp's *buccaneering* associates, and that they had decamped together with the booty; others surmised that the negro was nothing more nor less than a devil incarnate, who had now accomplished his ends, and made off with his dues.

Events, however, vindicated the negro from this last imputation. His skiff was picked up, drifting about the bay, bottom upward, as if wrecked in a tempest; and his body was found, shortly afterward, by some Communipaw fishermen, stranded among the rocks of Gibbet-Island, near the foot of the pirates' gallows.

The fishermen shook their heads, and observed that old Pluto had ventured once too often to invite Guests from Gibbet-Island.

A Tale From *The Alhambra*

Legend of the Arabian Astrologer

In old times, many hundred years ago, there was a Moorish king named Aben Habuz, who reigned over the kingdom of Granada. In his youthful days he had been a great conqueror, but now that he had grown old, he desired nothing more than to live at peace with all the world and to enjoy in quiet the possessions he had taken from his neighbours.

It so happened, however, that he had young rivals to deal with; princes full of the desire for fame and fighting, who had some old scores to settle with him which he had run up with their fathers. He also had some discontented districts in his own kingdom, which in his days of warfare he had treated with a high hand, and which, now that he languished for repose, were prone to rise in rebellion and threaten to invade him in his capital. Thus he had foes on every side; and as Granada is surrounded by wild and craggy mountains, which hide the approach of an enemy, the unfortunate Aben Habuz was kept in a constant state of watchfulness and alarm.

He built watchtowers on the mountains, and stationed guards at every pass with orders to make fires at night and smoke by day, on the approach of an enemy. But it was all in vain. His foes baffled him at every turn, and were sure to break out of some unthought-of pass, plunder his lands under his very nose, and then make off to the mountains with their prisoners and booty.

It chanced that while Aben Habuz was thus so sadly perplexed, an ancient Arabian arrived at his court. His white beard hung to his girdle, and he had every mark of extreme age, yet he had travelled almost the whole way from Egypt on foot, with no other aid than a staff marked with hieroglyphics. His fame had preceded him. His name was Ibrahim, and it was said that he had lived ever since the days of Mahomet. He had, when a child, followed the Arabian army into Egypt, where he had remained many years studying magic among the priests, and there he had learned the secret of prolonging life.

This wonderful old man was honourably entertained by the king. He invited him to remain in an apartment in his palace, but the old Arab preferred a cave in the side of the hill which rises above the city of Granada. He had the cave enlarged to form a spacious hall, with a circular hole at the top, through which he could see the heavens and behold the stars. The walls of this hall were covered with Egyptian hieroglyphics, and with the figures of the stars in their signs.

In a little while the sage Ibrahim became the bosom friend of the king, who applied to him for advice on every occasion. One day the king was as usual lamenting over the injustice of his neighbours and the strict watchfulness he was obliged to observe to guard himself against their invasions. The old Arab remained silent a moment, and then replied:

"Know, O king, that when I was in Egypt, I beheld a great marvel. On a mountain, above the city of Borsa, and overlooking the great valley of the Nile was a figure of a ram, and above it a figure of a cock, both of brass, and turning upon a pivot. Whenever the country was threatened with invasion, the ram would turn in the direction of the enemy, and the cock would crow. Upon this the inhabitants of the city knew of the danger, and of the quarter from which it was approaching, and could take timely means to guard against it."

"God is great!" exclaimed Aben Habuz, "what a treasure would be such a ram to keep an eye upon these mountains around me: and then such a cock, to crow in time of danger! How securely I might sleep in my palace with such sentinels on the top!"

"Listen, king," said the Arab. "When the city was conquered, this talisman was destroyed, but I was present and examined it and studied its secret and mystery, and I can make one of even greater power."

"O wise one," cried Aben Habuz, "better were such a talisman than all the watchtowers on the hills, and sentinels upon the borders. Give me such a safeguard, and the riches of my treasury are at your command."

And so the old Arab set to work at once to carry out the wishes of the king. He caused a great tower to be built upon the top of the royal palace. It was built of stones brought from Egypt, and taken, it is said, from one of the pyramids. In the upper part of the tower was a circular hall, with windows looking toward every point of the compass, and before each window was a table, on which was arranged, as on a chessboard, a mimic army of horse and foot, with an image of the monarch who ruled in that direction, all carved of wood.

To each of these tables there was a small lance, no bigger than a bodkin, on which were engraved certain Chaldaic characters. This hall was kept constantly closed, by a gate of brass, with a great lock of steel, the key of which was in possession of the king.

On the top of the tower was a bronze figure of a Moorish horseman, fixed on a pivot, with a shield on one arm and a lance. The face of this horseman was toward the city, as if keeping guard over it. But if any foe were at hand, the figure would turn in that direction, and would level the lance as if for action.

When this talisman was finished, Aben Habuz was all impatient to try it. And he now longed as much for an invasion as he had before sighed for peace. He soon had his wish. Tidings were brought, early one morning, that the face of the bronze horseman was turned toward the mountains of Elvira, and that his lance pointed directly against the Pass of Lope.

"Let the drums and trumpets sound to arms, and all Granada be put on the alert," said Aben Habuz.

"Let not your city be disturbed," said the Arab, "nor your

warriors called to arms. Send your attendants away and let us go alone to the secret hall of the tower."

So the ancient Aben Habuz mounted the staircase, leaning on the arm of the still more ancient Ibrahim. They unlocked the door and entered. The window that looked toward the Pass of Lope was open.

"In that direction," said the astrologer, "lies the danger. Behold, O king, the mystery of the table."

The king stepped close to the board on which were placed the small wooden figures, and, to his surprise, saw that they were all in motion. The horses pranced, the warriors brandished their weapons, and there was a faint sound of drums and trumpets, and a clang of arms, and the neighing of steeds: but all no louder, nor more distinct, than the hum of a bee.

"Behold," said the astrologer, "a proof that your enemies are even now in the field. They must be advancing through the mountains, by the Pass of Lope. If you wish them to retreat without loss of life, strike these images with the head of the magic lance, but if you would cause bloodshed among them, strike with the point."

Aben Habuz seized the lance with trembling eagerness.

"Son of Abu Ayub," exclaimed he, in a chuckling tone, "I think we will have a little blood!"

So saying, he thrust the magic lance into one of the images, and beat others with the head, upon which the former fell as dead upon the board, and the rest turned upon each other and began fighting pell-mell.

It was hard for the astrologer to stay the hand of the old king, and prevent him from killing all of his foes, but at last he persuaded him to leave the tower, and scouts were at once sent out to the mountains.

They returned with the news that a Christian army had advanced through the heart of the Sierra, almost within sight of Granada, where disagreement had broken out among them. They had turned upon each other, and after much killing had retreated over the border.

Aben Habuz was overjoyed.

"At length," said he, "I shall lead a life of peace, and have all my enemies in my power."

And to the Arab he said:

"What can I give you in reward for so great a blessing?"

"The wants of an old man and a philosopher are few and simple. Grant me but the means of fitting up my cave and I am content," answered Ibrahim.

The king was secretly pleased to know that he asked so small a reward. He ordered his treasurer to give him whatever sums might be required to furnish and complete his cave.

The astrologer now gave orders to have various chambers hewn out of the solid rock. These he caused to be furnished with beautiful ottomans and divans, and the walls to be hung with rich silks from Damascus.

"I am an old man," said he, "and can no longer rest my bones on stone couches. These damp walls require covering."

He had the apartments hung with silver and crystal lamps, which were filled with a fragrant oil made according to a recipe which he had found in the tombs of Egypt. These lights diffused a soft radiance.

"The light of the sun," said he, "is too bright for the eyes of an old man. The light of these lamps is better suited to the studies of a philosopher."

The treasurer of King Aben Habuz groaned at the sums daily demanded by the astrologer, and he finally carried his complaints to the king. The royal word, however, had been given. Aben Habuz shrugged his shoulders.

"We must have patience," said he. "All things have an end, and so will the furnishing of this cavern."

And he was right. The hermitage was at last complete, and formed a sumptuous underground palace.

While the Arab passed his time in his cave, Aben Habuz carried on furious battles in the tower. It was a glorious thing for an old man, like himself, to have war made easy, and to be able to amuse himself in his chamber by brushing away whole armies like so many swarms of flies. And by degrees, his enemies grew weary from repeated failures and tried no more to invade his kingdom.

At length, one day, the bronze horseman turned suddenly round, and lowering his lance, made a dead point towards a certain range of mountains. Aben Habuz hastened to his tower, but the magic table in that direction was quiet—not a single warrior was in motion. The king was perplexed and sent out a troop to scour the mountains. They returned after three days' absence.

"We have searched every mountain pass," said they, "but not a helm nor spear was stirring. All that we have found was a Christian damsel of great beauty, sleeping at noon-tide beside a fountain."

"Let her be brought before me," said the king.

So the Christian damsel was brought into the king's presence. She was dressed in the style of the Spaniards at the time of the Arabian conquest. Pearls were entwined in her hair, and jewels sparkled on her forehead. Around her neck was a golden chain, to which was suspended a silver lyre which hung by her side.

The flashes of her dark eyes were like sparks of fire on the old yet combustible heart of Aben Habuz,

"Fairest of women," cried he, "who and what are you?"

"The daughter of a Spanish prince who but lately ruled over this land. The armies of my father have been destroyed, as if by magic, among these mountains. He has been driven into exile, and his daughter is a captive."

"Beware, O king!" whispered Ibrahim. "This may be some evil spirit sent by your foes to do you harm—I think I read witchcraft in her eye. Doubtless this is the enemy pointed out by the talisman."

"You are a wise man I grant," replied the king, "but you are little versed in the ways of women. In that knowledge I yield to no man. As to this damsel, I see no harm in her. She is fair to look upon and finds favour in my eyes."

"Hearken, king!" said the astrologer. "I have given you many victories by means of my talisman, but have never shared any of the spoil. Give me this stray captive, to solace me in my solitude with her silver lyre."

"What!" cried Aben Habuz. "You have already dancing-women to solace you."

"Dancing-women I have, it is true," said Ibrahim, "but I would have a little minstrelsy to refresh my mind when weary with the toils of study."

But the king would not listen to the Arab's request, and they parted in high displeasure.

All kinds of festivities were devised for the entertainment of the princess—minstrelsy, dancing, tournaments, bull-fights. Granada for a time was a scene of perpetual pageant. But she treated all this as a matter of course, and seemed to take delight in causing expense as if she wished to drain the treasury of the king.

Aben Habuz could not flatter himself that he had made any impression on the heart of the princess. She never frowned on him, it is true, but then she never smiled. Whenever he began to plead his suit, she struck her silver lyre, and in an instant the old monarch began to nod and gradually sink into a deep sleep. All Granada scoffed at his infatuation.

At length the danger burst on the head of Aben Habuz, but this time the talisman gave him no warning. His palace was surrounded by an armed rabble, and both his life and that of the princess were in danger. At the head of a handful of guards he sallied forth, put the rebels to flight, and crushed the insurrection in the bud.

When quiet was again restored, he went in great alarm to the astrologer who still remained shut up in his cave.

"Wise Ibrahim," said he, "what you foretold has in some sort come to pass. The princess has brought trouble and danger upon me. How can I be secure from my enemies? Show me some safe retreat where I can stay in peace."

A gleam shone from the eyes of the Arab under his bushy eyebrows.

"You have heard, no doubt," said he, "of the palace and garden of Irem named in the *Koran*."

And the king answered:

"I have heard of that garden: wonderful things are told of it by the pilgrims who visit Mecca, but I have thought them only wild fables."

"Listen," said Ibrahim. "In my younger days, when I was a mere Arab of the desert, I tended my father's camels. Once one of them strayed from the rest and was lost. I searched after it for several days, but in vain, until, weary and faint, I laid myself down and slept under a palm tree by the side of a well. When I awoke, I found myself at the gate of the city. I entered and saw noble streets and squares and market places, but all were silent and without an inhabitant. I wandered on until I came to a palace with a garden adorned with fountains and fish ponds and groves and flowers and orchards of delicious fruits. But still no one was to be seen.

"I became frightened and hastened to depart, and when I had gone through the gate of the city, I turned to look upon the palace once more, but it was no longer to be seen—nothing but the silent desert before my eyes. I met an ancient Arabian, who knew the secrets of the land, and told him what had befallen me: 'This,' said he, 'is the Garden of Irem, one of the wonders of the desert. It only appears at times to some wanderer like yourself.' In after years, when I had been in Egypt and made myself master of all kinds of magic spells, I made up my mind to visit again this wonderful garden. I did so.

"It was revealed to me and I passed several days in the palace. The *genii* who watch over the palace obeyed my magic power, and from them I learned how the whole garden came into existence, and how it was made invisible. What say you, king, would you have a palace and garden like that of Irem, filled with all manner of delights, but hidden from the eyes of mortals?"

"O wise one," exclaimed the king eagerly, "make me such a garden and ask any reward even to the half of my kingdom."

"Alas," replied the other, "you know I am an old man and a philosopher, and easily satisfied. All the reward I ask is the first beast of burden with its load, which shall enter the gates of the garden."

The king gladly agreed and the Arab began his work. On the top of the hill just above his underground hall, he had a great gateway built. There was an outer porch with a lofty arch, and within was a portal secured by massive gates. On the top stone of the portal, the Arab, with his own hand, made the figure of a huge key, and on the top stone of the outer arch, which was loftier than that of the portal, he carved a gigantic hand. Over these he repeated many sentences in an unknown tongue.

When this gateway was finished, he shut himself up for two days in his hall, engaged in secret incantations. The third day he went to the summit of the hill, and passed the whole day there. At a late hour he came down and appeared before the king.

"My work is finished," said he. "On the summit of the hill stands one of the most wonderful palaces that ever the head of man devised, or the heart of man desired. It contains beautiful halls, galleries, gardens, cool fountains, and fragrant baths. The whole mountain is like paradise. Like the garden of Irem, it is hidden from the sight of mortals, except those who know the secret of the talismans."

"Enough!" cried Aben Habuz joyfully. "Tomorrow morning with the first light we will take possession."

Scarcely had the rays of the sun begun to play about the mountains when Aben Habuz mounted his steed, and with a few of his attendants ascended a steep and narrow road leading up the hill. Beside him on a white palfrey rode the princess. Her whole dress sparkled with jewels, and round her neck was suspended her silver lyre. The Arab, who never mounted a steed of any kind, walked beside the king carrying his staff.

Aben Habuz looked to see the towers of the palace, the terraces and gardens, but as yet nothing of the kind was to be seen.

"That is the mystery of the place," said the Arab; "nothing can be discerned until you have passed the spell-bound gateway."

As they drew near, Ibrahim paused, and pointed out the hand and key carved upon the portal of the arch.

"These," said he, "are the talismans which guard the entrance to this paradise. Until the hand shall reach down and seize the key no evil can prevail against the lord of this mountain."

While the king was gazing in silent wonder at these signs, the palfrey of the princess went on and bore her in at the portal, to the very centre of the barbican.

"Behold," cried the astrologer, "my promised reward: the first animal with its burden that should enter the gateway."

The king smiled at first, not thinking the old man in earnest, but when he found that he was, his gray beard trembled with indignation.

"You know the meaning of my promise," said he sternly, "the first beast of burden, with its load, that should enter this portal. Take the strongest mule in my stables, load it with the most precious things of my treasury, and it is yours, but dare not to think that I shall give you the princess."

"What need I of wealth?" cried the Arab scornfully. "The princess is mine by right. Your word is pledged. I claim her as my own."

The princess looked down haughtily from her palfrey, as she listened to this dispute between two gray heads.

"Base son of the desert," cried the king, "you may be master of many arts, but know me for your master, and do not try to juggle with your king."

"My master!" echoed the Arab, "my king indeed! Farewell, Aben Habuz, reign over your petty kingdom! As for me, I shall laugh at you in my retirement."

And saying this, he seized the bridle of the palfrey on which the princess was seated, smote the earth with his staff, and sank with her through the centre of the barbican. The earth closed and no trace remained of the opening.

Aben Habuz was struck dumb for a time. Then he ordered a thousand workmen to dig into the ground where the Arab had disappeared. They digged and digged, but in vain. As soon as they threw the earth out, it filled in again. They sought the Arab's cavern at the foot of the hill, but there was no entrance to be found.

All of the king's talismans now ceased to be of use. The bronze horseman remained fixed with his face turned toward the hill and his spear pointed to the spot where the Arab had descended, as if there still lurked the king's deadliest foe.

The top of the mountain, the site of the promised palace and garden, remained a desolate waste. And the neighbours of the king, finding him no longer protected by magic spell, invaded his lands from all sides, and the remainder of his life was a tissue of turmoils.

At length Aben Habuz died and was buried.

Ages have since rolled away. The Alhambra has been built on the mountain, and in some measure resembles the fabled garden of Irem. The spell-bound gateway still stands with the mystic hand and key, and now forms the entrance to the fortress. Under the gateway, it is said, the old Arab still remains in his underground cavern, nodding on his divan, lulled by the silver lyre of the princess.

The old sentinels, who guard the gate, hear the music of the lyre sometimes in the summer nights, and doze quietly at their posts.

It is said that even those who watch by day are generally found nodding on the stone benches, or sleeping under the trees, so that in truth it is the drowsiest military post in all the world.

And the legends tell us that this will endure. From age to age the Christian princess will remain a captive to the old Arab, and by the music of her lyre he will remain in magic slumber, unless the mystic hand shall grasp the fated key and dispel the whole charm of this enchanted mountain.

A Tale From *The Alhambra*

Legend of Prince Ahmed Al Kamel; or, The Pilgrim of Love

There was once a Moorish king of Granada, who had but one son, whom he named Ahmed, to which his courtiers added the surname of al Kamel, or the Perfect, from the signs of super-excellence which they perceived in him in his very infancy. The astrologers predicted everything in his favour that could make a perfect prince and a prosperous sovereign. One cloud only rested upon his destiny. Unless he could be kept from falling in love until he was of mature age, he would run great perils.

To prevent this danger, the king wisely determined to rear him in a seclusion where he would never see a woman. For this purpose he built a beautiful palace on the brow of the hill above the Alhambra, in the midst of delightful gardens, but surrounded by lofty walls, being, in fact, the same palace known at the present day as the Generalife. In this palace the youthful prince was shut up and entrusted to the care of Eben Bonabben, one of the wisest and driest of Arabian sages, who had passed the greatest part of his life in Egypt, studying hieroglyphics, and making researches among the tombs and pyramids, and who saw more charms in an Egyptian mummy than in a living beauty.

The prince grew up in the seclusion of the palace and its gardens, under the vigilant care of Eben Bonabben, who sought to instruct him in the abstruse lore of Egypt. But in this he made little progress, and it was soon evident that he had no turn for philosophy.

He was, however, amazingly ductile for a youthful prince, ready to follow any advice, and always guided by the last counsellor. He suppressed his yawns, and listened patiently to the long and learned discourse of Eben Bonabben, from which he imbibed a smattering of various kinds of knowledge, and thus happily attained his twentieth year, a miracle of princely wisdom.

About this time, however, a change came over the conduct of the prince. He completely abandoned his studies, and took to strolling about the gardens, and musing about the side of the fountains. He had been taught a little music among his various accomplishments. It now engrossed a great part of his time, and a turn for poetry became apparent. The sage Eben Bonabben took the alarm, and endeavoured to work these idle humours out of him by a severe course of algebra: but the prince turned from it with distaste.

"I cannot endure algebra," said he. "I want something that speaks more to the heart."

The sage Eben Bonabben shook his dry head at the words.

"Here is an end to philosophy," thought he. "The prince has discovered he has a heart."

As algebra was not to be mentioned, and he had exhausted almost all kinds of agreeable knowledge, he now tried to instruct him in the language of birds. This Eben Bonabben had learned in Egypt, and the prince applied himself to the study with such avidity that he soon became as great an adept as his master.

The tower of the Generalife was no longer a solitude: he had companions at hand with whom he could converse.

The first acquaintance he formed was with a hawk, who built his nest in a crevice of the lofty battlements, whence he soared far and wide in quest of prey. The prince, however, found little to like or esteem in him. He was a mere pirate of the air, swaggering and boastful, whose talk was all about carnage and desperate exploits.

His next acquaintance was an owl, a wise-looking bird, with a huge head and staring eyes, who sat blinking and goggling all day in a hole in the wall, but roamed forth at night. He had great pretensions to wisdom, talked of the moon, hinted at the dark sciences, and was grievously given to metaphysics, and the prince found him even more ponderous than Eben Bonabben.

Then there was a bat, that hung all day by his heels in the dark corner of a vault, but sallied out in slipshod style at twilight. He, however, had but twilight ideas on all subjects, and seemed to take delight in nothing.

Besides these there was a swallow, with whom the prince was at first much taken. He was a smart talker, but restless, bustling, and forever on the wing. He turned out in the end to be a mere smatterer, who did but skim over the surface of things, pretending to know everything, but knowing nothing thoroughly.

These were the only feathered associates with whom he had any opportunity of exercising his newly acquired language. The tower was too high for any other birds to frequent it. He soon grew weary of his new acquaintances whose conversation spoke so little to the head and nothing to the heart, and gradually relapsed into his loneliness. A winter passed away, spring opened with all its bloom and verdure, and the time arrived for birds to build their nests. Suddenly, as it were, a universal burst of song broke from the groves and gardens of the Generalife, and reached the prince in the solitude of his tower. From every side he heard the same universal theme—love—love—love—chanted, and responded to in every variety of note and tone. He listened in silence and perplexity.

"What can this love be?" thought he, "of which the world seems to be so full, and of which I know nothing?"

He applied for information to his friend the hawk. The bird answered in a tone of scorn.

"You must apply," said he, "to the vulgar, peaceable birds of earth, who are made for the prey of us princes of the air. My trade is war, and fighting my delight. I am a warrior, and know nothing of this thing called love."

The prince turned from him with disgust and sought the owl in his retreat.

"This is a bird," said he, "of peaceful habits, and may be able to solve my question."

So he asked the owl to tell him what was this love about which all the birds in the groves below were singing.

Upon this the owl put on a look of offended dignity.

"My time," said he, "is taken up with study and research. As to these singing birds of whom you talk, I never listen to them—I despise them and their themes. Allah be praised, I cannot sing: I am a philosopher, and know nothing of this thing called love."

The prince now repaired to the vault, where his friend the bat was hanging by the heels, and asked the same question. The bat wrinkled up his nose into a most snappish expression.

"Why do you disturb me in my morning's nap with such an idle question?" said he peevishly. "I only fly by twilight, when all birds are asleep, and never trouble myself with their concerns. I am neither bird nor beast, and I thank Heaven for it. I have found out the villainy of the whole of them, and hate them one and all. I know nothing of this thing called love."

As a last resort, the prince now sought the swallow, and stopped him just as he was circling about the summit of the tower. The swallow, as usual, was in a hurry, and had scarce time to make a reply.

"Upon my word," said he, "I have so much public business to attend to, and so many pursuits to follow, that I have had no time to think on the subject. I have every day a thousand visits to pay; a thousand affairs of importance to examine into, that leaves me not a moment of leisure for these little sing-song matters. In a word, I am a citizen of the world—I know nothing of this thing called love."

So saying, the swallow dived into the valley and was out of sight in a moment.

The prince remained disappointed and perplexed, and while he was still in this mood, Eben Bonabben entered the tower. The prince advanced eagerly to meet him.

"O Eben Bonabben," cried he, "you have revealed to me much of the wisdom of the earth; but there is one thing of which I remain in utter ignorance, and would fain be informed. Tell me, most profound of sages, what is the nature of this thing called love?"

Eben Bonabben was struck as with a thunderbolt. He trembled and turned pale, and felt as if his head sat but loosely on his shoulders. What could have suggested such a question to the prince? Where could he have learnt so idle a word?

The prince led him to the window of the tower.

"Listen, O Eben Bonabben," said he. The sage listened. The nightingale sat singing in the thicket below the tower, and from every grove rose a strain of melody; and love—love—love—was still the unvarying strain.

"*Allah Akbar!* God is great! "cried the wise Bonabben. "Who shall pretend to keep this secret from the heart of man, when even the birds of the air conspire to betray it?"

Then turning to Ahmed:

"O prince," cried he, "shut your ears to these strains. Close your mind against this dangerous knowledge. Know that this love is the cause of half the ills of wretched mortality. It is this which produces bitterness and strife between brethren and friends; care and sorrow, weary days and sleepless nights, are its attendants. It withers the bloom and blights the joy of youth, and brings on the ills and griefs of premature age. *Allah* preserve you in total ignorance of this thing called love!"

The sage Eben Bonabben hastily retired, leaving the prince plunged in still deeper perplexity. It was in vain he attempted to dismiss the subject from his mind. It still continued uppermost in his thoughts.

"Surely," said he to himself, as he listened to the tuneful strains of the birds, "there is no sorrow in those notes. If love be a cause of such wretchedness and strife, why are not these birds drooping in solitude, or tearing each other in pieces, instead of fluttering cheerfully about the groves, or sporting with each other among the flowers?"

One morning, as the prince sat at his window in the tower, there was a sudden rushing noise in the air. A beautiful dove, pursued by a hawk, darted in at the window, and fell panting on the floor, while the pursuer, balked of his prey, soared off to the mountains.

The prince took up the gasping bird and smoothed its feathers. When he had soothed it, he put it in a golden cage, and offered it the finest and whitest of wheat and the purest of water. The bird, however, refused food, and sat drooping and pining, and uttering piteous moans.

"Have you not everything your heart can wish?" said Ahmed.

"Alas, no!" replied the dove. "Am I not separated from my mate and that too in the happy spring-time, the very season of love?"

"Pray, pretty bird," said the prince. "Can you then tell me what is love?"

"Too well can I," replied the dove. "It is the torment of one, the felicity of two, the strife and enmity of three. It is the charm which draws two beings together, and unites them by tender sympathies, making it happiness to be with each other, but misery to be apart. Is there no being to whom you are drawn by such ties?"

"I like my old teacher, Eben Bonabben, better than any other being. But he is often tedious, and I occasionally feel myself happier without his society."

"That is not the sympathy I mean. I speak of love, the great principle of life. Every created being has its mate. The very beetle wooes its lady-beetle in the dust. Is there no beautiful princess nor lovely damsel who has ensnared your heart?"

"I begin to understand," said the prince, sighing.

A little further conversation ensued, and the first lesson was complete.

"Alas!" said he, "if love be such a delight, and its interruption such a misery, *Allah* forbid that I should mar the joy of any of its votaries."

He opened the cage, took out the dove, and carried it to the window.

"Go, happy bird," said he, "rejoice with your mate in the days of youth and springtime. Why should I make you a fellow prisoner in this dreary tower, where love can never enter?"

The dove flapped its wings in rapture, gave one vault into the air, and then swooped downward to the blooming bowers of the Darro.

A few mornings afterward, as the prince was ruminating on the battlements of the tower, the dove came hovering in the air, and alighted fearlessly upon his shoulder.

"Happy bird," said he, "who can fly, as it were, with the wings of the morning to the uttermost parts of the earth, where have you been since we parted?"

"In a far country, prince, whence I bring you tidings in reward for my liberty. In the wild compass of my flight, which extends over plain and mountain, as I was soaring in the air, I beheld below me a delightful garden with all kinds of fruits and flowers. It was in a green meadow, on the banks of a winding stream: and in the centre of the garden was a stately palace. I alighted in one of the bowers to rest after my weary flight. On the green bank below me was a youthful princess. She was surrounded by female attendants, young like herself, who decked her with garlands, but no flower of the field could compare with her for loveliness. 'Here,' thought I, 'is the being formed by Heaven to inspire my prince with love.'"

The resolution of the prince was taken. He addressed a letter to the princess: "To the Unknown Beauty, from Ahmed al Kamel," and gave it to the dove.

"Away, trustiest of messengers!" said he. "Fly over mountain and valley, river and plain. Rest not until you have given this letter to the princess."

The dove soared high in the air, and taking his course, darted away. The prince followed him with his eye until he was a mere speck on a cloud, and gradually disappeared behind a mountain.

Day after day he watched for the return of the messenger, but he watched in vain. At last, one evening toward sunset, the faithful bird fluttered into his apartment, and, falling at his feet, expired. The arrow of some archer had pierced his breast, yet he had struggled with the lingerings of life to deliver the message. As the prince bent with grief over the gentle martyr, he beheld a chain of pearls round his neck, attached to which, beneath his wing, was a small enamelled picture. It represented a lovely princess in the very flower of her years, and was doubtless the unknown beauty of the garden. But who and where was she? And was this picture sent as a token of her approval of his letter?

Unfortunately the death of the faithful dove left everything in mystery and doubt. The prince gazed on the picture. "I will fly from this palace," said he, "which has become an odious prison, and will seek this unknown princess throughout the world." To escape from the tower in the day, when everyone was awake, might be a difficult matter; but at night the palace was slightly guarded, for no one thought of the prince making any attempt of the kind. He had always been passive in his captivity. How was he to guide himself, however, in his flight, being ignorant of the country? He bethought him of the owl, who was used to roaming at night, and must know every by-lane and secret path. Seeking him in his hermitage, he questioned him touching his knowledge of the land. Upon this the owl put on a mighty self-important look.

"You must know, O prince," said he, "that we owls are of a very ancient and extensive family, though rather fallen to decay, and possess ruinous castles and palaces in all parts of Spain. There is scarcely a tower of the mountains, or a fortress of the plains or old citadel, but has some brother, or uncle, or cousin, quartered in it. And in going the rounds to visit my numerous kindred, I have pried into every nook and corner, and made myself acquainted with every secret of the land."

The prince was overjoyed to find the owl so deeply versed in topography, and now informed him of his intended elopement, urging him to be his companion and counsellor.

"Go to!" said the owl, with a look of displeasure. "Am I a bird to engage in such an affair as this?—I whose whole time is devoted to meditation and the moon?"

"Be not offended, most solemn owl," replied the prince. "Abstract yourself for a time from meditation and the moon. Aid me in my flight, and you shall have whatever heart can wish."

"I have that already," said the owl. "A few mice are sufficient for my frugal table, and this hole in the wall is spacious enough for my studies. What more does a philosopher like myself desire?"

"But think, wise owl, that while moping in your cell and gazing at the moon, all your talents are lost to the world. I shall one day be a sovereign prince, and may advance you to some post of honour and dignity."

The owl, though a philosopher, and above the ordinary wants of life, was not above ambition, so he was finally prevailed on to elope with the prince and be his guide in the pilgrimage.

The prince collected all his jewels, and concealed them about his person as travelling funds. That very night he lowered himself by his scarf from a balcony of the tower, clambered over the outer walls of the Generalife, and, guided by the owl, made good his escape before morning to the mountains.

He now held a council with his guide as to his future course.

"Might I advise," said the owl, "I would recommend you to repair to Seville. You must know that many years since I was on a visit to an uncle, an owl of great dignity and power, who lived in a ruined wing of the Alcazar. In my hoverings at night over the city, I frequently remarked a light burning in a lonely tower. At length I alighted on the battlements, and found it to proceed from the lamp of an Arabian magician. He was surrounded by his magic books, and on his shoulder was perched an ancient raven, who had come with him from Egypt. I am acquainted with that raven, and owe to him a great part of the knowledge I possess. The magician is since dead, but the raven still inhabits the tower, for these birds are of wonderfully long life. I would advise you, O prince, to seek that raven, for like all ravens, especially those of Egypt, he is a renowned soothsayer and a conjuror."

The prince was struck with the wisdom of this advice, and accordingly bent his course towards Seville. He travelled only in the night to accommodate his companion, and lay by during the day in some dark cavern or mouldering watchtower, for the owl knew every hiding place of the kind, and had a great taste for ruins.

At length one morning, at daybreak, they reached the city of Seville, where the owl, who hated the glare and bustle of crowded streets, halted without the gate, and took up his quarters in a hollow tree.

The prince entered the gate and readily found the magic tower, which rose above the houses of the city as a palm tree rises above the shrubs of the desert. It was in fact the same as the tower standing today, and known as the Giralda.

The prince ascended by a great winding staircase to the summit of the tower, where he found the raven—an old, mysterious, gray-headed bird, ragged in feather, with a film over one eye. He was perched on one leg, with his head turned on one side, poring with his remaining eye on a diagram described on the pavement.

The prince approached him with awe and reverence.

"Pardon me, most ancient and wise raven," exclaimed he, "if for a moment I interrupt those studies which are the wonder of the world. You behold in me a pilgrim of love, and I would seek your counsel how to obtain the object of my devotion."

"And can you be at any loss for an object in Andalusia?" said the old raven, leering upon him with his single eye. "Above all, can you be at a loss in Seville, where black-eyed damsels dance the *zambra* under every orange grove?"

The prince was somewhat shocked at hearing an old bird with one foot in the grave talk thus loosely.

"Believe me," said he gravely, "I am on no such light errand as that. The black-eyed damsels of Andalusia who dance among the orange groves are naught to me. I seek the original of this picture. And I beseech you, most potent raven, if it be within the scope of your knowledge or reach of your art, inform me where she may be found."

The gray-headed raven was rebuked by the gravity of the prince.

"What know I," replied he dryly, "of youth and beauty? My visits are to the old and not the young and fair. I am the harbinger of fate who croak bodings of death from the chimney-top and flap my wings at the sick man's window. You must seek elsewhere for tidings of your unknown princess."

"And where can I seek if not among the sons of wisdom? Know that I am a royal prince, fated by the stars, and sent on a mysterious enterprise on which may hang the destiny of empires."

When the raven heard that it was a matter of vast moment, he changed his tone and manner, and listened with profound attention to the story of the prince. When it was finished, he replied:

"Touching this princess, I can give you no information of myself, for my flight is not among gardens, or around ladies' bowers. But go to Cordova, seek the palm tree which stands in the court of the principal mosque. At the foot of it you will find a great traveller who has visited all countries and courts. He will give you tidings of the object of your search."

"Many thanks for this information," said the prince. "Farewell."

"Farewell," said the raven dryly, and again fell to pondering on the diagram.

The prince sallied forth from Seville, sought his fellow-traveller, the owl, who was still dozing in the hollow tree, and set off for Cordova.

He approached it along hanging gardens, and orange and citron groves, overlooking the fair valley of the river. When they arrived at the city gates, the owl flew up to a dark hole in the wall, and the prince proceeded in quest of the palm tree which had been planted in days of yore. It stood in the midst of the great court of the mosque towering from amidst orange and cypress trees. Men were seated in groups under the cloisters of the court, and many of the faithful were washing at the fountains, before entering the mosque.

At the foot of the palm tree was a crowd listening to the words of one who appeared to be a great talker.

"This," said the prince to himself, "must be the great traveller who is to give me tidings of the unknown princess."

He mingled in the crowd, but was astonished to perceive that they were all listening to a parrot, who, with his bright-green coat, pragmatical eye and consequential top-knot, had the air of a bird on excellent terms with himself.

"How is this," said the prince to one of the bystanders, "that so many grave persons can be delighted with a chattering bird?"

"You know not whom you speak of," said the other. "This parrot is a descendant of the famous parrot of Persia, renowned for his story-telling talent. He has all the learning of the East at the tip of his tongue, and can quote poetry as fast as he can talk. He has visited various foreign courts, where he has been considered an oracle of erudition."

"Enough," said the prince, "I will have some private talk with this distinguished traveller."

He sought a private interview, and told the parrot the nature of his errand. He had scarcely mentioned it when the parrot burst into a fit of dry rickety laughter, that brought tears into his eyes.

"Excuse my merriment," said he, "but the mere mention of love always sets me laughing."

The prince was shocked at this ill-timed mirth.

"Is not love," said he, "the universal bond of sympathy?"

"A fig's end!" cried the parrot, interrupting him. "Prithee where have you learned this jargon? Trust me, love is quite out of vogue. One never hears of it in the company of wits and people of refinement."

The prince sighed as he recalled the different language of his friend the dove. He then directed his inquiries to the immediate purport of his visit.

"Tell me," said he, "have you in the course of your travels met with the original of this portrait?"

The parrot took the picture in his claw, turned his head from side to side, and examined it curiously with either eye.

"Upon my honour," said he, "a very pretty face, a very pretty face. But then one sees so many pretty women in one's travels that one can hardly—but hold—bless me! now I look at it again—sure enough, this is the princess Aldegonda. How could I forget one who is such a favourite with me!"

"The Princess Aldegonda!" echoed the prince. "And where is she to be found?"

"Softly, softly," said the parrot: "easier to be found than gained. She is the only daughter of the Christian king who reigns at Toledo, and is shut up from the world until her seventeenth birthday. You will not get a sight of her. No mortal man can see her. I was admitted to her presence to entertain her, and I assure you, on the word of a parrot who has seen the world, I have conversed with much sillier princesses in my time."

"A word in confidence, my dear parrot," said the prince. "I am heir to a kingdom, and shall one day sit upon a throne. I see that you are a bird of parts, and understand the world. Help me to gain possession of this princess, and I will advance you to some distinguished place about my court."

"With all my heart," said the parrot. "But let it be a sinecure, if possible, for we wits have a great dislike to labour."

Arrangements were promptly made. The prince sallied forth from Cordova through the same gate by which he had entered. He called the owl down from the hole in the wall, introduced him to his new travelling companion as a brother savant, and off they set on their journey.

The prince was impatient, but they travelled much more slowly than he wished. The parrot was accustomed to high life, and did not like to be disturbed early in the morning. The owl, on the other hand, was for sleeping at midday, and lost a great deal of time by his long *siestas*. His antiquarian taste also was in the way, for he insisted on pausing and inspecting every ruin, and had long legendary tales to tell about every old tower and castle in the country.

The prince had supposed that he and the parrot, being both birds of learning, would delight in each other's society, but never had he been more mistaken. They were eternally bickering. The one was a wit, the other a philosopher. The parrot quoted poetry, was critical on new readings and eloquent on small points of erudition: the owl treated all such knowledge as trifling, and cared for nothing but metaphysics. Then the parrot would sing songs and crack jokes upon his solemn neighbour, and laugh at his own wit. The owl considered all this as an invasion on his dignity, and he would scowl and sulk and swell, and be silent for a whole day together.

The prince, being wrapped up in the dreams of his own fancy, gave no heed to the wranglings of his companions. In this way they journeyed through the stern passes of the mountains, across the sunburnt plains of La Mancha and Castile, and along the banks of the Tagus, which winds its wizard mazes over one half of Spain and Portugal.

At length they came in sight of a strong city with walls and towers built on a rocky promontory, round the foot of which the Tagus circled with brawling violence.

"Behold!" exclaimed the owl, "the ancient city of Toledo. Behold those venerable domes and towers, in which so many of my ancestors have meditated."

"Pish!" cried the parrot, interrupting his solemn rapture. "What have we to do with legends and your ancestry? Behold what is more to the purpose—behold at length, O prince, the abode of your long-sought princess."

The prince looked in the direction indicated by the parrot, and beheld, in a delightful green meadow on the banks of the Tagus, a stately palace rising from amidst the bowers of a garden. It was just such a place as had been described by the dove as the residence of the original of the picture. He gazed at it with a throbbing heart.

"Perhaps at this moment," thought he, "the beautiful princess is sporting beneath those shady bowers, or pacing with delicate step those stately terraces, or reposing beneath those lofty roofs!"

As he looked more closely, he perceived that the walls of the garden were of great height, so as to defy access, while numbers of armed guards patrolled around them.

The prince turned to the parrot.

"Most accomplished of birds," said he, "you have the gift of human speech! Hie you to yon garden. Seek the princess, and tell her that Prince Ahmed, guided by the stars, has arrived in quest of her."

The parrot, proud of his embassy, flew away to the garden, mounted above its lofty wall, and, after soaring for a time over the lawns and groves, alighted on the balcony of a pavilion that overhung the river. Here, looking in at the casement, he beheld the princess reclining on a couch, with her eyes fixed on a paper, while tears gently stole after each other down her pallid cheek.

Pluming his wings for a moment, and adjusting his bright-green coat, the parrot perched himself beside her with a gallant air. Then he assumed a tenderness of tone.

"Dry your tears, most beautiful of princesses," said he; "I come to bring solace to your heart."

The princess was startled on hearing a voice, but turning and seeing nothing but a little green-coated bird bobbing and bowing before her:

"Alas! what solace can you yield," said she, "seeing you are but a parrot?"

The parrot was nettled at the question.

"I have consoled many ladies in my time," said he; "but let that pass. At present I come ambassador from a royal prince. Know that Ahmed, the prince of Granada, has arrived in quest of you, and is encamped even now on the banks of the Tagus."

The eyes of the princess sparkled at these words.

"O sweetest of parrots," cried she, "joyful indeed are your tidings, for I was faint and weary with doubt of the constancy of Ahmed. Tell him that the words of his letter are engraven in my heart, and that his poetry has been the food of my soul. Tell

370

him, however, that he must prepare to prove his love by force of arms. Tomorrow is my seventeenth birthday, when the king, my father, holds a great tournament. Several princes are to enter the lists, and my hand is to be the prize of the victor."

The parrot again took wing, and flew back to where the prince awaited his return. The rapture of Ahmed on finding the original of the portrait, and finding her kind and true, can only be understood by those favoured mortals who have had the good fortune to realize daydreams and turn a shadow into substance.

Still there was one thing that alloyed his transport—this impending tournament. In fact, the banks of the Tagus were already glittering with arms, and resounding with trumpets of the various knights, who were prancing on toward Toledo.

Like the prince, the princess had been shut up from the world until her seventeenth birthday, but the fame of her charms had been enhanced by this seclusion. Several powerful princes had contended for her hand; and her father, who was a king of wondrous shrewdness, to avoid making enemies, had referred them all to the power of arms. Among the rival candidates were several renowned for strength and prowess. What a predicament for the unfortunate Ahmed, unprovided as he was with weapons, and unskilled in the exercise of arms!

"Luckless prince that I am!" said he, "to have been brought up in seclusion under the eye of a philosopher! "

"*Allah Akbar!* God is great!" exclaimed the owl. "In his hands are all secret things: he alone governs the destinies of princes! Know, O prince, that this land is full of mysteries hidden from all but those who, like myself, can grope after knowledge in the dark. Know that in the neighbouring mountains there is a cave, and in that cave there is an iron table, and on that table there lies a suit of magic armour, and beside that table there stands a spell-bound steed, which have been shut up there for many generations."

The prince stared with wonder.

"Many years since," continued the owl, "I accompanied my

371

father to these parts on a tour of his estates, and we sojourned in that cave; and thus I became acquainted with the mystery. It is a tradition in our family which I have heard from my grandfather, when I was yet but a very little owlet, that this armour belonged to a Moorish magician who took refuge in this cavern when Toledo was captured by the Christians, and died here leaving his steed and weapons under a mystic spell, never to be used but by a Moslem, and by him only from sunrise to midday. In that time, whoever uses them will overthrow every opponent."

"Enough: let us seek this cave!" exclaimed Ahmed.

Guided by the owl, the prince found the cavern, which was in a wild, rocky cliff. A lamp of everlasting oil shed a solemn light through the place. On an iron table in the centre of the cavern lay the magic armour, against it leaned the lance, and beside it stood an Arabian steed, ready for the field, but motionless as a statue. When Ahmed laid his hand upon the steed's neck, he pawed the ground and gave a loud neigh of joy that shook the walls of the cavern. Thus provided with "horse and rider and weapon to wear," the prince determined to defy the field in the coming tourney.

The eventful morning arrived. The lists for the combat were prepared in the Vega just below the walls of Toledo, where stages and galleries were erected for the spectators, covered with rich tapestry, and sheltered from the sun by silken awnings. All the beauties of the land were assembled in those galleries, while below pranced plumed knights with their pages and esquires, among whom were the princes who were to contend in the tourney.

All the beauties of the land, however, were eclipsed when the princess Aldegonda appeared in the royal pavilion, and for the first time broke forth upon the gaze of an admiring world.

The princess, however, had a troubled look. The colour came and went from her cheek, and her eye wandered with a restless expression over the plumed throng of knights. The trumpets were about sounding for the encounter, when the herald announced the arrival of a strange knight, and Ahmed rode into the field.

A steel helmet rose above his turban. His *cimeter* and dagger were of the workmanship of Fez, and flamed with precious stones. A round shield was at his shoulder, and in his hand he bore the charmed lance. The lofty and graceful demeanour of the prince struck every eye, and when his name was announced, a flutter prevailed among the fair dames in the gallery.

When Ahmed presented himself at the lists, however, they were closed against him. None but princes, he was told, were admitted to the contest. He declared his name and rank. Still worse!—he was a Moslem, and could not engage in a tourney when the hand of a Christian princess was the prize.

With haughty looks the rival princes surrounded him; and one sneered at his light and youthful form. The ire of the prince was aroused. He defied his rival to an encounter. They took distance, wheeled and charged; and at the first touch of the magic lance the scoffer was tilted from his saddle.

Here the prince would have paused, but, alas! nothing would control his horse and armour. The Arabian steed charged into the thickest of the throng. The lance overturned everything that presented. The gentle prince was carried pell-mell about the field, strewing it with high and low, gentle and simple. The king stormed and raged at this outrage on his subjects and his guests. He ordered out his guards—they were unhorsed as fast as they came up.

The king threw off his robes, grasped buckler and lance, and rode forth to awe the stranger with the presence of majesty itself. Alas! majesty fared no better than the vulgar. The steed and lance were no respecters of persons. To the dismay of Ahmed, he was borne full tilt against the king, and in a moment the royal heels were in the air, and the crown was rolling in the dust.

At this moment the sun reached the meridian. The magic spell resumed its power. The Arabian steed scoured across the plain, leaped the barrier, plunged into the Tagus, swam its raging torrent, bore the prince breathless and amazed to the cavern, and resumed his station beside the iron table.

The prince dismounted right gladly, and replaced the armour. Then he seated himself in the cavern, and began to think. Never again should he dare to show his face at Toledo after inflicting such disgrace upon its chivalry, and such an outrage on its king. What, too, would the princess think? Full of anxiety, he sent forth his winged messengers to gather tidings.

The parrot resorted to all the public places and crowded resorts of the city, and soon returned with a world of gossip. All Toledo was in consternation. The princess had been borne off senseless to the palace. The tournament had ended in confusion. Everyone was talking of the Moslem knight. Some thought him a Moorish magician; while others thought he might be one of the enchanted warriors who were said to be hidden in the caves of the mountains. All agreed that no ordinary mortal could have wrought such wonders.

The owl flew out at night and hovered about the dusky city, perching on the roofs and chimneys. He then wheeled his flight up to the royal palace, and went prowling about, eavesdropping at every cranny, and glaring in with his big goggling eyes at every window where there was a light, so as to throw two or three maids of honour into fits. It was not until the grey dawn began to peer above the mountains that he returned from his expedition and related to the prince what he had seen.

"As I was prying about one of the loftiest towers of the palace," said he, "I beheld through a casement a beautiful princess. She was reclining on a couch, with attendants and physicians around her, but she would have none of their ministry and relief. When they retired, I beheld her draw a letter from her bosom, and read it, and give way to loud lamentations, at which, philosopher as I am, I could but be greatly moved."

Ahmed was distressed at these tidings.

"Too true were your words, O Eben Bonabben!" cried he. "Care and sorrow, and sleepless nights are the lot of lovers. *Allah* preserve the princess from the blighting influence of this thing called love."

Further news from Toledo showed that the report of the owl

374

was true. The city was a prey to uneasiness and alarm. The princess was conveyed to the highest tower of the palace, every avenue to which was strongly guarded. In the meantime, a devouring melancholy had seized upon her, of which no one could divine the cause. She refused food, and turned a deaf ear to every consolation. The most skilful physicians had essayed their art in vain. It was thought some magic spell had been practised upon her, and the king made proclamation, declaring that whoever should effect her cure should receive the richest jewel in the royal treasury.

When the owl, who was dozing in a corner, heard of this, he rolled his large eyes and looked more mysterious than ever.

"*Allah Akbar!*" exclaimed he, "happy the man that shall effect that cure, should he but know what to choose from the royal treasury."

"What mean you, most reverend owl?" said Ahmed.

"Hearken, prince, to what I shall relate. We owls, you must know, are a learned body, and much given to dark and dusty research. During my late prowling at night about the domes and turrets of Toledo, I discovered a college of owls, who hold their meetings in a great vaulted tower where the royal treasury is deposited. Here they were discussing ancient gems and jewels, and golden and silver vessels, heaped up in the treasury, the fashion of every country and age. But mostly they were interested about certain relics and talismans which have remained in the treasury since the time of Roderick the Goth.

"Among them was a box of sandal-wood, secured by bands of steel, and inscribed with mystic characters known only to the learned few. This box and inscription had occupied the college for several sessions, and had caused much long and grave dispute. At the time of my visit a very ancient owl, who had recently arrived from Egypt, was seated on the lid of the box lecturing upon the inscription, and he proved from it that the coffer contained the silken carpet of the throne of Solomon the Wise."

When the owl had concluded his harangue, the prince remained for a time absorbed in thought.

"I have heard," said he, "from the sage Eben Bonabben of the wonderful properties of that talisman, which disappeared at the fall of Jerusalem and was supposed to be lost to mankind. Doubtless it remains a sealed mystery to the Christians of Toledo. If I can get possession of the carpet, my fortune is secure."

The next day the prince laid aside his rich attire, and arrayed himself in the simple garb of an Arab of the desert. He dyed his complexion to a tawny hue, and no one could have recognized in him the splendid warrior who had caused such admiration and dismay at the tournament. With staff in hand, and a small pastoral reed, he repaired to Toledo, and presenting himself at the gate of the royal palace, announced himself as a candidate for the reward offered for the cure of the princess. The guards would have driven him away with blows.

"What can a vagrant Arab like you pretend to do," said they, "in a case where the most learned of the land have failed?"

The king, however, overheard, and ordered the Arab to be brought into his presence.

"Most potent king," said Ahmed, "you behold before you a Bedouin Arab, the greater part of whose life has been passed in the solitudes of the desert. These solitudes, it is well known, are the haunts of demons and evil spirits, who beset us poor shepherds in our lonely watchings, enter into and possess our flocks and herds, and sometimes render even the patient camel furious. Against these, our counter-charm is music: and we have legendary airs handed down from generation to generation, that we chant and pipe, to cast forth these evil spirits. I am of a gifted line, and possess this power in its fullest force. If it be any evil influence of the kind that holds a spell over your daughter, I pledge my head to free her from its sway."

The king, who was a man of understanding, and knew the wonderful secrets often possessed by the Arabs, was inspired with hope by the language of the prince. He conducted him immediately to the lofty tower, in the summit of which was the chamber of the princess. The windows opened upon a terrace, commanding a view over Toledo and all the surrounding country. The windows were darkened, for the princess lay within, a prey to devouring grief.

The prince seated himself on the terrace, and performed on his pastoral pipe several wild Arabian airs which he had learnt from his attendants in the Generalife at Granada. The princess continued insensible, and the doctors who were present shook their heads, and smiled with contempt. At length the prince laid aside the reed, and, to a simple melody, chanted the verses of the letter which he had sent to the princess.

The princess recognized the strain—she raised her head and listened. She would have asked for the minstrel to be brought into her presence, but maiden coyness held her silent. The king read her wishes, and at his command Ahmed was conducted into the chamber. The prince and princess exchanged glances which spoke volumes. Never was triumph of music more complete. The rose had returned to the soft cheek of the princess, and the light to her eyes.

All the physicians present stared at each other with astonishment. The king regarded the Arab minstrel with admiration and awe.

"Wonderful youth!" exclaimed he, "you shall henceforth be the first physician of my court, and no other prescription will I take but your melody. For the present receive your reward, the most precious jewel in my treasury."

"O king," replied Ahmed, "I care not for silver or gold or precious stones. You have one relic in your treasury, handed down from the Moslems, who once owned Toledo—a box of sandal-wood containing a silken carpet. Give me that box, and I am content."

All present were surprised at the moderation of the Arab, and still more when the box of sandal-wood was brought and the carpet drawn forth. It was of fine green silk.

The court physicians looked at each other, shrugged their shoulders, and smiled.

"This carpet," said the prince, "once covered the throne of Solomon. It is worthy of being placed beneath the feet of beauty."

So saying, he spread it on the terrace beneath an ottoman that had been brought to the princess—then seating himself at her feet:

"Who," said he, "shall counteract what is written in the book of fate? Behold the prediction of the astrologers verified. Know, O king, that your daughter and I have long loved each other in secret."

These words were scarcely said when the carpet rose in the air, bearing off the prince and princess. The king and the physicians gazed after it with open mouths and straining eyes until it became a little speck, and then disappeared in the blue vault of Heaven.

The king in a rage summoned his treasurer.

"How is this," said he, "that you have suffered an *infidel* to get possession of such a talisman?"

"Alas, sir, we knew not its nature. If it be indeed the carpet of the throne of Solomon, it is possessed of magic power, and can transport its owner from place to place through the air."

The king assembled a mighty army, and set off for Granada in pursuit of the fugitives. His march was long and toilsome. Encamping in the Vega, he sent a herald to demand his daughter. The king of Granada himself came forth with all his court to meet him, and in him the Christian king beheld the minstrel, for Ahmed had succeeded to the throne on the death of his father, and the beautiful Aldegonda was the *sultana*.

The Christian king was easily pacified when he found that his daughter continued in his faith; not that he was particularly pious, but religion is always a point of pride and etiquette with princes. Instead of battles, there was a succession of feasts and rejoicings, after which the king returned well pleased to Toledo, and the youthful couple continued to reign as happily as wisely in the Alhambra.

It is proper to add that the owl and the parrot had severally followed the prince by easy stages to Granada: the former travelling by night, and stopping at the various hereditary possessions of his family—the latter figuring in gay circles of every town and city on his route.

Ahmed gratefully requited the services which they had rendered on his pilgrimage. He appointed the owl his prime minister, and the parrot his master of ceremonies. It is needless to say that never was a realm more sagely administered, nor a court conducted with more exact *punctilio.*

Legend of the Moor's Legacy

Just within the fortress of the Alhambra, in front of the royal palace, is a broad open space, called the Place of the Cisterns, so called from being undermined by reservoirs of water. At one corner of this place is a Moorish well, cut through the rock to a great depth, the water of which is cold as ice and clear as crystal. This well is famous throughout Granada, and water-carriers, some bearing great water-jars on their shoulders, others driving donkeys before them laden with earthen vessels, are going up and down the woody avenues, from early morning until a late hour of the night.

Fountains and wells have always been noted gossiping-places in hot climates; and at this well there is a kind of perpetual club kept up during the livelong day, by the invalids, old women, and other curious do-nothing folk, who sit on the stone benches, and dawdle over the gossip of the fortress, and question every water-carrier that arrives about the news of the city, and make long comments on everything they hear and see. Not an hour of the day but loitering housewives and idle maid-servants may be seen, lingering with pitcher on head or in hand, to hear the last of the endless tattle.

Among the water-carriers who once resorted to this well, there was a sturdy, strong-backed, bandy-legged little fellow, named Pedro Gil, but called Peregil for shortness. Like all the water-carriers he was a Gallego, or native of Gallicia.

Peregil had begun business with merely a great earthen jar

which he carried upon his shoulder; but by degrees he rose in the world, and was enabled to purchase a donkey. On each side of his long-eared companion, in a kind of pannier, were slung his water-jars, covered with fig-leaves to protect them from the sun. There was not a more industrious water-carrier in all Granada, nor one more merry withal. The streets rang with his cheerful voice as he trudged after his donkey, singing the usual summer note that resounds throughout the Spanish towns:

"Who wants water—water colder than snow? Who wants water from the well of the Alhambra, cold as ice and clear as crystal?"

When he served a customer with a sparkling glass, it was always with a pleasant word that caused a smile; and if, perchance, it was a comely dame or dimpling damsel, it was always with a sly leer and a compliment to her beauty that was irresistible. Thus Peregil was noted throughout all Granada for being one of the civilest, pleasantest, and happiest of mortals. Yet it is not he who sings loudest and jokes most that has the lightest heart. Under all this air of merriment, honest Peregil had his cares and troubles. He had a large family of ragged children to support, who were hungry and clamorous as a nest of young swallows, and beset him with their outcries for food whenever he came home of an evening.

He had a wife, too, who was anything but a help to him. She had been a village beauty before marriage, noted for her skill at dancing the *bolero* and rattling the *castanets*; and she still retained her early propensities, spending the hard earnings of honest Peregil in frippery, and laying the very donkey under requisition for junketing parties into the country on Sundays and Saints' Days, and those innumerable holidays, which are rather more numerous in Spain than the days of the week. With all this she was a little of a slattern, something more of a lie-abed, and, above all, a gossip of the first water; neglecting house, household, and everything else, to loiter slipshod in the houses of her gossip neighbours.

He, however, who tempers the wind to the shorn lamb, accommodates the yoke of matrimony to the submissive neck. Peregil bore all the heavy dispensations of wife and children with as meek a spirit as his donkey bore the water-jars; and, however he might shake his ears in private, never ventured to question the household virtues of his slattern spouse.

He loved his children, too, even as an owl loves its owlets, seeing in them his own image multiplied and perpetuated; for they were a sturdy, long-backed, bandy-legged, little brood. The great pleasure of honest Peregil was, whenever he could afford himself a scanty holiday, to take the whole litter with him, some in his arms, some tugging at his skirts, and some trudging at his heels, and to treat them to a gambol among the orchards of the Vega, while his wife was dancing with her holiday friends in the Angosturas of the Darro.

It was a late hour one summer night, and most of the water-carriers had desisted from their toils. The day had been uncommonly sultry. The night was one of those delicious moonlights which tempt the inhabitants of summer climes to linger in the open until after midnight. Customers for water were therefore still abroad. Peregil, like a considerate, painstaking father, thought of his hungry children.

"One more journey to the well," said he to himself, "to earn a Sunday's *puchero* for the little ones."

So saying, he trudged up the steep avenue of the Alhambra, singing as he went, and now and then bestowing a hearty thwack with a cudgel on the flanks of his donkey, either by way of cadence to the song, or refreshment to the animal; for dry blows serve in lieu of provender in Spain for all beasts of burden.

When arrived at the well, he found it deserted by everyone except a solitary stranger in Moorish garb, seated on a stone bench in the moonlight. Peregil paused at first and regarded him with surprise, not unmixed with awe, but the Moor feebly beckoned him to approach.

"I am faint and ill," said he: "aid me to return to the city, and I will pay you double what you could gain by your jars of water."

The honest heart of the little water-carrier was touched at the appeal of the stranger.

"God forbid," said he, "that I should ask fee or reward for doing an act of kindness,"

He accordingly helped the Moor on his donkey, and set off slowly for Granada, the poor Moslem being so weak that it was necessary to hold him on the animal to keep him from falling to the ground.

When they entered the city, the water-carrier demanded whither he should conduct him.

"Alas!" said the Moor faintly, "I have neither home nor habitation; I am a stranger in the land. Suffer me to lay my head this night beneath your roof, and you shall be amply repaid."

Honest Peregil thus saw himself unexpectedly saddled with an infidel guest, but he was too humane to refuse a night's shelter to a fellow-being in so forlorn a plight; so he conducted the Moor to his dwelling. The children, who had sallied forth open-mouthed, as usual, on hearing the tramp of the donkey, ran back with affright when they beheld the turbaned stranger and hid themselves behind their mother. The latter stepped forth like a ruffling hen before her brood.

"What *infidel* companion," cried she, "is this you have brought home at this late hour?"

"Be quiet, wife," replied Peregil: "here is a poor sick stranger, without friend or home. Would you turn him forth to perish in the streets?"

The wife would still have remonstrated, for although she lived in a hovel, she was a furious stickler for the credit of her house. The little water-carrier, however, was for once stiff-necked, and refused to bend beneath the yoke. He assisted the poor Moslem to alight, and spread a mat and a sheepskin for him on the ground, in the coolest part of the house, being the only kind of bed that he had.

In a little while the Moor was seized with violent convulsions, which defied all the skill of the water-carrier. He called Peregil to his side and addressing him in a low voice:

"My end," said he, "I fear is at hand. If I die, I bequeath you this box as a reward for your charity."

So saying, he opened his cloak, and showed a small box of sandal-wood, strapped round his body.

"God grant, my friend," replied the little Gallego, "that you may live many years to enjoy your treasure, whatever it may be."

The Moor shook his head. He laid his hand upon the box, and would have said something more about it, but his convulsions returned, and in a little while he expired.

The water-carrier's wife was now as one distracted.

"This comes," said she, "of your foolish good nature, always running into scrapes to oblige others. What will become of us when this corpse is found in our house? We shall be sent to prison as murderers."

Poor Peregil almost repented of having done a good deed, for, in truth, he was as distracted as his wife. At length a thought struck him.

"It is not yet day," said he. "I can convey the dead body out of the city, and bury it in the sands on the banks of the Xenil. No one saw the Moor enter our dwelling, and no one will know anything of his death." So said, so done. The wife aided him: they rolled the body of the Moor in the mat on which he had expired, laid it across the donkey, and Peregil set out with it for the banks of the river.

As ill-luck would have it, there lived opposite to the water-carrier a barber named Pedrillo Pedrugo, one of the most prying, tattling, and mischief-making of his gossip tribe. He was a weasel-faced, spider-legged varlet. The famous barber of Seville could not surpass him for his universal knowledge of the affairs of others, and he had no more power of retention than a sieve. It was said that he slept with but one eye at a time, and kept one ear uncovered, so that even in his sleep he might see and hear all that was going on. Certain it is, he was a sort of chronicle for the *quidnuncs* of Granada, and had more customers than all the rest of his fraternity.

You may be sure that he heard Peregil arrive at an unusual hour of the night. His head was instantly popped out of a little window which served him as a look-out, and he saw his neighbour assist a man in Moorish garb into his dwelling. This was so strange an occurrence, that Pedrillo Pedrugo slept not a wink that night. Every five minutes he was at his loophole, watching the lights that gleamed through the chinks of Peregil's door, and before daylight he beheld Peregil sally forth with his donkey unusually laden.

The barber was in a fidget. He slipped on his clothes, and silently followed the water-carrier at a distance, until he saw him dig a hole in the sandy bank of the Xenil, and bury the dead body.

He then went back to his shop. At sunrise he took a basin under his arm, and sallied forth to the house of his daily customer, the *alcalde*. The *alcalde* was just risen. Pedrillo Pedrugo seated him in a chair, threw a napkin round his neck, put a basin of hot water under his chin, and began his work.

"Strange doings," said he: "robbery and murder and burial all in one night"

"Hey!—how!—what is that you say?" cried the *alcalde*.

"I say," replied the barber, rubbing a piece of soap over the nose and mouth of the dignitary,—"I say that Peregil the Gallego has robbed and murdered a Moor, and buried him this blessed night. Accursed be the night for the same!"

"But how do you know all this?" demanded the *alcalde*.

"Be patient, *Señor*, and you shall hear all about it," replied Pedrillo, taking him by the nose and sliding a razor over his cheek. He then told all he had seen, shaving his beard, and washing his chin, while he was robbing, murdering, and burying the Moor.

Now it so happened that this *alcalde* was one of the most overbearing and greedy judges in all Granada. It could not be denied, however, that he set a high value upon justice, for he sold it at its weight in gold. He presumed the case in point to be one of murder and robbery. Doubtless there must be a rich spoil. It was not long before he had the poor water-carrier before him.

"Hark you, culprit," roared he in a voice that made little Peregil's knees shake, "everything is known to me. A gallows is the proper reward for the crime you have committed, but I am merciful. The man that has been murdered in your house was a Moor, an *infidel*, the enemy of our faith. Render up the property of which you have robbed him, and we will hush the matter up."

The poor water-carrier called upon all the saints, but alas! not one of them appeared.

He related the whole story of the dying Moor truthfully, but it was all in vain.

"Will you persist in saying," demanded the judge, "that this Moslem had neither gold nor jewels?"

"He had nothing but a small box of sandal-wood," said Peregil, "which he gave me in reward for my services."

"A box of sandal-wood! a box of sandal-wood!" exclaimed the *alcalde*, his eyes sparkling at the idea of jewels. "And where is this box? Where have you concealed it?"

"Please, your grace," replied the water-carrier, "it is in one of the panniers of my mule, and heartily at the service of your worship."

He had hardly spoken the words, when the keen *alguazil* darted off, and reappeared in an instant with the box of sandal-wood. The judge opened it with an eager and trembling hand. All pressed forward to gaze upon the treasure it was expected to contain; when, to their disappointment, nothing appeared within but a parchment scroll, covered with Arabic characters, and an end of a waxen taper.

The *alcalde*, finding that there was no booty in the case, discharged Peregil from arrest, permitting him to carry off the Moor's legacy, the box of sandal-wood and its contents; but alas, he kept his donkey in payment of costs and charges.

Poor unfortunate Peregil! He now had to be his own water-carrier and trudge up to the well of the Alhambra with a great earthen jar upon his shoulder. As he toiled up the hill in the heat of a summer noon, his usual good humour forsook him.

"Dog of an *alcalde!*" would he cry, "to rob a poor man of the best friend he had in the world!"

And then at the remembrance of his beloved companion, he would exclaim:

"Ah, donkey of my heart! I warrant me you think of your old master! I warrant me you miss the water-jars—poor beast!"

To add to his trouble, he had to endure the railings and reproaches of his wife. He was much grieved in flesh and spirit. At length, one evening, when, after a hot day's toil, she was scolding him as usual, he seized the sandal-wood box, and dashed it to the floor.

"Unlucky was the day I ever set eyes on you," he cried, "or sheltered your master beneath my roof."

As the box struck the floor, the lid flew open, and the parchment scroll rolled forth.

"Who knows," thought Peregil, "but this may be of some importance, as the Moor seems to have guarded it with such care?"

Picking it up, therefore, he put it in his bosom, and the next morning, as he was crying water through the streets, he stopped at the shop of a Moor, a native of Tangiers, and asked him to explain the contents.

The Moor read the scroll attentively.

"This manuscript," he said, "is a form of incantation for the recovery of enchanted treasures."

"Bah!" cried the little Gallego, "what is all that to me? I am no enchanter."

So saying, he took his water-jar and trudged forward on his daily rounds.

That evening, however, as he rested himself about twilight at the well, he heard some of the gossips who had gathered at the place—they were as poor as rats—talking about the enchanted riches left by the Moors in different parts of the Alhambra. They told marvellous tales of the treasures which they believed were buried deep in the earth under the tower of the seven floors. These stories made an unusual impression on the mind of the honest Peregil, and they sank deeper and deeper into his thoughts as he returned alone down the darkling avenues.

"If, after all," thought he, "there should be treasure hid beneath that tower; and if the scroll I left with the Moor should enable me to get at it!"

He well nigh let fall his water-jar at the thought.

That night he tumbled and tossed, and could scarcely get a wink of sleep for his thoughts. Bright and early he went again to the Moor's shop and told him all that was passing in his mind.

"You can read Arabic," said he: "suppose we go together to the tower, and try the effect of the charm; if it fails, we are no worse off than before; but if it succeeds, we will share equally all the treasure we may discover."

"This writing is not sufficient of itself," said the Moor: "it must be read at midnight, by the light of a taper singularly prepared of certain ingredients, which are not within my reach. Without such a taper the scroll is of no avail."

"Say no more!" cried the little Gallego. "I have such a taper at hand, and will bring it here in a moment."

So saying, he hastened home, and soon returned with the end of a yellow wax taper that he had found in the box of sandalwood. The Moor smelt of it.

"Here are rare and costly perfumes," said he. "While this burns, the strongest walls and most secret caverns will remain open, but woe to him who lingers within until it goes out. He will remain enchanted with the treasure."

It was now agreed between them to try the charm that very night. At a late hour when only bats and owls were stirring, they climbed the woody hill of the Alhambra and made their way to the awful tower. By the light of a lantern they groped their way through bushes, and over fallen stones, to the door of a vault beneath. With fear and trembling they descended a flight of steps cut into the rock. It led to an empty chamber, damp and drear. Then they went down another flight into a deeper vault, and so on until they had gone down four flights of stairs, and into four different vaults. The floor of the fourth was solid. The air was damp and chilly. Here they waited until they heard the clock in the watchtower strike midnight. Then they lit the taper which diffused an odour of myrrh and frankincense and storax.

The Moor began to read in a hurried voice. He had scarce finished when there was a noise as of thunder beneath them. The earth shook, and the floor opened, showing a flight of steps. They went down and found themselves in another vault covered with Arabic inscriptions. In the centre stood a great chest, secured with seven bands of steel, at each end of which sat an enchanted Moor in armour. Before the chest were several jars filled with gold and silver and precious stones. In the largest of these they thrust their arms up to the elbow, and at every dip hauled forth handfuls of broad pieces of Moorish gold, or bracelets and ornaments of the same precious metal. Sometimes a necklace of pearl would stick to their fingers. And all the time the enchanted Moors sat glaring at them with unwinking eyes.

They fancied they heard a noise from above and both rushed up the staircase, falling over each other as they went. They overturned the waxen taper, and when it went out, the floor closed again with a thundering sound.

Filled with dismay, they did not pause until they had groped their way out of the tower, and beheld the stars shining through the trees. Then seating themselves upon the grass, they divided their treasures and deter mined to return some night for more. To make sure of each other's good faith, also, they divided the talismans between them, one taking the scroll, the other the taper. This done, they set off with light hearts and well-lined pockets for Granada.

As they wended their way down the hill, the shrewd Moor whispered a word of counsel in the ear of the simple little water-carrier.

"Friend Peregil," said he, "all this affair must be kept a profound secret until we have secured the treasure, and conveyed it out of harm's way. If a whisper of it gets to the ear of the *alcalde*, we are undone!"

"Certainly," replied the Gallego, "nothing can be more true."

"Friend Peregil," said the Moor, "you are a discreet man, and can keep a secret, but you have a wife."

"She shall not know a word of it," replied the little water-carrier sturdily.

Never was promise more sincere; but alas! what man can keep a secret from his wife? Certainly not such a one as Peregil the water-carrier. On his return home, he found his wife moping in a corner.

"You've come at last," she cried," after rambling about until this hour of the night. I wonder you have not brought home another Moor."

Then bursting into tears, she began to wring her hands.

"What will become of us?" she cried. "My husband a do-no-good that no longer brings home bread to his family, but goes rambling about day and night, with *infidel* Moors! O my children! my children! what will become of us? We shall all have to beg in the streets!"

Honest Peregil was so moved by her tears that he could not help whimpering also. Thrusting his hand into his pocket, he hauled forth three or four gold pieces, and slipped them into her bosom. Then he took out a golden chain and dangled it before her, all the time smiling from ear to ear.

"What have you been doing, Peregil?" exclaimed the wife. "Surely you have not been committing robbery!"

But she became so sure of it, after the idea entered her brain, that she fell into violent weeping. What could the poor man do? He had no other way to ease her mind than to tell her the whole story of his good fortune. Her joy was boundless. And, of course, she promised to keep the secret.

"Now, wife," exclaimed the little man with honest exultation, "what say you now to the Moor's legacy? Henceforth never abuse me for helping a fellow-creature in distress."

Peregil slept soundly that night. Not so his wife. She emptied the whole contents of his pockets upon the mat, and sat counting gold pieces of Arabic coin, trying on necklaces and earrings, and fancying the figure she should one day make when permitted to enjoy her riches.

On the following morning the honest Gallego sold one of the coins to a jeweller, and with the money bought new clothes for his little flock, and all kinds of toys, and good things to eat, and returning to his dwelling, set all his children dancing around him, while he capered in their midst, the happiest of fathers.

What was surprising, his wife kept the secret. For a whole day and a half she went about with a look of mystery and a heart almost bursting, yet she told not a word of it. It is true, she gave herself a few airs. She talked of buying a new *basquiila* all trimmed with gold lace, and a new *mantilla*. She threw out hints of her husband's intention of leaving off his trade of water-carrying, as it did not altogether agree with his health.

The gossips stared at each other and thought she had lost her wits, and the moment her back was turned, they were quite merry over her airs and graces. When she got home, she put a string of pearls round her neck, bracelets on her arms, a diamond aigrette on her head, and sailed backwards and forwards in her rags, admiring herself in a piece of broken mirror. And she could not resist showing herself at the window to enjoy the effect on the passersby.

As the fates would have it, Pedrillo Pedrugo, the meddlesome barber, was at this moment sitting idly in his shop on the opposite side of the street, when his ever-watchful eye caught the sparkle of the diamonds. In an instant he was at his loophole watching Peregil's wife decorated with the splendour of an eastern bride. No sooner had he taken an accurate inventory of her ornaments than he posted off with all speed to the *alcalde*, and before the day was over the unfortunate Peregil was once more dragged into the presence of the judge.

"How is this, villain! "cried the *alcalde*, in a furious voice. "You told me that the Moor who died in your house left nothing behind but an empty coffer, and now I hear of your wife flaunting in her rags decked out with pearls and diamonds. Wretch that you are! Prepare to render up the spoils of your miserable victim and to swing on the gallows that is already tired of waiting for you."

The terrified water-carrier fell on his knees and confessed the whole secret. The Moor was sent for. He entered half-frightened out of his wits. When he beheld the water-carrier, he understood the whole matter.

"Miserable animal," said he, as he passed near him, "did I not warn you against babbling to your wife?"

The story of the Moor coincided exactly with that of Peregil: but the *alcalde* affected to be slow of belief and threw out menaces of imprisonment.

"Softly, good *Señor Alcalde*," said the Moor, who by this time had recovered his usual shrewdness and self-possession. "Let us not mar fortune's favours in a scramble for them. Nobody knows anything of this matter but ourselves. Let us keep the secret. There is wealth enough in the cave to enrich us all. Promise a fair division and all shall be produced. Refuse, and the cave shall remain forever closed."

The *alcalde* consulted apart with the *alguazil*. The latter was a fox in his profession.

"Promise anything," said he, "until you get possession of the treasure. You may then seize upon the whole, and if they dare to murmur, threaten them with the faggot and the stake."

The *alcalde* relished the advice. Smoothing his brow, and turning to the Moor, he said:

"This is a strange story and may be true, but I must have proof of it. This very night you must repeat the incantation in my presence. If there be really such treasure, we will share it between us and say nothing further of the matter. If you have deceived me, expect no mercy at my hands."

Towards midnight they started out. Everything turned out as before. The scroll was produced, the yellow waxen taper was lighted, and the Moor read the form of incantation. The earth trembled, and the pavement opened with a thundering sound, disclosing the narrow flight of steps. The *alcalde*, the *alguazil*, and the barber were struck aghast, and could not summon courage to descend. The Moor and the water-carrier entered the lower vault, and found the two Moors seated as before, silent and motionless. They removed two of the great jars, filled with golden coin and precious stones. The water-carrier bore them up one by one upon his shoulders and slung them on each side of his donkey. Peregil staggered beneath their weight, and they were as much as the animal could bear.

"Let us be content for the present," said the Moor. "Here is as much treasure as we can carry off without being seen, and enough to make us all wealthy."

"Is there more treasure remaining?" demanded the *alcalde*.

"The greatest prize of all," said the Moor: "a huge coffer bound with bands of steel, and filled with pearls and precious stones."

"Let us have up the coffer by all means," cried the grasping *alcalde*.

"I will descend for no more," said the Moor. "Enough is enough for a reasonable man."

"And I," said the water-carrier, "will bring up no further burden to break the back of my poor donkey."

Finding commands, threats, and entreaties equally vain, the *alcalde* turned to his two adherents.

"Aid me," said he, "to bring up the coffer, and its contents shall be divided between us."

So saying, he descended the steps, followed by the *alguazil* and the barber.

No sooner did the Moor behold them fairly earthed than he blew out the yellow taper. The pavement closed with its usual crash, and the three remained buried.

He then hastened up the different flights of steps, nor stopped until in the open air. The little water-carrier followed him as fast as his short legs would permit.

"What have you done?" cried Peregil, as soon as he could recover breath. "The *alcalde* and the other two are shut up in the vault."

"It is the will of *Allah!*" said the Moor devoutly.

"And will you not release them?" demanded the Gallego.

"*Allah* forbid!" replied the Moor, smoothing his beard. "It is written in the book of fate that they shall remain enchanted until some future time when the charm shall be broken."

So saying, he hurled the waxen taper into the gloomy thickets of the glen.

There was now no remedy, so the Moor and Peregil, with the richly laden donkey, proceeded toward the city. The honest little water-carrier was so happy to have his long-eared companion restored to him once more, that he could not refrain from hugging him. It is doubtful which gave him the most joy at that moment—the rich treasures, or the recovery of his beloved donkey.

The two partners in good luck divided their spoil fairly, except that the Moor made out to get into his heap the most of the pearls and precious stones, but then he always gave the water-carrier in lieu magnificent jewels of massive gold, of five times the size, with which the latter was heartily content.

They took great care not to linger within reach of accidents, but made off to enjoy their wealth undisturbed in other countries. The Moor returned to Africa, to his native city of Tangiers, and the Gallego, with his wife, his children, and his donkey, made the best of his way to Portugal. Here he became a personage of some consequence, for his wife made him array his long body and short legs in doublet and hose, with a feather in his hat and a sword by his side—and change his name to Don Pedro Gil. His children grew up as merry hearted as himself, while Senora Gil, befringed, belaced, and betasselled from her head to her heels, with glittering rings on every finger, became a model of fashion and finery.

As to the *alcalde* and his adjuncts, they remained shut up under the great tower of the seven floors, and there they remain spellbound at the present day.

A Tale From *The Alhambra*

Legend of the Three Beautiful Princesses

In old times there reigned a Moorish king in Granada, whose name was Mohamed, to which his subjects added the title of "The Left-handed." Some say he was so called on account of his being really more expert with his left than his right hand; others, because he was prone to take everything by the wrong end, or, in other words, to mar wherever he meddled. Certain it is he was continually in trouble. Thrice was he driven from his throne, and on one occasion barely escaped to Africa with his life, dressed as a fisherman. Still he was as brave as he was blundering; and, though left-handed, wielded his *cimeter* to such purpose that he always succeeded in keeping his throne.

As this Mohamed was one day riding forth with a train of his courtiers, he met a band of horsemen returning from a foray into the land of the Christians. They were conducting a long string of mules laden with spoil, and many captives, among whom the monarch was struck with the appearance of a beautiful damsel, who sat weeping on a low *palfrey*, and heeded not the consoling words of a *duenna* who rode beside her.

The monarch noted her beauty, and on inquiring of the captain of the troop, found that she was the daughter of an *alcayde*. Mohamed claimed her as his royal share of the booty, had her taken to the Alhambra, and soon sought to make her his queen.

At first the Spanish maid would not listen to him. He was an *infidel*, a foe to her country, and, what was worse, he was stricken in years!

Finding his addresses of no avail, Mohamed decided to enlist in his favour the services of the *duenna*, who had been captured with the lady. She was an Andalusian whose name was Kadiga. No sooner had he had a little private conversation with her than she promised to undertake his cause with her young mistress.

"Go to, now!" cried she. "What is there in all this to weep and wail about? Is it not better to be mistress of this beautiful palace, with its gardens and fountains, than to be shut up within your father's tower? As to this Mohamed being an *infidel*, what is that to the purpose? You marry him, not his religion. At any rate, you are in his power, and must either be a queen or a slave."

The arguments of Kadiga prevailed. The Spanish lady dried her tears, and became the queen of Mohamed, the Left-handed. She even conformed in appearance to the faith of her royal husband.

In process of time, Mohamed was made the happy father of three daughters, all born at the same time, and, as was usual with Moorish kings, he sent for his astrologers.

"Your daughters," said they, "will most need your watchfulness when they arrive at a marriageable age. At that time gather them under your wings, and trust them to no one else."

Mohamed the Left-handed had little fear of not being able to outwit the fates, for he considered himself a wise king, as did also his courtiers.

Within a few years, the queen died, leaving her infant daughters to his love, and to the fidelity of Kadiga. Many years had yet to pass before they would arrive at the period of danger—the marriageable age.

"It is good, however, to be cautious in time," said the shrewd Mohamed, so he determined to have the princesses reared in a distant castle, on the summit of a hill overlooking the Mediterranean sea. It was a royal retreat, and here they remained, separated from the world, but surrounded by every pleasure.

In this abode, the three princesses grew up into wondrous beauty; but, though all reared alike, they gave early tokens of a difference of character. Their names were Zayda, Zorayda and Zorahayda.

Zayda, the eldest, was of an intrepid spirit, and took the lead of her sisters in everything. She was curious and inquisitive, and fond of getting at the bottom of things.

Zorayda had a great feeling for beauty, which was the reason, no doubt, of her delighting to regard her own image in a mirror or a fountain, and of her fondness for flowers and jewels, and other tasteful ornaments.

As to Zorahayda, the youngest, she was soft and timid, and very sensitive, with a vast deal of tenderness, as was evident from her number of pet flowers, and pet birds, and pet animals, all of which she cherished with the fondest care. Her amusements, too, were of a gentle nature, and mixed with musing and reverie. She would sit for hours in a balcony, gazing on the stars of a summer's night, or on the sea when lit up by the moon; and at such times the song of a fisherman, faintly heard from the beach, or the notes of a Moorish flute, elevated her feelings into ecstasy. The least uproar of the elements, however, filled her with dismay, and a clap of thunder was enough to throw her into a swoon.

Years rolled on serenely. Kadiga was faithful to her trust, and attended the three princesses with unremitting care.

The castle, as has been said, was built on the sea-coast. One of the outer walls straggled down the hill, until it reached a rock overhanging the sea. A small watchtower on this rock had been fitted up as a pavilion, with latticed windows to admit the sea-breeze. Here the princesses used to pass the sultry hours of midday.

The curious Zayda was one day seated at a window of the pavilion, as her sisters, reclining on ottomans, were taking their siesta, when her attention was attracted to a galley which came coasting along. As it drew near, she saw that it was filled with armed men. The galley anchored at the foot of the tower. A number of Moorish soldiers landed on the narrow beach, conducting several Christian prisoners.

Zayda awakened her sisters, and all three peeped cautiously through the lattice. Among the prisoners were three Spanish cavaliers, richly dressed. They were youthful and noble, and though loaded with chains and surrounded with enemies, carried themselves in a lofty manner. The princesses had been cooped up in the castle so long that it is not to be wondered at that they should gaze with breathless interest at three gallant cavaliers in the pride of youth.

"Did ever nobler being tread the earth than the cavalier in crimson?" cried Zayda. "See how proudly he bears himself, as though all around him were his slaves!"

"But notice the one in green!" exclaimed Zorayda. "What grace! what elegance! what spirit!"

The gentle Zorahayda said nothing, but she secretly gave preference to the cavalier in blue.

The princesses remained gazing until the prisoners were out of sight, and then sat down, musing and pensive, on their ottomans.

Kadiga found them in this situation, and they related to her what they had seen.

"Poor youths!" exclaimed she. "I'll warrant their captivity makes many a fair and high-born lady's heart ache in their native land! Ah! my children, you have little idea of the life these cavaliers lead in their own country. Such devotion to the ladies! Such courting and serenading!"

The curiosity of Zayda was fully aroused.

She plied the *duenna* with questions, and drew from her tales of her youthful days and native land.

The beautiful Zorayda slyly regarded herself in a mirror, when the theme turned upon the charms of the Spanish ladies.

Zorahayda suppressed a sigh at the mention of moonlight serenades.

Every day the curious Zayda renewed her inquiries, and every day Kadiga repeated her stories. The old woman awoke at length to the mischief she might be doing. She had been used to thinking of the princesses only as children, but she realized now that there bloomed before her three damsels of the marriageable age.

"It is time," thought she, "to give notice to the king."

Mohamed the Left-handed was seated one morning on a divan in a cool hall of the Alhambra, when a slave arrived with a message from Kadiga, congratulating him on the anniversary of his daughters' birthday. The slave at the same time presented a delicate little basket decorated with flowers, within which lay a peach, an apricot, and a nectarine, all three in a stage of ripeness. The king being versed in the language of fruits and flowers at once understood the meaning of this offering.

"So," said he, "the critical period pointed out by the astrologers has arrived. My daughters are at a marriageable age. What is to be done? They are shut up from the eyes of men under the care of Kadiga—all very good—but still they are not under my own eye. I must gather them under my wing, and trust them to no one else."

So saying, he ordered that a tower of the Alhambra should be prepared for them, and departed with his guards for the castle, to conduct them home in person.

It had been three years since Mohamed had beheld the princesses, and he could scarcely believe his eyes at the wonderful change which that small space of time had made in them.

Zayda was tall and finely formed, with a lofty manner. She entered with a stately step, and made a profound reverence to Mohamed, treating him more as her sovereign than her father.

Zorayda was of the middle height, with an alluring look heightened by the assistance of the toilette. She approached her father with a smile, kissed his hand, and recited several *stanzas* from an Arabian poet. The king was delighted.

Zorahayda was shy and timid, smaller than her sisters, and with a beauty of that tender kind which looks for fondness and protection. She was little fitted to command like Zayda or to dazzle like Zorayda. She drew near to her father, with a faltering step, and would have taken his hand to kiss, but on looking up into his face, and seeing it beam with a smile, she threw her arms about his neck.

Mohamed the Left-handed looked at the three princesses with mingled pride and perplexity, for while he exulted in their charms, he bethought him of the prediction of the astrologers.

"Three daughters! three daughters!" said he to himself, "and all of a marriageable age! Here's tempting fruit that requires a dragon watch!"

He prepared for his return to Granada by sending heralds before him, commanding everyone to keep out of the road by which he was to pass, and that all doors and windows should be closed at their approach. This done, they set forth.

The princesses rode beside the king, closely veiled, on beautiful white palfreys.

The bits and stirrups were of gold and the silk bridles were adorned with precious stones. The palfreys were covered with little silver bells, which made the most musical tinkling as they ambled along. Woe to the unlucky wight, however, who lingered in the way when he heard the tinkling of these bells!—the guards were ordered to cut him down without mercy.

The cavalcade was drawing near to Granada, when it overtook, on the banks of the River Xenil, a small body of Moorish soldiers with some prisoners. It was too late for the soldiers to get out of the way, so they threw themselves on their faces on the earth, ordering their captives to do the like. Among the prisoners were the three cavaliers whom the princesses had seen from the pavilion. They either did not understand, or were too proud to obey the order, and remained standing and gazing upon the cavalcade as it approached.

The ire of the monarch was kindled at this defiance of his orders. Drawing his *cimeter*, and pressing forward, he was about to deal a left-handed blow that might have been fatal to at least one of the gazers when the princesses crowded round him, and implored mercy for the prisoners.

Even the timid Zorahayda forgot her shyness.

Mohamed paused, with uplifted *cimeter*, when the captain of the guard threw himself at his feet.

"Let not your highness," said he, "do a deed that may cause great trouble throughout the kingdom. These are three brave and noble Spanish knights, who have been taken in battle, fighting like lions. They are of high birth, and may bring great ransoms."

"Enough!" said the king. "I will spare their lives, but they must be punished. Let them be taken to the Vermilion Towers and put to hard labour."

Mohamed was making one of his left-handed blunders. In the tumult of this blustering scene, the veils of the three princesses had been thrown back. In those days people fell in love much more suddenly than at present, as all ancient stories will tell you. And therefore it is not a matter of wonder that the hearts of the three cavaliers were completely captured, each of them with a several beauty. As to the princesses, they were more than ever struck with the noble demeanour of the three cavaliers.

The cavalcade resumed its march. The princesses rode pensively along on their tinkling palfreys, now and then glancing back in search of the Christian captives who were being conducted to their allotted prison.

The residence provided for the princesses was in a tower, somewhat apart from the main palace of the Alhambra, though connected with it by the wall which encircled the whole summit of the hill. On one side it looked into the interior of the fortress, and had, at its foot, a small garden filled with flowers. On the other side it overlooked a deep embowered ravine, separating the grounds of the Alhambra from those of the Generalife.

The interior of the tower was divided into small fairy apartments, ornamented in light Arabian style, surrounding a lofty hall, the roof of which rose almost to the summit of the tower. The walls and ceilings of the hall were adorned with arabesque and fretwork, sparkling with gold and bright pencilling. In the centre of the marble pavement was an alabaster fountain, set round with shrubs and flowers, and throwing up a jet of water that cooled the whole place. Round the hall were hung gold and silver cages, containing singing birds.

The princesses had always been cheerful when in the castle, and the king had expected to see them enraptured with the Alhambra.

To his surprise, however, they began to pine and grow melancholy, and dissatisfied with everything around them. They did not like the flowers—the song of the nightingale disturbed their night's rest—and they were out of all patience with the fountain with its drop-drop and splash-splash, from morning till night and from night till morning.

The king at first took this in high displeasure. Then he reflected that his daughters were no longer children.

"They are women grown," said he, "and need suitable objects to interest them."

He therefore had all the dressmakers and jewellers in Granada set to work, and the princesses were overwhelmed with robes of silk and brocade, and cashmere shawls, and necklaces of pearls and diamonds, and rings and bracelets and anklets and all manner of precious things.

All, however, was of no avail. They continued pale and languid in the midst of their finery and looked like three blighted rosebuds, drooping from one stalk. The king was at his wits' end, and called in the aid of the *duenna*.

"Kadiga," said he, "I wish you to find out the secret malady that is preying upon the princesses, and devise some means of restoring them to health and cheerfulness."

Kadiga promised obedience. In fact she knew more of the malady of the princesses than they did themselves.

"My dear children," said she, "what is the reason you are so dismal and downcast in so beautiful a place, where you have everything that heart can wish?"

The princesses looked vacantly round the apartment, and sighed.

"What more, then, would you have? Shall I get you the wonderful parrot that talks all languages?"

"Odious!" exclaimed the princess Zayda. "A horrid, screaming bird, that chatters without ideas."

"Shall I send for a monkey from the rock of Gibraltar, to divert you with his antics?"

"A monkey! faugh!" cried Zorayda. "The detestable mimic of man. I hate the animal."

"What say you to the famous black singer, Casem, from Morocco? They say he has a voice as fine as a woman's."

"I am terrified at the sight of these black slaves," said the delicate Zorahayda. "Besides I have lost all relish for music."

"Ah, my child, you would not say so," replied Kadiga slyly, "had you heard the music I heard last evening from the three Spanish cavaliers whom we met on our journey. But bless me, children! what is the matter that you are all in such a flutter?"

"Nothing, nothing, good mother: pray proceed."

"Well, as I was passing by the tower last evening, I saw the three cavaliers resting after their day's labour. One was playing on a guitar, and the others sang by turns, and they did it in such style that the very guards seemed like statues. Allah forgive me! I could not help being moved at hearing the songs of my native country. And then to see three such noble and handsome youths in chains and slavery!"

Here the kind-hearted old woman could not keep back her tears.

"Perhaps, mother, you could manage to procure us a sight of these cavaliers," said Zayda.

"I think," said Zorayda, "a little music would be quite reviving."

The timid Zorahayda said nothing, but threw her arms round the neck of Kadiga.

"Mercy on me!" cried she. "What are you talking of, my children? Your father would be the death of us all if he heard of such a thing. To be sure, these cavaliers seem well-bred and high-minded; but what of that? They are the enemies of our faith, and you must not think of them."

But her argument was of no avail. The princesses hung around her and coaxed, and declared that a refusal would break their hearts.

What could she do? She certainly was a most faithful servant to the king. But was she to see three beautiful princesses break their hearts for the mere tinkling of a guitar? Besides, though she had been so long among the Moors, she was a Spaniard born, and had the lingerings of Christianity in her heart. So she set about to contrive how the wish of the princesses might be gratified.

The Christian captives, confined in the Vermilion Towers, were under the charge of a big-whiskered, broad-shouldered man, called Hussein Baba, who was said to have a most itching palm. Kadiga went to him privately and slipped a broad piece of gold into his hand.

"Hussein Baba," said she, "my mistresses the three princesses who are shut up in the tower are in sad want of amusement. They have heard of the musical talents of the three Spanish cavaliers, and wish to hear a specimen of their skill. I am sure you are too kind-hearted to refuse so innocent a request."

"What! and to have my head set grinning over the gate of my own tower! for that would be the reward if the king should discover it"

"No danger of anything of the kind: the affair may be managed so that the king will know nothing about it. You know the deep ravine outside the walls, which passes below the tower. Put the three Christians to work there, and at the intervals of their labour, let them play and sing, as if for their own pleasure. In this way the princesses will be able to hear them from the windows of the tower."

As the good old woman finished speaking, she kindly pressed the rough hand of Hussein Baba, leaving in it another piece of gold.

The very next day the three cavaliers were put to work in the ravine. During the noontide heat, when their fellow labourers were sleeping in the shade, and the guard nodding at his post, they seated themselves at the foot of the tower and sang a Spanish roundelay to the music of the guitar.

The glen was deep, the tower was high, but their voices rose distinctly in the stillness of the summer noon.

The princesses listened from their balcony. They had been taught the Spanish language by their *duenna*, and were moved by the tenderness of the song. Kadiga, on the contrary, was terribly shocked.

"*Allah* preserve us!" cried she. "They are singing a song addressed to yourselves. I will run to the slave-master and have them punished."

But the three princesses were filled with horror at the idea. Besides the music seemed to have a beneficial effect upon them. Their eyes sparkled, and a bloom came to their cheeks, so with all her indignation, Kadiga was soon appeased and made no further objection to the song.

When it was finished, Zorayda took up a lute, and with a sweet, though faint and trembling voice, warbled a little Arabian air, the burden of which was:

The rose is concealed among her leaves, but she listens with delight to the song of the nightingale.

From this time forward the cavaliers worked almost daily in the ravine. Hussein Baba became more and more indulgent and daily more prone to sleep at his post. By degrees the princesses showed themselves at the balcony, when they could do so without being seen by the guards, and conversed with the cavaliers. The change effected in their looks and spirits surprised and gratified the left-handed king, but no one was more elated than Kadiga, who considered it all owing to her able management.

At length there was an interruption. For several days the cavaliers ceased to make their appearance in the glen. The princesses looked out from the tower in vain. In vain they stretched their swan-like necks from the balcony: in vain they sang like captive nightingales in their cage. Nothing was to be seen of their Christian lovers—not a note responded from the groves. Kadiga sallied forth in quest of intelligence, and soon returned with a face full of trouble.

"Ah, my children!" cried she. "I saw what all this would come to, but you would have your way. You may now hang your lutes on the willows. The Spanish cavaliers are ransomed by their families. They are down in Granada preparing to return to their native country."

The three beautiful princesses were in despair at the tidings.

Zayda was indignant at the slight put upon them, in thus being deserted without a parting word.

Zorayda wrung her hands and cried, and looked in the glass and wiped away her tears, and cried afresh.

The gentle Zorahayda leaned over the balcony and wept in silence, and her tears fell drop by drop among the flowers where the faithless cavaliers had so often been seated.

Kadiga did all in her power to soothe their sorrow.

"Take comfort, my children," said she, "this is nothing when you are used to it. This is the way of the world. Ah I when you are as old as I am, you will know how to value these men. I'll warrant these cavaliers have their loves among the Spanish beauties of Cordova and Seville, and will soon be serenading under their balconies, and thinking no more of the Moorish beauties in the Alhambra. Take comfort, therefore, my children, and drive them from your thoughts."

But the words of Kadiga only redoubled their distress, and for two days they could not be consoled. On the morning of the third, the good old woman entered their apartment all ruffling with indignation.

"Who would have believed such insolence in mortal man!" exclaimed she, as soon as she could find words to speak. "But I'm rightly served for helping to deceive your worthy father. Never talk more to me of your Spanish cavaliers."

"Why, what has happened, good Kadiga? "exclaimed the princesses.

"What has happened?—treason has been proposed; and to me, the trustiest of *duennas*! Yes, my children, the Spanish cavaliers dared to ask me to persuade you to fly with them to Cordova, and become their wives!"

Here Kadiga covered her face with her hands, and gave way

to a violent burst of grief. The three beautiful princesses turned pale and red and trembled, and looked at each other, but said nothing. Meantime the old woman sat rocking backward and forward in violent agitation.

At length the eldest princess, who had the most spirit and always took the lead, approached her, and laid her hand upon her shoulder.

"Well, mother," said she, "supposing we were willing to fly with these Christian cavaliers—is such a thing possible?"

Kadiga paused suddenly.

"Possible," echoed she, "to be sure it is possible. Have not the cavaliers already bribed Hussein Baba to arrange the whole plan? But then, to think of deceiving your father!"

And here she gave way to a fresh burst of grief.

"But our father has never placed any confidence in us," said the eldest princess, "but has trusted to bolts and bars, and treated us as captives."

"Why, that is true enough," replied the old woman, again pausing in her grief: "he has indeed treated you unreasonably, keeping you shut up here in a moping old tower, like roses left to wither in a flower-jar. But then, to fly from your native land!"

"And is not the land we fly to the native land of our mother, where we shall live in freedom? And shall we not each have a youthful husband in exchange for a severe old father?"

"Why, that again is all very true, but what then," again giving way to grief, "would you leave me behind to bear the brunt of his displeasure?"

"By no means, my good Kadiga: cannot you fly with us?"

"Very true, my child, and to tell the truth, when I talked the matter over with Hussein Baba, he promised to take care of me, if I would fly with you. But then, bethink you, children, are you willing to renounce the faith of your father? "

"The Christian faith was the original faith of our mother," said Zayda. "I am ready to embrace it, and so, I am sure, are my sisters."

"Right again," exclaimed the old woman, brightening up.

"It was the original faith of your mother, and bitterly did she lament, on her death-bed, that she had renounced it. I promised her then to take care of your souls, and I rejoice to see that they are now in a fair way to be saved. Yes, my children, I too was born a Christian, and have remained a Christian in my heart, and am resolved to return to the faith. I have talked with Hussein Baba, who is a Spaniard, by birth, and comes from a place not far from my native town. He is equally anxious to see his own country, and the cavaliers have promised that if we are disposed to become man and wife, on returning to our native land, they will provide for us handsomely."

In a word, it appeared that Kadiga had consulted with the cavaliers and Hussein Baba, and had made the whole plan of escape.

Zayda and Zorayda agreed to the plan at once, but Zorahayda hesitated, for she was gentle and timid of soul. At last, however, with silent tears and stifled sighs, she prepared herself for flight.

In old times, the rugged hill on which the Alhambra is built had many underground passages cut through the rock, leading from the fortress to various parts of the city, and to distant sally-ports on the banks of the Darro and Xenil. They had been built at different times by the Moorish kings, as a means of escape from sudden insurrections, and by one of these passages Hussein Baba had undertaken to conduct the princesses beyond the walls of the city, where the cavaliers were to be ready with fleet steeds, to bear the whole party over the borders.

The appointed night arrived. The tower of the princesses had been locked up as usual, and the Alhambra was buried in deep sleep. Towards midnight, Kadiga listened from the balcony of a window that looked into the garden. Hussein Baba was already below, and gave the signal. The *duenna* fastened the end of a ladder of ropes to the balcony, lowered it into the garden and descended. The two eldest princesses followed with beating hearts, but when it came to Zorahayda, she hesitated and trembled.

Several times she placed her foot upon the ladder, and as often drew it back, while her poor little heart fluttered more and more the longer she delayed. She cast a wistful look back into the silken chamber. She had lived in it, to be sure, like a bird in a cage, but within it she was secure. Who could tell what dangers might beset her, should she flutter forth into the wide world! Now she bethought her of her Christian lover, and her little foot was instantly upon the ladder: and anon she thought of her father and shrank back.

In vain her sisters implored, the *duenna* scolded, and Hussein Baba blasphemed beneath the balcony. The gentle Moorish maid stood doubting and wavering. Every moment increased the danger of discovery. A distant tramp was heard.

"The patrols are walking their rounds!" cried Hussein Baba. "If we linger, we perish. Princess, descend instantly or we leave you."

Zorahayda was for a moment in fearful agitation; then loosening the ladder of ropes, she flung it from the balcony.

"It is decided!" cried she: "flight is now out of my power! *Allah* guide and bless you, my dear sisters!"

The two eldest princesses were shocked at the thoughts of leaving her behind, and would fain have lingered, but the patrol was advancing, Hussein Baba was furious, and they were hurried away to the passage. They groped their way through the heart of the mountain, and succeeded in reaching an iron gate that opened outside of the walls. The Spanish cavaliers were waiting to receive them, disguised as Moorish soldiers.

The lover of Zorahayda was frantic when he learned that she had refused to leave the tower, but there was no time to waste in lamentations. The two princesses were placed behind their lovers, Kadiga mounted behind Hussein Baba, and they all set off at a round pace in the direction of the Pass of Lope, which leads through the mountains towards Cordova.

They had not gone very far when they heard the noise of drums and trumpets from the battlements of the Alhambra.

"Our flight is discovered! "said Hussein Baba.

"We have fleet steeds, the night is dark, and we may distance all pursuit," replied the cavaliers.

They put spurs to their horses, and scoured across the Vega. When they reached the foot of the mountain of Elvira, Hussein Baba paused and listened.

"As yet," said he, "there is no one on our traces. We shall make good our escape to the mountains."

While he spoke a light blaze sprung up on the top of the watchtower of the Alhambra.

"Confusion!" cried he, "that bale fire will put all the guards of the passes on the alert. Away! away! Spur like mad—there is no time to be lost."

Away they dashed—the clattering of their horses' hoofs echoed from rock to rock, as they swept along the road. As they galloped on, the bale fire of the Alhambra was answered in every direction. Light after light blazed on the watch-towers of the mountains.

"Forward! forward!" cried Hussein Baba, "to the bridge, before the alarm has reached there!"

They doubled the mountains and arrived in sight of the famous Bridge of Pinos that crosses a rushing stream. To their confusion, the tower of the bridge blazed with lights and glittered with armed men.

Hussein Baba pulled up his steed, rose in his stirrups and looked about him for a moment; then beckoning to the cavaliers, he struck off from the road, skirted the river for some distance, and dashed into its waters. The cavaliers called upon the princesses to cling to them, and did the same. They were borne for some distance down the rapid current, the surges roared round them, but the princesses clung to their Christian knights, and never uttered a complaint. The cavaliers attained the opposite bank in safety, and Hussein Baba conducted them, by rude and unfrequented paths, through the heart of the mountains, so as to avoid all the regular passes. In a word they succeeded in reaching the ancient city of Cordova.

Their restoration to their country and friends was celebrated with great rejoicings, for they were of the noblest families. The beautiful princesses were forthwith received into the bosom of the Church, and after being in all due form made Christians, were rendered happy wives.

In our hurry to make good the escape of the princesses across the river, and up the mountains, we forgot to mention the fate of Kadiga. She had clung, like a cat, to Hussein Baba in the scamper across the Vega, screaming at every turn, and when he prepared to plunge his steed into the river, her terror knew no bounds.

"Grasp me not so tightly," cried Hussein Baba. "Hold on my belt and fear nothing."

She held firmly with both hands by the leather belt, but when he halted with the cavaliers to take breath on the mountain summit, the *duenna* was no longer to be seen.

"What has become of Kadiga?" cried the princesses in alarm.

"*Allah* alone knows!" replied Hussein Baba. "My belt came loose in the midst of the river, and Kadiga was swept with it down the stream. The will of *Allah* be done! But it was an embroidered belt and of great price."

There was no time to waste in idle regrets; yet bitterly did the princesses bewail the loss of their faithful *duenna*. That excellent old woman, however, did not lose more than half of her nine lives in the water. A fisherman, who was drawing his nets some distance down the stream, brought her to land, and he was not a little astonished at his miraculous draught. What further became of her, the story does not tell; but it is certain that she never ventured within reach of Mohamed the Left-handed.

Almost as little is known of the conduct of that wise monarch when he discovered the escape of his daughters, and the deceit practised upon him by the most faithful of servants. It was the only instance in which he had called in the aid of counsel, and he was never afterwards known to be guilty of a similar weakness.

He took good care, however, to guard his remaining daughter who had no disposition to elope. It is thought, indeed, that she secretly repented having remained behind. Now and then she was seen leaning on the battlements of the tower, and looking in the direction of Cordova, and sometimes the notes of her lute were heard as she sang plaintive songs in which she was said to lament the loss of her sisters and her lover, and to bewail her solitary life. She died young, and, according to popular rumour, was buried in a vault beneath the tower, and her untimely fate has given rise to more than one traditionary fable.

Legend of the Rose of the Alhambra

For some time after the surrender of Granada by the Moors, that delightful city was a frequent and favourite residence of the Spanish kings, until they were frightened away by shocks of earthquakes, which toppled down houses, and made the old Moslem towers rock.

Many, many years then rolled away, during which Granada was rarely honoured by a royal guest. The palaces remained silent and shut up, and the Alhambra, like a slighted beauty, sat mournfully among her neglected gardens. The tower, which was once the residence of the three beautiful princesses, partook of the general desolation. The spider spun her web across the gilded vault, and bats and owls nestled in those chambers that had been graced by the presence of Zayda, Zorayda, and Zorahayda. The neglect of this tower may have been partly owing to some superstitious notions of the neighbours.

It was said that the spirit of Zorahayda was often seen by moonlight seated beside the fountain in the hall, or heard moaning about the battlements, and that the notes of her silver lute could be heard at midnight by wayfarers passing along the glen.

At length the city was once more to welcome the king and queen, and the Alhambra was repaired and fitted up with all possible expedition for the visit. The arrival of the court changed the whole aspect of the lately deserted palace. The clamour of drum and trumpet, the tramp of steed about the avenues, the glitter of arms and display of banners, recalled the ancient and warlike glories of the fortress. Within the palace, there was the rustling of robes and the cautious tread and murmuring voice of courtiers about the ante-chambers, a loitering of pages and maids of honour about the gardens, and the sound of music stealing from open casements.

Among those who attended in the train of the monarchs was a favourite page of the queen, named Ruyz de Alarcon. He was just turned of eighteen, light and lithe of form, and very graceful. To the queen he was all deference and respect, yet he was at heart a roguish stripling, petted and spoiled by the ladies about the court.

This loitering page was one morning rambling about the groves of the Generalife, and had taken with him for his amusement a favourite ger-falcon of the queen. In the course of his rambles, seeing a bird rising from a thicket, he unhooded the hawk and let him fly. The falcon towered high in the air, made a swoop at his quarry, but missing it, soared away, regardless of the calls of the page. The page followed the bird with his eye, until he saw it alight upon the battlements of a remote and lonely tower, in the outer wall of the Alhambra, built on the edge of a ravine that separated the fortress from the grounds of the Generalife. It was, in fact, the "Tower of the Princesses."

The page descended into the ravine and approached the tower, but it had no entrance from the glen, and its lofty height made any attempt to scale it useless. Seeking one of the gates of the fortress, therefore, he made a wide circuit to that side of the tower facing within the walls.

A small garden overhung with myrtle lay before the tower. Opening a wicket, the page passed between beds of flowers and thickets of roses to the door. It was closed and bolted. A crevice in the door gave him a peep inside. There was a small Moorish hall with fretted walls, light marble columns, and an alabaster fountain surrounded with flowers.. In the centre hung a gilt cage containing a singing-bird. Beneath it, on a chair, lay a tortoise-shell cat among reels of silk, and a guitar leaned against the fountain.

Ruyz de Alarcon was struck with these traces of female taste in a lonely, and, as he had supposed, deserted tower. They reminded him of the tales of the enchanted hall of the Alhambra; and the tortoise-shell cat might be some spell-bound princess.

He knocked gently at the door. A beautiful face peeped out from a little window above, but was instantly withdrawn. He waited, expecting that the door would be opened, but he waited in vain. No footstep was to be heard within—all was silent. Had his senses deceived him, or was this beautiful apparition the fairy of the tower? He knocked again, and more loudly. After a little while the beaming face once more peeped forth. It was that of a blooming damsel of fifteen.

The page immediately doffed his plumed bonnet, and entreated in the most courteous way to be permitted to ascend the tower in pursuit of his falcon.

"I dare not open the door, Señor," replied the little damsel: "my aunt has forbidden it."

"I do beseech you, fair maid—it is the favourite falcon of the queen. I dare not return to the palace without it."

"Are you then one of the cavaliers of the court?"

"I am, fair maid. But I shall lose the queen's favour and my place if I lose this hawk."

"Santa Maria! It is against you cavaliers of the court my aunt has charged me specially to bar the door."

"Against wicked cavaliers doubtless, but I am none of these, only a simple harmless page, who will be ruined and undone if you deny me this small request."

The heart of the little damsel was touched by the distress of the page. It was a thousand pities he should be ruined for the want of so trifling a boon. Surely he could not be one of those dangerous beings whom her aunt had described. He was gentle and modest, and stood so entreatingly with cap in hand, and looked so charming.

The page redoubled his entreaties in such moving terms that it was not in the nature of mortal maiden to deny him, and the little warden of the tower descended and opened the door. The page was charmed with her appearance. Her Andalusian bodice and trim *basquiña* set off her round form. Her glossy hair was parted on her forehead and decorated with a fresh plucked rose, according to the custom of Spain. It is true her complexion was tinged with the southern sun, but it served to give richness to the bloom of her cheek, and heighten the lustre of her eyes.

Ruyz de Alarcon beheld all this with a single glance, for it became him not to tarry. He thanked her, and then bounded lightly up the spiral staircase in quest of his falcon.

He soon returned with the truant bird upon his fist. The damsel, in the meantime, had seated herself by the fountain in the hall and was winding silk. In her agitation she let the reel fall upon the pavement. The page sprang and picked it up, then dropping on one knee, presented it to her. In doing so, he seized her hand, and imprinted on it a kiss more fervent than he had ever imprinted on the fair hand of his sovereign.

"*Ave Maria, Señor*," exclaimed the damsel.

The page made a thousand apologies, assuring her that it was the way at court of expressing the most profound homage.

Just then a shrill voice was heard at a distance.

"My aunt is returning from mass!" cried the damsel in affright. "I pray you, *Señor*, depart."

"Not until you grant me that rose from your hair as a remembrance."

She hastily untwisted the flower.

"Take it," cried she, "but pray begone."

The page took the rose, again kissing the fair hand that gave it. Then placing the flower in his bonnet, and taking the falcon upon his fist, he bounded off through the garden, bearing away with him the heart of the gentle Jacinta.

When the aunt arrived at the tower, she remarked the agitation of her niece, and an air of confusion in the hall.

"A ger-falcon pursued his prey into the hall," said Jacinta.

"Mercy on us!" said the aunt. "To think of a falcon flying into the tower. Did ever one hear of so saucy a hawk?"

The aunt's name was Fredegonda and she was one of the

most wary of ancient spinsters. Jacinta was the orphan of an officer who had fallen in the wars. She had been educated in a convent, and had only recently been placed under the care of her aunt. Her fresh and dawning beauty had caught the public eye, even in her seclusion, and with that poetical turn common to the people of Andalusia, the peasantry of the neighbourhood had given her the name of "The Rose of the Alhambra."

The wary aunt kept a faithful watch over her little niece till at length the king cut short his sojourn at Granada, and departed with his court. Fredegonda watched the royal pageant as it issued from the gate and descended the great avenue leading to the city. When the last banner disappeared from her sight, she returned exulting to her tower, for all her cares were over.

To her surprise, a light Arabian steed pawed the ground at the wicket gate of her garden. To her horror she saw through the thickets of roses a youth in gayly embroidered dress at the feet of her niece. At the sound of her footsteps he gave a tender *adieu*, bounded lightly over the barrier of reeds and myrtles, sprang upon his horse, and was out of sight in an instant.

The tender Jacinta, in the agony of her grief, lost all thought of her aunt's displeasure. Throwing herself into her arms, she broke into sobs and tears.

"He's gone!—he's gone!" she cried, "and I shall never see him more!"

"Gone!—who is gone?—what youth is that I saw at your feet?"

"A queen's page, aunt, who came to bid me farewell."

"A queen's page, child!" echoed Fredegonda, "and when did you become acquainted with the queen's page?"

"The morning that the ger-falcon came into the tower. It was the queen's ger-falcon, and he came in pursuit of it."

"Ah silly, silly girl I" said the indignant aunt. "There are no ger-falcons half so dangerous as these young prankling pages, and it is precisely such simple birds as you that they pounce upon."

Days, weeks, months elapsed, and nothing more was heard of

the page. The pomegranate ripened, the vine yielded up its fruit, the autumn rains came down in torrents from the mountains, and the Sierra Nevada became covered with a snowy mantle. Still he did not come. The winter passed away. Again the genial spring burst forth with song and blossom. Still nothing was heard of the forgetful page.

In the meantime poor little Jacinta grew pale and thoughtful. Her former occupations and amusements were abandoned, her silk lay entangled, her flowers were neglected, and her eyes were dimmed with weeping.

"Alas, silly child!" the staid Fredegonda would say. "What could you expect from one of a haughty family—you an orphan, the descendant of a fallen line? Be assured, if the youth were true, his father, who is one of the proudest nobles about the court, would prohibit his union with one so humble and portionless as you. Therefore, drive these idle notions from your mind."

But the words of Fredegonda only served to increase Jacinta's melancholy.

At a late hour one midsummer night, after her aunt had gone to rest, Jacinta remained alone in the hall of the tower, seated beside the alabaster fountain. The poor little damsel's heart was overladen with sad recollections, her tears began to flow, and slowly fell drop by drop into the fountain. By degrees the water became agitated, and—bubble—bubble—bubble—boiled up and was tossed about, until a female figure, richly clad in Moorish dress, slowly rose to view.

Jacinta was so frightened that she fled from the hall, and was afraid to return. The next morning she related to her aunt what she had seen, but the good lady thought she had fallen asleep and dreamt beside the fountain.

"You have been thinking of the story of the three Moorish princesses that once lived in this tower," said she, "and it has entered into your dreams."

"What story, aunt? I know nothing of it."

"You have certainly heard of the three princesses, Zayda,

Zorayda and Zorahayda, who were shut up in this tower by the king, their father, and agreed to fly with three Christian cavaliers. The first two accomplished their escape, but the third failed in her resolution, and, it is said, died in this tower."

"I now remember to have heard it," said Jacinta, "and to have wept over the fate of the gentle Zorahayda."

"You may well weep," continued the aunt, "for the lover of Zorahayda was your ancestor. He long bemoaned his fate, but time cured him of his grief, and he married a Spanish lady from whom you are descended."

"If indeed it be the spirit of the gentle Zorahayda, which I have heard lingers about this tower, of what should I be afraid?" thought Jacinta. "I'll watch by the fountain tonight—perhaps the visit will be repeated."

Towards midnight, when everything was quiet, she again took her seat in the hall. As the bell in the distant watch-tower struck the midnight hour, the fountain was again agitated: and bubble—bubble—bubble—it tossed about the waters until the Moorish woman again rose to view. She was young and beautiful. Her dress was rich with jewels, and in her hand she held a silver lute. Jacinta trembled and was faint, but was reassured by the soft and plaintive voice of the apparition.

"Daughter of mortality," said she, "why do your tears trouble my fountain, and your sighs disturb the quiet watches of the night?"

"I weep because of the faithlessness of man, and I bemoan my solitary and forsaken state."

"Take comfort. Your sorrows may yet have an end. Behold in me a Moorish princess, who was, like you, unhappy. A Christian knight, your ancestor, would have borne me to his native land, but I lacked courage equal to my faith, and lingered till too late. For this the evil *genii* have power over me, and I remain enchanted in this tower until some pure Christian will deign to break the magic spell. Will you undertake the task?"

"I will," replied Jacinta, trembling.

"Come hither, then, and fear not. Dip your hand in the foun-

419

tain, sprinkle the water over me, and baptize me after the manner of your faith. So shall the enchantment be dispelled, and my troubled spirit have repose."

Jacinta advanced with faltering steps, dipped her hand into the fountain, collected water in the palm, and sprinkled it over the pale face of the phantom.

The latter smiled benignly. She dropped her silver lute at the feet of Jacinta, crossed her white arms, and melted from sight, so that it seemed merely as if a shower of dewdrops had fallen into the fountain.

Jacinta retired from the hall filled with awe and wonder. She scarcely closed her eyes that night; but when she awoke at daybreak out of a troubled slumber, the whole appeared to her like a dream. On descending into the hall, however, she beheld the silver lute lying beside the fountain, glittering in the morning sunshine.

She hastened to her aunt, to relate all that had befallen her, and called her to behold the lute as a proof of the reality of her story. If the good lady had any doubts, they were removed when Jacinta touched the instrument, for she played such a beautiful melody that Fredegonda's frigid heart was entirely thawed, and nothing but supernatural music could have produced such an effect.

The power of the lute became every day more and more apparent. The wayfarer, passing by the tower, was detained, as it were, spellbound. The very birds gathered in the trees, and, hushing their own strains, listened in charmed silence. Rumour soon spread the news abroad. The inhabitants of Granada thronged to the Alhambra to catch a few notes of the wonderful music that floated about Jacinta's tower.

The lovely little minstrel was at length drawn from her retreat. The rich and powerful of the land contended who should entertain and do honour to her. Wherever she went, her vigilant aunt kept a dragon watch at her elbow, awing the throngs of admirers who listened to her strains. The report of her wonderful powers spread from city to city. Malaga, Seville, Cordova, all became mad on the theme. Nothing was talked of throughout Andalusia but the beautiful minstrel of the Alhambra.

While all Andalusia was thus music mad, a different mood prevailed at the court of Spain. The king, as was well known, was subject to all kinds of fancies. Sometimes he would keep to his bed for weeks together, groaning under imaginary complaints. At other times he would insist upon abdicating his throne, to the great annoyance of his royal spouse, who had a strong relish for the splendours of a court and the glories of a crown, and guided the sceptre of her lord with an expert and steady hand.

At the moment we treat of, a freak had come over the mind of the king that surpassed all former moods. After a long spell of imaginary illness, the monarch, fairly in idea, gave up the ghost, and considered himself absolutely dead.

This would have been harmless enough, and even convenient both to the queen and courtiers, had he been content to remain in the quietude befitting a dead man. But to their annoyance, he insisted upon having the funeral ceremonies performed over him, and began to grow impatient because they left him un-buried.

In the midst of this fearful dilemma, a rumour reached the court of the female minstrel who was turning the brains of all Andalusia. Nothing was so efficacious in dispelling the royal megrims as the power of music, so the queen dispatched messengers in all haste to summon Jacinta to the court.

Within a few days, as the queen with her maids of honour was walking in the stately gardens of the palace, the far-famed minstrel was conducted into her presence. The queen gazed with surprise at the youthful and unpretending appearance of the little being that had set the world madding. She was in her picturesque Andalusian dress, her silver lute in hand, and stood with modest and downcast eyes, but with a simplicity and freshness of beauty that still bespoke her "the Rose of the Alhambra."

As usual, she was accompanied by the ever-vigilant Fredegonda, who gave the whole history of her parentage and descent to the inquiring queen. The queen was pleased when she learnt that her father had bravely fallen in the service of the crown.

"If your powers equal your renown," said she, "and you can cast forth this evil spirit that possesses the king, your fortune shall henceforth be my care, and honours and wealth attend you."

The queen was impatient to make trial of her skill, and led the way at once to the apartment of the moody monarch.

Jacinta followed with downcast eyes through the files of guards and crowds of courtiers. They came at length to a great chamber hung with black. The windows were closed to exclude the light of day. A number of yellow wax tapers in silver sconces diffused a light which dimly revealed the figures of the courtiers as they glided about with noiseless step and woebegone visage. In the midst of a funeral bier, his hands folded on his breast and the tip of his nose just visible, lay extended this would-be-buried monarch.

The queen entered the chamber in silence, and pointing to a footstool in an obscure corner, beckoned to Jacinta to sit down and commence.

At first she touched her lute with a faltering hand, but gathering confidence as she proceeded, drew forth such wonderful harmony that all present could scarce believe it mortal. As to the king, who had already considered himself in the world of spirits, he set it down for some angelic melody or the music of the spheres.

By degrees the theme was varied, and the voice of Jacinta accompanied the lute. She sang one of the legendary ballads treating of the ancient glories of the Alhambra and the achievements of the Moors. The funeral chamber resounded with the strains. It entered into the gloomy heart of the monarch. He raised his head and gazed around. He sat up on his couch. His eyes began to kindle. At length, leaping upon the floor he called for sword and buckler.

The triumph of music, or rather of the enchanted lute, was complete. The demon of melancholy was cast forth, and, as it were, a dead man brought to life. The windows of the apartment

422

were thrown open and the glorious Spanish sunshine burst into the chamber. All eyes sought the lovely enchantress, but the lute had fallen from her hand, she had sunk upon the earth, and the next moment was clasped to the heart of Ruyz de Alarcon.

The wedding of the happy couple was celebrated soon afterwards with great splendour, and "The Rose of the Alhambra" became the ornament and delight of the court.

"But hold—not so fast—" I hear the reader exclaim. "This is jumping to the end of a story at a furious rate! First let us know how Ruyz de Alarcon managed to account to Jacinta for his long neglect."

Nothing more easy: the venerable, time-honoured excuse— the opposition to his wishes by a proud pragmatical old father.

"But how was the proud pragmatical old father reconciled to the match?"

O! as to that, his scruples were easily overcome by a word or two from the queen, especially as dignities and rewards were showered upon the blooming favourite of royalty. Besides, the lute of Jacinta, you know, possessed a magic power, and could control the most stubborn head and hardest breast.

Governor Manco and the Soldier

While Governor Manco, or "the one-armed," kept up a show of military state in the Alhambra, he became nettled at the reproaches continually cast upon his fortress, of being a nestling place of rogues and *contrabandistas*. On a sudden, the old potentate determined on reform, and setting vigorously to work, ejected whole nests of vagabonds out of the fortress and the gipsy caves with which the surrounding hills are honeycombed. He sent out soldiers, also, to patrol the avenues and footpaths, with orders to take up all suspicious persons.

One bright summer morning, a patrol, consisting of the testy old corporal who had distinguished himself in the affair of the notary, a trumpeter and two privates, was seated under the garden wall of the Generalife, beside the road which leads down from the mountain of the sun, when they heard the tramp of a horse, and a male voice singing in rough, though not unmusical tones, an old Castilian campaigning song.

Presently they beheld a sturdy, sunburnt fellow, clad in the ragged garb of a foot-soldier, leading a powerful Arabian horse, caparisoned in the ancient Morisco fashion.

Astonished at the sight of a strange soldier descending, steed in hand, from that solitary mountain, the corporal stepped forth and challenged him.

"Who goes there?"

"A friend."

"Who and what are you?"

"A poor soldier just from the wars, with a cracked crown and empty purse for a reward."

By this time they were enabled to view him more narrowly. He had a black patch across his forehead, which, with a grizzled beard, added to a certain dare-devil cast of countenance, while a slight squint threw into the whole an occasional gleam of roguish good humour.

Having answered the questions of the patrol, the soldier seemed to consider himself entitled to make others in return. "May I ask," said he, "what city is that which I see at the foot of the hill?"

"What city!" cried the trumpeter; "come, that's too bad. Here's a fellow lurking about the mountain of the sun, and demands the name of the great city of Granada!"

"Granada! *Madre de Dios!* can it be possible?"

"Perhaps not!" rejoined the trumpeter; " and perhaps you have no idea that yonder are the towers of the Alhambra."

"Son of a trumpet," replied the stranger, "do not trifle with me; if this be indeed the Alhambra, I have some strange matters to reveal to the governor."

"You will have an opportunity," said the corporal, "for we mean to take you before him." By this time the trumpeter had seized the bridle of the steed, the two privates had each secured an arm of the soldier, the corporal put himself in front, gave the word, "Forward-march!" and away they marched for the Alhambra.

The sight of a ragged foot-soldier and a fine Arabian horse, brought in captive by the patrol, attracted the attention of all the idlers of the fortress, and of those gossip groups that generally assemble about wells and fountains at early dawn. The wheel of the cistern paused in its rotations, and the slip-shod servant-maid stood gaping, with pitcher in hand, as the corporal passed by with his prize. A motley train gradually gathered in the rear of the escort.

Knowing nods and winks and conjectures passed from one to another. "It is a deserter," said one. "A *contrabandista*," said another. "A *bandalero*," said a third-until it was affirmed that a captain of a desperate band of robbers had been captured by the prowess of the corporal and his patrol. "Well, well," said the old crones, one to another, "captain or not, let him get out of the grasp of old Governor Manco if he can, though he is but one-handed."

Governor Manco was seated in one of the inner halls of the Alhambra, taking his morning's cup of chocolate in company with his confessor, a fat Franciscan friar, from the neighbouring convent. A demure, dark-eyed damsel of Malaga, the daughter of his housekeeper, was attending upon him. The world hinted that the damsel, who, with all her demureness, was a sly buxom baggage, had found out a soft spot in the iron heart of the old governor, and held complete control over him. But let that pass—the domestic affairs of these mighty potentates of the earth should not be too narrowly scrutinized.

When word was brought that a suspicious stranger had been taken lurking about the fortress, and was actually in the outer court, in durance of the corporal, waiting the pleasure of His Excellency, the pride and stateliness of office swelled the bosom of the governor. Giving back his chocolate cup into the hands of the demure damsel, he called for his basket-hilted sword, girded it to his side, twirled up his moustaches, took his seat in a large high-backed chair, assumed a bitter and forbidding aspect, and ordered the prisoner into his presence. The soldier was brought in, still closely pinioned by his captors, and guarded by the corporal. He maintained, however, a resolute self-confident air, and returned the sharp, scrutinizing look of the governor with an easy squint, which by no means pleased the punctilious old potentate.

"Well, culprit," said the governor, after he had regarded him for a moment in silence, "what have you to say for yourself-who are you?"

"A soldier, just from the wars, who has brought away nothing but scars and bruises."

"A soldier—humph—a foot-soldier by your garb. I understand you have a fine Arabian horse. I presume you brought him too from the wars, besides your scars and bruises."

"May it please Your Excellency, I have something strange to tell about that horse. Indeed I have one of the most wonderful things to relate. Something too that concerns the security of this fortress, indeed of all Granada. But it is a matter to be imparted only to your private ear, or in presence of such only as are in your confidence."

The governor considered for a moment, and then directed the corporal and his men to withdraw, but to post themselves outside of the door, and be ready at a call. "This holy friar," said he, "is my confessor, you may say any thing in his presence—and this damsel," nodding toward the handmaid, who had loitered with an air of great curiosity, "this damsel is of great secrecy and discretion, and to be trusted with anything."

The soldier gave a glance between a squint and a leer at the demure handmaid. "I am perfectly willing," said he, "that the damsel should remain."

When all the rest had withdrawn, the soldier commenced his story. He was a fluent, smooth-tongued varlet, and had a command of language above his apparent rank.

"May it please Your Excellency," said he, "I am, as I before observed, a soldier, and have seen some hard service, but my term of enlistment being expired, I was discharged, not long since, from the army at Valladolid, and set out on foot for my native village in Andalusia. Yesterday evening the sun went down as I was traversing a great dry plain of Old Castile."

"Hold," cried the governor, "what is this you say? Old Castile is some two or three hundred miles from this."

"Even so," replied the soldier, coolly; "I told Your Excellency I had strange things to relate; but not more strange than true; as Your Excellency will find, if you will deign me a patient hearing."

"Proceed, culprit," said the governor, twirling up his moustaches.

"As the sun went down," continued the soldier, "I cast my eyes about in search of quarters for the night, but as far as my sight could reach, there were no signs of habitation. I saw that I should have to make my bed on the naked plain, with my knapsack for a pillow; but Your Excellency is an old soldier, and knows that to one who has been in the wars, such a night's lodging is no great hardship."

The governor nodded assent, as he drew his pocket handkerchief out of the basket-hilt, to drive away a fly that buzzed about his nose.

"Well, to make a long story short," continued the soldier, "I trudged forward for several miles until I came to a bridge over a deep ravine, through which ran a little thread of water, almost dried up by the summer heat. At one end of the bridge was a Moorish tower, the upper end all in ruins, but a vault in the foundation quite entire. Here, thinks I, is a good place to make a halt; so I went down to the stream, took a hearty drink, for the water was pure and sweet, and I was parched with thirst; then, opening my wallet, I took out an onion and a few crusts, which were all my provisions, and seating myself on a stone on the margin of the stream, began to make my supper, intending afterwards to quarter myself for the night in the vault of the tower; and capital quarters they would have been for a campaigner just from the wars, as Your Excellency, who is an old soldier, may suppose."

"I have put up gladly with worse in my time," said the governor, returning his pocket handkerchief into the hilt of his sword.

"While I was quietly crunching my crust," pursued the soldier, "I heard something stir within the vault; I listened—it was the tramp of a horse. By and by a man came forth from a door in the foundation of the tower, close by the water's edge, leading a powerful horse by the bridle. I could not well make out what he was by the starlight. It had a suspicious look to be lurking among the ruins of a tower, in that wild solitary place. He might be a mere wayfarer, like myself; he might be a *contrabandista*; he might be a *bandalero*! what of that? thank heaven and my poverty, I had nothing to lose; so I sat still and crunched my crust.

"He led his horse to the water, close by where I was sitting, so that I had a fair opportunity of reconnoitring him. To my surprise he was dressed in a Moorish garb, with a *cuirass* of steel, and a polished skull-cap that I distinguished by the reflection of the stars upon it. His horse, too, was harnessed in the Morisco fashion, with great shovel stirrups. He led him, as I said, to the side of the stream, into which the animal plunged his head almost to the eyes, and drank until I thought he would have burst.

"'Comrade,' said I, 'your steed drinks well; it's a good sign when a horse plunges his muzzle bravely into the water.'

"'He may well drink,' said the stranger, speaking with a Moorish accent; 'it is a good year since he had his last draught.'

"'By Santiago,' said I, 'that beats even the camels I have seen in Africa. But come, you seem to be something of a soldier, will you sit down and take part of a soldier's fare?' In fact, I felt the want of a companion in this lonely place, and was willing to put up with an *infidel*. Besides, as Your Excellency well knows, a soldier is never very particular about the faith of his company, and soldiers of all countries are comrades on peaceable ground."

The governor again nodded assent.

"Well, as I was saying, I invited him to share my supper, such as it was, for I could not do less in common hospitality. 'I have no time to pause for meat or drink,' said he, 'I have a long journey to make before morning.'

"'In which direction?' said I.

"'Andalusia,' said he.

"'Exactly my route,' said I, 'so, as you won't stop and eat with me, perhaps you will let me mount and ride with you. I see your horse is of a powerful frame, I'll warrant he'll carry double.'

"'Agreed,' said the trooper; and it would not have been civil and soldier-like to refuse, especially as I had offered to share my supper with him. So up he mounted, and up I mounted behind him.

"'Hold fast,' said he, 'my steed goes like the wind.'

"'Never fear me,' said I, and so off we set.

"From a walk the horse soon passed to a trot, from a trot to a gallop, and from a gallop to a harum-scarum scamper. It seemed as if rocks, trees, houses, everything, flew hurry-scurry behind us.

"'What town is this?' said I.

"'Segovia,' said he; and before the word was out of his mouth, the towers of Segovia were out of sight. We swept up the Guadarama mountains, and down by the Escurial; and we skirted the walls of Madrid, and we scoured away across the plains of La Mancha. In this way we went up hill and down dale, by towers and cities, all buried in deep sleep, and across mountains, and plains, and rivers, just glimmering in the starlight.

"To make a long story short, and not to fatigue Your Excellency, the trooper suddenly pulled up on the side of a mountain. 'Here we are,' said he, 'at the end of our journey.' I looked about, but could see no signs of habitation; nothing but the mouth of a cavern. While I looked I saw multitudes of people in Moorish dresses, some on horseback, some on foot, arriving as if borne by the wind from all points of the compass, and hurrying into the mouth of the cavern like bees into a hive. Before I could ask a question the trooper struck his long Moorish spurs into the horse's flanks, and dashed in with the throng.

"We passed along a steep winding way, that descended into the very bowels of the mountain. As we pushed on, a light began to glimmer up, by little and little, like the first glimmerings of day, but what caused it I could not discern. It grew stronger and stronger, and enabled me to see everything around. I now noticed, as we passed along, great caverns, opening to the right and left, like halls in an arsenal. In some there were shields, and helmets, and *cuirasses*, and lances, and cimeters, hanging against the walls; in others there were great heaps of warlike munitions, and camp equipage lying upon the ground.

"It would have done Your Excellency's heart good, being an old soldier, to have seen such grand provision for war. Then, in other caverns, there were long rows of horsemen armed to the teeth, with lances raised and banners unfurled, all ready for the field; but they all sat motionless in their saddles like so many statues. In other halls were warriors sleeping on the ground beside their horses, and foot-soldiers in groups ready to fall into the ranks. All were in old-fashioned Moorish dresses and armour.

"Well, Your Excellency, to cut a long story short, we at length entered an immense cavern, or I may say palace, of grotto work, the walls of which seemed to be veined with gold and silver, and to sparkle with diamonds and sapphires and all kinds of precious stones. At the upper end sat a Moorish king on a golden throne, with his nobles on each side, and a guard of African blacks with drawn cimeters. All the crowd that continued to flock in, and amounted to thousands and thousands, passed one by one before his throne, each paying homage as he passed. Some of the multitude were dressed in magnificent robes, without stain or blemish and sparkling with jewels; others in burnished and enamelled armour; while others were in mouldered and mildewed garments, and in armour all battered and dented and covered with rust.

"I had hitherto held my tongue, for Your Excellency well knows it is not for a soldier to ask many questions when on duty, but I could keep silent no longer.

"'Prithee, comrade,' said I, 'what is the meaning of all this?'

"'This,' said the trooper, 'is a great and fearful mystery. Know, O Christian, that you see before you the court and army of Boabdil the last king of Granada.'

"'What is this you tell me?' cried I. 'Boabdil and his court were exiled from the land hundreds of years agone, and all died in Africa.'

"'So it is recorded in your lying chronicles,' replied the Moor; 'but know that Boabdil and the warriors who made the last struggle for Granada were all shut up in the mountain by powerful enchantment. As for the king and army that marched forth from Granada at the time of the surrender, they were a mere phantom train of spirits and demons, permitted to assume those shapes to deceive the Christian sovereigns. And furthermore let me tell you, friend, that all Spain is a country under the power of enchantment. There is not a mountain cave, not a lonely

431

watchtower in the plains, nor ruined castle on the hills, but has some spell-bound warriors sleeping from age to age within its vaults, until the sins are expiated for which *Allah* permitted the dominion to pass for a time out of the hands of the faithful. Once every year, on the eve of St. John, they are released from enchantment, from sunset to sunrise, and permitted to repair here to pay homage to their sovereign! and the crowds which you beheld swarming into the cavern are Moslem warriors from their haunts in all parts of Spain.

"For my own part, you saw the ruined tower of the bridge in Old Castile, where I have now wintered and summered for many hundred years, and where I must be back again by day-break. As to the battalions of horse and foot which you beheld drawn up in array in the neighbouring caverns, they are the spell-bound warriors of Granada. It is written in the book of fate, that when the enchantment is broken, Boabdil will descend from the mountain at the head of this army, resume his throne in the Alhambra and his sway of Granada, and gathering together the enchanted warriors, from all parts of Spain, will reconquer the Peninsula and restore it to Moslem rule.'

"'And when shall this happen?' said I.

"'*Allah* alone knows: we had hoped the day of deliverance was at hand; but there reigns at present a vigilant governor in the Alhambra, a stanch old soldier, well known as Governor Manco. While such a warrior holds command of the very outpost, and stands ready to check the first irruption from the mountain, I fear Boabdil and his soldiery must be content to rest upon their arms.'"

Here the governor raised himself somewhat perpendicularly, adjusted his sword, and twirled up his moustaches.

"To make a long story short, and not to fatigue Your Excellency, the trooper, having given me this account, dismounted from his steed.

"'Tarry here,' said he, 'and guard my steed while I go and bow the knee to Boabdil.' So saying, he strode away among the throng that pressed forward to the throne.

"'What's to be done?' thought I, when thus left to myself; 'shall I wait here until this *infidel* returns to whisk me off on his goblin steed, the Lord knows where; or shall I make the most of my time and beat a retreat from this hobgoblin community? A soldier's mind is soon made up, as Your Excellency well knows. As to the horse, he belonged to an avowed enemy of the faith and the realm, and was a fair prize according to the rules of war. So hoisting myself from the crupper into the saddle, I turned the reins, struck the Moorish stirrups into the sides of the steed, and put him to make the best of his way out of the passage by which he had entered.

"As we scoured by the halls where the Moslem horsemen sat in motionless battalions, I thought I heard the clang of armour and a hollow murmur of voices. I gave the steed another taste of the stirrups and doubled my speed. There was now a sound behind me like a rushing blast; I heard the clatter of a thousand hoofs; a countless throng overtook me. I was borne along in the press, and hurled forth from the mouth of the cavern, while thousands of shadowy forms were swept off in every direction by the four winds of heaven.

"In the whirl and confusion of the scene I was thrown senseless to the earth. When I came to myself I was lying on the brow of a hill, with the Arabian steed standing beside me; for in falling, my arm had slipped within the bridle, which, I presume, prevented his whisking off to Old Castile.

"Your Excellency may easily judge of my surprise, on looking round, to behold hedges of aloes and Indian figs and other proofs of a southern climate, and to see a great city below me, with towers, and palaces, and a grand cathedral.

"I descended the hill cautiously, leading my steed, for I was afraid to mount him again, lest he should play me some slippery trick. As I descended I met with your patrol, who let me into the secret that it was Granada that lay before me; and that I was actually under the walls of the Alhambra, the fortress of the redoubted Governor Manco, the terror of all enchanted Moslems. When I heard this, I determined at once to seek Your Excellency, to inform you of all that I had seen, and to warn you of the perils that surround and undermine you, that you may take measures in time to guard your fortress, and the kingdom itself, from this intestine army that lurks in the very bowels of the land."

"And prithee, friend, you who are a veteran campaigner, and have seen so much service," said the governor, "how would you advise me to proceed, in order to prevent this evil?"

"It is not for a humble private of the ranks," said the soldier, modestly, "to pretend to instruct a commander of Your Excellency's sagacity, but it appears to me that Your Excellency might cause all the caves and entrances into the mountains to be walled up with solid mason work, so that Boabdil and his army might be completely corked up in their subterranean habitation. If the good father, too," added the soldier, reverently bowing to the friar, and devoutly crossing himself, "would consecrate the *barricadoes* with his blessing, and put up a few crosses and relics and images of saints, I think they might withstand all the power of infidel enchantments."

"They doubtless would be of great avail," said the friar.

The governor now placed his arm *akimbo*, with his hand resting on the hilt of his Toledo, fixed his eye upon the soldier, and gently wagging his head from one side to the other.

"So, friend," said he, "then you really suppose I am to be gulled with this cock-and-bull story about enchanted mountains and enchanted Moors? Hark ye, culprit!—not another word. An old soldier you may be, but you'll find you have an older soldier to deal with, and one not easily outgeneralled. Ho! guards there! put this fellow in irons."

The demure handmaid would have put in a word in favour of the prisoner, but the governor silenced her with a look.

As they were pinioning the soldier, one of the guards felt something of bulk in his pocket, and drawing it forth, found a long leathern purse that appeared to be well filled. Holding it by one corner, he turned out the contents upon the table before the governor, and never did freebooter's bag make more gorgeous delivery. Out tumbled rings, and jewels, and rosaries of pearls, and sparkling diamond crosses, and a profusion of ancient golden coin, some of which fell jingling to the floor, and rolled away to the uttermost parts of the chamber.

For a time the functions of justice were suspended; there was a universal scramble after the glittering fugitives. The governor alone, who was imbued with true Spanish pride, maintained his stately decorum, though his eye betrayed a little anxiety until the last coin and jewel was restored to the sack.

The friar was not so calm; his whole face glowed like a furnace, and his eyes twinkled and flashed at sight of the rosaries and crosses.

"Sacrilegious wretch that thou art!" exclaimed he; "what church or sanctuary hast thou been plundering of these sacred relics?"

"Neither one nor the other, holy father. If they be sacrilegious spoils, they must have been taken, in times long past, by the *infidel* trooper I have mentioned. I was just going to tell His Excellency when he interrupted me, that on taking possession of the trooper's horse, I unhooked a leathern sack which hung at the saddle-bow, and which I presume contained the plunder of his campaignings in days of old, when the Moors overran the country."

"Mighty well; at present you will make up your mind to take up your quarters in a chamber of the Vermilion Tower, which, though not under a magic spell, will hold you as safe as any cave of your enchanted Moors."

"Your Excellency will do as you think proper," said the prisoner, coolly. "I shall be thankful to Your Excellency for any accommodation in the fortress. A soldier who has been in the wars, as Your Excellency well knows, is not particular about his lodgings: provided I have a snug dungeon and regular rations, I shall manage to make myself comfortable. I would only entreat that while Your Excellency is so careful about me, you would have an eye to your fortress, and think on the hint I dropped about stopping up the entrances to the mountain."

Here ended the scene. The prisoner was conducted to a strong dungeon in the Vermilion Tower, the Arabian steed was led to His Excellency's stable, and the trooper's sack was deposited in His Excellency's strong box. To the latter, it is true, the friar made some demur, questioning whether the sacred relics, which were evidently sacrilegious spoils, should not be placed in custody of the church; but as the governor was peremptory on the subject, and was absolute lord in the Alhambra, the friar discreetly dropped the discussion, but determined to convey intelligence of the fact to the church dignitaries in Granada.

To explain these prompt and rigid measures on the part of old Governor Manco, it is proper to observe, that about this time the Alpuxarra mountains in the neighbourhood of Granada were terribly infested by a gang of robbers, under the command of a daring chief named Manuel Borasco, who were accustomed to prowl about the country, and even to enter the city in various disguises, to gain intelligence of the departure of convoys of merchandise, or travellers with well-lined purses, whom they took care to waylay in distant and solitary passes of the road.

These repeated and daring outrages had awakened the attention of government, and the commanders of the various posts had received instructions to be on the alert, and to take up all suspicious stragglers. Governor Manco was particularly zealous in consequence of the various stigmas that had been cast upon his fortress, and he now doubted not he had entrapped some formidable desperado of this gang.

In the meantime the story took wind, and became the talk, not merely of the fortress, but of the whole city of Granada. It was said that the noted robber Manuel Borasco, the terror of the Alpuxarras, had fallen into the clutches of old Governor Manco, and been cooped up by him in a dungeon of the Vermilion Tower; and everyone who had been robbed by him flocked to recognize the marauder. The Vermilion Tower, as is well known, stands apart from the Alhambra on a sister hill, separated from the main fortress by the ravine down which passes the main avenue. There were no outer walls, but a sentinel patrolled before the tower.

The window of the chamber in which the soldier was confined was strongly grated, and looked upon a small esplanade. Here the good folks of Granada repaired to gaze at him, as they would at a laughing hyena, grinning through the cage of a menagerie. Nobody, however, recognized him for Manuel Borasco, for that terrible robber was noted for a ferocious physiognomy, and had by no means the good-humoured squint of the prisoner. Visitors came not merely from the city, but from all parts of the country; but nobody knew him, and there began to be doubts in the minds of the common people whether there might not be some truth in his story.

That Boabdil and his army were shut up in the mountain, was an old tradition which many of the ancient inhabitants had heard from their fathers. Numbers went up to the mountain of the sun, or rather of St. Elena, in search of the cave mentioned by the soldier; and saw and peeped into the deep dark pit, descending, no one knows how far, into the mountain, and which remains there to this day—the fabled entrance to the subterranean abode of Boabdil.

By degrees the soldier became popular with the common people. A freebooter of the mountains is by no means the opprobrious character in Spain that a robber is in any other country: on the contrary, he is a kind of chivalrous personage in the eyes of the lower classes. There is always a disposition, also, to cavil at the conduct of those in command, and many began to murmur at the high-handed measures of old Governor Manco, and to look upon the prisoner in the light of a martyr.

The soldier, moreover, was a merry, waggish fellow, that had a joke for everyone who came near his window, and a soft speech for every female. He had procured an old guitar also, and would sit by his window and sing ballads and love-ditties to the delight of the women of the neighbourhood, who would assemble on the esplanade in the evening and dance boleros to his music. Having trimmed off his rough beard, his sunburnt face found favour in the eyes of the fair, and the demure handmaid of the governor declared that his squint was perfectly irresistible.

This kind-hearted damsel had from the first evinced a deep sympathy in his fortunes, and having in vain tried to mollify the governor, had set to work privately to mitigate the rigor of his dispensations. Every day she brought the prisoner some crumbs of comfort which had fallen from the governor's table, or been abstracted from his larder, together with, now and then, a consoling bottle of choice Val de Penas, or rich Malaga.

While this petty treason was going on, in the very centre of the old governor's citadel, a storm of open war was brewing up among his external foes. The circumstance of a bag of gold and jewels having been found upon the person of the supposed robber, had been reported, with many exaggerations, in Granada. A question of territorial jurisdiction was immediately started by the governor's inveterate rival, the captain-general. He insisted that the prisoner had been captured without the precincts of the Alhambra, and within the rules of his authority.

He demanded his body therefore, and the *spolia opima* taken with him. Due information having been carried likewise by the friar to the grand inquisitor of the crosses and rosaries, and other relics contained in the bag, he claimed the culprit as having been guilty of sacrilege, and insisted that his plunder was due to the church, and his body to the next *auto-da-fe*. The feuds ran high; the governor was furious, and swore, rather than surrender his captive, he would hang him up within the Alhambra, as a spy caught within the purlieus of the fortress.

The captain-general threatened to send a body of soldiers to transfer the prisoner from the Vermilion Tower to the city. The grand inquisitor was equally bent upon dispatching a number of the familiars of the Holy Office. Word was brought late at night to the governor of these machinations. "Let them come," said he, "they'll find me beforehand with them; he must rise bright and early who would take in an old soldier." He accordingly issued orders to have the prisoner removed, at daybreak, to the *donjon* keep within the walls of the Alhambra. "And d'ye hear, child," said he to his demure handmaid, "tap at my door, and wake me before cock-crowing, that I may see to the matter myself."

The day dawned, the cock crowed, but nobody tapped at the door of the governor. The sun rose high above the mountain-tops, and glittered in at his casement, ere the governor was awakened from his morning dreams by his veteran corporal, who stood before him with terror stamped upon his iron visage.

"He's off! he's gone!" cried the corporal, gasping for breath.

"Who's off—who's gone?"

"The soldier—the robber—the devil, for aught I know; his dungeon is empty, but the door locked: no one knows how he has escaped out of it."

"Who saw him last?"

"Your handmaid, she brought him his supper."

"Let her be called instantly."

Here was new matter of confusion. The chamber of the demure damsel was likewise empty, her bed had not been slept in: she had doubtless gone off with the culprit, as she had appeared, for some days past, to have frequent conversations with him.

This was wounding the old governor in a tender part, but he had scarce time to wince at it, when new misfortunes broke upon his view. On going into his cabinet he found his strong box open, the leather purse of the trooper abstracted, and with it, a couple of corpulent bags of *doubloons*.

But how, and which way had the fugitives escaped? An old peasant who lived in a cottage by the road-side, leading up into the Sierra, declared that he had heard the tramp of a powerful steed just before daybreak, passing up into the mountains. He had looked out at his casement, and could just distinguish a horseman, with a female seated before him.

"Search the stables!" cried Governor Manco. The stables were searched; all the horses were in their stalls, excepting the Arabian steed. In his place was a stout cudgel tied to the manger, and on it a label bearing these words, "A gift to Governor Manco, from an Old Soldier."

Legend of the Two Discreet Statues

There once lived in a poor part of the Alhambra a merry little fellow, named Lope Sanchez, who worked in the gardens, and was as brisk and gay as a grasshopper, singing all day long. He was the life and soul of the fortress. When his work was over, he would sit on one of the stone benches, strum his guitar, and sing songs about Spanish heroes, or strike up a merrier tune, and set the girls dancing *boleros* and *fandangos*.

Like most little men. Lope had a buxom dame for a wife, who could almost have put him in her pocket. They had but one child, a little black-eyed girl named Sanchica, who was as merry as her father, and the delight of his heart. She played about him as he worked in the gardens, danced to his guitar as he sat in the shade, and ran as wild as a young fawn about the groves and alleys and ruined halls.

It was now the eve of St. John, and the men, women, and children of the Alhambra went up at night to the mountain of the sun to keep their midsummer vigil on its summit. It was a bright moonlight night, and all the mountains were grey and silvery, and the city lay in shadows below. The Vega was like a fairyland, with haunted streams gleaming among its dusky groves. On the highest part of the mountain they lit a fire. The people of the country round were keeping a similar vigil, and fires here and there in the Vega, and along the folds of the mountains, blazed palely in the moonlight.

The evening was gayly passed in dancing to the guitar of

Lope Sanchez, who was never so joyous as on a holiday of this kind.

While the dance was going on, Sanchica and some of her friends were playing among the ruins of an old Moorish fort, when she found among the pebbles a small hand curiously carved of jet. She ran to her mother with her prize.

"Throw it away," said one of the women. "It 's Moorish and there 's witchcraft in it."

"By no means," said another. "You may sell it for something to the jewellers."

An old soldier drew near who was as dark as a Moor.

"I have seen things of this kind," said he, "among the Moors of Barbary. It is a great virtue to guard against all kinds of spells and enchantments. I give you joy, friend Lope: this bodes good luck to your child."

Upon hearing this, the wife of Lope Sanchez tied the little hand to a ribbon, and hung it round the neck of her daughter. The dance was neglected, and they sat in groups on the ground, telling old legends about the Moors. Some of the stories were about the very mountain on which they were seated. One old crone gave a long account of the palace which was inside the mountain where Boabdil and all his court are said to remain enchanted.

"Among yonder ruins," said she, pointing to some old walls, "there is a deep black pit that goes down into the very heart of the mountain. For all the money in Granada I would not look into it. Once upon a time a poor man of the Alhambra, who tended goats up on this mountain, scrambled down into that pit after a kid that had fallen in. He came out again and told such things of what he had seen, that everyone thought he had gone mad. He raved about hobgoblin Moors, and they could hardly get him to take his goats up there again. He did so at last, but, poor man, he never came down. They found his hat and mantle near the mouth of the cavern, but he was never more heard of."

Sanchica listened to all this story. She felt a great longing to peep into this dangerous pit, so she stole away from her companions, and after some time, found the hollow near the brow of the mountain. In the centre of this was the mouth of the pit. She peeped in. All was as black as pitch. Her blood ran cold. She drew back, then peeped in again—then would have run away—then took another peep. She pushed a large stone into it. For some time it fell in silence—then it struck with a crash, rebounding from side to side, rumbling and tumbling with a noise like thunder. Then it made a splash into water, far, far below—and all was still again.

A murmuring sound gradually rose out of the pit like the buzz and hum of bees. It grew louder and louder. Sanchica could hear voices, and the sound of arms and trumpets, as if some army were marshalling for battle in the very inside of the mountain.

The child became frightened, and hastened back to the place where she had left her father and mother and their companions, but all were gone. The fire was going out, and its last wreath of smoke was curling up in the moonshine. Everything seemed to be asleep. Sanchica called, but there was no answer. She ran down the side of the mountain, and by the gardens of the Generalife, until she came to the alley of trees leading to the Alhambra. Here she seated herself on a bench of a woody recess, to recover breath.

The bell in the watchtower tolled midnight. All she could hear was the tinkling of a stream. The sweet air was lulling her to sleep, when her eye was caught by something glittering, and to her surprise she beheld a long line of Moorish warriors pouring down the mountain side and along the leafy avenues. Their horses pranced proudly, but their tramp caused no more sound than if they had been shod with felt, and the riders were all as pale as death. Among them rode a beautiful lady, with a crowned head and long yellow hair entwined with pearls. The housings of her palfrey were crimson velvet and swept the earth; but she rode all disconsolate, looking ever at the ground.

Then came a train of men belonging to the court. They were arrayed in robes and turbans of divers colours. With them rode

King Boabdil. His royal mantle was covered with jewels, and he wore a crown sparkling with diamonds. Sanchica knew him by his yellow beard, for she had often seen his portrait in the picture gallery of the Generalife. She gazed in wonder as they passed among the trees, but though she knew they were enchanted, yet she looked on with a brave heart, for the talisman gave her courage.

When they had passed by, she rose and followed them to the great gate which stood wide open. The old men who watched there were sound asleep on the stone benches.

The train swept by them noiselessly, with banners flaunting. Sanchica would have followed them, but to her surprise she saw an opening in the earth leading down beneath the tower. She entered for a little way, and found steps hewn in the rock, and a passage here and there lit up by a silver lamp which diffused besides light a grateful fragrance.

Going on, she came at last to a great hall in the heart of the mountain. It was furnished in Moorish style, and lighted by silver and crystal lamps. Here sat an old man in Moorish dress, with a long white beard, nodding and dozing. He had a staff in his hand which seemed ever to be slipping from his grasp. Near him sat a lady in ancient Spanish dress, wearing a crown. She was softly playing on a silver lyre. Sanchica now remembered a story she had heard about a Spanish princess who was imprisoned in the centre of the mountain by an old Arab whom she kept bound up in magic sleep by the power of music.

The lady paused at seeing Sanchica.

"Is it the eve of the blessed St. John?" said she.

"It is," replied Sanchica.

"Then for one night the charm is broken. Come hither, child, and fear not. I am a Christian like yourself. Touch my chain with the talisman which hangs about your neck, and for this night I shall be free."

Sanchica touched a broad golden chain that fastened her to the earth, as the lady had told her, and it fell to the ground. At the sound the old man woke and began to rub his eyes: but the lady ran her fingers over the lyre and again he fell asleep.

"Now," said the lady, "touch his staff."

The child did so, and as it fell from his grasp, he sank into a deep, deep sleep. The lady laid the silver lyre beside him.

"Now follow me, my child," said she, "and you shall behold the Alhambra as it was in the days of its glory."

Sanchica followed her and they passed up through the entrance in the cavern.

Everywhere were Moorish soldiers with floating banners, and here and there were royal guards and rows of African slaves. No one spoke a word, and Sanchica passed on fearlessly, following the lady. The moon lit up all the halls and courts and gardens, almost as if it were day. The scene was far different from what she was used to seeing. The walls were no longer stained and old. Instead of cobwebs, they were now hung with rich silks, and the gildings and paintings looked bright and fresh. The halls were set out with divans and ottomans of rare stuffs, and all the fountains in the courts and gardens were playing.

Cooks were busy in the kitchens, and servants were hurrying to and fro with silver dishes heaped up with dainties, preparing a banquet. The Court of Lions was thronged with guards and courtiers, and at the upper end sat Boabdil on his throne. Not a sound was to be heard except the splashing of the fountains.

Sanchica followed the lady about the palace until they came to an opening beneath a great tower. On each side of the portal sat the figure of a nymph wrought out of alabaster. Their heads were turned aside and they seemed to be looking at the same spot within the vault. The lady paused.

"Here," said she, "is a great secret, which I will reveal to you in reward for your faith and courage. These discreet statues watch over a treasure hidden long ago by an old Moorish king. Tell your father to search the spot on which their eyes are fixed, and he will find what will make him richer than any man in Granada. Your hands alone, however, gifted as you are with the talisman, can remove the treasure."

When the lady had spoken these words, she led Sanchica to

the little garden hard by.

The moon trembled upon the waters of the fountain, and shed a tender light upon the orange and citron trees. The lady picked a branch of myrtle and wreathed it round the head of the child.

"Let this be a memento of what I have told you. My hour is come. I must return to the enchanted hall. Do not follow me lest evil befall you—farewell. Remember what I have said and pray for my freedom."

Then the lady entered a dark passage leading beneath the tower and was no longer seen.

The faint crowing of a cock was now heard from the cottages in the valley, and a pale streak of light began to appear above the eastern mountains. A slight wind arose, there was a sound like the rustling of dry leaves through the courts, and door after door shut to with a jarring sound.

Sanchica returned to the place where she had so lately beheld a throng, but Boabdil and his court were gone. The moon shone into empty halls stained by time and hung with cobwebs. Bats flitted about and frogs croaked from the fishpond.

Sanchica made her way to the staircase which led up to the place where she lived. The door as usual was open, for Lope Sanchez was too poor to need bolt or bar. She crept quietly to bed, and putting the myrtle wreath under her pillow, soon fell asleep.

In the morning she related all that had befallen her to her father. Lope Sanchez thought it was a mere dream and laughed at the child. He went to his work in the garden, but had not been there long when his little daughter came running to him.

"Father! father!" cried she, "see the myrtle wreath which the lady bound round my head!"

Lope Sanchez looked with wonder, for the stalk was pure gold, and every leaf was a sparkling emerald! He then went to the place where the two statues stood and found that they both seemed to be looking at the same spot on the wall. He drew a line from the eyes of the statues, made a mark on the wall, and went away. He feared that the secret might be found out and trembled when any one went near the place. He wished that he might turn their heads, forgetting that they had looked precisely in the same direction for some hundreds of years, without any person being the wiser.

"A plague upon them," he would say to himself, "they'll betray all. Did ever mortal hear of such a way to guard a secret?"

And if he heard anyone coming, he would steal away, then return, peeping from a distance to see if all was secure.

"There they stand," he would say, "always looking and looking, just where they should not. They are just like all their sex: if they have not tongues to tattle with, they'll be sure to do it with their eyes."

At last, the long day drew to a close. The sound of footsteps was no longer heard and it was quiet in the halls of the Alhambra. When the night was well advanced, Lope Sanchez went with his little daughter to the hall of the two statues. He found the place on the wall which he had marked and laid it open. In the recess stood two great jars of porcelain. He tried to draw them out, but they could not be moved until they were touched by the hands of Sanchica. With her aid he drew them from the niche, and found to his great joy, that they were filled with Moorish gold, and jewels and precious stones. Before daylight he had conveyed them to his house and left the two statues with their eyes still fixed on the wall.

Lope Sanchez had thus become a rich man. But riches, as usual, brought a world of cares which he had never known before. For the first time in his life he was in fear of robbers, so he went to work and made bolts and bars for his windows and doors, but even then he could not sleep soundly. He was no longer merry. He no longer had a joke for his friends. He became the most unhappy man in the Alhambra. His old friends, observing the change, pitied him and began to desert him, for they thought he must be falling into want and might look to them for assistance. Little did they think that his only trouble was riches.

We ought before this to have mentioned that in all grave matters Lope's wife sought the advice of her confessor. Fray Simon, a sturdy, broad-shouldered friar, and he was soon acquainted, in great secrecy, with the story of the hidden treasure.

The friar opened his eyes and mouth in great surprise.

"Daughter of my soul," said he, "know that your husband has committed a double sin—a sin against both state and church! The treasure was found in the royal domains, and so it belongs to the crown. But as it belonged to the Moors, who were not Christians, it should be devoted to the church. Bring hither the myrtle wreath."

When he saw the gold and emeralds, his eyes twinkled with delight.

"This," said he, "I will hang in the church and earnestly pray that Lope may keep the remainder of his wealth in peace."

The friar put the wreath under his robe, and with saintly step, departed. Lope's wife was delighted to make her peace with Heaven at so cheap a rate.

When Lope returned, and his wife told him what had passed, he was very angry, but there was no use of complaining. The secret was told, and, like water spilled on the sand, was not again to be gathered.

The next day the friar came again. He said to Lope's wife:

"Daughter, I have earnestly prayed and in the dead of night a saint appeared to me. 'Go to the house of Lope Sanchez,' said he, 'crave in my name enough of the Moorish gold to furnish two candlesticks for the church, and let him keep the rest in peace.'"

When the good woman heard this she crossed herself with awe, and going to the place where the treasure was hid, she filled a great leathern purse with pieces of Moorish gold and gave it to the friar. He blessed her, then slipped the purse into the sleeve of his habit and departed.

When Lope Sanchez heard of this second donation to the church, he well-nigh lost his senses.

"What will become of me," cried he. "I shall be robbed by

piecemeal: I shall be brought to beggary."

The friar kept coming from day to day for offerings until poor Lope was driven to despair, and found that unless he got out of reach of this holy friar, he should have to make offerings to every saint in the calendar. Therefore he made up his mind to pack what he had left, and go away in the night to another part of the kingdom.

He bought a stout mule for the purpose and sent off his family during the day, with orders to wait for him at a distant village. When night came he loaded his mule, and very quietly went down the dark avenue.

Honest Lope had made his plans with the utmost secrecy, telling them to no one but his faithful wife. Fray Simon, however, in some miraculous way learned of them. He determined to have one more dash at the treasure for the benefit of the church: and that night when all the Alhambra was quiet, he hid among the thickets of roses and laurels that bordered the great avenue. Here he remained counting the quarters of hours as they were sounded on the bell of the watchtower and listening to the dreary hooting of owls, and the distant barking of dogs from the gypsy caverns.

At length he heard the tramp of hoofs, and through the gloom saw a steed coming towards him. He tucked up his skirts and sat like a cat watching for a mouse. Then when the steed was directly before him, he darted forth from his leafy covert, and putting one hand on the shoulder and the other on the crupper made a vault and alighted well-forked astride the steed.

"Ah, ha!" said he, "we shall now see who best understands the game."

He had hardly said the words when the mule began to kick, and rear, and plunge, and then set off full speed down the hill. He bounded from rock to rock and bush to bush. The friar's habit was torn to ribbons and fluttered in the wind. His head received many a hard knock from the branches of the trees and many a scratch from the brambles.

To add to his terror, he found a pack of seven hounds in full cry at his heels, and then did he know that he was not mounted on Lope's mule at all, but upon the terrible goblin horse which was said to scour the streets of Granada at midnight.

Away they went down the great avenues. Never did huntsman and hound make a more furious run or greater uproar. In vain did the friar invoke every saint in the calendar: every time he mentioned a name of the kind the horse bounded as high as a house. Through the rest of the night the unlucky Fray Simon was carried hither and thither and whither he would not, until every bone in his body ached.

At last a cock crowed. At the sound the steed wheeled short and galloped back for his tower. The seven dogs yelled and barked and leaped and snapped at the poor friar. The first streak of day had just appeared as they reached the tower. Here the goblin kicked up his heels, sent the friar a somerset through the air, and plunged into the dark vault, followed by the dogs.

Was ever such a trick played upon a holy friar? A peasant going to his work at early dawn found Fray Simon lying under a fig-tree, so bruised and bedevilled that he could neither speak nor move. He was taken with all care to his cell, and the story went that he had been waylaid by robbers.

It was a day or two before he could use his limbs. Then his first care was to look under his pillow where he had hidden the myrtle wreath and leathern pouches of gold which dame Sanchez had given him. What was his dismay at finding the wreath but a withered branch of myrtle, and the pouches filled only with sand and gravel!

Nothing was heard of Lope Sanchez for a long time after he left the Alhambra. He was always remembered as a merry companion, though it was feared from the care observed in his conduct just before his departure that poverty and distress had driven him away.

Some years afterwards one of his old friends, being at Malaga, was nearly run over by a coach and six. The carriage stopped and an old gentleman magnificently dressed, with a wig and sword, stepped out to assist him. What was the astonishment of the latter to behold in this grand cavalier his old friend, Lope Sanchez, who was celebrating the marriage of his daughter Sanchica with one of the first *grandees* in the land.

The carriage contained the bridal party. There was Dame Sanchez, dressed out with feathers, and jewels, and necklaces of pearls, and necklaces of diamonds, and rings on every finger, as fine as the Queen of Sheba. The little Sanchica had now grown to be a woman, and for grace and beauty might have been mistaken for a duchess if not a princess outright. The bridegroom sat beside her—rather a spindle-shanked little man, but this only proved him to be of the true-blue blood. The match had been of the mother's making.

Riches had not spoiled the heart of honest Lope. He kept his old friend with him for several days, feasted him like a king, took him to plays and bull-fights, and at length sent him away with a big bag of money for himself, and another for his old friends of the Alhambra.

Lope always gave out that a rich brother had died in America and left him a copper mine, but the gossips of the Alhambra insist that he got his wealth from discovering the secret guarded by the two marble nymphs. And it is said that these statues, even to the present day, stand with their eyes on the same spot on the wall, which leads many people to think that there is still some treasure hidden there.